Sign of the Qin

OUTLAWS OF MOONSHADOW MARSH

BOOK ONE

Sign of the Qin

HYPERION PAPERBACKS

NEW YORK

Text copyright © 2004 by L. G. Bass

Title hand lettering by Leah Palmer Preiss

Chinese calligraphy by Jiaxuan Zhang

Printed in the United States of America

First Hyperion Paperbacks edition, 2006

1 3 5 7 9 10 8 6 4 2

This book is set in Centaur MT.

ISBN 0-7868-5566-5 (pbk.)

Library of Congress Cataloging-in-Publication Data on file.

Visit www.hyperionteens.com

FOR ETHAN

ACKNOWLEDGMENTS

Thanks to my husband, Tony Bass, to my editor, Donna Bray, to my publisher, Lisa Holton, and to my agent, Nancy Rose; to Gopal Sukhu, Chairman of the Chinese Studies department at Queens College, for his role as consultant; to Linh Thai, martial arts instructor, who introduced me to *The Marsh Chronicles* and *The Journey to the West*, featuring the Monkey King. Additional thanks to art director Christine Kettner; to Peter Hassinger for his constant encouragement and help; to Graham Bass; and to Rebecca Ballantine, who enjoyed this story in its early stages. And a very special thanks to Samantha Mitchell, and to my son, Ethan Bass, for his excellent notes, guidance, and advice.

CONTENTS

PART TWO: *Scorpion*

PART THREE: Leopard

CAST OF CHARACTERS

The Imperial Family
Emperor Han
Father Han, former Emperor
Silver Lotus, the First Consort
Prince Zong, the Starlord

Guardians
The Tattooed Monk (General Calabash)
Monkey

Outlaws
White Streak
Mother Gu
Black Whirlwind
Chiko Chin
Day Rat
Jade Mirror

Immortals

The Master Hand, King of Heaven
The Immortal Beggar, the Eighth Genie
Emperor Hung Wu
Zheng
Yin Dang, River Goddess
Chac, Dragon King of the North Sea
Yamu, Lord of the Dead

Members of the Celestial Court
The Celestial Detective
Thousand-League Eye
Down-the-Wind Ear
The Red-Legged Ones
The Three Judges

Demons

Old Bones, King of the Land Dragons
The Nokk
Puk
Malia
The Ponaturi
The Bunyip
The Wahwee
The Norn
The Kappa

Bandits

Spotted Leopard

T'sao T'sao

Golden Wings

Peasants

Gong Sun (Order of the Silver Lotus)

Kuan

Iron Ox

Wang Tinghong

Little Grandmother

Yongle

Qilin

Yu Yu

Sign of the Qin

Streaked with soot, the Tattooed Monk followed the wavering tracks of a lone fox into the woods. Herds of yak stood like black boulders on the windswept cliffs, their shadows sharp against the snow in the pale morning light. Burning prayer flags snapped thinly in the acrid wind, and the bell from the smoking ruins of the monastery below sounded eerily across vast spaces.

The single shrill call of a crane cut the air. Leaning heavily upon his staff, the monk limped along over splintered rockfalls, struggling to maintain his footing. At every step a hot jolt of pain shot through his leg. As he labored up the mountain, his breathing calmed.

In the turmoil of his grief, the monk's memories loomed like a storm about to break. With one fiery stroke, the Lord of the Dead had erased the sacred order of the Silver Lotus. Were the kung fu secrets of the Twelve Scrolls soon to be destroyed as well?

The monk's tattoos began to swirl, reflecting his thoughts. Perhaps he had lived too long. He remembered a time when Sleeping Giant Mountain rose up out of the boreal swamp. He remembered a time much like this one when ancient demons had been summoned from the Netherworld and a Starlord had opposed them, sacrificing his Imperial Throne to dragon fire in order to save the earth. It would take another Starlord to save the unsuspecting earth now.

The vibrating call of the red-crowned crane came again. Drawn by the sound, the monk lifted his face to the sky but saw no birds overhead. He neared a solid wall of locusts trapped in ice at the base of a frozen waterfall. Impulsively, he broke through the ice on the surface of the ghostly stream and plunged into the frigid waters, no longer feeling the agony of his wound. Leaping onto a boulder with the lightness of a bird, the Tattooed Monk knew that he must climb the waterfall.

Seizing hold of strong vines, he swung like a monkey, lifted by some inverted sense of gravity. He clung to the slippery precipice, advancing toward the peak. One false move and he would go careening down in an avalanche of stone. He groped for footholds, desperately clawing at the side of the gorge as the gusting wind threatened to throw him over the edge. The world lay beneath him—the scorched forest, the flooding river, and even, at a great distance, the open sea.

At the summit a graceful flock of red-crowned cranes danced in a deep blue crater lake cradled in clouds. Bowing and leaping, preening and springing into the air, they lifted their long bills and unfurled their necks, trumpeting their mating call.

The monk's heart lifted, but still he held back. The White Crane was his fighting form, but he was not yet ready to fight. He was a shadow brooding over the fate of other shadows, striving to remember all that he had once possessed and lost. He was a yeti, a wraith of the marsh, a spirit of the sea, a ghost of the snow, marching aimlessly through time. He had been scoured by the meteoric heat of a dragon's breath and had known himself in that instant to be utterly mortal. By whose hand, while others more worthy foundered and died without mercy, had the tide turned once again and the Tattooed Monk been spared?

He lifted his face to the heavens and let out a clangorous, unearthly cry. Flaring his arms like wings and arching his back, he moved with the cranes, pumping his head up and down and leaping madly into the air. He had lived so long, he no longer remembered his childhood, but he remembered this dance. When it was finished, he stood motionless and one-legged in the shallow water, cranelike except for the absence of a mate. He stood there perfectly balanced for a long time, until the rainbow of shifting tattoos across his back ceased to change. The pictures took the repeating shape of overlapping V's— cranes flying, their blazing red caps fanning out like spots of blood across a continent of snow.

PART ONE

Monkey

*Our sleep is troubled by dreams
we cannot forget we have forgotten.*
—Emperor Hung Wu

CHAPTER ONE

Sign of the Qin

*A Starlord appears suddenly and moves from the forgotten
to the unexpected. This is a miracle, but no more so
than the birth of any other child.*—The Master Hand

Some said the newborn's first cry was so loud and lusty it summoned the Lord of the Dead and his demons from the Netherworld. Others said it called the ancient Starlord Hung Wu down from Heaven to help the deteriorating kingdom of Han in its hour of need. Perhaps both interpretations were true and perhaps not. But it could not be contested that from the hour Prince Zong first announced his arrival, the moon rocked in the sky like a cradle, and nothing was ever the same in the province of Shandong.

The Prince's earsplitting howl floated up from the Emperor's private chambers, echoing loudly through the palace halls until it reached the Tower of the Water Clock, setting off a blare of trumpets, a beating of valves, a shimmering of bells, and a precipitous spinning of gears. The clock's twelve animal automata began to move all at once, and the sapphire eyes in the head of the monkey rolled from left to right three times.

In his eagerness to view the baby boy, the Emperor signaled his circle of twelve worried counselors to clear the servants from the birthing room. The stubborn nurse, however, would not relinquish her charge for the traditional viewing. She glared daggers at the Emperor's guards, insisting that the infant's first meal was more important than his first meeting with his father. In the headlong rush of events, no one had time to reprimand her.

And so, the official meeting took place less formally than had been planned, and the Prince was a bit underdressed for the occasion. Clasped firmly in his nurse's arms, Emperor Han's firstborn, only minutes old, drank his fill before calmly studying his father for the first time, staring at him appraisingly with big bright eyes.

Han saw that the boy was handsome, with noble features and a thick thatch of black hair framing his well-shaped head. He breathed a sigh of relief and felt his fatigue creeping back, the long sleepless vigil taking its toll. Suddenly, his ceremonial robes weighed heavily upon his shoulders, and his tasseled cap pressed into his skull, giving him a headache. Signaling his desire to withdraw, he turned away, but something in the nurse's triumphantly protective stance as she cradled the infant set off a small alarm bell in his mind, and he turned back to take one last look.

At that moment, the cooing of an amorous pair of turtle-doves rose in the garden and the infant turned his head to listen. Emperor Han fell back, pale as a ghost. Emblazoned on the

Prince's left cheek was a tiny ink-black birthmark, an exact replica of the sign of the Qin. It looked as if it had been burned into the baby's face like the brands on condemned criminals in Han's prisons below. The outlaws of Moonshadow Marsh, the gang most defiant of the Emperor's authority, identified themselves with this symbol. The Emperor's own flesh and blood had been born with the clear mark of the outlaw!

Beside himself with shame, the Emperor roared an order for Silver Lotus, the child's mother, to be brought before him. Torn from her bed, where she had been resting after the labor of childbirth, she was forced to kneel in the courtyard like a common thief, before he sentenced her to be stripped of all her worldly possessions and banished. By sunrise, she would be gone from his sight forever, or preparations for her execution would immediately commence.

The lady's attendants began to wail, tearing their hair and ripping their clothes, mourning the fate of their unfortunate mistress. Their cries incited the servants and workers who had spontaneously gathered. Many in the mob of cooks and kitchen helpers, sweepers and smiths, gardeners and artisans had withstood severe beatings and worse in this very courtyard. And the gentle Silver Lotus, the one they called Sacred Mother, had brought them all soothing comfort and charity when the Emperor punished them harshly.

The crowd began to push forward toward the guards, murmuring and invoking her name. "Sacred Mother," they intoned, and ironically, "Fortunate Mother," and some, already giving her the title that would now never be bestowed upon her: "Venerable Mother."

But Silver Lotus ignored the moaning and the lamentations. When she heard the Emperor's proclamation, she rose and with steady hands began to remove her outer robes, letting them drop to the cold flagstones.

A shocked hush fell over the spectators. The Emperor watched her, and for a moment time froze as their eyes locked. Her loyal maidservants rushed to her aid, but she waved them aside, asking in a clear voice for the simple clothes she had worn when she first came to the Forbidden City.

Still the Emperor watched as the First Consort, mother of his only child, deliberately removed the red-and-gold garments of rank layer by layer, and let them blow away in the icy winter wind like burnt paper cutouts at the Festival of the Dead.

Finally, Silver Lotus stood shivering in her yellow slip. Then she put on the dress she had brought from home four long years before, lovingly stitched by her own mother's hand, a poor farmer's attempt to simulate the splendor of the court. She stood there, erect and proud, refusing to bow her head or to lower her eyes. At last, it was Emperor Han who lowered his, disappearing into a circle of soldiers who ushered him rapidly out of sight.

The youngest of the palace maids stepped forward and silently offered Silver Lotus her arm. The new mother smiled gratefully and allowed herself to lean upon it for a moment. Then she called for her dulcimer. When it was brought to her she ran her fingers lightly over the strings, remembering how she had brought it with her when she first entered the court as a young girl, hoping that day, against all odds, to attract the Emperor's attention. With great care, she wrapped the instrument in its silken sack and slung it across her back.

Whereas once her happiness had hung upon each summons into her master's royal presence, in the last year she had grown to hate the Emperor with a passion as strong as the love she bore her new son. To be free of her nightly visits to his bed was a blessing she had long prayed to deserve, although the granting of her wish seemed now to carry with it a death sentence. Her own father had long ago abandoned her, and what remained of her family had been dispersed by flood and famine. Without a home to which she could return, she had no faith she would survive in the world outside the Forbidden City.

As the Emperor's eunuchs led her away, the Prince began to wail inconsolably in his nurse's arms. Pulling away from the guards, she ran to him and, leaning down, touched her lips lightly to his birthmark, covering with a kiss the mark of the Qin.

As Silver Lotus straightened, a young soldier, attempting to dispel the idle onlookers, lashed her with his whip. She cried out and, caught off balance, bent closer to the baby. As she steadied herself, her last piece of jewelry, a heavy locket stamped with the sign of the phoenix, dangled before his eyes. He reached up to play with it, attracted by the glimmer of tiny seed pearls depicting the constellations. Taking it from around her neck, his mother slipped it over his head, tenderly placing the sign of the imperial phoenix on his tiny chest, over his heart, where it shone like a golden shield.

"Whatever happens, little one," she whispered into his ear so that only the child could hear, "you are a prince. Never forget your heritage. Last night the Starlord Hung Wu spoke to me in a dream, claiming to be your father. May he watch over you, for I cannot. Always remember that I love you. One day, perhaps you will rule, and truth and justice will once again reign supreme. Good-bye, my little Starlord."

The baby fingered the phoenix as he held his mother's moon face in his steady gaze. He gave her a small nod, as if he understood. At that same moment, the sun rose, marking the end of her time in the Forbidden City. And two bright drops of blood from the gash the soldier had inflicted fell upon the golden phoenix, solidifying into a gleaming pair of ruby eyes. Silver Lotus bowed her head and submitted to being escorted toward the imposing marble gates.

Under the white arch of the Gate of First Snow, she stood a moment, looking back over her shoulder at the Garden of Pleasant Sounds. There she had spent many peaceful hours by the marble wishing well, anticipating this day of joy when her son would be born and she would be crowned Empress. One agonized, shuddering sob escaped her. Then, cradling her dulcimer, she stepped out into the road and headed toward the teeming streets of Bai Ping, where, if luck stayed with her, she might lose herself among the anonymous poor and live to sing for her supper in the town square.

CHAPTER TWO

The Phoenix

As above, so below.
—The Master Hand

"Our Starlord has arrived," announced the Master Hand, King of Heaven, fingering his own phoenix necklace. "A suitable guardian and teacher must be found. Summon the Tattooed Monk. I must read the signs."

"The monk in question is not in Heaven, Your Majesty," replied the Celestial Detective. "He has been delayed by a natural disaster and the unforeseen appearance of several demons."

The Master Hand sighed. Natural disaster indeed. It was just like the general to be absent from high council. The warrior monk hated meetings. This time, however, matters on earth had gone too far, and the Master Hand would have to begin without him. Perhaps he would show up after the tribunal.

Donning his magistrate's cap, the King of Heaven took his

place in front of his favorite mural depicting his historic victory over Yamu, Lord of the Dead, on the day he trapped ten thousand demons in the Tomb of the Turtle. Some of the immortals had criticized the style of this monumental work of art, hinting that so realistic a portrait of the Lord of the Dead and his demons belonged in the Netherworld, not in Heaven, but the Master Hand enjoyed contemplating his triumph and had commissioned the artist to spare no detail in depicting the horror of those vanquished. Bowing his head, he now took longer than usual with the opening prayer, still hoping the Tattooed Monk would appear. Finally, he called the Celestial Court to order.

The first and only offender, bound in chains, was brought before the Heavenly Throne.

"What, again?" said the Master Hand, sighing mightily when he saw the prisoner. "You are looking the worse for wear, Monkey."

"Have mercy, master," said Monkey, wringing his hands. "It's not dying I fear; it's the rebirth that's the hard part. Please, let me come back as something else—anything else. I just can't stand being Monkey any longer."

"Let's see," said the Master Hand, stroking his long white beard. "It's been three thousand years, has it not? And you still can't seem to get it right."

"My point, exactly," said Monkey, looking truly repentant. "Maybe I'd do better as a dung beetle, sir. Or an ant." He hung his head.

"Perhaps you would," agreed the Master Hand thoughtfully. "Better an insect than a thief—even a master thief."

Monkey looked alarmed. "Or you could give me a job in Heaven to keep me out of trouble," he said, brightening. "I'd be your stable boy, my lord, and groom your nine thousand nine hundred and ninety-nine horses. Or your leaf sweeper in the royal peach orchard."

"Yes, I'm sure you'd like to get close to those peaches," observed the Master Hand. "One bite of the white ones and you'd be as strong as the Dragon King of the North Sea. One bite of the yellow ones and you'd be as wise as the Tattooed Monk. One bite of the purple ones and you'd never grow old. But what have you done to deserve such a feast?"

"Oh, sir, are you implying I would take the fruit without your permission? " asked Monkey plaintively, looking hurt.

The Master Hand signaled his officers, Thousand-League Eye and Down-the-Wind Ear, to come forward. "What are the charges this time? " he asked wearily. Dutifully the Eye unrolled a very long scroll. Monkey cringed, and the Master Hand glared at him sternly.

"Just the main points please," he said.

The Eye scanned the document and began to read: "Charge: breaking and entering. Filed against the accused by the Guardian of the Precious Pearl Gates in the World Beneath the Waves."

"Your Majesty . . ." Monkey began.

"Silence!" thundered the Master Hand. Monkey began tapping his foot impatiently.

"Charge: theft. Filed against the accused by the Dragon King of the South," the Eye continued. "Item: one pair of cloud-stepping shoes."

Monkey stopped tapping his foot.

"Charge: theft. Filed against the accused by the Dragon King of the West. Item: one heirloom chain-mail vest of pure gold."

Monkey crossed his arms over his chest.

"Charge: theft," the Eye droned on. "Filed against the accused by the Dragon King of the East. Item: one magic phoenix-plumed cap of invisibility."

Monkey stuffed the blue feathered cap into his pocket. He scratched his ear and jumped up and down, trying to distract the solemn jury of immortals.

"Charge: theft. Filed against the accused by Chac, the Dragon King of the North . . ."

"Uh-oh, sir, you're not going to like this one. But I can explain, truly I can. . . ."

"Shall I read that last charge again, sir?" asked the Eye.

"No, that won't be necessary," said the Master Hand. "Just tell the court what this thieving Monkey took from the most powerful dragon of the Four Seas."

"Item: iron rod," read the Eye in the same nasal monotone. "Two blue sapphires set in a handle of yellow jade. Shrinks to the size of a sewing needle; expands to the height of the thirty-third Heaven and reaches to the depth of the eighteenth pit of the Netherworld upon command."

"Why, that's my wishing rod!" the Master Hand interrupted. "I used it to pound the Milky Way flat when I created the constellations and subdued Yamu's army of demons. I gave it to Chac for safekeeping after I sealed the Tomb of the Turtle. Impudent ape, did you steal my wishing rod?"

"I never knew it was yours, Your Majesty," Monkey cried. "I'd return it to you right now except—I, uh, lost it while flying here in my cloud-stepping shoes. You see, I wasn't used to the shoes and—"

"Liar!" shouted the Eye. "It's right behind your ear!" He reached out to snatch it, but Monkey danced away, put his cap back on, and turned invisible.

Leaping all around the courtroom, Monkey easily dodged the Eye, who could not see him, and the Ear, who could not keep up with him, as well as the three Red-Legged Ones, who waved their long arms at him, reciting priestly incantations. Monkey, a quick study, repeated the magical chants with slight variations, altering their meaning entirely, so that instead of weakening him, the spells invoked a small tornado that swept through the Celestial Courtroom, tossing legal documents everywhere. The chaos pleased Monkey so much that he laughed out loud, and hopped around so hard his hat fell off, revealing his location in the room.

But he sobered when one of the Red-Legged Ones, indignant at having his spell turned against him, grabbed Monkey firmly by the scruff of his neck and suggested the Master Hand have the scoundrel beheaded immediately, before he could turn invisible again.

"Oh, oh, not the head, not the head," babbled Monkey. "Haven't we done that already? Yes, yes, you had me beheaded in 1068, a very bad year, but I put it right back on again, don't you remember? I learned that trick from a traveling snake charmer. 'Head, come back!' I said. And it did. Yes, and I'll do it again, just you watch!"

Now the proceedings were interrupted by the tardy arrival of the Tattooed Monk, who swept into the Hall of Mists, followed by the Three Judges, all dressed in black.

"General Calabash—late but always welcome," said the Master Hand, smiling as he rose from his throne. But the smile faded when he saw the Tattooed Monk's stormy face.

"I am sorry to interrupt, sir," said the monk, bowing briefly. "These gentlemen have further evidence to present against this . . . Monkey." He spat out the last word like sour wine and glared at the ape with pure hatred.

The Three Judges pressed forward, seizing the opportunity to state their case. The Master Hand sat back on his throne with a resigned sigh.

"This wretched baboon is guilty of high treason. He works for Yamu now," said the first. At this accusation, the other judges nodded furiously.

"He broke into our chambers with your wishing rod, sir," cried the second judge, sending the others into loud lamentation. "The blow caused a fissure in the earth near the Tomb of the Turtle, and several of Yamu's demons leaked through."

"I think he may have loosened the lock to the Tomb of the Turtle, Your Majesty," said the third. "And then he tried to steal the Book!"

"I didn't steal the Book, sir," cried Monkey earnestly.

Dropping his defiant pose, he prostrated himself before the Master Hand, banging his head on the floor three times.

"I said he *tried* to steal it," answered the third judge, shaking with indignation. "He did not succeed, Your Honor. But he did find his name and crossed it out with my ink brush! He has upset the whole balance between darkness and light. No mortal may erase his name from the Book of the Living and the Dead!"

"I only wanted to be immortal!" wailed Monkey piteously. "But I didn't make that volcano erupt, Your Honor. I swear, that was just a coincidence. Yes, I tried to steal the Book. But the rest was Yamu's doing. Do you think I would have gone there at all if I had known it was going to blow up?"

Now the Tattooed Monk could contain himself no longer. His tattoos began to glow and move in shifting patterns, and his head began to shine like a fortune-teller's globe. The colors blurred and blended and rearranged themselves into discernible pictures and symbols that spread up and down his back, crisscrossed with scars. It was an irritating procedure that made his skin itch ferociously, as if a thousand mosquitoes were biting at once, worse even than the slow healing of battle wounds. But he was used to it. Only the Master Hand could read the signs with unerring accuracy, although others had tried with varying success. The monk could not read them himself, of course, and that always irked him.

It was more than a little disconcerting to be undergoing the changes in the middle of a trial. Normally, he was sitting or standing still in meditation when the transformations occurred. But these were strange times, and nothing was as it should be.

The monk tried to put what he had recently witnessed on Sleeping Giant Mountain out of his mind. But the horrific eruption replayed in his brain over and over again—the black smoke, the chanting and prayers replaced by bloodcurdling screams, the smell of fear and burning flesh, the excruciating heat, the electric crackle of holy books consumed in flame, the crumbling of the ancient monastery, and the ashy aftermath. He had risked his own life to save three scrolls. But he had failed to drag his old friend Gong Sun from the wreckage in time. Nor had he managed to save the others in the Order of the Silver Lotus.

"The Lord of the Dead has won a terrible victory today," cried the monk, pointing an accusing finger at Monkey. "One atrocious act has erased the wisdom of generations. And all because of this stupid, shortsighted ape!"

"Please, sir, in the name of all my ancestors, that is not true!" Monkey pressed his hands together in supplication. "I freely admit to the other charges. I am sorry I stole the shoes and the vest and the cap. I am even sorrier I stole your wishing rod. Punish me, lord, and I will submit. But I cannot be blamed for things beyond my control."

Ignoring Monkey, the Tattooed Monk urgently directed his plea to the Master Hand: "With all due respect, sir, Yamu is about to engineer the most devastating jailbreak in history. If he wakes the land dragons and succeeds in tricking Emperor Han into unlocking the Tomb of the Turtle, all hell will break loose. Are we just going to stand here, listening to this lowlife protest his innocence?"

The Master Hand sadly shook his head. "I am disappointed in you, Monkey. Extremely disappointed."

"I just wanted to look like an immortal, Your Honor, that's all," begged Monkey, but the Master Hand was no longer paying attention, distracted by the monk's tattoos, which now showed the martyred Gong Sun's face, a pale mask of agony wreathed in smoke.

"I am your loyal subject," Monkey tried again. "I have died many times, but I swear I have never worked for the Lord of the Dead. I would do almost anything to be immortal. But I would never betray you to serve Yamu. You believe me, don't you?"

"I don't know what to believe about you anymore, Monkey," answered the Master Hand grimly. He turned to the Tattooed Monk. "Have you anything more to report, General Calabash?" he asked.

The monk frowned, his tattoos fading. He let his mind linger on his friend Gong Sun, smiling in welcome only a few brief days ago, exhorting him to rest from his travels and take his ease at the sanctuary. The scholarly farmer's most fervent prayer had been that his youngest daughter forgive him for abandoning her to join the order. He had managed to see her only once since he had become a monk long ago. His dying wish was that General Calabash find her and tell her how much he had loved her. But in all the years they had known one another, the two monks had never spoken much about the lives they had left behind, and Gong Sun breathed his last before he could tell his friend her name or even the name of the village where he had once lived.

Overcome with grief, the monk hid his face in his hands. Shocked by this rare display of emotion, the other immortals cried for retribution. The accused covered his ears against the clamor, knowing his final hour had come.

"I am lost," Monkey cried desperately. "Oh, I am lost, I feel it in my heart!"

"And what does a monkey heart weigh?" asked the monk coldly, recovering his composure.

The Master Hand rose from his throne, commanding silence, and pronounced sentence: "Once again, Monkey, you have not tried to earn your immortality but selfishly attempted to steal it. You have resorted to common thievery as a shortcut. You have been unable to love anyone but yourself. And you have been unwilling to sacrifice anything but your morality. Worst of all, you have caused innocent lives to be lost. And so, you must die."

Then, sternly ordering the Celestial Detective to complete the proceedings and bring him Monkey's ashes, he thanked the Tattooed Monk and all who had testified and hurried from the hall.

With a nod from the Celestial Detective, a Red-Legged One marched Monkey to the block. At the word "Strike!" the royal executioner swung mightily, and Monkey's head fell upon the ground and rolled away like a melon. But miraculously, Monkey shed no blood.

"Head come back!" called Monkey to his head, just as he had boasted he would. But he should not have boasted, for the Red-Legged Ones had used a charm to root Monkey's head to the ground as soon as it fell from his shoulders, and it stayed firmly where it was, about twenty paces away.

Monkey had to think fast. "Grow!" he commanded. And to the immortals' amazement, a new head magically replaced the old one.

"It didn't hurt at all," Monkey boasted, regaining his bravado.

"Put him in the Crucible of Eight Trigrams," the Tattooed Monk commanded.

So Monkey was placed inside the holy crucible, where the

forces of the heavenly winds would freeze and crack him; the crashing tides of the earth's four seas would turn him to sludge and primordial mud; and the explosive powers within the earth's crust would burn and grind him into volcanic rock, reducing him finally to dust. "Is this how it will all end?" he lamented loudly. He wriggled into the section marked Wind, hoping that Wind would blow out Fire, but when the lid was lifted, all that was left of Monkey after the elements had done their work was a thin soft layer of dusty ash at the bottom of the crucible.

The Celestial Detective delivered Monkey's ashes to the Master Hand, who locked them away inside the golden phoenix locket around his neck.

Although the Tattooed Monk would certainly advise against it, the Master Hand intended to give Monkey another chance. In spite of repeated sins and shortcomings, the Master Hand still had faith in the ridiculous ape. No soul yearned for immortality more than Monkey. And no soul had pursued it through as many lives without success. Soon, like the phoenix, he would rise out of the ashes. But not too soon. For the present, the Master Hand had a new Starlord to attend to and more important things to worry about.

Although patience was not one of Monkey's virtues, the misbehaving ape would just have to wait.

CHAPTER THREE

The Immortal Beggar

The listening gods bring us to speech through their silence.
—Emperor Hung Wu

A lone wolf prowled through the dry cattails, searching for prey. Gulls fought over herring caught in Mother Gu's brush traps, and black-crowned herons stirred in the groaning branches of the nearby nesting tree. It was not yet dawn and the outlaws' hut, nestled in dune grass, still vibrated with the familiar sounds of the marsh at night.

White Streak sat up, listening intently. There was a faraway vibration in the morning wind, a disturbance he could not name. He sprang from his pallet and dressed quickly, turning the faint foreign note over in his mind. It most resembled the high-pitched, underwater wailing of an approaching tribe of demon ponaturi.

White Streak was born with hearing so acute he would sit or stand as still as a stone for hours as a child, listening. When he did finally begin to speak, he answered his family not in words but in whatever language happened to draw his attention, from the quick flutter of the song swallows living in the eaves, and the eerie whales' song beneath the waves, to the bell-like tones of a colony of bats, deep in the cedar woods to the north.

"When he's ready, he'll talk," Mother Gu told her friends. "And when that time comes," she added with confidence, "you would all do well to listen."

White Streak grew up strong, and as his mother had predicted, well-spoken for his years. Now, at eighteen years of age, he was leader of the small gang of outlaws most feared by the Emperor. By virtue of his frequent attacks on the imperial soldiers who dared enter his domain, and his bold defense of the poor against the injustice of the Emperor's taxes, he was considered the most dangerous criminal on the royal wanted list.

In the gloomy early morning chill, Mother Gu was already alert and fully dressed, a mountain of a woman, clad in a long-sleeved jacket and wide trousers of rough brown cotton with a red sash wound around her barrel-like torso and a second just below her waist, supporting her paunch. She busied herself with breakfast, pouring two steaming cups of tea and hastily preparing a platter of crisp fried trout. An accomplished wrestler, she had already performed fifteen hundred deep knee-bends that morning and had weighted her sleeves with iron balls. Gathering the cloth in her hands and whirling her huge body with surprising grace and speed, she had practiced for hours before sunrise in her vegetable garden, demolishing a straw opponent over and over again with unerring and deadly accuracy.

She set the food before her son, slamming it down as she always did when serving her customers at the Golden Phoenix. Then she added a steaming platter of his favorite dumplings stuffed with sweet bean paste.

"Eat up," she said brusquely. "It's a long way to Morning Cloud Cove—and I've heard the ponaturi are moving upriver."

White Streak helped himself to a generous serving of dumplings.

"I guess I'm not the only one with ears," he said. "But why the cove? Out with it, Mother! What else have you heard?"

When she wasn't fishing or minding her garden, Mother Gu was a first-class spy, tending bar and swapping gossip at the Golden Phoenix. The inn stood at the entrance to Moonshadow Marsh, and no one who entered escaped her notice.

"A monk claiming to be the sole survivor of the fire at Sleeping Giant Mountain came to our door during the sixth watch," she answered. "He was a big man, bald as a baby, with strange tattoos all over him. He wanted me to wake you."

"Why didn't you, Mother?"

She hesitated, reddening. "He frightened me," she admitted.

"Mother Gu, frightened?" he teased her. "The one who's been attacked by tigers, poisoned by serpents, and buried alive? The one who's met Yamu and his demons face to face and returned to tell the tale? The one who married my father when all the other girls sensibly ran the other way? Frightened by a monk?"

His mother shrugged, and, choosing to ignore his sarcasm,

shook her head, genuinely puzzled.

"I don't know why he frightened me," she mused.

White Streak smiled, patting her large hand. Mother Gu's face broke into a million anxious wrinkles. "You must go see your father," she said, searching his face. White Streak's smile faded and he turned away, lowering his eyes. His father appeared infrequently and only when there was real trouble. White Streak had a long scar on his chest, close to his heart, as a permanent memento of his last visit. As dreadful as an advancing army of ponaturi might be, he sensed something worse was about to descend on Moonshadow Marsh.

No longer hungry, White Streak stood, thanking his mother for the meal. She was right, of course. He would have to go to Morning Cloud Cove where the tides turned and the swamp gave way to the open sea. It was the only place his father would show himself. The meeting would require a day's intricate journey along the murky Great River, where a treacherous web of meandering creeks and misty waterways posed a terrible threat to sailors, even to those like himself and his twin brother, Black Whirlwind, who knew the territory well enough not to take a dead-end turn.

For the trip, White Streak would need his trusted navigator, Chiko Chin, and perhaps his spies, Day Rat and Jade Mirror, who were also his most accomplished marksmen. But no, he would have to do without Jade Mirror, he remembered, sighing. She was in the palace, attending the First Consort, who had just given birth to the heir to the Imperial Throne. And if Jade Mirror was in the Forbidden City, Day Rat would most likely be there as well.

Eager to be gone now, White Streak took up his harpoon and knife, preparing to leave, but his mother blocked the door and placed both hands on his shoulders, looking earnestly into his eyes.

"Demons that haven't surfaced for centuries have been seen not far from the cove," she warned. "A small boy named Kuan from Banpo Village has disappeared. His parents think he's been kidnapped by the Nokk, or perhaps a demon wahwee. . . ."

"Any more bogey stories before I say good-bye?" White Streak laughed.

"Remember, the Nokk is a shapeshifter, the lowest of the low," she said gruffly, stepping aside. "Be careful." As an answer, he gave her a brief affectionate squeeze around the middle before racing down the rough tumble of rocks that camouflaged their fisherman's hut toward the stony beach below. He turned back and waved, but she had already gone inside.

As he made his way to the hidden landing, White Streak startled two giant gray herons who snaked their long-beaked heads in his direction and froze. With his warrior's topknot, his five-pronged harpoon, and the black sign of the Qin branded upon his chest, bare even in winter, White Streak was a formidable sight to any stranger. But he was a familiar figure to the local birds, and his sudden towering appearance did not warrant more than a brief pause in the regal pair's peaceful patrol of the estuary.

It was high tide, and the current was fierce as White Streak waded through the mud, disturbing the cormorants who nested thickly on the slippery black boulders surrounding his sand skiff. There it was—his pride and joy and true home. As soon as he saw it, he was comforted. At least whatever had exploded on Sleeping Giant Mountain, shaking loose the ponaturi and who knows what other demons, had not touched his boat, the *Immortal Beggar*. It was still the same, cheerfully bobbing on the waves.

The *Immortal Beggar* was named after the Eighth Genie, a poor student adept in the magical arts who was good at detaching his soul from flesh and bone and floating at will through the universe. One day he forgot his body in a field and, according to the legend, lost it forever. Forced to enter the corpse of a crippled old mendicant lying by the road, he had to keep that shape all his life, and entered Heaven with only a crooked crutch to his name. During the Festival of Lanterns honoring the dead, White Streak always set out alms for the wandering spirit of the Immortal Beggar, asking him to watch over his beloved boat. Inside the lantern on its prow was a tin effigy of the craft's guardian, waving his single crutch. Dark now, the figure creaked as it spun slowly in the wind. But when lit, its cheerful shadow would project out over the shifting water, dancing wildly, and seemingly beckoning the outlaws to safety.

White Streak hacked at the mass of tangled weeds that hid the *Immortal Beggar*, and when it was free, sprang aboard, guiding it effortlessly through a maze of twisting channels that ended in an overgrown salt pond. Darting in and out among the familiar islands, he was suddenly surrounded by an eerie chorus of wood frogs. Before he could react, his paddle was pulled from his hand and a dark wet seal-like head emerged from the water.

"Ho, there, where are you going in such a hurry?" bellowed Black Whirlwind, blocking White Streak's quick thrust of the steering pole. "Don't you say hello to your big brother anymore?"

"You're only four minutes older, remember?" White Streak laughed.

"I can't say—I wasn't there. We'll have to take Mother's word for it. And where is she, by the way?"

"Home, practicing her fatal swing. It's a miracle I survived breakfast. What brings you out so early? And where's Chiko Chin?"

On cue, another muddy head popped up a few yards away, like a river goblin. Brown water ran in rivulets down his bushy beard, framing his broad grin. "Here," he said, jumping into the boat and taking the oar. "Let me have that before you knock yourself out with it."

"I wouldn't count on it." White Streak lunged for him and almost dumped him overboard. "Hey, steady, I thought you knew how to steer."

"Only when extra cargo isn't weighing me down," grunted Chiko Chin, tackling him. "Whirlwind, let's toss this ugly one back—he stinks"; and he made to throw White Streak over the side.

"Hold there, Chiko," yelled his mate, pointing to his giant double-bladed ax, sheathed in leather and strapped to his back. "If you hurt my twin I'll have to use these twins on you. And if you have no head, how will you read a map? Anyway, you stink, too."

"And you stink worst of all," said Chiko Chin, holding

his nose. Having established that they all stank, the three out-laws good-naturedly settled down, filling one another in on their lives and changes in the gang's fortunes since the last time they had all been together. None of the three noticed a darkening of the waters under their speeding craft, and a gradual change of color from brown to blood red.

Dragon Scroll

There is a crack in everything. That's how the light gets in.
—Monkey

Deep beneath the overpopulated dungeons of the Imperial Palace, where the innocent outnumbered the guilty, in the crumbling tunnels and unexcavated tombs, lay the foul cave of a long-forgotten land dragon. Clouds of red vapor whirled around the massive serpent's head as black volcanic sands settled in powdery lines along his plated spine. Scarred by the flow of molten lava that had trapped him thousands of years ago, he stirred restlessly in a deathlike sleep.

"Awake," whispered Yamu hoarsely. "Stir yourself, Old Bones."

The behemoth slowly opened his heavily lidded eyes, staring sightlessly at Yamu, Lord of the Dead. He shook his gigantic armored head and shifted his ponderous tail, revealing in the ruins of his soiled lair a defiled and battered scroll like those the Tattooed Monk had, at the risk of his life, rescued from the burning Temple of the Five Blessings.

Yamu had satisfied himself earlier with a tour of the royal prisons. Of those arrested and branded by the Emperor's corrupt law enforcers, very few were criminals. Some were poor starving lads, caught robbing as a last resort. But most were hardworking farmers, taxed beyond endurance, ensnared in Han's cruel system of justice, and punished for debts they could do nothing to avoid. He was certain now, after making the rounds, that Emperor Han was the long-sought key to the Tomb of the Turtle and the perfect instrument of his wrath. That fool of a Monkey had unwittingly played directly into his hands by stealing the wishing rod and breaking the lock. But he needed a more exalted fool to open the sealed subterranean chambers and release the Spellbinders.

"Han is weak, dwarfed by the shadow of the former Emperor. He will never live up to his father's name. Unless, Old Bones, we decide to help him. What do you say, eh?" asked Yamu, stroking his pet where he most enjoyed it, along the spiny roots of his gargantuan wings. "Shall we set off a few fireworks for this cowardly dolt and show him how to unleash the ravaging plagues of living hell? Shall we toss his false pride into a boiling stream of sulfur? Shall we melt his vanity with red-hot tongs and lead him and his dull bell-clanking worshippers by their lying tongues into the eternal abyss? Shall we raise the ghostly Spellbinders and, banners flying, march our demon army to victory?"

Old Bones closed his eyes, soothed by his master's deeply

hypnotic voice. He was not the most intelligent of dragons, but he made up for his lack of imagination with his brute strength and gigantic wingspan.

Yamu smiled indulgently, injecting the dragon's dream state with a vision of a tall warrior on a golden horse, dressed in blazing golden armor. "Look at her, my darling," he crooned softly. "Trained by Spotted Leopard himself. Magnificent and ruthless. See how she gleams like a metal bird of prey? Her name is Golden Wings, my pet. Shake off this hibernation and serve me well one last time, and she's yours, the spoils of victory, to keep in your treasure hoard, until she tarnishes with time. But not quite yet," he cautioned, as the ancient veteran snorted black smoke and stirred restlessly, clawing the flagstones. "Soon, very soon, I will call you, Old Bones. And then, my dear one, you will come."

Far above the dragon's resting place, in the Tower of the Water Clock, the sharp grating of metallic scales against stone sent a shudder through the agitated Emperor Han. Pacing back and forth, through the echoing Hall of Earthly Tranquillity, Han had surrounded himself with his twelve most trusted counselors, all of whom paced with him.

They had begun their vigil two nights before, to the clamor of bells and the beating of ceremonial drums, and as the third morning dawned, they were the worse for wear. In all that time, their lord, who normally never exited the royal bedchamber before noon, had not closed his eyes once. When the Emperor went without sleep, no one around him slept either, for fear of awakening in the spirit world without a head.

In the adjoining Hall of Supreme Harmony, banquet

tables heavily laden with meat and fruit stood ready for the celebration. Three thousand honored guests from the four corners of the Empire would soon arrive in their finest ceremonial attire to pay their respects to the Emperor's successor. The Prince's name would be written on the sacred tablet and entered into the sealed box behind Father Han's coffin: Prince Zong, Heir to the Imperial Throne.

As Han stood staring blindly out at the barren winter landscape beyond the Meridian Gate, a wisp of reddish vapor snaked through a crack in the copper-tiled floor and wrapped around his head. Absently, he brushed it away like an evil odor. But in that fleeting moment, one of his weary advisers noticed his master's long, sickly face take on a strange reptilian cast, closely resembling the fearsome features of the two gigantic gilded dragons decorating the vaulted ceiling above the Imperial Throne.

Old Bones, in the meantime, had once again fallen asleep. With a great putrid sigh, the dragon blew shards of rubble around his subterranean nest, burying the briefly revealed scroll.

CHAPTER FIVE

Black Swans of the Red Tide

Nature has no outline.
—The Master Hand

"Dragon phlegm!" muttered Chiko Chin, jutting out his jaw as he strained to propel the *Immortal Beggar* through the crimson tide. As the mist rolled in, the three outlaws grew less talkative, turning their attention to the tortuous route toward Morning Cloud Cove. The landscape, shrouded in hemlocks, began to take on a blighted look, with slanting patches of sea grass withered by relentless winds from the north.

Black Whirlwind frowned at the change in weather and hunched his shoulders against the chilly air. "Feels like a baku flying over," he said.

The male baku was said to herald rain but was more notorious for its lack of fatherly feeling. With its powerful bill and sharp claws, the giant seabird caressed its young so fiercely that often it made a bloody mess of the nest.

"It's no surprise you'd be thinking of the rain bird," said White Streak. "After all, we're on our way to see Father."

Black Whirlwind studied his brother's gloomy face. "I used to wonder why Father always took you into battle and left me at home," he said thoughtfully.

"You're the eldest, and heir to his gold. I'm the more expendable son, I guess."

Black Whirlwind shook his head. "Father has no heir. He would never part with his hoard. If flood, famine, and pestilence were to threaten us all at once, he might toss Mother a bag of gold, but he would probably ask for interest on the loan. He always loved you best, though—you know that. Even Mother admits it. He's made no secret of it."

"Count yourself blessed for being unloved then," said White Streak bitterly.

"Blessed, eh? I'll bet you all his gold, should it ever be mine, that when we see him after all this time, he'll speak only to you. As far as he's concerned, I don't exist."

"Then you can return the favor by pretending he doesn't either," answered White Streak. "That way, maybe you'll live to a ripe old age."

"Quiet, both of you!" growled Chiko Chin, shaking his shaggy head at the twins. "I can't steer through this soup with your dreary whining clogging my ears."

Through the fog, a bevy of black swans appeared, silently following the boat. Suddenly, their silence was echoed by a surrounding silence so profound, White Streak had the sensation of tumbling into it, as if falling down a deep dark hole.

The outlaw could not remember a time in Moonshadow Marsh, even in the frozen months of winter, when he had heard nothing at all—no salamanders burrowing through submarine tunnels, no rhythmic drops of rain falling from clouds of fog in the trees, no pipers, no birdsong—no sounds at all from the galaxy of small things alive in the wetlands, not even the soft whisper of an unfurling fern leaf in a receding bank of snow. It was as if the whole land held its breath or had died for a moment. The river was now a deep muddy red and so shallow it was nearly impossible to move.

"I've never seen a tide like this," muttered Chiko, who knew the local tides so well, many thought he had some influence over them. "We'll soon be stranded on the flats like a bunch of toads."

Black Whirlwind spat over the side. "Some old sea slug is drinking the streams dry," he said.

White Streak looked sharply at his brother. "Mother warned me that the Nokk was nearby, but I didn't take her seriously," he said, eyeing the swans uneasily.

"Your mistake," rasped Black Whirlwind, slowly unsheathing his double ax. Chiko Chin made no move toward his knives but continued to row, calmly maneuvering through the tight passageway. He tried to put more power into his strokes, but roots and tangled cranberry vines dragged the *Immortal Beggar* almost to a standstill. Distant thunder broke the silence and the sky darkened.

The swans quietly formed a tight circle around the boat, their yellow beaks glowing strangely in the stormy light.

Impulsively, Chiko leaned toward the prow and lit the night

lantern. "Pray to your patron, mate," he said to White Streak, as the projected silhouette of the Immortal Beggar danced out over the shallow water.

The sudden apparition seemed to frighten the swans. They milled about, trumpeting. Then, as quickly as they had come, they disappeared like ghosts.

A suffocating odor filled the air. Suddenly, the craft spun to a halt. Although they were hardly moving at all, the impact was so violent, Black Whirlwind was thrown off balance, toppling overboard.

A jellyfish larger than any White Streak had ever seen oozed out from its own glistening center, curling around Black Whirlwind. The living mass was transparent, and White Streak could see its coiled entrails, pulsing and clenching in the churning water. It was swallowing his brother alive!

In a fury, Black Whirlwind let out a hair-raising battle cry and began striking left and right. The more ferociously he struck, the faster he sank, until he was waist deep in crimson slime. Like a human tornado, he cut and cut again, swinging the double blades of his enormous ax, but the sea of flesh continued to squeeze, relentlessly drawing him down. At last, Black Whirlwind sank so deep into the swamp, he could no longer maneuver his bloody weapon. Held in a death grip, he struggled desperately. At that moment, a serpentlike tentacle reached out and wrapped itself around his neck.

Now White Streak saw that the colossal thing had eight strong arms, each with two rows of deadly suckers. And at their center was a terrible glassy eye. Hooking his fishing knife into the edge of the boat to steady himself, he hurled his harpoon into the monster, holding on with all his strength. Impaled, the Nokk loosened its grip and Black Whirlwind took a great gulp of icy air, filling his lungs. But just as the whiplike stalk that held him began to loosen, another wrapped itself tightly around his waist. Violently twisting, he slashed at the Nokk with all his might as it carried him under.

White Streak resisted the temptation to release his knife and attack the Nokk's writhing tendrils. Even if he should succeed in amputating one or two, he didn't have time to cut off all eight before his brother drowned. He remembered Mother Gu's first principle of combat: *When fighting an opponent stronger than yourself, use his own strength against him.*

The Nokk's power seemed to emanate from its hunger. White Streak held on as hard as he could, working the ragged edge of the Nokk's gargantuan body toward its own predatory center. Greedily, the monster's gut began to fold over into itself as the horrible beak continued to suck. Still, the outlaw held on as the Nokk drew itself into its own lashing intestines. Senselessly, it gorged upon its own fat, eating itself into extinction.

White Streak grimaced and pulled his arm away just in time as the Nokk twisted into one long corkscrew, spooling tighter and tighter until it swallowed itself completely—all but its mouth. Finally, the insatiable creature vanished entirely in a violent red whirlpool.

With a banshee yell, Black Whirlwind dived straight into that snaking maelstrom. Pulling his knife and harpoon free, White Streak followed after him, leaving the challenge of righting the *Immortal Beggar* to Chiko Chin.

White Streak knew the Nokk was not defeated. Although blinded by its frothing trail, he swam with eyes wide open, watching for the shapeshifter's next transformation.

CHAPTER SIX

Puk

Surprise is the triumph of the future over the past.
—Mother Gu

Having feasted upon itself, the Nokk was still hungry. Tossing in the chaotic current, White Streak had no chance to adjust to the underwater darkness before he was viciously assaulted by a deadly set of slashing teeth. Stabbing his harpoon into the roof of that toothy steel trap, White Streak watched as a massive head materialized.

There was no scourge of the sea more ferocious than Puk, Yamu's overgrown hound, and that was who the shapeshifter had elected to become next. Sharks and octopi were breakfast and lunch to Puk, but dinner and dessert were often human. The demon dog's great glowing eyes illuminated the water with a strange light, attracting phosphorescent fairy shrimp in droves. The tiny crustaceans danced in greenish clouds, obscuring White Streak's vision. Flailing about, he tried to swipe at them, but they only grew thicker and more persistent. Puk attempted to free himself from the shooting pain of White Streak's well-aimed harpoon, but White Streak dug his weapon in deeper.

Now the Nokk had managed a full transformation, and White Streak could see the rest of the mammoth mutt's body. Puk was as big as a bull calf and twelve times as powerful. But White Streak did not sense any evil emanating from the cur, just a houndlike love of the hunt.

"Reckless pup!" he said, startling the demon by addressing him underwater. "You are young and I don't wish to kill you. I think you haven't been a demon long. Is Yamu so kind a master that you wish to be a slave to his bidding? Did he buy you from your mother with a few gems and coins? Or did he kidnap you from her ocean cave?"

Puk growled deeply, trying to bite off his tormentor's fighting arm. This human who could magically speak underwater seemed to know him and had somehow guessed his secret. His own monster mother had sold him to the Lord of the Dead for a pair of golden earrings as big as chariot wheels set with diamonds as bright as the crashing surf surrounding their rocky home. And all because Puk had given his father a nasty bite before he was old enough to know any better.

Would his mother be sorry if she could see him now? Would she even know him, now that he was part Nokk? He had let the Nokk absorb him to escape Yamu. But it was terribly confusing to see the world as the Nokk saw it. He never knew how long he would be one thing or another. Whose eyes was he looking out of now, for example—his own or the Nokk's? And what Puk hated most about being joined to the shapeshifter was life as a stupid jellyfish between changes. Little wonder the Nokk needed him. Puk was by far the shapeshifter's best self. If he could only find a way to resist the changes and keep his own shape a little longer. If he could only find a way of staying Puk at least for a while.

"Look, you're bleeding," said White Streak, "and I promise to free you if you listen to me. I'm a hunter too. Help me hunt the demon who has stolen the boy Kuan from Banpo village, and your reward will be great. If you refuse"—here he punctuated his threat with another twist of his harpoon—"the sharks will feast upon your carcass for weeks to come."

Puk did not like to be threatened, and there was nothing he hated worse than sharks. Although by now he was in great pain and his wound was bleeding profusely, this puny hunter was becoming an irritation. Why not just eat him and be done with it? Stretching his sinewy neck to its limit, he bit through White Streak's harpoon. Then, fiercely gnashing his bloody teeth, he lunged forward to bite off the outlaw's head when a crushing blow from behind stunned him into a defensive dive.

White Streak was never so happy to see his brother. Grabbing Black Whirlwind's arm so as not to lose him again, the two plunged in pursuit of the fleeing menace, down to the black depths of the ocean floor.

They would have to work quickly, for in addition to speaking to beasts of the woods and sea, White Streak had been born with the ability to breathe underwater for seven days and seven nights—but this was not a talent shared by his twin brother, who had already almost drowned that day.

The farther they sank, the thicker grew the hordes of fairy shrimp surrounding them, until they could hardly propel themselves through the glowing multitude. Though still reeling from the blunt end of Black Whirlwind's double-bladed ax bashing into his skull, Puk was in a feeding frenzy, and had disappeared into the swarming throng. Only his flashing teeth were still visible, bared in an ecstatic grin of satisfied gluttony. He appeared to have lost interest in the outlaws now that he was hunting smaller prey. Very soon his trail of blood would attract sharks.

White Streak signaled his brother to give up the chase. Together, they began to rise toward the surface. But the glowing army pressed in around White Streak, and now the floaters were turning as green as sea worms and gibbering in a garbled language. Although the words were indecipherable, the sound was familiar. As one or two attached themselves to him, others followed until his chest was shrouded in bristling luminescence. They spread toward his face, sealing his mouth and nose, spinning him around like a revolving underwater mummy.

Too late, White Streak realized these were not fairy shrimp as he had assumed, but the same devilish tribe of ponaturi he had heard from a distance that morning, a thousand times more dangerous than the demon dog. In fact, it seemed now that Puk had disappeared altogether. Surprisingly, White Streak felt a pang of loss; but it was quickly replaced by a surge of fear as he understood that the Nokk had changed yet again.

Of all the dangers, Mother Gu had taught him, *the greatest is to think lightly of the foe.* Struggling to breathe as the jabbering ponaturi cut off his supply of air, White Streak was struck once again by his mother's wisdom. He had misjudged his present enemy, discounting a harmless host of tiny sea scavengers when he should have been girding himself for a surprise attack. He had grown arrogant in the fight against Puk, an inexperienced opponent, forgetting that his battle was truly with an enemy many thousands of years old. His guard had slipped, and now he would surely die.

As he struggled, trying to rip the malevolent pests off his skin, he searched his mind for what he knew about his enemy, but their incessant babble rose in volume and invaded his brain. Beset on all sides, he began to feel numb as they latched on wherever they found a hold. Now he noticed a thin thread of blood snaking out from each place they had attached themselves, and it took him a moment to realize it was his own blood. White spots danced before his eyes, bursting like small explosions inside his head. He began to feel dizzy as the demon tribe continued to drag him down toward the mossy bottom.

He struggled not to lose consciousness, his power to reason almost gone. He knew he must not enter the kingdom of the ponaturi, and he clung to that knowledge like a lifeline, summoning all his strength to resist. Once there, his father had warned him many times, it was almost impossible to find one's way back.

His father! It was all his fault he was here at all. A wave of rage surged through him like fire. With renewed strength he snatched at his attackers, crushing them in his hands and popping their goggle-eyed heads like seaweed pods. They shrieked horribly, leaking a yellowish phosphorescent glow that covered him in a sulfurous cloud. Instantly, many more took their places, sinking their tiny hooks into his face.

The ponaturi were leading him farther and farther from the light, down through the layers of rotting leaves, beneath the sunken taproots and dead tree snags into their putrid caves. There, he had been told, they kept the pickled body parts of captured sailors in urns salvaged from ancient shipwrecks, as well as the poor drowned children they had managed to kidnap at sea, preserved in pots and jars.

He held his breath and played dead, hoping if the ponaturi thought him lifeless they would release their grip. But the scavengers only tightened their hold. Oddly, White Streak found himself thinking of Puk. If he only had the demon dog by his side, he could slash these little ghouls to pieces. But what was he thinking? Puk was the ponaturi, the ponaturi were Puk, and both were the Nokk. The shapeshifter was playing games.

Suddenly, White Streak went rigid with panic. In his battle to stay alive, he had lost track of his brother. If White Streak, the better swimmer, was hard pressed to keep from drowning, surely his twin had already lost the battle.

Tortured by demon pincers digging deeply into his flesh, he was aware that with every passing moment, he was losing more blood. If he didn't find Black Whirlwind soon, he was not sure he would have the remaining strength to make his way back up to the surface.

As it grew darker, the ponaturi grew larger and brighter. With long spikes along their spines and whiplike tails, they slashed back and forth at high speeds. White Streak stretched out his arms, waving his fingers like water plants, trying to attract the ponaturi to his hands. Light, he needed more light. Suddenly, like a pinpoint of candlelight through the thick fog in his mind, appeared the story his father used to tell about the bravest of fathers who tried to rescue his human son from the ponaturi, tricking them by exposing them to the sun. Light was their enemy—sunlight, lantern light, light from his world. It would kill them outright. But where in this abysmal chasm would he find light?

As if some malevolent intelligence were responding to this thought, it grew even darker over his head. Looking up, he saw a giant shadow pursuing him. He tried to swim away; but it followed him, growing larger and more solid, like the eagle wing of Yamu, Lord of the Dead, reaching out to claim him.

Now White Streak swam as if possessed, knowing he must rid himself of this black shadow or die. And then he thought he must have died after all, for dancing before his half-blinded eyes, in the blackest part of the pursuing shadow, was the deep purple hunchbacked silhouette of the Immortal Beggar, dazzling the astonished outlaw with a brilliant flash of light. The ponaturi began to screech in torment, curling and turning black like burning shrouds on a funeral pyre. And then, as suddenly as they had descended upon him, the demons weren't there at all!

Two strong hands plunged down through the flickering gloom, grabbed him roughly by the hair and hoisted him up. He thought his head would burst from the sudden ascent, and he screamed in pain as he breached out of the icy water, blinking furiously.

"Steady now, little brother," came a familiar voice. Hearing it, White Streak took a deep rasping breath and gratefully fell back into Black Whirlwind's arms as Chiko Chin, holding the lantern high in one hand, continued to project the weirdly wavering shape of the Immortal Beggar onto the rising waters, banishing the demon ponaturi into the darkness from which they had come.

CHAPTER SEVEN

The Guardian

One cannot step twice into the same river.
—Gong Sun, Order of the Silver Lotus

General Calabash removed his yellow monk's robes, revealing a bronzed muscular torso, every inch of which was covered in tattoos. Taking a large gourd from his belt and twirling it in his hands, he seated himself before the Heavenly Throne. Chanting, he began to meditate.

The Master Hand leaned forward, watching as the tattoos shifted and changed, revealing ancient writings that documented a mystical form of kung fu, and diagrams similar to those on the scrolls the Tattooed Monk had rescued from the burning Temple of Five Blessings. The magic signs and symbols glowed like constellations in the northern sky but soon dissolved, giving way to the face of a fierce white tiger, fading into a bird's-eye view of a snow-covered mountaintop. A ragged procession of rough-looking men emerged, winding through the icy ravines, their clothing tattered, their feet bleeding and bound in rags. That picture, too, disappeared, replaced by a terrifying dragon, hurling fiery bolts at the frozen earth. Then came the gaping mouth of a demon wahwee, swallowing an entire village in a roaring tidal wave. And out of that terror rose the image of a hero in white, a tall warrior with a five-pronged harpoon and a chest as bare as the day he was born, branded with the sign of the Qin. Beside him stood his wild-haired twin dressed all in black, a formidable figure twirling a double-bladed ax with one arm and nestling a crying child with the other.

"Ah," said the Master Hand, rubbing his knees. "Now we're getting somewhere. These two look like suitable guardians. Twin brothers, eh?"

But the twins disappeared as well, and an inferno of fire dominated the scene, out of which stepped Monkey, smoking and fiery-eyed. Fiercely striking a martial pose, Monkey leaped straight up into the air, as if he intended to jump right out of the picture onto the Tattooed Monk's shoulder. Then he too faded and the monk stopped chanting, and sat silently twirling the gourd with his eyes firmly shut. Finally, the tattoos receded and were still, and General Calabash opened his eyes.

Now the immortals crowded around the throne, pleading with the Master Hand to remember Monkey's recent trial and to consider his troubled past.

"There's been a mix-up," chorused the Red-Legged Ones.

"The tattoos are not always correct," agreed the Celestial Detective. "The twin brothers are an excellent choice, although they did not appear last. Didn't you see how the dark one held a small boy in his arms? Surely that boy is the Prince!"

The Master Hand silenced them with a glance. "What have you to say, General Calabash?" he asked. "It is your advice I seek."

"Can you be entertaining the notion of appointing Monkey as the Starlord's guardian?" asked the Tattooed Monk incredulously. "The ape is a thief and has shown himself to be entirely without honor. Would you entrust the next Emperor, our only hope, to him?"

"So you agree with the Celestial Detective? Shall we pass over Monkey and appoint the outlaw brothers against the advice of the celestial message? Yet the outlaws, too, are thieves, are they not?"

"They steal not for themselves but to help the starving and the poor," answered the Tattooed Monk angrily.

"And you too were a thief once," said the Master Hand pointedly.

"I was an outlaw, yes," conceded General Calabash, frowning.

"Can you deny a fellow thief another chance, then?"

The Tattooed Monk clenched his fists. "I do not claim to know what is written in the stars, sir," he answered slowly. "The Master Hand must interpret the message. I can only deliver it. But thanks to Monkey, the monks of the faithful Order of the Silver Lotus are all dead and buried beneath Sleeping Giant Mountain."

"Accident and coincidence, sir. History is rotten with both. Monkey was not entirely responsible for that horror, although he deserved his punishment. You, Calabash, know better than anyone what it is to be falsely accused. Monkey has been persistently selfish, not evil. But I am not interested in debating recent testimony with you. I assure you I had no intention of bringing Monkey back this soon. However, will you abide by my decision and be guardian to the guardian, whoever that may be? I need your pledge."

"As always, sir, I obey," said the Tattooed Monk, bowing his head.

"Good, it's settled, then," said the Master Hand, smiling radiantly now. "In serving Monkey, you serve me."

All the immortals groaned, and the Celestial Detective threw himself to his knees. "Please, master, Monkey cannot be the new Starlord's guardian, or I fear Yamu has already won."

"Monkey has had several lives to learn his lesson," answered the Master Hand evenly.

"Monkey never learns," the Celestial Detective protested loudly. "General Calabash! How can you be silent now when the fate of the universe hangs in the balance?"

"I thought my life had touched rock bottom years ago," said the Tattooed Monk bitterly. "But now I see I can sink lower still. It seems I am to serve an ambitious ape. You are correct, detective. Monkey never learns. But then, neither do I." Bowing respectfully to the Celestial Detective and to the Master Hand, the general withdrew.

The Master Hand dismissed the irate Celestial Detective, the fuming Red-Legged Ones, and all the courtiers he had assembled for the reading. Standing alone in the empty, echoing hall, he strode to the Mirror of Peaceful Longevity, a gigantic glass peach cut down the middle, with each half reflecting his image. Directing his gaze to the phoenix necklace, a twin to the

Prince's, he removed it from around his neck, gently cradling it in the center of his hand. The tiny pearls shone like stars in the sky, and the ruby eye of the phoenix stared brightly up at him. He placed a weighty finger upon the gem. It warmed and softened at his touch, spreading like blood upon new snow. He rubbed the red into the gold, rubbing faster and faster as if chafing it to life, until the metal grew hot and hotter still and finally burst into flame. He closed his hand over the burning jewel.

"For your sake, Monkey, I have enraged my loyal general and all the immortals in Heaven," he whispered fiercely. "This time, if you fail me, rest assured, there will be no next time. A great responsibility has settled upon your skinny shoulders, ape. I pray you are up to it. I have said it before, but listen well, for I mean it, now. *This is your last chance!*"

CHAPTER EIGHT

The Bunyip

We travel from—and with—our point of departure.
—Emperor Hung Wu

As the chill wind from the north nudged the outlaws toward Morning Cloud Cove, a horrendous bellow rent the air. Before White Streak could react, the cry came again and again, each time amplifying until it was louder than the pounding ocean surf ahead, taking his breath away. In a flash he understood why men could be driven insane by the mind-rending call of the bunyip. It violated all his senses at once, driving him to the brink of an echoing abyss where nothing mattered but the cessation of sound. The bunyip's baleful voice sucked all hope from his heart and replaced it with a terrible vacuum, an emptiness that threatened to collapse his resolve.

Regrets and sorrowful memories flooded White Streak's mind as he listened. Struggling to keep from drowning in a paralyzing sea of sadness, he marshaled his rage to protect himself from this new attack by the Nokk.

The bunyip's lamentation reopened a wound that had never healed. On his last visit, his father had led White Streak into a battle the twelve-year-old was too young to fight, almost getting the boy killed. In fact, if Mother Gu had not stepped in to save him, White Streak would have died. And yet his father's look of disappointment haunted him, as if he had been a traitor instead of just a child.

Soon after that, his father had left them and had not reappeared since. Although Mother Gu denied it, White Streak felt his father's absence as a personal rebuke. He convinced himself that his defeat and near demise had been his own fault and that his parent had judged him unworthy.

White Streak's old grief swelled, filling his scarred chest until he thought he would burst apart. Mother Gu had not adequately warned him about the bunyip. Could it be that his mother's sorrows were not as great as his own? He looked over at Black Whirlwind. His brother's eyes were alert and he was turning in all directions, searching for the source of the prolonged din, eager to split the demon in two with his twin blades. His face reflected nothing but anger and bloodlust. For him, the task was simple: put a stop to the offensive noise by beheading the noisemaker.

They turned sharply into the cove, and then White Streak saw it, reclining on a flat rock just ahead of them like an oversized walrus in repose. It was grotesquely ugly, with a thick wrinkled pelt, a flat puckered snout, stiff brown whiskers, and long yellowish tusks. Lying in a pile of half-rotting carcasses and skeletons, it reeked of dead fish. Its little doleful red-veined eyes were buried so far into its folding flesh that they would have been invisible had they not been overflowing with tears which traced slow trails down its hairy jowls. As soon as the outlaws came into sight, the bunyip's bulging throat began to vibrate, building toward a crashing crescendo of complaint.

By all reasonable standards, the bunyip was too far away to shoot. But White Streak was no longer bound by reason. Before the monster could again release the full power of its voice, White Streak threw his harpoon. Black Whirlwind froze, willing his brother's impossible shot to hit its mark as the bunyip's sobbing dirge filled the cove.

Moaning and digging his fingers into his eyes, White Streak fell to his knees, rocking back and forth and whimpering helplessly. Black Whirlwind had never seen his brother so abject, even when their father had punished them as boys for infractions of his iron laws. He wondered what strange power the bunyip held over his twin, but before he could try to guess, White Streak's harpoon grazed its faraway target, its point sticking there like a burr, just barely piercing the startled demon's throat. Poling forward with a roar of his own, Black Whirlwind slashed into the monster's gut, and before it could dive into the sea, lopped off its head with a quick backhanded sweep of his ax. A gurgling death rattle replaced the bunyip's thunder. Its albino coat turned scarlet with blood. As it expired, it slapped the water with its rear flippers, raising a huge wave that threatened to overturn the *Immortal Beggar* and throw the outlaws overboard.

As the hideous creature breathed its last, an uneasy silence descended. Chiko Chin maneuvered toward the bunyip, deftly avoiding the foaming shoals around its rocky perch. Recklessly reaching out over the side of the boat, he wrenched White Streak's harpoon from its flesh, spilling the demon's intestines into the sea.

White Streak rose swiftly, grabbing a slippery piece of the bunyip's innards.

"Nokk!" he cried. "You have changed three times and still, I have you. You must obey!"

"He's held me through three—but who is 'he'?" came the high-pitched answer through the beaky mouth of what was now, once again, a giant mass of jelly. "I'm the Nokk. Am I not . . . the Nokk? What is . . . my name? What is my . . . ? What?"

The Nokk trailed off, sinking lower into the water. White Streak spoke up, knowing that if he did not, the Nokk would escape and the wish he had won would be irrevocably lost. Impulsively, he blurted out the first desire that came into his mind.

"I wish Puk to be my loyal pet."

"A Nokk . . . cannot be tamed," answered the Nokk, still sinking.

"Perhaps as Puk you can love your master."

"I cannot love."

"Yet that is my wish," insisted White Streak.

"Make another. . . . Ask your brother."

One of Mother Gu's many warnings sounded in White Streak's mind. *Never bargain with the Nokk.* In the time it took to ask Black Whirlwind, he knew the shapeshifter would disappear.

"If you do not grant the wish you owe me, you will die," answered White Streak resolutely.

"Then it shall be so . . . on one condition," replied the Nokk immediately. "You must tell no one. The moment you do, I will disappear. If you keep your word, you may keep me as Puk for twelve lunar months. After that, I shall return to the sea. Do you agree?"

"I do," said White Streak.

"There is one more thing," added the Nokk.

"The deal is done."

"That is true," said the Nokk, waiting.

"What is this 'one more thing'?" asked White Streak reluctantly.

"A dog is loyal to the master who loves him. But Puk is a demon. He will hate you for what you show him of love."

"Unless I free him," said White Streak. He knelt down, peering closely at the repulsive Nokk, and dangled a hand before its unblinking eye. "Do you wish to be loved, Nokk?" he asked. "Do you wish to be free of Yamu?"

"I am a shapeshifter," cried the Nokk, viciously whipping the outlaw's extended hand with one of his tentacles.

"Then I shall try to love you in all your shapes," promised White Streak earnestly, drawing his hand back and rubbing the sting.

"Love demands no less," hissed the Nokk, submerging. And then with an nasty gurgle and a inky burp, the jellyfish was gone.

CHAPTER NINE

Dragon of the North Sea

To move toward a horizon is to seek a new horizon.
—The Tattooed Monk

"I suppose you expect me to thank you," said Puk sullenly as he circled the *Immortal Beggar*. He was paddling so fast he was making himself dizzy, his powerful legs churning and his dark head held high.

"That depends how much you liked hanging around with ponaturi," answered White Streak, smiling.

"Is hanging around with you any better?" asked Puk, sniffing haughtily and slowing down but still not climbing on board. He squinted at White Streak and for a moment his eyes grew terribly sad, reminding the outlaw leader of the bunyip.

"Being a bunyip wasn't so bad," he observed darkly. "It was depressing, but all I had to do was sit on a rock and cry."

On the horizon, a giant wave, even larger than the one the

bunyip had created, was gathering and coming their way.

"We'll have to make for shore in a hurry or the *Beggar* may capsize," observed Chiko Chin calmly, ignoring the dog's complaint.

"If you'd like to help," suggested Black Whirlwind to Puk politely, "take this rope in your teeth and pull."

Puk stared at the oncoming wave. An unnatural wash of dolphins and sharks, caught together in the boiling tide, rushed toward them. To his horror, Puk could see the unmistakable spiked head of an enormous dragon breaking through the turbulence, its forehead jutting out like a jagged cliff.

It was Chac, King of the North Sea!

The dog heaved and clawed himself up onto the deck in a hurry, shedding sheets of muddy water and shifting his weight back and forth frantically, almost sinking the boat. White Streak and Black Whirlwind exchanged looks as they prepared the *Immortal Beggar* for the onslaught.

"I'm told you're pretty handy with sharks, mutt," said Chiko Chin. "Here's your chance for a real banquet."

Puk started to shake, causing the *Immortal Beggar* to wallow dangerously.

"We've heard you're the scourge of the sea, Yamu's right arm," said White Streak. "You look like you're going to throw up, pup. What's wrong with you?"

"We're counting on you to save us, demon dog," said Chiko Chin.

"Oh, why was I ever born?" cried Puk, shivering so hard his teeth rattled loudly. "First ripped from my mother's cave, then sold to Yamu, then absorbed by the nasty shapeshifting Nokk, and now this! Can't you sorry sailors see? Do I look like a match for . . . Oh, my god—"

"The Dragon King of the North Sea?" White Streak finished for him, flourishing his trusty harpoon. As Chac drew closer, he rose from the water like a green scaly island. "Well, Puk, if you won't save us, perhaps my brother and I can do the honors. We're pretty good with dragons, especially the half-human sort. Why don't you just take care of the sharks and leave the dragon to us?"

Puk hunkered down to avoid being hit by the thundering fall of ocean spray as the most powerful king of the Four Seas drew closer. "No disrespect intended, but when I was in Yamu's service, I had the misfortune of watching Chac fight," he said.

"More of a privilege than a misfortune for the likes of you, I'd wager," said Chiko Chin.

"And a nightmare for the likes of *you*," answered Puk in disgust, his voice turning once again into the Nokk's. "Do you think a harpoon, an ax, and a few knives stand a chance against *him*? When he's finished roasting and eating you for lunch, he'll use your miserable weapons as toothpicks. Fortunately," he concluded smugly, in his own voice, "dragons aren't too keen on dogmeat."

As he said "dogmeat," Puk clamped down hard on a large silvery shark that had spun up over the side of the boat, slashing it in half and splattering the already bloodied brothers with fresh gore.

Raising his harpoon, White Streak brandished it in a military salute to the approaching dragon. Black Whirlwind did the same with his double-bladed ax. Chiko Chin placed a knife between his teeth like a pirate and raised one oar. Puk took one fearful look at the three and, whimpering, dove for cover under a great pile of fish nets and wooden buoys, dragging his meal with him.

Spraying fog out of his nostrils, the Dragon King of the North Sea towered over the little group of outlaws, shrouding their inlet in heavy mist. He was smaller than Old Bones or any of the clan of land dragons, but he was the largest of sea dragons, and he seemed to be enjoying his dramatic entrance. Chiko Chin knelt down, bowing his head, and Black Whirlwind did the same. But White Streak stood his ground at the prow, glaring defiantly into the dragon's lamplike eyes.

"You're a little late, Father," he shouted. "You missed the battle."

Puk stuck his head out from under the nets. Scraps of shark gut hung from his shaggy fur.

"Father?" he growled.

"Did I miss it? Well, there's always another to look forward to, isn't there?" observed the King of the North Sea, baring his fangs. White Streak frowned. "You've grown," his father added in a deep rumbly voice.

"What did you expect?" snapped White Streak. "It's been seven years!" He longed to tell his father he had beaten the Nokk, but he dared not break his word to the shapeshifter.

"Time is of little importance in the ocean," said the dragon, bowing his gigantic head apologetically.

"Yes, if you have the good luck to be immortal," answered White Streak resentfully.

"Luck has little to do with it, my son," said the old king.

"Fate is more to the point. Listen to me. Ponaturi and a bunyip are the least of what you'll be up against. The Nokk is no challenge compared to what you will soon see rising from the Netherworld. Does the name *Spellbinder* mean anything to you?" He paused as if searching for the right words to communicate his message.

White Streak bristled. Suddenly, his remarkable victory over the Nokk seemed like child's play. Apparently, his father already knew about it and counted it as nothing. He felt small and insignificant as he always did when his father was near.

"Promise me you won't tell your mother a word of what I'm about to say," said the King of the North Sea in a confidential tone, glancing around fearfully, as if he half expected Mother Gu to materialize right behind him.

The familiar gesture of exaggerated concern made White Streak smile in spite of himself; and for the first time since he had heard the approaching wail of the ponaturi that morning, he relaxed.

"You try to keep a secret from her," he said, more warmly than he intended, patting Puk's gigantic head as the demon dog wriggled out from under the mess of smelly fishing gear to stand beside his new master.

"Phew, that dog stinks!" said the King of the North Sea, noticing Puk for the first time. The dog cringed defensively.

"Of course he stinks," said White Streak. "He's an outlaw, like the rest of us."

The Dragon King drew himself up to his full impressive height. "Are you saying I *stink*, boy?" he roared.

White Streak had not intended to include his father in his

statement, but as he looked up at Chac, his anger returned. Though a smile still played upon his lips, there was a steely note in his voice as he answered. "Yes, Father. I'm saying you stink. I've been saying it for years. You just haven't been around to hear me."

For a long moment, the King of the North Sea glared down at White Streak. Black Whirlwind shut his eyes, tensely fingering the handle of his ax. He looked as if he were praying. Chiko Chin pulled his head into his neck like a turtle. Puk whimpered and crouched down, hiding his head with his paws. Then he stopped whining and waited, licking his muzzle. Except for the musical splash of the leaping dolphins attending the Dragon King, there was utter silence in Morning Cloud Cove. Even the waves seemed to freeze for a suspended moment.

Finally, Chac's booming laughter rumbled out over the ocean like thunder.

"Listen closely, son," said the Dragon King, slowly lowering himself into the water. "You've fought the Nokk and won. I'm proud of you—very proud." White Streak raised one eyebrow in surprise. He had never heard those words from his father before. They triggered such strong emotion that he found it difficult to swallow.

Black Whirlwind threw his brother a knowing look, as if to say *I told you so—he doesn't even know I'm here.* But White Streak was ignoring his twin as well, drinking in his father's words with urgent attention. Chac now included Black Whirlwind and Chiko Chin in his smoldering gaze. "We will all soon be tested and challenged to our limits—no, beyond our limits," he said.

"In the war to come—and it will be nothing less than a full-scale war—I know I shall be proud of you all." Then he fixed upon White Streak again. "But you, White Streak, bear the biggest burden of all," his father said.

The Dragon King of the North Sea eyed his son and waited. Then he nodded, as if White Streak had spoken, although he had not.

"You can be sure I won't miss your next battle, my boy," he said quietly. "Tell your mother only this: next time, I shall not fail you."

White Streak suddenly felt too weary for a next time. The Nokk had absorbed all his energy. Or perhaps it was seeing his father again that had drained him of strength. All he wanted right now was to go home. But he had to find the demon that had kidnapped Kuan, the lost boy from Banpo village.

When White Streak still did not speak, Chac took a more businesslike tone. The demon invasion of the Lord of the Dead had already begun, he reported matter-of-factly. White Streak and his brother had that day rebuffed a few of the forward guard. But countless more were on their way. As foretold in the ancient scrolls, the Tomb of the Turtle would be cracked wide open like a walnut, releasing a demon horde. There would be no escape. There was only one on earth, the descendant of Starlord Hung Wu, who could truly stem the flood. White Streak must find that one to fight by his side. Only if he succeeded in finding him, would the outlaws stand a chance against the Spellbinders.

"And where will I look for this Chosen One?" asked White Streak skeptically, finally recovering his voice. Surely, his father would at least give him a clue to help him begin to track this Starlord warrior, if he existed.

"That, I do not know," his father admitted.

"You're charging me with finding a phantom to do battle with ghosts?" asked White Streak, clenching his fists.

"Not a phantom, son. A Starlord, heir to the Imperial Throne. And marked at birth with the sign of the Qin."

It seemed to White Streak that his father was repeating history. Where would it end? he thought bitterly. Would his father finally be satisfied when White Streak died trying to meet his impossible demands? Having failed to kill him once, had he come back to try again?

Yet Chac's large yellow eyes were so close and bright that White Streak felt warmed as if by the direct rays of the sun. And, strangely, the warm feeling did not leave him even as his father went on to speak about the Spellbinders and what that chilling name would shortly come to represent.

The truth of the matter was, White Streak had missed his father, although he had learned to live without him. He fingered his scar, remembering the horror of that long-ago battle, and the moment when he had been felled by bandits in the woods. He had suffered many wounds since, but none like that one. He remembered how it felt to think he was dying and to know that his father had failed to block the fatal blow. Now the Dragon King was back, leading his son once again toward the edge of a precipice.

"I do not know what the Starlord looks like," his father said, as he sank slowly back into the sea, "or even if he is a man or a boy."

"If he's a boy, he had better grow up fast," growled Black Whirlwind.

White Streak did not acknowledge his brother's comment. He did not even look his way. It was as if no one at all were there in the cove but himself and his father. *Next time I shall not fail you.*

Chiko Chin silently observed White Streak. Pulling the boat around abruptly, the outlaw navigator waited for the sudden shock and challenge of the dragon's departing wave.

"If he's a boy, we're dead," he said calmly.

CHAPTER TEN

Song of the Nightingale

The nightingales may sing of the flower's being too sweet
or not sweet enough, but from the flower's point of view,
this is just the chattering of birds.—Monkey

In the golden light of dawn, attendants in the royal nursery
were amazed to see that Prince Zong had grown miraculously
overnight. The Emperor's heir was only one day old, yet he walked
with confident steps and, although it was winter, flowers sprang
up beneath his feet. Hummingbirds and flocks of white doves
fluttered around his head. And his breath was as sweet as wild
honeysuckle in bloom.

At noontime, attracted to a bright pebble in the sun and
hungry perhaps for his lunch, the Prince put the stone in his
mouth. A guard rushed to take it out, but when he replaced it
on the ground, the pebble glittered more brightly than the gems
in the Emperor's crown and rolled after the handsome infant
as he walked away. And then, swore the guard when telling

the story to his fellows later, as Prince Zong walked, other rocks and pebbles pulled themselves out of the ground and followed!

The Prince loved the Pekinese puppies popular among the court ladies, and the next afternoon, he was found sitting in the sun surrounded by a circle of perfumed women, playing with the miniature dogs. As he walked among the potted plum trees in the Hall of Surpassing Brightness, crickets chirped at him from their bamboo cages. Suddenly, he opened the doors of all the cages and let the insects out. Coaxing them onto his outstretched arm, he calmed them by stroking their papery wings.

The next day, wearing a scarlet cap, Prince Zong joined the royal ice party in the Hall of Crystal Waters. To everyone's amazement, he flew across the ice in his tiny silver skates, cutting graceful circles around the trees and river rocks in that pavilion of winter sport, as if born to glide and soar as freely as any bird.

The servants found it impossible to keep up with the Prince as he ran about in the mazelike gardens, gathering crimson berries buried under the snow and scooping up goldfish from the heated lotus pools with his shimmering net before laughing and letting them go.

Since the hour when he had wailed for his mother, he had wept only once in those first few days. A servant informed his nurse that the Emperor had made the proper sacrifice on the Altar of the Moon, offering up incense and prayers for the Prince's long life. Fragrant smoke from several miles away billowed into the sky and stung the Prince's eyes. Although it was distant and smelled sweetly of pine and cypress logs, to the

Prince the air seemed suddenly filled with the acrid odor of death, and he shed tears over the beautiful animals slaughtered in his honor.

There had been, however, no ceremonial procession to the Round Mound with banners streaming and princes, nobles, guards, and eunuchs in their best robes snaking along the imperial highway. Although thousands had expectantly lined the road on their knees, knocking their heads upon the ground and crying "Ten thousand years, ten thousand years, ten thousand years!" the Emperor had decided to forgo all public celebration and instead retired to the Hall of Supreme Harmony to pray before the coffin of the deceased Father Han. Nor had he yet announced Prince Zong as the heir to the Imperial Throne.

The royal nursemaid, Jade Mirror, a handsome, strapping girl, having overheard his mother's last words to her son, fondly called her charge "little Starlord," and the name stuck. By the time he was only one week old, she was convinced he was the Chosen One.

Here at last was the long-awaited leader of the common people who, according to the ancient legends, would turn away from his birthright of wealth, rank, and privilege and travel the path of righteousness, fighting for justice. Here at last, she announced to all those who would listen, was the boy, born with the sign of the Qin, who would restore the wisdom of the first Starlord, Hung Wu, to the imperial court.

Gossip flew through the streets of the Forbidden City. Little wonder the Emperor refused to write the name of Zong on the sacred plaque behind Father Han's coffin, said the people. This prince was no descendant of Han but the heaven-sent son of Starlord Hung Wu, whose peaceful kingdom had been toppled in an attack of the land dragons and buried long ago beneath the frozen earth.

In the twilight, unaware of all that was being whispered about him, Prince Zong strolled through the bamboo grotto. As if acknowledging a kinship, little brown nightingales flew to his fingertips, and lightly perching there, sang melodiously, piercing the swift sonorous beat of the imperial drummer's end-of-day salute, and the quivering blast of the brass trumpets, and the triple stroke of the big brass bell, signaling sleep.

That night, the Prince did not sleep, for in the shadows, he sensed danger and a darkness deeper than night gathering around the Forbidden City. Sitting cross-legged in his bedroom on a padded platform of warm bricks, the boy stared straight ahead, his black eyes large, his body alert.

Rockets marking his birth sprayed the sky with light, but under the rhythmic explosions he heard the dry north wind rising. A fierce sandstorm was gathering, and soon the pagoda rooftops would be loaded with a layer of pale gold, blown in from the distant desert. In the morning, the sun would glitter upon the eaves, already dusted with snow, and every crack and crevice in the Forbidden City would be filled with sand. Wrapped in scarlet wool blankets, the Prince shivered as a bitter wind danced around his head, teasing the flaming lanterns and casting a white glare upon his round face, so like his mother's, yet even more moonlike and luminous.

He started as a long shadow fell across his bed. But it was only his nurse, Jade Mirror, come to smooth his pillows and lightly brush his forehead with her mothlike fingers. She smelled of nightblooming lilies and tree peonies, sesame toffee and dates, and he sighed, relaxing in her comforting presence. But her whispered words were not comforting at all, though she never suspected he understood.

"Poor little Starlord," she murmured softly. "No mother now, and your father almost as evil as the former Emperor, Father Han. What will become of you, my dumpling? Surely, they will murder you in your sleep if they have the chance. Those who would not name you true heir today conspire to kill you tomorrow. But do not fear, sweet one. Jade Mirror will keep you safe from harm. Jade Mirror is here beside you. Sleep now, Prince Zong, and in the morning, perhaps the world will look less dangerous."

Suddenly she whirled around, scanning the room, her hand on a fish knife she had stolen from the kitchen and concealed in her robe. She thought she heard something moving behind the screen. She waited but nothing emerged. "Did you hear that, little Starlord?" she asked. But Prince Zong was no longer listening. Exhausted by the day's activities and lulled by the swelling chorus of sweet nightingales singing outside his window, he had fallen fast asleep.

"How do they sing in such a chill wind?" wondered Jade Mirror, taking up her post beside the Prince's bedside. She put the knife back in her sleeve, removing a bean-paste roll she had hidden there. As she ate ravenously, her worried thoughts turned to Silver Lotus, wandering hungry through the bitter cold streets of Bai Ping, with no shelter from the sandstorm blowing in from the north. If only Jade Mirror had anticipated the Emperor's decree, perhaps she could have gotten word to

Day Rat. He could have watched out for Silver Lotus as she exited the Forbidden City and taken her to Mother Gu. Alas, she had been too slow, too stupid to protect her mistress. But she would keep her promise and protect the son. Yes, she would willingly give up her life for the little Starlord.

Day Rat

Each note of a nightingale's song echoes notes past and notes to come.—Emperor Hung Wu

Lost in thought and distracted by the delicious taste of her stolen dinner, Jade Mirror watched the Prince's moon face at rest as she listened to the sweet song of the nightingales. Suddenly the birds were silent. Out of the corner of her eye, she caught a slight movement of the gossamer netting above the boy's head and the warning glint of a silver dagger. Stifling a cry of horror and snatching the child to her breast, she saw a man's thick hand with a thumb ring of red jade coming through the widening gap in the cloth.

Instantly, another hand reached in and grabbed the bejeweled one, forcing the dagger back. The slit in the curtain tore apart and two men fell into the Prince's chamber, locked in deadly combat. Jade Mirror stood holding the little Starlord close, hardly breathing as the two masked intruders struggled.

They seemed unevenly matched. One was burly and barrel-chested, with a bloodstained scrap of leopard's fur wrapped around his right arm, identifying him as a member of Spotted Leopard's infamous bandit gang. The other, she realized with relief, was Day Rat, her fellow spy and comrade in arms. Small, agile, and an ace long-distance shot with blow pipe or bow and arrow, Day Rat seemed to be at a distinct disadvantage now as the bandit bludgeoned him to the floor with his fists. Jade Mirror tightened her grip on the Prince as Spotted Leopard's man closed in, his blade poised to strike. Then she leapt across the room, landing a powerful kick that threw the cutthroat off balance. He lunged at her, and the Prince screamed, one high-pitched cry so sharp it cracked the bedside mirror cleanly into two parts, as if the glass had been struck by lightning. The intruder hesitated for an instant and blinked.

It was all the time Day Rat needed. Before the great lumbering robber knew what hit him, the little spy suddenly somersaulted to his feet and flung a spiked iron ball no bigger than an egg at the other's weapon, flipping the blade right out of his hand and catching it in midair.

Without a second's delay, Day Rat knocked the mercenary square in the jaw with his weighted sleeve, cracking the bone. Stunned, his assailant flung himself backward, attempting to put some distance between his head and the twirling iron balls that suddenly filled the air. But Day Rat had him now, his small feet dancing so fast he looked as if he were flying, his whirling chains spinning with lightning speed.

Jade Mirror gave silent thanks to Mother Gu, who had

trained the Rat in chain fighting. On the back of each leg, she noticed, her friend had painted the character *su*, 速, to give him godspeed. He must have run all the way from Moonshadow Marsh in one day to find her, she thought warmly. He must have run so fast he had drummed the back of his head with his heels!

And now he was lashing her assailant with a ferocity heated by the love she knew he held for her in his heart.

"Don't kill him!" she cried.

"Why in the name of the Qin not?" cried Day Rat, continuing to batter the bigger man.

Slung over Day Rat's shoulder was a bulging blue cotton bag which he now tossed toward Jade Mirror. "Here, take this! I made it for you in case you should ever have to leave in a hurry with the Prince. Have you heard of the many faces of Hung Wu?" Jade Mirror shook her head. "No? Well, this is designed just like the ancient Starlord's. Turn it inside out as many times as you like. Each time you do, you'll see a different disguise— with all the tools of whatever trade suits you—fortune teller, scholar, poet, gardener, monk. Take your pick."

"Magistrate will do nicely, thank you," she said, taking the bag as the bandit crashed to the floor.

Day Rat threw her a look. "Black gauze cap. Official issue. Identity papers as well. It's all there. But you may do better as a poet."

The man on the floor rolled over and groaned.

"What's your name, scum?" Day Rat asked roughly, giving him a kick in the ribs for good measure.

"T'sao T'sao, dead man," gasped the other, spitting blood. "The next time you hear it, you'll have a knife in your back."

"T'sao T'sao—pardon me, the magistrate here won't be pleased if I send you to the Netherworld tonight as you deserve. So I'll just dump you out this window, if you don't mind. Watch your head on the rocks! Happy landing. You do know how to swim, don't you?" Hoisting the man on his back like a heavy sack of grain, he threw him into the moat. Then tucking the iron balls neatly back into his sleeves, Day Rat gave Jade Mirror a smile.

Jade Mirror threw her arms around him and kissed him to show her gratitude. "You saved our lives!" she exclaimed.

Day Rat blushed and shrugged her off. "If I hadn't shown up, you'd have done pretty well by yourselves," he said, grinning. "That's quite a pair of lungs you've got there, Prince," he added. Then, to cover his embarrassment, he grew stern. "Remember, Jade Mirror—that bag of tricks is only to be used if your lives are in danger and you need to disappear. Don't go disappearing just for fun. You're not to traipse around Bai Ping looking for Silver Lotus. It's dangerous outside the Forbidden City."

"No more dangerous than it is *inside*," said Jade Mirror, thrusting out her chin defiantly.

He shrugged and turned away from her, preparing to leave. She softened. "Any news?" she asked, placing a hand on his sleeve to keep him by her side a moment longer.

"White Streak and Black Whirlwind haven't come back from the cove. But there are rumors White Streak has stolen Yamu's own demon guard dog!"

Jade Mirror grinned.

Day Rat lightly hoisted himself up to the window and balanced gracefully there for a moment.

"I wish I could come with you," said Jade Mirror wistfully.

"White Streak wants you here," he answered. "Remember, I don't want to catch you spying in Bai Ping. That's *my* territory now."

Then he was gone before she could answer, and an instant before the nightingales in the garden again took up their song. A thin insistent rattling cut into the swelling music. The Prince pointed to the floor. Rolling across the copper bricks was the bandit's jade thumb ring! She stared at it, terrified for a moment as if she were seeing a ghost. Then she stooped to pick it up, turning it over and over in her hand.

It was neatly carved in the shape of a toad, and its eyes, inset with tiny specks of emerald, gave off a cold, green phosphorescent glow like fairy shrimp under the sea. Quickly, she dropped it into her bag.

CHAPTER TWELVE

Lady Dulcimer

*If a man wants to be sure of the road, he must close his eyes
and walk in the dark.*—The Tattooed Monk

Silver Lotus sat on a dirty straw mat in the littered alley
behind the Kingfisher Inn, plucking the strings of her dulcimer.
She had been chased away from a more advantageous spot in the
village square by a gang of beggars who had thrown stones at
her and stolen the few coppers in her cup. One particularly
nasty urchin had hit his target, raising a large red welt on her
cheek. Later, a merchant had whipped her away from his door
with a bamboo rod as she begged for a bit of rice. The deep
laceration on her leg prevented her from walking farther that
day. Trying to keep her voice steady and her back straight, she
shivered in the bitter cold as snow began to fall, dusting the
dead-end street with a thin layer of white.

Two chairbearers squatted nearby in the shelter of a

puppeteer's stall, cursing and gambling with stones. As daylight faded, dingy yellow lights went on in the paper windows of the ramshackle houses at the end of the road, casting an oily glow on the cobblestones. A few miles away, the crumbling stone ruins of the old East Gate loomed like an abandoned ship, silhouetted against the sky. It was said black foxes from the nearby forsaken shrine haunted that neighborhood, and occasionally an unsolved murder in the poor districts surrounding the Kingfisher Inn was attributed to vagrant animal spirits.

But mostly the poor preyed upon one another in that lawless region. Those who were toughest took whatever paltry prizes were to be won in an arena stripped bare by wintry necessity, leaving little behind for the stealthy scavengers following in their wake. This was a place of defeat and despair. The vagabonds and ragpickers lining the doorways all had desolate tales to tell of how they had anchored far from their ambitions and dreams, if they still remembered ever dreaming at all.

But none inhabiting that ravaged district that day had landed quite so far from her dreams or quite so suddenly as Silver Lotus. And perhaps the lingering ghosts of those privileged memories were what the cutthroats now approaching her sensed. A vicious beating reserved for the newcomer lay coiled in their fists. Leering, they named her Lady Dulcimer and closed in, their makeshift weapons raised in readiness. They had been wretched so long it seemed as if they had always been that way. And somehow, although her clothes were torn and grimy and her brow creased with care, they knew that she had not.

"Who knows where the waters may carry one Silver Lotus, plucked by the storm?" she sang, strumming her instrument.

The music calmed her, bringing back sunny afternoons when she would wander the garden grounds, her baby growing inside her, dreaming of his glorious future.

Silver Lotus thought often in those idle days of her father, a poor but learned man who in his advanced years had left their farm and retreated to a distant monastery, where he was initiated into the secret rites of an ancient sect. Her mother mourned for him as if he had died, but he confided to his daughter on his only visit home that he had in fact been reborn. When she was chosen by the Emperor, she took the name of his sect as her own, to honor her father and cherish the bond between them. And she took her most treasured possession, the dulcimer he had carved for her with its secret hidden inside.

It comforted her to think of her monklike father at peace in the mountains. How happy she would be, she thought, if her son grew up to be as wise as his grandfather. She had hoped, when the Prince was older, to pay a visit to his temple on Sleeping Giant Mountain. She had imagined he would be the one to introduce his grandson to the kung fu fighting forms, although he had refused to teach her.

After becoming the Emperor's favorite, she had stolen martial arts lessons from the imperial arms instructor, who found her to be an apt pupil, but even so acomplished a master could not satisfy her longing to learn the twelve animal forms of the Silver Lotus. Yet her father had given her one important lesson in self defense, a skill she had practiced every day after he had gone away. And she intended to use that secret skill tonight.

Silver Lotus stopped singing. She had seen the men approaching, six to overcome one woman, and her dark eyes widened with fear, but she continued to strum her dulcimer, not moving from the spot. The wound on her leg throbbed painfully now and it was too late to rise and flee.

Hunched beside Silver Lotus, hidden in the damp shadow of the damaged wall, sat an old beggar with the white cane of a blind man. She glanced his way, thinking to warn him. From his rice bowl and simple robes he looked to be a traveling monk, and as she observed his grizzled appearance, she noticed with surprise that he was younger and more powerfully built than she had at first assumed.

"Sir, if you are able, be gone. Vultures approach and their looks harbor no pity for infirmity. You'd best seek another spot. Night has fallen and we are unprotected here."

"And you, child? Will you fight them alone?" His voice was strong and deep, more like a soldier's than a holy man's.

"I am not defenseless," she assured him. "Though I doubt I can defend us both."

He smiled then, but his face was grave and he looked as if he rarely smiled. Unhitching a gourd from his belt, he placed his hands around it and asked her to place her hands there too. She hesitated.

"I will not hurt you," the monk assured her.

She leaned forward, gingerly brushing the tips of her fingers against his own. As she touched him, the gourd began to spin and she felt suddenly released from the tension of the upcoming struggle, as if she were already victorious. Confidence flooded through her and she felt she could take on an army. With a sharp intake of breath, she drew back. The calabash continued to spin, and though it was dark, she thought she saw a picture appear under the monk's left hand. The image seemed to move, like a flower opening in slow motion. And then in fact she thought it *was* a flower—a lotus blossom. As she stared, it began to shine as if moonbeams had painted it all in silver. She gasped.

"I will stay here with you," he said.

"What is your name?" she asked breathlessly.

"You may call me General Calabash. Others do. And yours?"

Wordlessly, she pointed to the flower that had appeared on the gourd. He smiled, a real smile this time that included his eyes. He had a handsome face, she thought in surprise, finely lined and chiseled like a warrior's. He looked as if he had indeed been a general at one time, overcoming much hardship in his life and conquering many on distant battlefields. And now, as he gazed intently at her, she realized with a start that he did not look blind at all.

Her heart beating wildly, Silver Lotus turned away from the mysterious monk and plucked a bold melody on the taut strings of her instrument. This time the song she chose contained a warning she hoped her assailants would heed.

"In a city of walls within walls," she sang, "the phoenix rises and soars over red rooftops. Those who shoot the fire bird shall lose their arrows, and their souls shall burn in blue flame, never to rise again."

The ruffians were very close now. Their faces were obscured in the deep shadows cast by the alley's crumbling walls, but the glimmer of knives drawn and the bulge of cudgels clumsily concealed under their rough clothing showed what they had in mind for her.

"Eh, boys, did you hear that?" guffawed the leader of the gang to his mates, drawing a heavy club from under his cloak and waving it in the air. "She's worried about our arrows. Says we'll lose them. What do you say, lads? Shall we show this war-bler our arsenal? From the looks of her, she's used to those fops at court. Eunuchs, most of them. Here's what a man's quiver looks like, Lady Dulcimer!" he roared, fumbling drunkenly with a frayed rope belt. "Blind man, you're our only witness. Perhaps you'd like a turn with this beauty too?" he taunted. "Ah, but what does it matter to you if she's good-looking or not, eh? Be off with you, imbecile, before we beat you senseless with your own stick." The others, following his lead, began to laugh while one suddenly slashed her silk belt with his knife so that her robe fell open.

Trembling, Silver Lotus drew one of the dulcimer strings so taut it produced a steely note that isolated itself from the others and a silver dart flew out, pinning the first lout to the wall by his sleeve. Then the hissing string itself suddenly tripled in length, wrapping him around the middle. Too surprised to yell as his club clattered to the ground, he opened his mouth wide, revealing rotten teeth.

With breathtaking skill and speed, Silver Lotus released dart after dart, pinning his followers to the ground and to one another. The men howled as if they had wandered into a nest of stinging bees. Silver Lotus began to chant like an avenging spirit. She downed them one by one, and her whining dulcimer accom-panied their lamentations as the monk watched motionless from the shadows.

By the time she had finished, the six unfortunate beggars were writhing upon the ground, trussed up tight and begging to be released. But if Silver Lotus felt merciful, she had no time to show it, for, attracted by the cries of a skirmish, two masked assassins stealthily approached. Having missed her musical performance, they thought to find a victim and finish whatever business the gang had begun.

Now she was truly afraid, for these two looked to be professionals and beyond her strength. They wore coarse black jackets tied with bloodstained rags of leopard fur, and their hair was bound up in strips of the same spotted pelts. She screamed as one pinned her arms, at the same time applying pressure to the small of her back with the point of his short pike. The other pulled out a sword and held it to her throat. His leering face close up was horrible to behold, bloated and scarred with recent bruises. His beard was flecked with dried blood. Silver Lotus kicked backward with all her might and tried to free her arms but the stranglehold tightened. The hulking pikebearer pulled a jade comb from her head, cutting off a lock of her hair and stuffing it into his sodden coat. Then without warning, he slumped forward, almost crushing her in his fall. His pike clattered to the cobblestones. With one stroke of his white cane, the monk had bashed his head from behind.

Again the white cane flashed, coming down with a ferocious crack on the head of the brigand holding the sword. He whirled and threw himself at the monk, who parried the thrust, effortlessly blocking with his staff. Silver Lotus watched in amazement as General Calabash raised his cane a third time. The monk was still seated quite comfortably on the ground, having not found it necessary to move at all. With a steady hand, he pointed the cane at the swordsman's throat. "Who sent you?" he asked sternly.

"Nobody sent us, you old wreck," answered the other, angrily executing a series of feints and thrusts, each of which the monk easily deflected without rising to his feet. "We heard the woman's voice. She squeals like royalty being robbed—our stock in trade. Just came for our fair share, that's all."

"And that you shall receive," said the monk. Without changing position, he lowered the point of his cane to the killer's heart. The other laughed incredulously but immediately jumped aside, swearing, as a blade shot out, inflicting a deep gash. With a howl, he began leaping crazily about the seated man, holding his ribs. He was a competent fighter and showered the monk with a barrage of lightning thrusts. But General Calabash, leaning back against the wall where he was hidden in darkness except for his flashing white cane, matched every blow with one of his own, taking his time with each in a relaxed manner, as if he were having a leisurely conversation. Sweat poured from the robber's matted brow as he labored on, aiming now for the monk's feet, slashing at his head, furiously lunging and backing away and lunging again. But no matter where he landed, the monk anticipated every move, shifting his cane from right hand to left as the maneuver required and always just exactly in time. Finally, frustrated beyond tolerance, the murderous thief raised his sword and let loose, aiming at the monk's heart. Intercepting the crude throw in midair, General Calabash sent the weapon smashing against the wall. Then seemingly in the same instant, he delivered a shattering blow to the man's ankle, toppling him into a pile of trash.

"Who sent you?" the monk asked again, rising and pressing his foot into the other's neck. "The truth, this time."

"We're Spotted Leopard's men," gasped the assassin. "But he didn't send us, I swear. We heard the ruckus, that's all. We have no orders to kill you. We went after the lady. We do not even know your name."

"And do you know your own name, footpad?" growled the monk, between gritted teeth, stepping down harder.

"Don't . . . kill . . . me. . . ." gasped the man.

"Please, leave him and come!" urged Silver Lotus, pulling on the monk's sleeve. She pointed down the street where a mob of lowlifes were gathering, attracted by the shouting. "There are more—we are only two."

In disgust, General Calabash released the wounded man, who doubled over, rocking from side to side.

"You had best pray we do not meet again," he said in parting.

Even as a newcomer to the city, Silver Lotus knew their pursuers would be reluctant to follow them over the Black Fox Bridge. In the isolated woods surrounding the notorious abandoned shrine, she hoped they would find shelter from the rising storm. Lifting his robes, the monk carefully picked his way through the group of moaning bodies, tapping gingerly with his white cane as Silver Lotus led him swiftly away toward the haunted ruins of the East Gate.

CHAPTER THIRTEEN

The Garden of Pleasant Sounds

As the past informs the present, it continues to change.
—Emperor Hung Wu

"It might be nice to be a magistrate, don't you think, little Starlord?" asked Jade Mirror as she settled her charge in the Garden of Pleasant Sounds, now silent with neglect. Ever since Silver Lotus had been banished, her favorite garden had been abandoned. No one wanted to be seen there, for fear of stirring the Emperor's displeasure. "I think I would make an excellent judge, don't you?"

With large solemn eyes, Prince Zong studied his nursemaid. Dressed in snowy white, she looked like a lily. But her mouth was pulled sternly down at the corners.

"Yes, certainly I'd make a much better magistrate than the one who sentenced my father to death for a few *taels*," she continued, buttoning his jacket against the wind and fiercely pulling his ermine hat down over his ears, tugging a little too hard. "Well, he didn't sentence him to death exactly, but it amounted to the same thing. Have you any idea what Emperor Han's jails are like, little one? No, you're too young. I was too young when my mother went to visit. But she would come home and tell me all she saw there. Well, perhaps not all . . ." Now her lips were trembling a bit, and she fell silent, stroking the Prince's round cheek.

She continued to caress him, gently. Then she bent down close to his ear, as if telling him a secret, her breath warm and smoky in the cold air. "They made my father wear a debtor's wooden cangue around his neck," she whispered. "And they beat him and wore him down, day after day, until there was nothing left." She trailed off, and for a moment all he could hear was her breathing. He watched the white mist curling from her lips into the frosty wind, and for one fleeting instant, her liquid eyes turned to steel, and he was frightened of her. Then she straightened and gave him a bright smile.

"Little Starlord, the Emperor is *not* your father," she said earnestly. "You must not do as he does. You must break free, little bird, and find your own way."

She stealthily slipped Day Rat's gift out from under her robe. Crouching like a cat in the shadow of the old wishing well, she turned it inside out and inside out again, searching for the magistrate's black cap and beard and robe. Ah, there! Shoes as well! Day Rat had thought of everything.

Dreamily, she fingered the fine silk and fur and thought of Silver Lotus, perhaps with a beggar's bowl, wandering the streets of Bai Ping. Day Rat had been wrong. It was stupid to stay here, idling in empty gardens, waiting for another assassin to come and try to kill the Prince. They were all in danger, the Prince most of all. It was up to Jade Mirror to find the little Starlord's mother before it was too late.

Jade Mirror had a plan, all worked out in her mind. She had decided on it the night before, after Day Rat had departed. First, she would kidnap the little Starlord and run away to Bai Ping, where she would find Silver Lotus. Then she would take the reunited mother and son to the Golden Phoenix and beg Mother Gu to take them in and train them herself. Often she had dreamed of confiding in the kind First Consort, telling her about the outlaws of Moonshadow Marsh and their good deeds. But although she knew her mistress was often at odds with the decisions of the Emperor, she could not trust her not to betray them. Now everything had changed. Silver Lotus had herself been betrayed.

She put on the cap and stood on tiptoe, staring at herself in the wind-rippled water of the ancient wishing well. Reflected beside her own dark head was the magnificently chiseled white marble head of the Dragon King of the North Sea. Some said this well was one door to his kingdom, and that the concubine who had recently fallen out of favor with the Emperor and accident- ally drowned there had been taken by Chac to the World Beneath the Waves. She gazed into the Dragon King's sculpted hollow eyes, praying for a dragon's courage. Then she looked at her own pale face, framed now by the impressive cap. Putting on the long scholar's beard, she fastened the edges behind her ears and under the cap. She studied herself again in the well, tucking in her two glossy coils of black hair. The transformation was complete. She thought she looked like a young man, a scholar or a poet, certainly a person of education. And yes, perhaps a person of importance.

Like a high judge bestowing the favor of his attention upon a poor supplicant, Jade Mirror smiled magnanimously at herself. She closed her eyes, imagining the scene as she had a thousand times before. She, the judge. Her father, the prisoner: guilty. He cannot pay. But he is a hardworking farmer, and the flood that took his crop was not his fault. Justice lives. The poor triumph this day. The verdict: a pardon. Go home to your family. And what of the greedy merchant who pressed charges? He will pay triple the debt as a fine to the imperial court.

She opened her eyes, satisfied with this revision of history. If only it had been true. If only she had been able to save her father! Regally, she turned her head, examining herself in profile with the magistrate's cap and beard. Even Day Rat would have to admit, she looked grand!

Jade Mirror slung Day Rat's changing bag over her shoulder like an ordinary traveling purse. It was comforting to know the first Starlord had carried one just like it as he traveled around the countryside, mingling with the commonfolk. "The many faces of Hung Wu," she thought, smiling to herself, but the smile faded almost as quickly as it had come. The punishment for kidnapping an Emperor's heir was too horrible to contemplate. If caught, she would be sentenced to slow torture and a humiliating death. She had once witnessed the death of a man who had been called a traitor. He had been flayed with barbed whips, then torn limb from limb in the public arena—the same courtyard where her mistress had stood stripped of her royal robes and cruelly sentenced to a life of exile.

Jade Mirror took a deep breath. She would leave immediately, before she had time to think further and frighten herself. She would not lose her nerve. She would not abandon her mistress now when Silver Lotus most needed her. Firmly taking Prince Zong by the hand, she left the unnaturally quiet Garden of Pleasant Sounds and began to walk with a steady stride toward the Gate of First Snow and the city of Bai Ping.

CHAPTER FOURTEEN

The Tattooed Monk

The gaps between stars are filled with stars.
—The Master Hand

Offerings of fresh fruit and rice to the elusive fox spirits haunting the glade behind the old East Gate tempted Silver Lotus, who had not eaten since the night before. As she stumbled along the crooked path, General Calabash strode on ahead, parting the thorny branches and beating his way through the tangled bracken.

The sounds of the wind and sifting snow blended with the soft whisper of gathering dust whirling in from the desert, softening their footsteps. Now and then they heard a spitting sound in the shadows, and a pair of eerie green eyes would stare out at them from the leaves and then vanish into the darkness. Once, the green eyes lingered. General Calabash threw a stone and they receded.

A circle of trees, sparse and half charred, stood out against the sky in stark silhouette, forming a gateway to a stretch of rattling elephant grass strewn with gigantic boulders. In the center of this barren ground stood the blackened ruins of the Black Fox Temple.

A distinct odor of decay hung heavily in the damp air, and Silver Lotus shuddered convulsively, regretting her impulse to take refuge here. Too exhausted to walk any farther, she nevertheless could not imagine spending the night in this evil place. But she knew she would not have the strength tonight to climb the steep and narrow mountain trails that led away from Bai Ping, nor would it be safe to do so until dawn. Aware that she was limping but too proud to acknowledge the infirmity, she looked down at her leg, which was still swollen and oozing blood. Surely it would stiffen overnight in this freezing weather, and she wondered if by morning she would be able to walk at all.

Panic seized her as she watched General Calabash striding purposefully on. He was a wanderer, a nomad. During their flight from the back alley of the Kingfisher Inn, they had thrown the bandits off their trail by hiding for several hours under the Black Fox Bridge. There, as they crouched together, shivering in the icy underbelly of the broken monument, he had held her for warmth. In whispers he had spoken of the sweeping spaces and starlit skies of the great desert. Although he said he had no home, she guessed the desert was his destination. As long as she could keep up, he would accompany her and act as her guide. But if she were crippled and unable to travel for days, she could not ask a stranger to wait until she was well.

As if reading her thoughts, the monk turned back, offering his arm. Stirred by his touch, Silver Lotus was suddenly flooded by memories of the Forbidden City. She thought of the Emperor who had introduced her to luxuries she would never have otherwise known, only to cast her out into the world alone and penniless. Yet strangely these memories prompted no yearnings in her heart, except the wish to see her son. The vast courtyards and manicured terraces of the gilded palace had always been a prison to her, never a home.

"Inside the temple, you may rest," said the monk encouragingly. "It is just over there. We are very close now."

They reached the decimated altar, and she leaned against it for support, then slid to the ground, faint with exhaustion. The pain of her wound seemed to melt her bones. She shook with the exertion of trying to stand but, like a bird shot through the wing, could not rise. Hugging the cold stone, Silver Lotus began to weep, and once she had begun, to her shame she could not stop. Clutching her dulcimer tightly to her breast, she bowed her head to her knees and cried as if her heart would break. The monk stood quietly by her side. Then swiftly, before she could protest, he bent and gathered her, dulcimer and all, in his arms. Lifting her easily like a child, he sheltered her tear-streaked face from the icy wind and carried her over the threshold.

It was no warmer inside, although the ruins did afford some protection from the whirling dust and wind. A family of yellow-winged bats hung upside down from the decaying rafters, regarding the intruders with tiny beady eyes. The bats beat the air, fluttering in protest, as if trying to prevent them from coming near. General Calabash smiled, and whispered to them softly. "Settle down, little ones," he crooned, waving them off. "We shall not disturb your hiding place. You are guardians too, and the scroll you protect is the Fourth, is it not? We are just passing through, night fliers, and we are friends of the fox. Quiet down now, return to your posts; you are too revealing of your treasure."

In the corner of the room lay a heap of rags covered in drifting leaves. Gently, the monk put Silver Lotus down, as if settling her on a magnificent goosedown bed. He removed his gourd and, taking some pale ash into the palm of his hand, rubbed it on her injury. She cried out, startled, but he kept his hand over the wound; and the next moment, the searing pain subsided. As she watched, wide-eyed, the inflamed edges of the gash closed and mended together. She gazed at him, puzzled. "Are you a healer, then?" she asked in wonder.

He shook his head. "I have inflicted more wounds than I have healed, child," he answered sadly. "Sleep now."

"But the foxes?"

"I will stand watch."

"Only a little sleep, then. Soon I shall take my turn, and you may sleep too, General Calabash."

He nodded, tenderly touching her snow-dusted hair in the rumpled place where Spotted Leopard's man had torn off a souvenir. He traced his finger over the remaining hair comb, a butterfly carved in rare white jade. She winced, thinking of the assault and letting herself imagine what might have happened had the monk not been there.

"Here, this will keep you warm," he said, removing his

jacket and wrapping it tightly around her thin shoulders. It was patched and its seams were unraveling, but she gave him a radiant smile of thanks. Then trusting her fate to her new guardian, she slept.

Impervious to the chill, the monk watched her for a while. He could not remember feeling so moved by the perfection of a face, even many years ago, when as a young man he had courted his bride. His brow darkened as he recalled how one short year after their wedding day, Yamu had taken her from him, along with his infant daughter. Ash had buried them and their whole sleeping village as it had buried his fellow monks on Sleeping Giant Mountain. And the few survivors of the tragedy had blamed him, the outsider, for calling down their doom.

Now, by some miracle, from that ash had sprung this flower, bearing the name of his order, Silver Lotus. This one, he vowed, would not die. At least, not while he was alive.

He became aware of sudden movement in the courtyard and was reminded of his task. Returning to the bats, he unsealed his calabash and gently drew the scroll from the beam they guarded. They protested shrilly, but settled down again as soon as they heard his voice. Squatting on the cold ground, he twirled the calabash until a small flame ignited and licked at the ancient parchment. In a moment, the tongue of fire flared and the scroll was consumed.

The monk scooped the ashes into his hands. Through the open doorway, he saw a huge black fox leap to the top of the tallest rock and balance there, so still it seemed to become a part of the stone. It was followed by another and another, not quite as large, each taking up a post at the base of a boulder so that faintly illuminated in the starlight, they looked like a circle of doglike gods turned to granite, sentinels of the Netherworld. Only their long plumed tails, waving softly, made them look like living creatures.

Calmly, the monk faced them, and at that very moment, the moon broke out from behind a cloud and shone down upon him. His tattooed arms rose slowly as he readied himself. The black ash lifted from each of his palms and began to twirl in two funnel-shaped clouds and then, combining into one minia-ture tornado, disappeared into the monk's calabash.

Now the monk stepped out into the center of the circle. The foxes watched silently, their green eyes gleaming. They looked frozen in time, as if they had stood there for thousands of years, unmoving. He flowed into the first fox position, his body beginning to warm as he followed the ancient kung fu form. And as he moved, so did his tattoos, glowing in the moonlight.

He had no idea how much time had elapsed when he found her by his side, mirroring his motion. Together, they moved har-moniously under the stars, the exiled empress and the fighting monk, as if participating in a dance choreographed long ago by a higher power.

One by one, the green-eyed foxes silently retreated and van-ished into the sacred grove, and in their places, each tall black boulder, like a miniature mountain, wore a thick cap of pow-dery snow as white as bone, topped by a shimmering halo of golden desert sand.

CHAPTER FIFTEEN

Jade Mirror's Justice

To call infinity a number does not make it one.
—The Immortal Beggar

J ade Mirror was stopped only once, at the Gate of First Snow, where she informed the guards that she was the famous poet, Chang Lang Po, hired by the Emperor and imported all the way from Canton to instruct the Prince in the ancient arts of versification and calligraphy. Digging into the blue bag, she brought out brushes and pens and a black ink stick of the best quality as proof of her profession. The guards looked at one another in surprise. They had heard nothing of this new poetry tutor and thought it odd that the Emperor would engage one when the Prince was still so young. But something in her tone made them reluctant to challenge her.

Upon demand she produced a false identity paper from the handful of documents Day Rat had thoughtfully stashed in the bag. A fully equipped studio by the Bridge of Prayer had been provided by the Emperor himself, she told the bewildered guards, and it was there that the Honorable Chang would take valuable time away from his own writings to introduce the Prince to the rigors of the muse. The Emperor had approved a demanding training schedule of three hours a day. The Prince would begin by reading the classics, and the poet was empowered to keep him longer if he proved slow at his studies.

After hesitating another moment, the guards consulted one another in whispers. The Emperor had been in a foul humor that day and none were willing to risk his wrath by questioning his orders. This poet, clearly an aristocrat of high standing, was surely an invited guest of the court and seemed the type to take offense and make trouble for them if thwarted. Only one guard voted for detaining him, but he was as reluctant as the rest to deliver the message. In the end, after much discussion, they let the poet through.

Jade Mirror squeezed the Prince's hand. They had passed the test! They were on their way to Bai Ping.

But as she looked back over her shoulder, she realized she and the Prince were not alone. The guards had decided to let her pass, but they knew better than to let the Prince out of their sight. A cadre of four was following them, keeping a respectful distance. She swallowed hard. Now her course was charted. There was no turning back. She wondered if she should try to lose them but decided to let them come. After all, she hadn't much choice, and perhaps in town their presence would be useful. Besides, if she needed to shake them, it would be less risky to try in the city, where it was easier to hide and Day Rat was not very far away.

She marched on until it began to rain and she came to the gates of a municipal courthouse, just outside Bai Ping. A restless crowd had gathered there, waiting to be admitted to the hall. A usurer was pressing charges against one of those from the village who had not paid back his loans. "We will stop here and get dry and listen to the proceedings," she told the Prince. Glancing over her shoulder, she saw that the palace guards were taking their time and had fallen far behind. Perhaps in the rain they would stop at the nearby inn and order some lunch and some wine. She ducked into an official-looking doorway framed by two golden lions.

The room was crowded with spectators, mostly peasants like the prisoners themselves, poor farmers who worked the land and hoped they would for one more year make ends meet so that they would not be dragged on their knees before the old judge. Quietly, she took her seat among them. A few stared at Prince Zong in his silk robe and fur hat, causing a stir in the aisles.

Now the debtor was brought forth, barefoot, with a heavy wooden collar clamped around his neck so that he could hardly hold up his head. All eyes turned to the dais, where the magistrate was seated on a thronelike seat. He was surrounded by his formidable staff of counselors, sergeants, lieutenants, and constables, wearing black lacquered helmets and chains around their thick waists from which hung a threatening array of thumbscrews and iron manacles.

Jade Mirror tensed, imagining her father as the man on

trial. He knelt in his ragged clothes on the unforgiving stone, shivering in the icy draft from the door where two officers of the court stood with whips and clubs, ready to silence him if he spoke the wrong words.

His accuser, a wealthy grain merchant, was pacing the platform above him, waving his hands in the air as he spoke. He had long pointy fingernails, which he flourished like tiny swords as he gestured toward the defendant.

This farmer had borrowed a sum of money three years before so that he could pay the taxes on his poor piece of land, which had never yielded much of a crop. The merchant had generously accepted this land as security. Now the debt with interest was worth much more than the land. Yet although the farmer did not deny that he could not pay the usurer back, he still refused to move.

At this point in the tale, the accused began to beat his head upon the floor and wail. "Your Honor, forgive me if I do not know how to speak to one as high as you, yet if I do not say something, no one will speak for me."

"Speak, then," said the magistrate.

The man, not lifting his eyes, addressed the floor and his words fell out all in a rush. "Sir, our land is poor and we are poor people with never enough to eat. But still, Your Honor, the land is all we have. My father farmed it and my father's father before him and now I work this same land and I live there with my wife and my son who helps me, and we barely make ends meet in a good year. Three years ago, you remember, sir, came the flood and it was a very bad year and we were starving, but still the taxes had to be paid. So to pay the taxes, we borrowed from this man."

Now the farmer began to cough, and the magistrate waited until he could catch his breath. When finally he could speak again, he raised his eyes to look pleadingly at the magistrate and pressed his hands together. "Sir, I borrowed ten pieces of silver," he said, "and now in three short years I owe fifty. How can I, who could not pay ten, pay fifty now when times are even harder than before? And so this merchant who has never been a farmer says, leave the land. But it is my land, given to me by my father and it is all I have. If I left the land, where would I go? Where would my family go? Sir, I have worked this poor farm since I was a child and I would not know what to do from the time the sun rises in the morning to the time it sets at night if I was no longer a farmer on my land. Your Honor, I mean no disrespect to this honorable gentlemen who lent me ten pieces of silver and now asks fifty in return. But I would rather die than leave my land." The farmer hung his head, as if exhausted by the unaccustomed exertion of saying so much at once. It was completely silent in the court as if all who had listened held their breath, waiting for the magistrate to speak.

Jade Mirror sat up very straight. She had been watching the old judge while the farmer spoke, and he had been listening with only half his attention. In fact, he seemed at one point to doze off and then wake himself with a little shudder as if from an uneasy dream. Now his long face grew wrinkled with worry as he scanned the spectators. He had the cloudy look of one just roused from a nap, dazed and confused, as if he had no idea how he had arrived at this difficult moment of decision. He looked almost as uncomfortable, in fact, as the man kneeling before him, and although not as frightened, perhaps equally lost.

He turned to his chief counselor, a younger man with beetling bushy brows and a large belly, almost as large as the moneylender's. This man had enjoyed many fine dinners with the usurer and had been paid for his favor with gifts of silver much weightier than the paltry sums the insignificant farmer owed. Stroking his chin slowly as if carefully considering the situation, he spoke, projecting his voice through the hall.

"Your Honor, does not the usurer live by collecting interest on his loans just as the farmer lives on the produce harvested from his land? If the moneylender cannot collect his debts, how will he live? This farmer has an obligation to pay back what he has borrowed with the lawful interest he agreed to at the time."

The lawyer produced a document with the farmer's mark upon it and waved it in the air. "Is this not your signature, sir?" he asked.

"Yes, it is mine," said the farmer.

"Did you not know what you were signing? Was it not read out to you?"

"Yes, sir, it was read to me, but I did not understand what was read."

"Did you ask to have what you did not understand explained to you?"

The farmer's face froze in a grimace of despair.

"No, sir," he said, his voice barely above a whisper.

"There, Your Honor. This man cannot be excused from his obligations under the law just because he is ignorant of the law. He acknowledges his debt. If he cannot pay, he must forfeit his land. It is the law. If he refuses, he must learn the law. He is obstructing justice in defiance of this court. He must be punished."

Each time the counselor said the word *law* he let his voice ring out so that the word seemed to linger in the air, like the tolling of a funeral bell.

An angry murmur rose from the crowd at this pronouncement, whereupon the magistrate rose nervously from his seat. But the chief counselor was not cowed by the spectators' protests.

"Let us take this farmer who does not know the law at his word, shall we, Your Honor?" he said with the air of one used to usurping his superior's authority. "Let us see if he would rather die than leave his land. One hundred lashes, I say. And who among you would like to share his fate?"

Now the magistrate's rheumy eyes blinked furiously, and tears ran down his cheeks in a fit of sneezing. "Carry on, Counselor Kao," he said softly, removing a silk handkerchief from his sleeve and blowing his nose. "I am not feeling well, I'm afraid. I must therefore leave this case in your capable hands." And, bowing, he backed away from the dais as if he hoped no one would take any further notice of him.

The constables closed in on the farmer, who could hardly make his legs work in order to rise. Desperately, the man looked for his wife and son, to catch one last glimpse of them before being led away to his cell to await a beating that would surely be the end of him. They were there in the audience, easy to see among all the others as they held their arms out to him, weeping openly.

Jade Mirror could bear it no longer. Instructing the Prince

to sit still in his seat, she thrust the blue bag into his lap and strode toward the wheezing magistrate. Since she wore a magistrate's cap and insignia of a higher rank than any had seen in that court before, nobody dared stop her. Even the chief counselor was taken by surprise and did not interfere with her approach. Jade Mirror bowed formally before the bench.

"The farmer shall go free and return to his land, by order of the Emperor and in the name of his heir apparent, Prince Zong," she announced in clear tones. "The usurer shall drop his charges immediately or receive the one hundred lashes this court has assigned an innocent man."

Gasps were heard and the chief counselor rose as if to challenge her, but she glared at him as she continued: "It has been brought to the Emperor's attention that the officers of this court have been accepting inappropriate gifts. I intend to stay as long as it takes to inspect your records and file a report. During my investigation, you will of course, provide me with food and appropriate lodging. You are aware, sir, of the current penalty for accepting bribes, are you not?" She did not wait for him to answer but hurried on as if reading from an official proclamation: "An officer found guilty of accepting gold, silver, gems, or gifts of any kind given with the intention of influencing the outcome of a municipal trial shall suffer beheading before a tribunal of his peers."

But the chief counselor cried out, "You are a fraud, sir! How dare you come here and threaten me in my own courtroom and make a mockery of the Emperor's justice? We have heard nothing of a pending investigation. Always in the past the magistrate has been notified well in advance so that we may be adequately prepared. Your sudden appearance is against all protocol. Where is your warrant to do this work? It is you who will lose your head, sir! Seize him," he instructed his lieutenants.

Now pandemonium broke loose. The four imperial guards had finally arrived at the court's door and looking in, saw a mob of angry peasants surrounding the Prince. They rushed in to protect the heir to the Imperial Throne, swinging in all directions with their swords. People began to scream and run to the exits. With a battle cry, Jade Mirror leapt into the fray. Out from under her magistrate's sleeves came her deadly iron balls, and she stood balancing atop the slippery backs of the polished wooden pews hitting in all directions in a blur of speed, cracking the heads of imperial guardsmen, constables, and counselors alike and sparing only the fleeing country folk.

The officers of the court covered their heads, running as fast as their legs would carry them. Fueled with the righteous rage she had nursed since childhood, Jade Mirror pursued them. Jumping lightly from the top of one head to another like a child leaping from stone to stone across a rushing river, she bore down mercilessly on all those who represented Han and his justice.

Seeing the poet transformed into a maddened warrior, the imperial guards went after Jade Mirror, weapons flashing.

But the farmer, thinking his savior was about to be murdered by imperial guardsmen, cried out to his neighbors to stay and protect the Emperor's new magistrate. Some of the braver peasants rallied around Jade Mirror as the guards pressed in from all sides. No longer free to let the ball and chains fly, she slipped a dagger from her belt, slashing the closest guard and earning herself some distance from the pack. Then, suddenly producing a whole armory of flashing knives from hidden places in her robes, she whirled as she threw them, pinning her pursuers to the walls as they raised their swords against her.

One of the guards seized the Prince and held him high above his head. Jade Mirror, seeing the danger, paused for a moment, no longer daring to throw knives. Her hesitation cost her dearly, for the guard behind her grabbed her and brought her down. Then all the remaining guards closed in, beating her as she writhed on the floor, trying in vain to avoid their blows.

But a big blacksmith in the crowd pointed at the Prince dangling in the air and bellowed: "Look, this kid's got the sign of the Qin!" and others cried out: "It's the outlaws! That's no magistrate. It's White Streak!" And the name White Streak was carried out to the courtyard where those who were fleeing turned back to get a glimpse of the famous outlaw. Then a true riot broke out in all the streets and alleys surrounding the court, and in the confusion, a masked figure entered like a shadow. Standing off in a corner unnoticed, he drew forth a blowpipe and picked off two of the imperial guardsmen holding Jade Mirror.

Now the blacksmith, whose name was Iron Ox, began picking up guardsmen and officers of the court as if they were straw dolls and smashing their heads together, yelling to all who would listen that he was fed up with this life of slavery and ready for Moonshadow Marsh. "Brand me with the sign of the Qin and take me with you!" he roared. Drawing a blacksmith's hammer from his belt, he bashed his way toward Jade Mirror. Seeing that the magistrate in disguise was hurt, he picked her up in his enormous arms and crashed his way to the door, clearing a swath for the farmer and his friends to follow.

As the big man carried her off, Jade Mirror screamed, ordering him to put her down so that she might rescue the Prince. Now he saw that she was a woman and not White Streak at all and almost dropped her. But Iron Ox, in the clarity of battle, also saw that death stood where she pointed. Should they attempt to wrest the child from the guardsmen who now held him fast, they would be overcome and captured. So he persisted against her cries, bearing her through the chaos in the square into the crowded markets of Bai Ping where he hoped their pursuers would lose the trail. As they exited, a shadow detached itself from the courtroom wall and followed, downing with his blowpipe all those who blocked their way.

The imperial guardsmen, holding the Starlord before them like a shield, staggered out of the blood-splashed tribunal back toward the Forbidden City. As soon as they stepped past the golden lions guarding the door, a rare ray of sunshine escaped from the solid gray bank of rain clouds and struck the boy's golden necklace, raising a ruby-red flare from the phoenix's eyes.

The peasants immediately quieted and bowed down before the child stamped with the sign of the Qin. Peddlers, chair-bearers, and street stall merchants lining the road threw flowers and rice in his path, shouting "Ten thousand years, ten thousand years, ten thousand years!" The undeclared heir to the Imperial Throne watched them, unsmiling, his young face bearing the mark of early sorrow. Robbed of his beloved mother and his nurse all in a few weeks of being born, the little Starlord was carried back to Han's palace on the uniformed shoulders of four men who loved him not at all but sought a temporary reprieve in his presence from the fate of being torn apart by the mob. None of the guards had any illusions about what would befall them upon their return, but good soldiers all, they preferred to be properly hanged for their bad judgment by the Emperor himself than to die like dogs by the side of the road.

As for the Prince, he clung tightly to all he had left of Jade Mirror, the strange lumpy blue bag she had hastily deposited in his lap when she had told him to sit still. Afraid the rough men would take it away, he hid it under his coat, and drawing it close like a doll, crushed it to his small chest, where it stayed for the entire bumpy journey, weighing warmly and heavily upon his heart.

CHAPTER SIXTEEN

Monkey

Whoever lingers long on earth will suffer more than enough.
What sorrow to be born again and again!
—Monkey

Rumors about the midnight attempt on the Prince's life and the little Starlord's magistrate who had ruled against the rich merchant in favor of the poor debtor spread like wildfire through the villages. Before long the Emperor was rudely awakened every morning by the sound of rattling carts and wagons as peasants from all over the countryside brought baskets of fruit, flowers, and other offerings to the palace gate.

A special coat of many colors, made up of twenty-four swatches, one for every hour of the day and night, handstitched by the nation's most talented seamstresses, was presented to the Prince. The jacket symbolized the unity of a kingdom welcoming its new heir, although the baby had not yet been recognized as such by the Emperor.

Like a beautiful bird in the exotic patchwork, the boy flitted in and out of the labyrinthine courtyards, playing his favorite game of hide-and-go-seek with the guards. Often he favored the same sequestered paths and quiet, peaceful places his mother had frequented, darting through the enchanting landscape bordering the white marble fountain of Chac in the Garden of Pleasant Sounds.

One day, Prince Zong's attendants, momentarily preoccupied by well-wishers in the courtyard, suddenly became aware that their charge had disappeared. Eager to see the world, and perhaps thinking he might find Jade Mirror, he had wandered beyond the limits of the imperial gardens. Frantically calling his name, the servants scanned the surrounding pools and bridges, terraces and manicured groves, but the Prince was already out of earshot, busily following a flying raven as it led him farther and farther away from the palace.

The longer he walked, the lighter he felt, and, determined to stay free of his entourage for as long as possible, he began to run on his sturdy legs—past eight magnificent temples, past a stream and the intricate rockeries where poets idly gathered, past the moat by the West Gate and over a bridge.

Rushing along, he met a group of young girls on the riverbank with flowers in their hair, tossing white pigeons into the air. As the birds circled, spiraling up into the clouds, they made a wondrously melodious sound. The Prince noticed that the girls tied bamboo whistles above the pigeons' tails before releasing them, and gourds of different sizes, carved into pitch pipes. Soon the pigeons disappeared into the sky, and his heart rose as their mysterious music lingered long after they were gone, like a concert of fairies and spirits of the air.

"Where is your mother?" the prettiest and boldest of the girls asked playfully, noticing his fur-lined satin hat and blue silk robe embroidered with pomegranates. "Shouldn't you be home sipping bird's nest soup and sugar, little man? I hear that's what the Emperor drinks in the morning to make him strong." The girls all covered their mouths with their hands and tittered, the sound of their laughter like tinkling glass.

The Prince cocked his head and gazed at them solemnly but did not answer. Although he could understand every word, he could not yet speak. Still laughing, the group dispersed to their duties and the Prince walked on, sadly now, following the river. He wished he too could be a bird so that he could fly away and find his mother, wherever she might be.

Soon he came to the edge of an evergreen forest, and catching sight of the giant raven once again, plunged on, tearing his brocaded sleeve on an alder thicket and muddying his yellow silk shoes on the piney trail as it sank into marshland. Suddenly, a duck exploded up out of the river reeds, its wingbeats shattering the heavy air like a roll of thunder. Then, without warning, separating itself from a border of bulrush, a looming shape, large and black, moved unhurriedly into view, loping toward the little Starlord.

It was a bear, sleek and smooth and blacker than ink, and it seemed to be coming straight for him. Instinctively, the child froze, his heart beating fast. The bear stopped, then rose to full height on its hind legs, looking straight at the Prince with beady eyes. It was the blackest thing the Prince could imagine, blacker than any midnight shadow, and its presence cut a hole as dark as death into the snow-dusted landscape.

The bear dropped to all fours again and continued along the swampy treeline, steadily making its way toward the boy. With rounded ears cocked, it stopped and again rose on its hind legs, towering over the high grasses, its muzzle raised, its nose twitching. The Prince stood where he was, rooted to the spot. He held his breath as the bear tested the wind, clearly sensing something unusual. After what seemed to the child like an eternity, the bear ambled back the way it had come.

Now the Prince realized he was lost, for in the excitement of discovering this wild new landscape, so different from the manicured imperial gardens, he had not kept careful track of the turns he had taken, nor was he sure how far he had wandered from home. He spotted the raven that had led him to this place and for lack of a better plan, he followed.

But the raven was, in fact, a harpy named Malia, sent to destroy the Prince. Infuriated by the clumsy stupidity of the bear, Malia's fertile mind had hatched another plan the instant the first had failed. Cheered by the prospect of seeing the Prince lying poisoned on the forest floor, she dived down to the mossy rocks between the swaying cattails to find the special grass-green breed of viper she needed to complete her task. Responding to her summons, the deadly worms whipped out of a watery hole and slithered toward Prince Zong. Swiftly, they wrapped themselves around his ankles and prepared to sink their fangs into his flesh before he even noticed they were there.

The harpy gloated. These miniature serpents were the most

venomous on earth. Once they bit the boy, he would die instantly. But then Malia heard the child laugh. She saw him playfully stretch out his arms to the bright pair, his rosy face framed by their identical diamond-shaped heads. Now he was humming as the serpents wound around his legs.

"Bite!" she crowed raucously. "Oh, why don't you bite?"

The Prince looked up at her as if he had at that moment understood. To the harpy's amazement, he calmly plucked the vipers off as if they were harmless damsel flies. Swiftly braiding one with the other, he flung them away. Stunned, they untwined and raced back toward their holes. But the harpy's punishment was swift. Swooping down, she caught the two green snakes in her claws and rising as high as a harpy can go without trespassing on Heaven, dropped them into the muddy river below, where they immediately drowned.

The consequence of returning to Yamu and admitting she had failed to kill the Starlord was not to be imagined. Yet she had been reluctant to kill the Chosen One with her own brass claws, for fear of instant retribution from the Master Hand. Descending fast, the frustrated harpy scooped up a large rock from the craggy cliffs above.

The boy ducked behind a tree, but Malia rose up very high and, aiming carefully, dropped the boulder. Hurtling down at top speed, the rock hit with a loud crack and teetered on the edge of the narrow mossy overhang just above Prince Zong's head. Instead of falling and crushing the Prince to death as she had planned, it crashed to the ground at his feet and split wide open.

The harpy shrieked, a long drawn-out cry of agonized

surrender. Too furious to see more, she flapped darkly away, and so did not witness what happened next. Out of the granite bounced a stone egg, as round as a moon and as large as a playing ball, which began to circle Prince Zong like a pet dog. In the fading light of day, it led the astonished and delighted child straight back to the Forbidden City. Safe in the palace, Prince Zong longed more than ever for Jade Mirror, but his new nursemaid, beside herself with worry, scolded him soundly and, paying no attention to his tears or his odd new toy, put him to bed without his supper.

That night, wild nightingales gathered once more in the trees by the Prince's window, singing sweetly, but again the little Starlord could not sleep. He placed the stone by his bedside and waited. A gale blew up from the marsh, spinning the stone egg around and around. Etched by the harsh winter wind, an ancient face slowly appeared on the ice-smooth surface. The cold wind moaned and rose in intensity, carving the creature's arms and legs—and its long tail. Then the storm passed suddenly and, there by the Starlord's bedside mirror, stood a huge stone monkey, busily bowing to the north, south, east, and west.

When Monkey completed his obeisance to the four quarters, a steely beam of light darted out of his fierce sapphire-blue eyes and a white flash electrified the air around him. As Zong watched, wide-eyed, the beast was transformed from stone into flesh and blood.

Monkey did not seem to see the Prince at first, so troubled was he with what he saw in the mirror.

"Again and again and again and again—" he moaned, rapping his forehead against the glass with each repetition of the word. "Monkey is Monkey is Monkey, eternally and forever. When will I be free of you?" he asked his own image, hitting his head once more, harder than before. The Prince raised a small hand in protest, but Monkey was so beside himself with grief, he still did not notice the boy.

"Oh, how I hate you, Monkey," he said. "And you look even uglier naked. Look at you, you miserable excuse for a warrior. No cloud-stepping shoes, no chain-mail vest, no phoenix cap, no—"

He broke off and felt behind his ear. Then his mournful face broke into a grin as he pulled out what looked like a rusty sewing needle with two tiny sapphires set in a cracked handle of yellow jade. He rolled his eyes to Heaven, dropping to his knees as if in prayer.

"Thank you, Master. I will not abuse your gift," he said. "I shall never use this wishing rod for destruction but only for good, and I shall deserve it so well that you will change your mind about me. Next time I shall be invited to Heaven as a hero, and you shall grant me my immortality. Wait and see."

Now Monkey noticed the handsome child watching him quizzically, and he smiled. And Prince Zong, intrigued by a beast who talked to himself, returned the smile with all the innocence in his heart.

The boy had seen many smiles during his first few weeks of life, but none had been like Monkey's. He had seen the smile of shame on the thunderstruck face of his father, the cruel smiles of Han's ministers, his mother's tearful smile as she kissed him for the last time and turned away, the adoring smiles of his subjects, full of hope in his ability to rescue them from oppression, the solicitous smile of his nurse, and the mocking smile of the girl with the whistling pigeons.

But Monkey's was a newborn's happy, carefree smile, for like Prince Zong, he was an old soul reborn. And every baby, even an Emperor's son, needs such a smile. The Prince, who had never smiled before, instantly smiled back with such love that the ape, not very loving by nature, spontaneously swept the lad into his arms and swung him up and down until the child laughed. The laugh tickled Monkey so much, he swung the Prince up and down again. And again the Prince laughed. And so the two, Starlord and Monkey, became fast friends in one spontaneously loving moment of smiling and laughing.

And that moment sealed their fate, and the fate of an empire, forever.

PART TWO

Scorpion

*Everything gains in grandeur every day,
becoming more and more unknown.*
—Master Zheng

CHAPTER SEVENTEEN

Father Han

Even the weakest must agree to be oppressed.
—Eunuch Zhao Gao

Emperor Han could not sleep. As the rising wind beat against the palace walls, he rose from his bed and made his unsteady way to the Hall of Supreme Harmony, where Father Han, embalmed for all eternity, rested in his golden coffin. Two eunuchs followed at a respectful distance, and their combined footsteps echoed down the polished corridors. Impatiently he waved the servants away, indicating that he wished to be alone in the temple of his ancestors.

Even now Han's heart beat faster in this room that housed his father's spirit. Many years before his death, Father Han had ordered the creation of nine sculpted demons to guard his final resting place, and the statues were lifelike and horrible to behold, some standing with raised whips, some holding gruesome instruments of torture. His father had explained that the threat to those who entered was intended for thieves who wished to rob the mausoleum of its treasures. But as a child, Han wondered about his father's choice of art and was sure the demons had been placed there to threaten him alone.

Mortally afraid of his father, who often secretly ordered him beaten by the head eunuch when the boy fell short of his expectations, Han was tormented by the notion that the old Emperor would someday take his assigned place in the Netherworld as Demon King, and order unspeakable torments inflicted upon his son in the afterlife.

As heir to the Imperial Throne, Han was taught that he was by ancient law exempt from all physical discipline. An underling was supposed to take the beatings meant for him. But he never had the courage to confront Father Han with this knowledge. He always felt that his father was testing him. If he had once had the audacity to refuse his father's command and invoke his right to reassign his punishment, he was sure the beatings would have ceased. Instead, they grew more frequent as he grew older, but he never summoned the nerve to defy his father. Rather than risk a confrontation, he chose to lie down abjectly before the head eunuch who, dressed all in black, with a black hood to hide his face, raised the rod against him with such enthusiasm and skill that, although each time Han was determined not to cry out, he was always made to shed tears in the end.

The man was careful to leave no mark that could be detected by the slaves who came to bathe the Prince in the morning, but the boy became obsessed with wondering who else besides his father and the head eunuch knew his shameful secret, a humiliation unknown to any other born to the Imperial Throne. As soon as Father Han died, the Prince ordered the public execution of the head eunuch, who was, to Han's great satisfaction, slowly sliced to death by a faceless executioner dressed all in black. Han had chosen this most severe of all imperial decrees to quiet any at the palace who might have been privy to the eunuch's privileged glimpse of his weakness. Yet even after the bloody display, Han wondered who else in the palace whispered of how he had cringed like a maid and pitifully begged for mercy during those terrible nocturnal meetings.

Now, years after the old Emperor's death, Han was still haunted by a constant sense of his father's stinging disapproval, and the nine demons guarding Father Han's tomb had begun of late to appear to his son in terrible nightmares. It had occurred to Han to order the effigies removed from the palace, but he found himself incapable of issuing the directive, as paralyzed by his father's authority as he had been when the old Emperor was alive. He realized he would rather suffer the dreadful nightly visitations than risk incurring the wrath of his father's ghost.

The painted wooden guardians of Father Han's tomb were indeed the most frightful of Yamu's minions, and they were pictured in painstaking detail inflicting cruel torments upon the sinners who fell into their clutches. It was not hard for Han to imagine himself in the place of those poor sufferers, trapped for eternity. Here was one tormented soul, lying spread-eagled on his back as a winged harpy with a red barbed beak feasted on his entrails. There across the aisle was a tribe of hideous tengu, with beet-red faces and beards of real white human hair, sawing a man in half with their pointy jagged teeth. Next came a group of grinning goblins boiling a silently screaming prisoner in a black cauldron. The artist knew his craft so well that each drop of sweat was visible on the victim's brow.

A monstrous norn with one huge bloodshot eye and no skin at all, its ropy sinews and bulging muscles dark and raw, snorted a suspended cloud of poisonous steam through its hideously wide mouth, felling a band of sailors with one puff of its congealed breath. Tonight, as Han watched, the vapor's hard sculpted edges softened and gradually turned red, spreading like gas through the chamber and enveloping him in a misty shroud.

He walked on until he came to the monumental wall plaque behind Father Han's coffin, where the Lord of the Dead was pictured in ornate relief, haloed by the old Emperor's rare collection of deadly chert knives, confiscated from the rebellious peasantry. Each golden dagger, forged by the kingdom's master craftsmen, represented a different fiery ray of the setting sun reflected from the divine orb which crowned and illuminated Yamu's terrible head.

The Emperor stared at Yamu's scowling brows. As depicted by the court sculptor, the Lord of the Dead bore an unmistakably strong resemblance to Father Han, his long black silky beard glistening like oil in the lantern light. As a child, Han had heard it whispered in court that each hair in that beard had been plucked from the heads of the condemned in his father's dungeons. The snakelike thing had continued to grow over the years, tended by slaves who combed and groomed it as they did the less luxuriant beard of the living Emperor. In fact it was rumored no servant would dare go near the figure of Yamu on certain nights of the year, particularly around the time of the Festival of the Dead, when it was said the beard dripped blood upon the floor.

Han knew every inch of this gallery of horrors by heart. After it was completed and consecrated with due ceremony, it became his father's preferred setting for disciplinary sessions, teaching his son that worse awaited him in the afterlife.

Han approached the gilded dais where his father sat, embalmed and dressed in full regalia, staring out at him from raisinlike eyes. His wasted legs and torso were encased in a body suit laboriously constructed of two thousand translucent wafers of precious green jade, giving his body a reptilian sheen. His shriveled right hand held Dragon Rain, the sword he had promised Han. The old Emperor had broken his promise and taken the weapon with him to the Netherworld by order of his last will and testament. To Han's chagrin, that document had been read out in court so that the entire nation knew the deceased had not deemed his heir worthy of the famous sword.

Han knelt down before Dragon Rain now, touching the golden dragon emblem with his lips and reverently bowing his head.

"I must kill him, Father," he whispered. "Had I been born with the sign of the Qin, you would have squashed me like a scorpion before I drew breath enough to utter my first cry. He is your heir as well as mine. Give me your dragon strength to do this deed, for you were always the assassin."

As he prayed, the reddish vapor closed around him. With a resounding crack like the breaking of brittle bone, Dragon Rain fell from Father Han's clawlike hand and clattered to the floor.

Cautiously, as if afraid of being burned, Han closed his fingers around the hilt and, grasping the forbidden blade, rose from his knees. He had his answer and, for the first time in his life, his father's blessing.

With this ancestral sword, Father Han had repelled the barbarian hordes and beaten back the nomadic tribes of the northern steppes, leading a cavalry of fifty thousand and chasing the legendary flying horsemen all the way to the black Gobi desert. With this fabled sword, he had subdued the brigand bands at home and repelled the rebel Red Beards and later, the Yellow Turbans. With this sword of the immortals, he had colonized the fierce kingdoms of Bactria and Ferghana and crossed the highest of the Pamir peaks, taking his war weary troops farther than any emperor had traveled before him, through Kucha, Khotan, Yarkand, Kashgar, Kushar, Tukmak, and Karashar to the distant shores of the Caspian Sea. And still, with all of Manchuria and Mongolia conquered, with subjects paying homage to the throne all the way to Turkestan, Father Han's sword had not been satisfied.

Now the weapon once again called for blood, but this time, it called for the sacrificial blood of Han. With his father's sword, he would go forth and kill his own son and heir, born with the mark of the Qin. He would do this now, tonight, before his courage left him and before the child grew strong enough to strike first. Afterward, perhaps, his father's demons would cease to haunt him, and Yamu would leave him in peace, to sleep without dreams until morning.

CHAPTER EIGHTEEN

Dragon Rain

A legless man may still have cold feet.
—Yamu, Lord of the Dead

In a daze of coiling red mist, Emperor Han exited his father's Gallery of Horrors. Clutching Dragon Rain in his fist so tightly that the carved hilt cut into his flesh, he walked slowly toward Prince Zong's chamber. His son was fast asleep, his smooth face half obscured in the shadow cast by a large statue silhouetted in the moonlight. Han shook his head, confused. He did not recall seeing such a statue in the nursery before. Coming closer, he examined the effigy—a monkey, larger than life and cleverly modeled in stone, resembling the mythical Monkey King, one of the twelve mechanical animals represented in the royal water clock. Perhaps it had come as a gift for the "little Starlord" that day.

Recalling the people's name for the Prince filled Han with

rage. The infant, in one month, had already become so popular with the peasants, he commanded a loyal following before he could even speak! How could Han hope to retain his throne in the face of this strange boy's magical hold over his kingdom? The rumors must be true—this was not his natural son but some resurrection of the Starlord Hung Wu, predestined to usurp his power.

Staring at the beautiful child, he raised his sword to strike. Wisps of scarlet vapor snaked around him and wove like vipers into the Prince's tousled hair, wrapping around the coarse blue cotton bag the child seemed to be using as a pillow. The Emperor groaned as he felt the all-too-familiar wave of nausea and terror overtake him. He had always been assailed by illness when faced with the necessity to kill. It was, he knew, no higher principle holding him back, no nobility of spirit or moral hesitation. It was cowardice in its purest form. Even with Dragon Rain in his hand, he began to shake violently. Paralyzed and fearful, he wondered how he had come to this sorry cross-roads. He must banish the only woman who had ever made him feel like a man, and stamp out their son—or be destroyed.

He knew he must not think of Silver Lotus now, for then even Father Han's nine demons pricking him all at once with their barbed spears could not force him to do what must be done. He had cast away his flower, his only joy. If she were not already maimed and trampled, lying dead in the slums of Bai Ping, it was likely he would have to kill her. He was Emperor. He would kill whom he pleased. And then, perhaps some day, he would be man enough to kill himself.

The stone statue's eyes moved, following Han's movements

as he stumbled blindly around the room. The Emperor failed to notice this witness to his indecision, so preoccupied was he with his own internal struggle. Suddenly, the heavy silence was broken by the nightingales' song. The Prince smiled peacefully and turned in his sleep, still clutching his makeshift pillow. By a trick of light, the wraiths of red mist clinging to his tangled hair were instantly bleached a dazzling silver, and the moonbeams streaming through the window starkly illuminated his birthmark.

Seeing the hated sign of the Qin once again, Han let out a cry, and raising Dragon Rain, plunged it toward his son's heart. But his battle cry melted into a scream of terror, and his murderous blow froze in midair as the stone monkey's eyes blazed, blinding him in a pulsing stream of light. The heavenly music of the nightingales swelled, drowning a second agonized scream as, dropping his father's sword, the Emperor turned and fled from the haunted chamber. And then it seemed as if the room were suddenly incandescent and the floating moon itself had entered on a ghostly gust of rainswept wind. Monkey swooped down for the sword and snatched the Prince, bedclothes and all. Holding the startled child tightly, he sprang out the window, fleeing over the rooftops into the night. The nightingales sang on as the two grew smaller and smaller, silhouetted against the sinking moon. Their only audience was a lone monk sitting cross-legged and motionless in the garden, a calabash slowly spinning in his tattooed hands as the constellations guided the Starlord and his monkey guardian toward Moonshadow Marsh.

CHAPTER NINETEEN

The Assassin

Evil sees love as power and loyalty as obligation.
—The Tattooed Monk

The song of the nightingales pursued Han as he staggered through the freezing corridors toward the shelter of his private chambers. But his feet had taken on a will of their own and, like magnets drawn to a buried vein of metal, they were pointing him relentlessly toward Father Han's coffin.

How could he appear before his father without having accomplished the deed? And Dragon Rain—had the Monkey god stolen it? Like a marionette trying to break free of its strings, Han forced himself back down the darkened hall toward the nursery. But he found he could make no progress against the invisible hand pushing him in the opposite direction. Panic seized him. No, he could not return there to retrieve the sword, so frightened was he of the living statue that had snatched his son.

Gathering his royal robes around his knees and hunching down, he scuttled, panting like a small hunted animal through the carved doorway of the Gallery of Horrors and down the aisle of painted statuary, trying to look straight ahead so as not to see the terrified faces of the victims in each of the tableaux. He did not stop until he reached the plaque of Yamu. There, he prostrated himself on the floor like one of his own petitioners before the throne, his forehead pressed hard against the tiles. A premonition of humiliating defeat and dishonor crept into his limbs like an injection of lead. He could not move or even call out as a masked assassin, dressed all in black, stepped out of the shadows.

Will I die here, then? wondered Han, too paralyzed to scream for a guard or to run away as the menacing figure drew near. Often as a child he had lain like this, wondering if he would die if his father's eunuch went too far and beat him into unconsciousness. Now, in a dull haze that could almost be mistaken for peace, he waited for the blow that would end his life; and for once he did not cower but just lay still, as if he had in spirit already departed and no longer inhabited the miserable body that had so often betrayed him.

As he listened to the murderer's heavy step, grating like gravel on glass, a new thought exploded in his brain, flooding him with alarm. This man in black—could he be the eunuch's ghost? He was much larger than the slave he had ordered sliced to pieces, but in the Netherworld, appearances did not always stay as those on earth remembered them. As if to confirm his worst fears, the apparition drew one of his father's precious chert knives from the wall, and made a show of testing its gleaming point on his muscular arm, drawing a thin line of blood. The Emperor leapt to his feet, recoiling and pressing his pale hands to his heart as if he thought the intruder was preparing to carve the beating organ out of his chest.

Instead, the thickset bandit groped in the pocket of his bulky coat, producing a clump of black hair. Han cried out when he saw the familiar butterfly comb of finely carved white jade he had given Silver Lotus on her nineteenth birthday.

"Remove your mask so that I may see who you are," said the Emperor, weakly attempting to summon a tone of command.

The man growled like a dog, holding his trophy high. Then slowly he turned to the imposing statue of Yamu and, looking back over his shoulder at Han with what the Emperor imagined to be a mocking expression, he took his time loosely braiding the hair of the former First Consort into the long black beard of the Lord of the Dead.

"I am T'sao T'sao, Your Majesty," he said, bowing and removing his mask. "I am not a pretty sight this evening. Your castle is riddled with outlaws who protect the prince, and I've had an icy dip in the moat. Your lady's comb cost me dearly as well. But of course, I inform you of nothing your spies have not already told you."

The Emperor continued to stare at the bandit's stolen dagger. "Did you murder her for a comb?" he asked hoarsely.

T'sao T'sao sneered, and now Han noticed the piece of leopard's fur wrapped around his arm. "I would not be here if I had," he answered.

"Spotted Leopard sent you, then?" Han asked with relief and renewed interest. "Why?"

"He told me you were in need of a hired assassin," said T'sao T'sao. "For the little Starlord, first. And then, perhaps, for Lady Dulcimer."

"Lady Dulcimer?" gasped the Emperor, turning scarlet and choking on the words. Was this rogue so familiar with his Lotus that he dared name her so?

"Answer directly!" he whispered. "Did you . . . harm her?"

A rush of memories suddenly flooded his mind, of the graceful girl playing song after song to soothe him to sleep, and wiping the sweat from his brow as she stroked him gently when he woke from his nightmares.

"I gladly would have, but she got me first," T'sao T'sao sneered. "She travels with a blind man, or some beggar pretending to be blind. He's fairly handy with his staff—almost killed me, but I'll have another go at him soon if the Leopard guesses your game correctly."

"My game?" repeated the Emperor dully, trying to focus on the business at hand, for now it was clear he would live a little longer and the criminal confronting him would draw cash, not blood. But for the moment he could think of nothing other than that Silver Lotus still lived.

"Four hundred silver taels for each," said T'sao T'sao flatly, taking an empty pouch from his sleeve and dropping it into Emperor Han's palm. "Although we should charge more for the lady," he added.

"Your price is high, even for a thief," Han answered.

"Kill them yourself, then," said T'sao T'sao disdainfully. "But first you must find them. And that could take months. What will you tell your people in the meantime? Will you say the little Starlord has been kidnapped? Will you post a reward for his safe return? Of course, whether you pay us or not, the Leopard will track them. Dead or alive, they'll fetch a tidy sum. When we find them, we'll sell to the highest bidder." He licked his lips and began to mumble as if to himself. "The Leopard hasn't seen the little lotus flower yet, but I'm sure when he does, he'll find a use for her. Why waste such talent in the Netherworld? Yes, yes, she's of much greater value to the Leopard alive." He bowed again and made as if to go.

"Wait!" said Han, "I agree to your price, but you must bring me the head of the Prince by the first night of the Festival of Lanterns!"

T'sao T'sao came a step closer and bent down confidentially to the Emperor's ear. "Murder is a delicate art, Your Majesty," T'sao T'sao murmured. "A double murder even more so. Not even an Emperor can rush a true artist, or the work may suffer. An enemy recovered from a bungled attempt on his life is surely the most dangerous kind, wouldn't you agree?"

"Nevertheless, the Festival of Lanterns is the date," said the Emperor, a steely note coming into his voice. "Or the Leopard forfeits his fee."

"And if we finish the work early?" asked T'sao T'sao, using a more respectful tone now that he had secured the job. "A bonus is customary," he insisted.

"A bonus?" mused the Emperor. "Bring me the head of the monk who travels with Silver Lotus, and you shall receive a bonus of five hundred silver taels."

"One thousand for the monk, Your Majesty," answered T'sao T'sao joyfully, knowing he had the jealous Emperor now.

"And a nice dagger just like this one when the job is done." Fingering the gleaming weapon he had taken, he moved to return it to its sheath on the wall.

Han did not hesitate. "Let it be done," he said.

"And the lady?" asked T'sao T'sao. "What are your instructions, Your Majesty?"

For a long moment, the Emperor said nothing at all, struggling visibly with himself. He stared at the statue of Yamu, almost expecting the beard to grow sticky with a flow of blood as he watched. In a kind of dream, he leaned forward and shamelessly caressed the new strands T'sao T'sao had added, wondering who this old warrior could be, this heroic monk who fought for her. The silence stretched like a long frozen road between the Emperor and the assassin. Finally, Han spoke.

"Bring me her head as well," he said softly.

CHAPTER TWENTY

Scourge of the Sea

The dead will always outnumber the living.
—Yamu, Lord of the Dead

As the outlaws put Morning Cloud Cove behind them, a tumultuous wind roughened the darkening waves, issuing from all directions at once. The sunset threw welts of deep purple across a glowering sky.

Without warning, a gargantuan head, more terrifying to Puk than his sighting of Chac earlier than day, rose up out of the waves. From the demon wahwee's blind eyes gushed a fountain of bile, one drop of which would have reduced the dog to a bleached pile of bones. Lodged in its gigantic mouth, trapped between two massive intestine-like lips, the lost boy Kuan stretched out his arms beseechingly toward White Streak's boat.

Flinging himself through the seething surf, Puk hit the

wahwee from the side so hard he almost knocked himself out. In a frenzy, he bit through tendon and muscle, causing the monstrous mouth to swing open in surprise.

White Streak dove into the foam, narrowly avoiding the bubbling pool which now all but surrounded the dog, and dragged Kuan out of the spewing cavity, heaving him into Black Whirlwind's waiting arms. But Puk was not finished with the wahwee. The giant head had scared him half to death. Now that he had discovered he could puncture the wahwee with his teeth, he plunged brashly underwater again, and continued to tear at the snarling face as if it were a tasty pile of blood sausage.

Suddenly White Streak understood why Puk had been nicknamed the Scourge of the Sea. But the pup was in danger of being eaten alive by the acid pouring from the wahwee's wounds.

"Puk!" he called urgently. "Stop biting now! Before that green bile bites you back!"

With a yelp of fright, Puk dove for the pole White Streak held out to him, latching on for dear life as White Streak hauled him in toward the *Immortal Beggar*. Then letting go, Puk heaved himself into the boat, panting and dripping shreds of wahwee all over the deck.

"Good dog! Good dog!" whooped Black Whirlwind, twirling his ax in the air.

Puk eyed the big outlaw. "Good dog?" he echoed contemptuously.

Kuan ran forward and threw his arms around Puk's neck, giving him a kiss on his messy snout. "Good dog!" he yelled, and hugged the hound hard. Somehow this praise, coming from the child, satisfied Puk, and he settled down, resting his head on his paws, and let the boy pat him all over.

"Father will be angry with me for going fishing by myself," Kuan confided.

"I'm sure your father has been hunting all over for you," said White Streak, smiling. "He'll be happy to find you safe."

"Do you think so?" asked the boy anxiously.

"You'll be greeted like a prince," Black Whirlwind chimed in. "Wait and see."

Reassured, Kuan grew talkative as they slid through the reeds in the fading light, headed for Banpo village. "Maybe Father will sing for us when we get there," mused the boy. "He plays the lute at weddings and funerals, and everyone says his songs come straight from Heaven. Sometimes, he plays just for us. And he tells ghost stories too, about the ponaturi and other evil spirits. But he never told me about the wahwee."

"I'd like to meet your father," said White Streak. Exhausted, the boy yawned wearily and nodded. To pass the time, White Streak told Kuan about Mother Gu and the Golden Phoenix and then, because there was something about the quiet way the boy listened that White Streak found restful, he found himself talking about his own father, and how the Dragon of the North Sea had met Mother Gu one stormy morning in the marsh when Chac had lost his way and become dangerously stranded in shallow water.

"Do you mean your father is a dragon?" asked Kuan, alert and hanging on every word now.

"Yes, and a king," White Streak answered, laughing. Usually the outlaw leader never spoke about his father except to complain about him. He asked himself why he enjoyed thinking about Chac now, when the mission his father had assigned to him was as murky as ever. Perhaps it was the comforting presence of Puk, reminding him of his victory over the Nokk, and of Kuan, whom he had stolen from the jaws of a wahwee, that cheered him.

Peacefully, White Streak followed the muskrat trails, disturbing a swarm of ghost moths illuminated in the glow of the setting sun. This was his favorite time of day in the marsh, when the white-tailed deer browsed the foliage along the banks, the snow hares rustled in the bushes, and the vacated nests of the summer birds stood out starkly against a painted sky. The scene was so restful, it was hard for White Streak to imagine it disturbed by demons the likes of which he had seen earlier that day.

But as the outlaws neared Banpo Village, White Streak noticed there was little evidence of life in the water larger than masses of tiny snails and pill clams. The strangled plants were laced with thick veins of black spittle-like slime, and a heavy silence hung over the hoary thickets like fungal moss. When they finally reached Banpo, they found that demons had discovered it before them, and after the demons, bandits had destroyed all that was left. From the moment they entered the town, they smelled the carnage, and death was everywhere as they walked through.

In a daze of sudden sorrow, Kuan led them to his house. It was razed to the ground, his mother and father, sister and brothers all gone. Bodies were tossed carelessly about in the still-smoking debris, burned beyond recognition. Too deeply shocked for tears, the boy wandered through the blackened beams and cinders, searching for something recognizable. A pile of bricks and stakes, a tangled nest of knotted cords and shredded nets, some singed matting, and a few shattered screens were all that remained.

Frantically, Kuan began to dig in the dirt, unearthing his grandmother's metal water jug and bowl. He continued to claw in the earth, sifting through the ashes. Pulling up his little sister's abacus, he dusted it on his shirt and slowly rolled the chipped beads up and down, one at a time, as if making sure they were all still there. Hugging the battered counting tool to his chest, he curled up on the ground and would not rise or respond when White Streak told him it was time to go, lest more bandits descend upon them, looking for whatever loot the first gang had left behind. Puk lay down beside Kuan and, whining mournfully, licked his salty cheek. Finally the boy raised his head, staring at them miserably. "Where will I go?" he croaked.

"We'll bring you home to Mother Gu," answered White Streak, kneeling down beside him. "She'll take good care of you, Kuan, and teach you how to fight."

"Will I be an outlaw, then?" asked Kuan, more alert now and sitting up, his face streaked with soot. "My father didn't want me to be an outlaw. He said it was better to mind your own business." He hung his head miserably. "But I suppose all that doesn't matter now," he muttered, almost to himself.

"We're fishermen like your father," answered White Streak. "We can train you to be as fine a fisherman as he would have wished."

Kuan slipped the abacus into his sleeve. Rising to his knees, he bowed three times on the smoking site of his demolished house, which had become his family's grave. He closed his eyes, and remained very still. Finally, he stood and walked unsteadily to a nearby tree. On a low-hanging branch, a man's long, mangled body hung from a blackened noose, swaying gently in the breeze. Wrapped around his broken wrist was a bloodied strip of spotted fur.

The boy choked and fell silent, gazing at the charred remains. He ran his tongue over his dry lips. Then he walked up to his father's corpse and untied the talisman, handing it to White Streak.

"Do those who wear the sign of the Qin hunt *this* kind of demon?" he asked.

White Streak hesitated, struggling with himself, reluctant to fill Kuan's mind with bitter thoughts of revenge. "Yes," he answered truthfully after a moment. The boy's eyes were bright with tears.

"Then I will be an outlaw too," he said.

Awkwardly, Black Whirlwind tried to envelop Kuan in a bear hug, but the boy quickly stepped aside. Puk growled and nuzzled his leg. Kuan embraced the demon dog, burying his face in Puk's matted fur. Then he turned and, with the giant mastiff close by his side, followed the three outlaws through the ruins of Banpo Village to the beach where the *Immortal Beggar* lay anchored and ready to sail.

CHAPTER TWENTY-ONE

General Calabash

We are here until we are somewhere else.
—The Immortal Beggar

Asea of gray, patched with the shadows of drifting clouds, stretched to the horizon. Silver Lotus tried to keep up with her tireless companion as they followed an ancient river bed, dry for centuries and snaking endlessly through the sandy gorge. Nothing but barren rock surrounded them. Here and there a dust devil spun upward, dissolving into the glare. A frigid sprinkling of rainbow-tinged rain evaporated as soon as it erased their footprints, leaving the land unmarked by their passage.

For a moment, the monk looked as if he were on fire, sending a pall of ashy smoke billowing out from behind, but as Silver Lotus struggled to keep up, she realized she too was on fire, a miragelike effect of stirring up the black dust of the Gobi.

This vast, forbidding place was her new home, Silver Lotus marveled, for she had decided to stay with General Calabash and learn all he could teach her of kung fu and the secrets of the sect whose name she shared. During their flight through the mountains, he had told her of his friendship with her father, Gong Sun. Together, they had mourned his death, and together, each evening, they said a prayer for his soul. As the days and nights passed in his company, Silver Lotus felt more and more strongly that she and the Tattooed Monk had been destined to meet, brought together by her father's dying wish.

The sun rose higher and the swarthy dunes revealed dark, dusty streaks of charcoal. A colony of spindly gorse bushes sat like squat little gods on the surface of the earth, their leaves aflame. In the distance, cracked slabs of flat stone thrust through the desert floor like the buried ruins of unsung cities. In front of one of these natural shelters, near a frozen patch of hummocks, the monk slowed and stopped, urgently beckoning her to come.

As soon as she stepped inside the cavernous space, she heard the song. A light breeze drifted up against her legs, carrying the soft sounds of distant camels, the barking of dogs, and the neighing of ponies, as well the faint approach of a ghostly cavalcade of travelers, some beating drums and others blowing ram's horns. And somehow she knew that the music was not from a distant place but from a distant time. Although she had never given much thought to ghosts, she had no doubt that spirits resided here and were singing to her, conjuring a life on the desert that had long ago disappeared.

The Tattooed Monk cast an enormous shadow on the wall. Suddenly, the monk's wavering shape reminded her of the cutouts she had seen as a child in her village on the night of the Festival of the Dead, black silhouettes dancing and trembling in the lantern light. Most common of all was the people's favorite—the Immortal Beggar with his cripple's cane and misshapen legs. Growing uneasy, she stared at the flickering shadow of General Calabash, which seemed to be growing taller by the moment, towering over her own wraithlike shade on the wall of the desert tabernacle. Then, turning slowly away from these phantoms, she stared at her companion directly, and her heart quieted. His look contained only gentleness and concern, and she knew she should not fear him.

The song, which seemed to have traversed time, drifting in on the gray sands, began to fade into a less insistent hum and then, sinking in volume, dropped to a soft steady hiss. Wishing the spirit music would linger a little longer, Silver Lotus knelt and took out her dulcimer. The monk stood as still as a statue, never taking his eyes from hers as she sang. Then he added his deep voice to hers, and by the time they both fell silent, the song of the sands had hushed as well. In the failing light, she saw that the Tattooed Monk had fallen into meditation, his eyes closed, his arms embracing air in the standing pose she had come to recognize as his stance for prayer. She took her place beside him, imitating his attitude, but she did not close her eyes. Something in this room alerted her to danger, yet it was entirely empty, except for the monk, whose tattoos had begun to move.

Silver Lotus watched in fascination as one animal after

another appeared upon the monk's back. First, a gigantic bat took shape, spreading its hinged wings; then a swift black fox; then a crane, as gray as the desert sands; then a great bear, rearing on its hind legs as tall as a tree and twice as thick, followed by something she could not quite make out resembling a sun dial with ancient symbols carved into it. No, now it became clear. It was a giant turtle with writing and signs inscribed on its shell in gold; then a bulging toad, huge and oily; and a darting orange lizard with a dizzying number of spots giving way to a galloping amber horse; a golden monkey swinging through the forest canopy; and finally, a fierce white tiger, which lingered longest and stared at her with uncompromising yellow eyes.

Silver Lotus gasped, for she had the distinct sensation that the tiger could see into her soul. Her surroundings dropped away for a moment and there was nothing to be seen or known in all the universe but the white tiger. Between two black velvet strokes in the middle of its broad forehead, a bright pearl blinked at her as round and pure as a baby's ear, and she knew if she plucked that pearl, she would live forever.

"Tiger," she breathed, reaching out, but the phantom melted into a flaming phoenix and then, last and most dreadful, a fearsome dragon, perfect in every hot brazen scale and armored joint, and displaying its formidable fangs.

Silver Lotus stood stunned, watching the mesmerizing transformation of the Tattooed Monk into living scripture. General Calabash had begun to teach her passages he had committed to memory from the scrolls destroyed in the fire, and she recognized these terrible animals and their sacred guardians as the twelve beasts that embodied the fighting forms of the Silver Lotus, her father's holy order.

"I thought perhaps you were a crane," came the Tattooed Monk's voice, echoing strangely. He was breathing heavily from what seemed to have been an ordeal, although his exertions had been entirely confined to one spot. He had not yet faced her. "But I see the white tiger is your spirit animal. You must learn that form first."

"Have I just been tested, then?" she asked meekly. The tattoos had stopped writhing now, and the monk turned slowly, studying her.

"No, *I* have," he answered. Crossing his powerful arms across his chest, he shivered, but it was more as if a strong vibration had passed through him, like an earth tremor after a quake. "Were you frightened . . . ?" He hesitated, letting the question dangle in midair.

"I was a bit, but I'm not afraid now," she admitted, smiling at him.

His heavy brows drew together, his face clouding. He seemed suddenly as old as when she had first seen him behind the Kingfisher's Inn, only then he had appeared to be blind and now his eyes drilled into her. He had told her about the mystery of his moving tattoos, but now she had actually seen the miracle for herself.

"I would never willingly let anything hurt you," he said, watching her.

Silver Lotus had been a girl when she came to live in the Forbidden City. She had known only duty there, never love.

Now, her heart was stirred by the Tattooed Monk's vow to protect her with his life, by the unexpected passion of his pledge. He continued to study her.

"I would rather die," he added, and the charged intensity of his voice swept through her, melting her bones.

CHAPTER TWENTY-TWO

First Journey

However far back we look into the past, we see the waves breaking into the future.—Emperor Hung Wu

Monkey tried to recall all he had learned in ninety-nine lifetimes about babies, but it was, he realized as he looked down at the one in his arms, precious little. He had heard that humans had a soft spot in their skulls until a certain age when the bones closed up, so it was important not to drop them, but this boy seemed to have a pretty hard head. He was also heavier than Monkey had imagined a child could possibly be.

Monkey wrapped his aching arms tightly around the clinging boy as he climbed from rock to rock in the rushing mountain stream, following the slippery tumble of boulders ever upward. He had hoped to reach Huang Ho by nightfall, but he had not counted on the rain-swollen waters blocking his access to the upper reaches of the Kunlun range. Now he was forced to seek firmer ground in one long muddy detour after another.

As Monkey struggled steadily up the treacherously steep and slippery incline with the large-eyed Prince Zong clutched firmly to his furry chest, he paused a moment to catch his breath, leaning for support against the scarred trunk of a fallen tree. Floods of surging whitewater had stunted the maples along the crumbling riverbank upon which Monkey now settled to rest, making himself more comfortable by pillowing his weary head upon the Prince's blue bag. The giant tree he reclined against had been downed by successive storms. But in stark defiance of gravity, it was still growing.

"Sometimes, life is as plain as a sock in the jaw." Monkey sighed, placing the child gently down on a tussock of frozen sedge grass. Unstrapping Dragon Rain, he propped his sore feet up on a scoured branch. Then, liking the sound of his own voice, he went on, addressing the Prince as his student: "Take this tree, for example. We judge its strength by the number of storms it has survived. Same as a man—or an ape for that matter." Monkey paused, considering the wisdom of this statement, and wondering how to elaborate. As no further words of philosophical weight came to mind, he dropped his pompous tone and shrugged apologetically. "It's as simple as that, Prince!" he concluded, with a shrug and a foolish grin.

The boy nodded, seeming to understand, and gazed back at Monkey with solemn sympathy. Monkey shook his finger at him, and sucked in his lips like an old man eating a sour lemon. "But perhaps not quite that simple, eh? Take Father Han, for instance. He mistook lack of mercy for strength. He measured power by the catastrophes he was able to visit upon his enemies and by the number of lives he snuffed out. Skulls on his belt, eh? Your father, Emperor Han, is the same, with one difference—he hasn't the courage to kill. Nor has he the courage to conquer nations or even to travel very far from the palace. I doubt he would stick his nose out the door at all if he didn't have to show himself on holidays. So he has to order others to do his killing for him. I expect by now he has ordered somebody to get rid of us."

The Starlord blinked and pulled his chin into his collar so that he resembled a turtle retreating into his shell. Monkey, regretting the harshness of this last remark, smiled encouragingly at him. He had not meant to frighten the boy. He searched his mind for something to make the Prince feel braver and his eyes lit upon Dragon Rain. It was unmistakably the famous weapon Emperor Hung Wu had earned from the Immortal Beggar to aid him on his long journey to the iron summit of the Mountain of the Five Elements.

"Do you know how you come by this legendary sword, Prince? It's a pretty one, isn't it? And it was no accident that it fell into our hands. The Master Hand himself saw to it that you own it now, and do you know what that means? It means Emperor Han, though born to the Imperial Throne, is a hairy toad—and you, my lord, have dragon blood in your veins and phoenix fire in your heart. Shall I tell you how I know that?"

Zong nodded. Monkey had his full attention now and he had relaxed out of his turtlelike pose and was watching his guardian with bright eyes, hanging on every word. Monkey warmed to his theme, letting the oft-told story roll through his mind. He realized with the surge of high spirits only a true storyteller experiences before launching into a familiar tale, that this was the first time he had told this particular favorite to someone who had never heard it before. He could not remember when he had first heard it himself but guessed it was probably when he was about Zong's age in some faraway lifetime, for it was part of every infant's education, human or animal.

"Once upon a time," he began, and then stopped, for he realized that he was about to speak of the Starlord as if he were a character in a fairy tale to the boy who was, according to all the cosmic signs and omens, the new Starlord. Monkey cleared his throat and began again:

"Even as a small boy, the Emperor-to-be, Hung Wu, excelled in the art of warfare. Though small of stature and very young, he was strong, fast, and subtle, and no other person of any age or class in his province could hurl a javelin so unerringly or twirl his sword so rapidly or utter growls of such terrifying menace while showing graceful proficiency in the use of blunt-edged weaponry.

"Yet Hung Wu had a gentle nature when not practicing battlefield tactics with his tutor, and would sooner resort to persuasion than force in his ordinary affairs, never relying upon his fighting skills or his rank to win an argument or make anyone—even the youngest son of the lowliest slave—feel inferior. For this reason, he was, unlike his father, popular with all who lived and worked in the palace.

"It was a chaotic time similar to our present one,

when the poor, wracked by a series of natural catastrophes, were hard-pressed to pay their burden of taxes. Floods, earthquakes, and waves of wind-borne locusts had transformed many hardworking farmers and craftspeople into homeless beggars, and some who could not bring themselves to beg had turned away from lawful commerce to thievery and worse. Bands of brigands roamed freely, and the poor robbed the poor. And many were robbed of more than their possessions. Stripped of all pleasure in living, there were reports every day of men and women who had jumped into dry wells or hung themselves from the rafters, preferring suicide to slowly starving to death or waiting to be murdered by the brutal gangs of bandits preying upon the ravaged countryside.

"When his son was ten, the Emperor required him to spend a good deal of his time sitting silently beside his throne at council sessions, listening to the reports from his emissaries and noting which issues raised their most heated debates. Hung Wu, accustomed to the demanding activity of his martial arts training, and also to speaking his mind, found this new duty to be oppressively dull. Upon occasion, he would burst out with opinions of his own, interrupting and shocking the ministers of state. For these displays of impatience and temper he would be severely reprimanded but never as severely as the insulted parties thought appropriate. Secretly, the Emperor delighted in his son's precocious grasp of politics and natural talent for military strategy."

Monkey broke off here and studied Prince Zong's face. The boy had closed his eyes, as if in pain, and at first Monkey was mystified as to the cause. "I wish you could speak, Prince," he said wistfully, scratching his head. "I guess I talk enough for both of us, but right now you look as if you'd like me to stop."

The Prince shook his head, but he looked so sad that Monkey hesitated for fear of saying something that would further upset the child. He sighed. "It's Hung Wu's father, isn't it? You're thinking you don't have a father to be proud of you, is that it, Prince? Emperor Han hasn't shown much fatherly pride, has he? Well, think of it this way, my friend, your *real* father is Hung Wu, the hero I'm telling you about. And if he had known you, I'm sure he would have been very proud. I've only known you a few hours and I'm already proud of you."

At this, Prince Zong smiled, although still sadly. "Forget about Han," said Monkey emphatically. "He isn't your true father. Think about it, Prince. Would your father try to kill you?"

The question hung in the air, growing heavier with each passing moment, like a cloud swelling with rain. The Prince turned his face away. Monkey saw his bony shoulders grow rigid, as if he were pushing at something weighty bearing down on him. When he turned back, his face had cleared and he gave Monkey a wan smile, nodding to him to continue. Monkey took the cue and resumed:

"As he grew older, Hung Wu's faithful hunch-backed tutor, Zheng, was finding it harder and harder to challenge his student. Already, Hung Wu, in addition to his widely known skills as a swordsman, could lie in a stupor and feign death for long periods of time, pass more stealthily than any spy through encamped ranks of armored men, and skewer several enemies with one arrow at a distance of one hundred paces. All attacks of course were performed upon dummies, with no real danger to Hung Wu. But the mysterious Zheng was known for his artistry in creating wonderfully realistic effigies for Hung Wu to engage with on their simulated field of battle. The man took pride in his lifelike models of the powerful warriors, both living and dead, arrayed against the Emperor, ranging from the seven-foot pirate Ma He with his glaring eyes and teeth as white as shells, to the greedy and treasonous merchant Zhu Qing, to the Mogul conqueror Ghengis Khan, as well as a scattered sampling of ferocious beasts of the forest, all wicker skeletons covered in painted cloth and tinted wax.

"People trembled when they saw Zheng's collection, for it seemed to all who viewed his convincing villains that the sculptor had drawn upon a supernatural gift and modeled his subjects true in every detail, save the divine spark that would bring them to life. And some believed the solitary artist, possessed the godlike power to breathe life into his creations at will.

"But no matter how realistically his resourceful master conjured the enemy, and no matter how much praise he garnered for his precise and elegant fighting forms, the young man complained of boredom and suffered a great restlessness of spirit. He could no longer bear to sit in his father's throne room listening to the injustices that permeated the kingdom, nor could he tolerate battling one more fabricated foe.

"One day, procuring the skin of a large gray wolf from a royal hunter, he concealed himself within it and at dawn, while the dew was still wet upon the ground, crept out of the palace toward Zheng's house, intending to startle him in this fearsome disguise into a genuine attack. He couldn't wait to see his teacher's face when the true identity of this beast of the woods was finally revealed. But before he could wake Zheng from his slumbers and engage him in combat, a laborer, hung over from a late night in the local tavern, crossed the royal compound on his way to the rice fields and spotted what he thought was a dangerous beast heading toward the sifu's garden.

"Thinking to defend himself and curry favor with Zheng, the worker dove at the Prince with a shocking lack of consideration for the proper fighting forms. Taking Hung Wu by surprise, he dealt the lad a great blow to the head with his staff, which would have surely knocked Wu out cold or even killed him had it not been for the protection of the wolf's already slightly cracked skull which, like a helmet, took the full brunt of the attack.

"The peasant began to cut what he thought was the carcass with his knife, intending to skin it on the spot. The pelt fell away with surprising ease and little blood, and imagine this man's shock and disbelief when he discovered the rumpled and semi-conscious form of Hung Wu, curled snugly inside!

"Apologizing profusely and fearing for his life, the rustic began to kowtow furiously, but seeing Hung Wu's confused and weakened state, he decided it would be best to revive the youth before kneeling before him and begging forgiveness.

"The embarrassment this incident caused Hung Wu was the last straw. Staring into his assailant's beady eyes, which, although terrified and remorseful, could not entirely disguise traces of amusement, the Prince decided then and there to run away from home, fleeing his imperial duties as the Emperor's son and heir.

"Hung Wu woke his beloved master and, pledging him to silence, said his farewells. Tears were shed on both sides, for the two men were as fond of one another as father and son. Zheng insisted on giving Wu his own horse, a steed worthy of an emperor, and sent him off with plenty of food in his saddlebags. The sifu also gave his single disciple a sum of money, a silk robe embroidered with the sign of the Silver Lotus (for he was a member of that ancient order), and his most reliable throwing spear. Then, commanding Hung Wu to treat him to a last demonstration of the sword techniques he had learned, the master took Dragon Rain down from its place on the wall and thrust it into his student's hands.

"Now, as you well know, this sword was no ordinary one. Zheng, though a hunchback, was a formidable fighter and he had altered it for his own use to perfectly match his distinctive style of combat. The blade emerged in the first light of morning like a blazing tongue of fire. Hung Wu had been taught his master's own repertoire of moves with a lighter replica of the weapon but had never held the actual ancient sword in his own hands before.

"Filled with the desire to gratify his teacher, Wu threw his whole heart into the moves he knew so well, showing Zheng a perfect slant hack, left and right slice, straight stab, and upward slash before moving as liquidly as lava into the overhead block, drag cut, and single- and double-armed swirls. Finally, Wu hoisted the heavy sword high and performed a flawless display of his master's own innovations, starting with *Looking Around at the Moon*, and *Emperor Strokes His Own Beard*, and ending with *Snowflakes Pour Down on Little Ghost's Head*, and *Lion Turns the Great Compass.*

"Moved beyond words, Zheng sent Hung Wu on his way, but not before pressing Dragon Rain into his hands, insisting that he had earned the treasure as his graduation present. Knowing full well how much his sifu loved this sword, which had been in his family for generations, Hung Wu protested the sacrifice, at first refusing to take the weapon from him; but in the end he was persuaded to do so and knelt before Zheng for his blessing like a true son.

"'Never mistake the map for the territory,' said his teacher, resting his hands on Hung Wu's shoulders. 'We *ask the same questions over and over again, but the soul never repeats itself. At any instant, the bush may flare, our feet may rise into the air, and whatever we look at hard, may look back at us.'*

"As he spoke, Zheng seemed to grow in stature until, when Hung Wu opened his eyes, his master was towering over him, and from his fingers as they pressed down upon the young man's shoulders came a strong light that penetrated to Hung Wu's bones. Even stranger was his voice, which had taken on a booming resonance and now, in addition to the hump on his back, his legs appeared to have become bent and twisted and he emphasized his last words with a tap of a crooked wooden crutch.

"'*Like the immortals,*' he said, '*we have the power to affect only what is in the nature of things. And all the known laws of science do little to explain why goodness shines from one face and evil betrays itself in another.*'

"Now Hung Wu understood the truth and gasped as he recognized Zheng as the Immortal Beggar, whom he had often addressed in prayer as a child. Stammering, he shook his head, trying to recall when Zheng first came to the palace, but the tutor was so much a part of every childhood memory, he could not conjure a time when Zheng was not by his side.

"'Did you come because I prayed to you? Or did I pray to you because you were here all along, right beside me?' he asked, stunned.

"'I do not know how to answer that question.' Zheng smiled. 'When you were born, you cried very loudly and your mother, rocking you in her arms, looked into your open mouth and saw, deep inside your throat, the night sky filled with all the stars in the universe, arranged as they were above, in orderly constellations. And so she called you little Starlord. You have my blessing, Hung Wu. Each day and night I shall pray for your continued health and joy.' "

Now Monkey once again checked Zong's face for signs of discomfort at this fatherly leave-taking, so different from what the Prince had experienced in the hands of his murderous parent, but he was gratified to see the child riveted, so rapt in the recitation of Hung Wu's first journey away from the Forbidden City, he seemed to forget for the moment to be anxious about his own. The lad was studying Dragon Rain with new interest, and reached out his hand toward the heavy broadsword resting on Monkey's lap.

"Ah, ah, not yet, Prince," laughed Monkey, springing up and leaning upon the long shaft. "Your story has just begun. Your arms need to grow, and you haven't earned this Emperor's weapon yet. Like Zheng, I'm keeper of the dragon sword now, and I don't intend to give it up until you can show me all those moves and more, for in ninety-nine lifetimes I've learned a trick or two, and I intend to teach you the highest of fighting forms—Monkey kung fu—when you're ready. You must learn to be a monkey before you can be a dragon or a phoenix, eh? But first," he said, suddenly shivering with cold, "we have to find our way out of these sun-forsaken mountains before the frost demons send an avalanche down upon our heads!"

CHAPTER TWENTY-THREE

Dragon Bone Lake

*Exile may darken the eyes, but the stars shine
as brightly as ever.*—The Tattooed Monk

As if the spirits of the mountain overheard Monkey's words, a terrible rending sound of screaming and wailing suddenly surrounded them, causing the ape to scoop the boy and the blue bag into his arms once again. Still reluctant to leave the comforting shelter of the tree, he peered over the ledge into the rocky valley below, digging the tip of the broadsword into the ground for balance. The echoing cries came from some distance down along the twisting trail, where a slow-moving caravan of villagers and farmers, fleeing their flooded homes with all their possessions, had been waylaid by a small group of armed bandits.

The thieves were encountering some weak resistance from the half-starved men in one of the families and had set fire to his provisions. The piercing lamentations were coming from that peasant's wife and her children. Dressed in blackened rags that fluttered like banners of defeat, they ran frantically around the flaming pile of debris, burning their hands in a futile attempt to retrieve their few remaining possessions from the ashy pyre.

An old toothy grandmother, so skinny it seemed a miracle she wasn't knocked over by the icy wind, crouched in the middle of the chaotic scene, weeping at the sudden blast of warmth issuing from the destruction of what little she had left in the world. Shaking her fist and shrieking, she held out her arms to her children and grandchildren, begging them to come away from the blaze into the imagined safety of her embrace.

As Monkey watched, the thieves slashed and beat their way through the entire sorry company of exiles. He tightened his grip on Dragon Rain. But it was over almost as soon as it had begun. The gang swiftly inflicted what damage they intended and moved on, leaving a few of the bravest who had opposed them dead by the road, a few wounded and bloodied, and those who had submitted and survived, stunned and more burdened by grief than before.

Monkey longed to pursue the scavengers and send them all to the Netherworld. He hated nothing worse than the vultures who stole from their own kind. But he could not risk appearing before them with the Prince. He knew that those he might offer to help would be likely to rob him of more than he could spare, since they had been left with so little.

Having reached the comforting conclusion that he could do nothing to alleviate the suffering of the unfortunate travelers, he looked down at the Prince, but his solicitous glance was met with a stern and accusatory glare. If the boy could speak, he could have communicated his glowering displeasure no more clearly. Monkey read the command in the royal toddler's clouded face and shook his head.

"You don't understand, Prince. We can't help those people or we'll die ourselves, and what good will that do, eh?" he said. "Perhaps they'll starve, and that's sad, very sad, but we don't have enough for all of them and after they've gobbled what we've got, what will keep our hungry ghosts from haunting these forsaken hills? Mark my words, that old one has a big appetite. I've seen her kind before. She looks like a dried-up pine twig, but I bet she can down twenty bowls of rice in one sitting! I'd wager my wishing rod on it. I want to do more than feed a few ragamuffins in this life, chief. It might be my last. We don't know those folks and they don't know us. Let's keep it that way. Anyway, what do you think they're going to do when they see your golden necklace?"

The boy listened calmly and continued to stare at Monkey. Then he pointed to the wishing rod, raising his eyebrows quizzically.

"No, Prince, you don't understand about the wishing rod. It's not what you think. Actually, I don't really know exactly what it does yet, but I know we can't bash those bandits with it, see? We can use it only in self-defense, but not to harm anyone who isn't threatening us, even our worst enemies. And it certainly can't feed all those people down there; it's not that kind of magic. . . ." He broke off and scratched his ear, looking puzzled. "Although I do think it might have *something* to do with multiplication. . . . The truth is, Prince, I haven't figured the thing out yet. . . . Whoa!"

Prince Zong had lost interest in Monkey's stammering explanation. With one supremely smooth leap, he was out of the ape's grasp. Turning his back on his startled guardian, the little Starlord began to stride with short, bold steps down the rock-strewn winding path toward the canyon below. A small avalanche of pebbles rolled after him as he walked, creating a strangely soothing sound like the surf grinding on stones.

Monkey muttered angrily to himself as he struggled to keep up with the Prince. "I must have been crazy to tote him about," he said, berating himself. "He's a Starlord, after all, and his fancy coat and necklace alone weigh more than any sane person would try to carry on these bumpy trails. It's a wonder I didn't cripple myself or turn into a hunchback like Zheng. Ouch, oh, look how fast he's going, and my poor legs are trembling so. Ow, my muscles feel like a team of tengu are beating them with hot rods. Prince, why are you doing this to me? You seemed like such a baby just a moment ago."

Shaking his head, Monkey lumbered along as best he could, for the lad was leaping from ledge to ledge like a billy goat, and he made such speedy progress downhill that Monkey's head started to spin trying to keep him in sight. To encourage and amuse himself, Monkey continued his story, talking loudly and gesticulating dramatically, as if the Prince were listening by his elbow instead of blazing ahead without seeming to care at all whether Monkey followed or not.

"So the Starlord Hung Wu began to walk," said Monkey to himself, "and after several days of walking, he reached the tundra. The stones of the steppe ripped themselves from their ancient hollows and followed him, sparking a holy fire that warmed all growing things." Here Monkey broke off, for he could see that the Prince had taken a wrong turn, and he began to shout at Zong to turn around and go the other way.

The dangerous path the little Starlord had chosen wrapped around an icy glacial kettle known to the locals as Dragon Bone Lake, a beautiful but accursed body of water shrouded in a thick haze that obscured the precipitous cliffs surrounding it.

Local lore told of a whole mendicant order of monks who had once been swallowed in fog on precisely the sharp turn Prince Zong was nearing now. Several of their prayer bells and begging bowls had been found buried deep in red mud by the stony shore. Some said they had all died, others that they were catapulted into one of the many hidden hermits' caves reputed to exist in these hills, where deities were said to reside when they visited earth. But scattered human skulls and skeletons by the silty shores of the lagoon indicated that whatever the fate of the monks, many a stranger to these parts had fallen to his death.

Zong was either too far ahead to hear Monkey's warnings or he chose to ignore them, disappearing into a shroud of vapor. Monkey had no choice but to plunge in after him, and soon his teeth were chattering with the strain of deciding where to put his feet when he could hardly see the ground.

Suddenly, a white wall of mist rose so thickly from the frigid water it seemed fanned by a monster's giant wings or expelled from the belly of one of the legendary scaled leviathans rumored to reside at the bottom of the lake. Soon Monkey felt as if he were composed of fog himself, a spirit hovering between worlds and walking on mountains of air. But unlike a creature of the wind accustomed to balancing on the border between earth and sky, his heart was beating so rapidly that the drumming drowned out all other sounds. Gripped by a fear of falling so intense that it took all his will power to continue on, he cursed rapidly beneath his breath at the absurd situation in which he found himself. A lone raven soared over the ravaged plateau, its beak as red as the garnet streaks in the surrounding gorge, its shadow gliding smoothly over the cracked cliffs.

And then, abruptly, the fog parted, and Monkey was staring at his own startled face, upside down and quite tiny in the smooth surface of the glassy tarn below. But the instant he recognized himself, the hiss of sliding stone sounded a tardy warning all around him as a shower of falling rock broke his reflection into flying fragments.

Too late to duck the deluge, Monkey instinctively thrust Dragon Rain forward like a balancing pole and desperately tried to steady himself on the razor-thin ledge. Perhaps in another long-forgotten life, Monkey had perfected just such a trick, or perhaps his desire to help Prince Zong registered like a blessing upon the Starlord's magical sword. Whatever the root of the miraculous suspension of ape in air, Monkey did not plummet to his destruction at that moment but stayed, poised like a hovering dragonfly over the beckoning abyss.

"When the moon is reflected in the water, it does not get wet," whispered Monkey to himself. And for one instant, the shattered pieces of his frightened face in the water came together and he thought he saw the serene and shimmering heart-shaped face of the River Goddess Yin Dang instead, with heavy black brooding eyebrows and a luminous white pearl planted in her noble forehead. The apparition nodded to him, the moon pearl glowing brightly like a third eye.

And then, ridiculously, Monkey found himself thinking, Look at me, Yin Dang! I'm holding an immortal's sword! Perhaps, before long, I shall be immortal too! And with that thought, the River Goddess disappeared, moon pearl and all, and he fell, tumbling headfirst through space with terrible speed toward the multiple monkey heads glittering like facets of a diamond in the frigid water below.

I'm dead, he thought. Good-bye, Monkey. You'll need another guardian now, little Starlord. And then, because he thought he would be making a watery exit this time, he began, in the few moments remaining to him, to pray fervently to Yin Dang and to every other water god and goddess he could think of, starting with Chac. But as soon as he invoked the Dragon King of the North Sea, he remembered the stolen wishing rod behind his ear and cursed himself for not remembering it sooner. He could not reach it now without dropping Dragon Rain and anyway, it was too late—he was falling too fast.

"Stupid Monkey! You do not deserve to live," he ranted as he tumbled toward his demise. The full irony of beseeching the very water god who would most bear him a grudge came to roost like one of Yamu's black ravens of doom on his last miserable moment. He shut his eyes and braced himself for the shattering crash of his unworthy skull into the frigid water. But the air thickened like soup around him and as his eyes flew open in shock, there he dangled, like an unraveling bundle of laundry, suspended inches above a rough slab of barren stone in the middle of Dragon Bone Lake. And then, ever so gently, he felt himself being slowly rotated and rolled in an invisible palm and tossed not quite as gently onto the rock.

The small island welcomed his knees with surprising softness, like a satin cushion, and Monkey just knelt there, a stunned supplicant handed a last-minute reprieve, hugging himself and Dragon Rain. He rubbed his head hard. "In one more second my brains would have been splattered all over this ridge," he whispered, looking around him in all directions as if quite expecting to see the Master Hand nearby, wagging an admonishing finger in his direction. "But it's strange I did not see this rock until I had almost crashed into it." He lowered his forehead to his lap, trying to catch his breath and dispel the wave of nausea that assailed him as he allowed himself to realize how very close he had come to extinction.

As he huddled there, he noticed an inscription chiseled deeply into the pockmarked surface. Tracing the characters with shaking fingers, he strained to read the archaic script:

Up high it is not always bright.
Down below it is not always dark.
Earth follows the way of the sky,
Sky follows the way of the sea,
And, like the dragon,
The sea follows its own way.
 –Chac, King of the North Sea

"Chac!" Monkey mused. "Was it you who saved me after all? And if it was, you old bully, why are you following me? Do you want your wishing rod back? Or is it something more?"

With a soft, ripping sound, the sea dragon's verse lifted into the air, inscribed on a thin yellow layer of shell as translucent as ancient parchment, as if cut from the boulder with a razor-sharp blade. Hovering, the strange scroll rolled itself tightly and neatly and landed precisely in Monkey's outstretched hand. Stashing the treasure in his vest, Monkey was reminded he had left his charge in danger too long.

But now the rock began to lurch as if it were alive, like the cracked armor of a giant sea monster. Jumping to his feet, Monkey dug the tip of his sword shaft into the silty platform and vaulted high up into the air. Confident beyond any reasonable expectation that he would once again be catapulted to safety on the other side by the same unknown benevolent force that had just saved his neck, he disappeared into a floating cloud of blinding white mist. And as he faded from sight, the limpet-covered rock did as well, submerging slowly into the indigo depths of Dragon Bone Lake.

CHAPTER TWENTY-FOUR

Yu Yu

*The sighting of divinity is divinity itself. But if the light
is not seen in the present, it is not seen at all.*
—Emperor Hung Wu

The old grandmother was the first to spot the Prince's approach. She gave a croak like a frog and slid to her knees upon the ground, kowtowing furiously. Her son, noticing his mother's strange behavior, followed her gaze, fearing the worst. Now Monkey hove into sight as well, a few strides behind the holy one, and the family all gathered in wonder, their eyes wide.

"Ten thousand years," murmured the matriarch, and her son, the clan's headman, followed suit, kneeling and banging his head upon the frozen earth. "Ten thousand years, ten thousand years," they chanted, and even the children joined in, slowly inching forward on their knees to be closer to the beautiful boy in his bright patchwork jacket who had descended so suddenly from the mountaintop like a god from Heaven.

"Little Starlord," quavered the ancient one hoarsely, "do you visit us because we are about to die? Or do you come to rescue us from those who would rob us of our last bit of rice?"

The Prince stopped walking and stared at her silently.

"Perhaps you have come to lead me to the throne of final judgment?" she asked sharply. "I have seen one drought, one flooding of the Yellow River, one plague of locusts, one fire, one famine too many, and now I am ready to die." Each time she intoned *one* she raised a trembling finger, and when she said *die*, she raised her open shaking hand in front of her wrinkled face, as if to screen out a view of the afterlife she was not yet prepared to see.

Now her son pleaded with the Prince to lead them all to safety, for he was certain the Starlord had been sent from on high to save them in their hour of need.

Monkey was enjoying this clan's subservient bowing and scraping a little too much. He began to bask in the Prince's reflected glory as he fingered his wishing rod. Flexing his long scrawny arms and flaring his matted chest, he swung Dragon Rain around from his back to his side, where he could more easily draw the sword out of its sheath.

Prince Zong threw Monkey a sideways look of warning as if to say, *Watch it, ape. Don't frighten these people, or you'll regret it.*

The look reminded Monkey painfully of the Master Hand. He mustn't be tempted to strut and show off, or his last chance to prove himself worthy of immortality would vanish like a snake into a hole. He was Prince Zong's protector, only that. If the Starlord were threatened, then he would flare forth like lightning in a stormy sky. Until then, he scolded himself, he would remain quiet and stand by the Prince's side like a good servant, awaiting orders.

But now the knot of men who had just lost friends, fathers, and brothers in the brief massacre shouldered their way forward toward the worshipful group gathered around Prince Zong. One of their number, a tall muscular farmer with a sour, down-turned mouth, began to yell and shake his fist. Then another angrily stepped in front of the first, and striding up to the little Starlord, tore open Prince Zong's shirt, revealing the imperial necklace to all who now pressed close.

Monkey quickly pinned the burly troublemaker's arm behind his back, but the Prince made an impatient sign to Monkey to release him. Monkey snarled at his prisoner, baring his teeth, and would not budge, so that for a long moment they just stood there as if frozen in a museum tableau, and the crowd began to hoot the fellow's name to encourage him to stand his ground. "Wang Tinghong, Wang Tinghong!" they roared, over and over again but still, Monkey did not relent.

Finally, Tinghong, sensing Monkey's powers, stepped back, and the others followed, but the leader spat contemptuously into the dirt. "We would not hurt a child," he rasped with controlled rage. "That would make us as low as your imperial soldiers."

Then, clenching his huge fists and raising them to the sky, he called curses down upon the Emperor and the Emperor-to-be, for all emperors were the same, he cried bitterly, taxing the poor until they were forced to steal and then allowing those who would not rob and murder to be killed off like flies.

"You who rule are the lowest of the low," he bellowed, "for you were born rich enough to do right. But you choose instead to oppress us and turn a blind eye to our suffering."

Stirred by the big man's indignation, an elderly farmer stood forth and spoke in a quavering voice, clutching at his own throat as if the words were jumping out like ugly toads and he could not hold them back. He was known to them all jokingly as Yongle, meaning "lasting joy," for he never smiled. "Last year, Prince, we had no rain for the spring tilling. Then no rain for the summer harvest. And no rain for the fall planting. No rain, no crops. No water to cook the rice and no rice to cook. How could we pay our taxes? But your tax collector came, crawling like a scorpion over the dry fields, and he taxed us just the same."

"A tax on dust," the men rumbled, shaking their heads. The old man nodded and continued: "And after your scorpion left, a thousand locusts came. Have you ever seen a locust, Prince? They flew into our fields and laid their eggs. They crawled into our cracking walls and into our clothes and down our chimneys and ate what was left of our wheat."

Now more voices joined in, some mournfully, some with mounting fury. "Yes, and after the locusts left, the bandits came, and they were worse."

And here the old farmer's voice broke, for his wife and daughters had been ruthlessly murdered in the last raid. Overwhelmed by memories, the entire group fell silent for a moment, each nursing his own sorrow.

Then Tinghong spoke again: "But did our taxes pay for decent burials? No! Our loved ones were piled into graves like cattle. And did the government dogs protect us in return for all those taxes? Hah! The troops came but only to do more harm. Your soldiers are without mercy, Prince, and they stop at nothing. And when your soldiers left, most of us prayed for death."

Now Yongle raised a trembling hand. "And our prayers were answered," he quavered, "for then the floods came."

"Yes, the floods," said the villagers, shaking their heads in unison. And now everyone spoke at once, a cavernous sound like distant thunder before the rains, but a few strong voices made themselves heard above the rest:

"Our soil turned to muck. . . ."

"Our fields turned to water. . . ."

"Our dikes caved in. . . ."

"And the river flooded. . . ."

"And again, no crops. No rice."

"And again, your tax collector showed his scorpion face," concluded Yongle.

"In a paddleboat this time," added Tinghong, "taking all that was left and more."

"But even that wasn't enough!" they all cried, in another rising chorus of lamentation.

Listening to this account of the stunning series of plagues and ill fortune that had collectively befallen them, Monkey tensed and stepped forward, shielding the Prince, for he felt a storm brewing perhaps as violent as the one they were describing. Nervously he touched his ear, behind which the Master Hand's powerful wishing rod, shrunken to the size of a toothpick, lay hidden. But again the Prince signaled Monkey not to interfere.

Having found its voice, the gathering swelled now with men and women eager to finish the tale, and each came forward offering a brief piece of evidence to lay before the Prince, who was judge, jury, and the accused:

"The day the scorpion left . . ."

"Jets of black water spurted up into the air!"

"The ground shook. . . ."

"And we saw our children swallowed by earth demons!"

"We saw our fathers and mothers buried alive. . . ."

"And our temples smashed to smithereens."

"We saw our altars, crushed. . . ."

"And buried with the bones of our ancestors."

"And would you believe it?" cried Yongle, shaking a shriveled fist. "That spring, the scorpion came to us again! 'Why are you here?' we asked him, for we could not imagine what he thought he could tax this time. And do you know what he replied—to us, who had watched the blood of our parents and children run into the red earth? He said: 'To wring blood from the stones!'"

"We should have murdered him on the spot," cried Tinghong.

"But we're law-abiding citizens," said Yongle, wheezing with indignation.

"The Emperor's loyal subjects," they all agreed.

"So again we stood about and did nothing. This time, he robbed us of our heritage," Tinghong concluded. "The ancient relics our forefathers buried deep in the earth were tossed out of yawning pits like corpses and hauled away."

"And then, we were left truly naked," said the old man, sighing. "Without a history, without a future. Yet still we knew the scorpion would come again. . . ."

"And again . . ." echoed another.

"Until we became skeletons picked to the bone," finished Yongle bitterly, "with nothing left even for the ravens."

The Prince rose now, his face pale as a lily, his black brows drawn together over eyes dark with pain. Who was this evil tax collector they spoke of as "the scorpion" and why did they say "your tax collector" when he had never met the person in question? And why did they say "your soldiers" when they were Emperor Han's troops and not his own? Surely the scorpion that had robbed them of their hope came from Han, for Prince Zong himself had witnessed the Emperor's red scorpion smile before running away with Monkey.

Confused, the Prince stroked his mother's parting gift, the precious phoenix medallion. Tinghong caught the gesture and patted his own neck as if an invisible jewel rested there. "Is the Prince perhaps thinking he'd like to make a charitable contribution?" he mocked. "Or is the boy just petting his gold for the pleasure of feeling it around his royal neck? We could make good use of that gold, Prince, were you to part with it. We have children who are eating dirt so that you may wear gold."

The Prince turned to Monkey now, for he wanted to help the burly farmer and his people, but he would rather have died than relinquish his mother's necklace. His guardian had warned him not to show the necklace to anyone on the road or they would force it from him. He was deeply moved by the villagers' tale. But the Prince did not think of himself as an Emperor-to-be, and so he did not truly understand why the sight of the golden necklace had drawn such wrath upon him. By wearing the phoenix, did he become his father?

"Fools," came the grandmother's crackly voice. "Don't you

know the Emperor has set a price on his own son's head and there is a handsome reward for the return of this boy who bears the phoenix necklace and the sign of the Qin?"

"Then let's turn him in without delay and be done with it!" cried Tinghong.

"And how soon would your own empty head roll after that?" screamed the old woman. "Are you as dumb as the ox that used to plow your fields when you still had fields to plow? For a few silver taels, you would put the next Starlord to death and ruin us all? Does the sign of the Qin mean nothing to you?"

Wang Tinghong flushed a deep crimson. "I do not know if this one is a Starlord or not," he answered, his voice shaking with fury. "But it takes no reading of the stars to see he is an Emperor's son, sign of the Qin or no. And the outlaw White Streak himself might turn this little golden god in for a price, if his own mother and brothers were starving!"

Monkey had heard enough. Slowly, Dragon Rain had come out in plain view during this exchange. The outspoken Tinghong might not have fared too well had not Qilin, the old one's daughter-in-law, quietly approached.

She was painfully thin and her cheekbones stood out like stone mounds in the desert, altars to a beauty recently wasted by hunger. The angry men, many of whom had courted her and lost, made way for her. They saw Qilin as a stately queen among them, wife of their headman, taller and stronger than he, and gifted. Her fingers were long and delicately shaped, smoother and better cared for than the other wives, and she wore a boldly colored, intricately embroidered shawl around her shoulders that called attention to her regal bearing. Slowly, she pointed to the Prince's jacket, touching the largest of the colorful patches. Then she traced the beautiful embroidery with a trembling hand.

The quilted square pictured a graceful white deer in a lush green forest, fleeing from the Emperor's hunters. Many ornamented spears of gold were trained at its bloodied side, but in spite of its wound, it was shown performing a miraculously high leap. Its flight was almost birdlike, and in fact, it had magically sprouted a fledgling pair of pale dovelike wings bearing it aloft. From puffy clouds in a sky of turquoise blue, a glimpse of a benevolent god could be seen, smiling down on the scene in the knowledge that in a moment, the danger would be past and all would be well.

Tears sprang to Qilin's eyes as she recognized the tableau, for she had sewn it, taking great pains with every stitch, working far into the night for an entire month. She was known in her village and in neighboring towns as a true artist with needle and thread and on the occasion of the birth of the Emperor's son, her friends and relatives had eagerly taken on her work in the fields so that she might execute this gift and bring honor to their family clan and to the entire province.

Now there was no doubt in Qilin's mind that the boy standing before them was indeed the reincarnation of the Starlord Hung Wu, just as the rumors had spoken, for how else could all the fervent prayers she had woven into that scrap of cloth be coming home to her just when life's burdens had grown too heavy to bear?

Her husband saw the familiar detail in the piece of fabric on the Prince's coat and recognized it as Qilin's fine handiwork, and he was struck dumb by this coincidence of fate. All he could do was stand there and point, and he too began to weep, silently. And then the Starlord startled Monkey, for above their weeping, he spoke for the first time: "Thank you," he said, simply.

He smiled sweetly at them all, but his eyes lingered on the woman and he stretched out his hands to her, for he missed his mother and, like his mother and Jade Mirror, she had given him a gift of love. She responded by rising and, before Monkey could protest, wrapped him in a bear hug, as if he were one of her own children. And her wet cheek brushed his round moon face, leaving the mark of a tear there.

That single tear miraculously doused the fire in the hearts of the assemblage surrounding the Prince and turned the tide. But before the angry men even realized what had just occurred, the headman's youngest daughter barreled out from behind her father and, running with her head down like a small bull, rammed the Prince hard in the belly, knocking him into the dirt. Startled at what she had just accomplished, she crashed down beside him and began to wail inconsolably, pointing to his pretty jacket as if her heart would split in two.

Her name was Yu Yu, and she had watched her mother working on the glowing coat of colors with jealous eyes, longing to wrap it around her skinny shoulders. Late each night when her mother folded the jacket away, hiding it in her old dowry chest to keep it clean and away from the children, Yu Yu had prayed to possess it, knowing her prayer would never be answered. Some other child would own the coat, she knew, a boy born in a palace in a city far away, who could have anything he wanted but chose her mother's sewing over all the fine seam-stresses in Bai Ping. He needed this lucky jacket to guard him from demons. Or so her grandmother said.

But it was hard to imagine this fortunate boy threatened by evil. And what would keep demons away from Yu Yu? No one seemed concerned about that, for she was a just a girl and not worthy of even a demon's notice.

The desire to wear the luminous coat ate at Yu Yu's heart until one night she broke into her mother's lacquered chest and ever so carefully unwrapped the half-finished garment. In an ecstasy of stolen pleasure, she put it on and sat until dawn, rocking back and forth on the dirt floor. Toward sunrise, exhausted, Yu Yu nodded off to sleep, slumped against the clay daubed wall, and there her mother had found her, and slapped her awake, furious at her daughter for disobeying her. Even her grandmother had been stern and unsympathetic to Yu Yu's grief. And then her mother had given Yu Yu her first real beating with the bamboo rod she sometimes used on her older sister, cutting into her bare legs until she yelped with pain. And her grand-mother had not interfered.

Yu Yu had resolved never to forgive her mother for the beating. The little girl who had been everyone's pet, with an easy smile for all, grew silent and brooding. On the day the jacket was sent to the baby Emperor, Yu Yu said not a word all day and all night. And she had not spoken since, even though her mother had softened and promised to sew Yu Yu her own patchwork jacket some day, just as beautiful as the one she had made for the Starlord, only even better, for she would sew every patch herself.

Now, the little Starlord, the Chosen One, had come to Purple Mountain. He was as beautiful and round as the sun while she had become as bleak and ugly as a stormy night. How she hated him!

Yet there was her own mother hugging him as if he were her very own child while she had not received such a hug for how long? It was just too much for Yu Yu to endure.

Rising to his knees, the Prince looked directly into her streaming eyes and read the yearning in her heart. Taking off his jacket and smiling, he wrapped it around her shoulders. Yu Yu turned to her mother and then to her grandmother, clasping her hands together and silently begging permission to keep the gift. Then she turned back to the Prince.

"Thank you," she said, echoing his own words to her mother. And to her great relief, her mother, hearing those words, opened her arms and drew Yu Yu into them as she had the Starlord a moment before.

The Prince, pleased at his peacemaking, stood up, signaling to Monkey that it was time to depart. But now Monkey let out a shrill cry of warning, for a new threat had appeared out of the mist on the mountain and was slowly coming their way.

CHAPTER TWENTY-FIVE

Flight

Once in a great while, there is one who gets away.
—Yamu, Lord of the Dead

T'sao T'sao worked his way along the rocky crevasse, trying not to look down into the sheer drop on his right where the ravine plunged into oblivion. His crablike movements came in awkward spasms. Frequently, he had to pause to catch his breath and to rest the injured leg he dragged behind him.

Still suffering from the head wound the blind monk had inflicted upon him, the bandit's hair had frozen into black slivers of ice that sent stinging droplets into his swollen eyes. Each time this happened, a low rumble, starting deep down in his broad chest, erupted into a string of curses so explosive that the red-beaked ravens dotting the ledges just above the frozen waterfall ahead took notice and rose up into the sky, a spiraling black plume silhouetted against the pale clouds. Their flight set off a wild chorus of loud, rasping calls and a fierce metallic drumming of wings. *Rrack, rrack, rrack,* they cried, in an echoing gonglike clatter that threatened, even at a distance, to tip T'sao T'sao over the edge.

"Damned birds," he muttered, not realizing that the largest in the group was the harpy Malia, damned indeed.

From a cliff not very far away, Puk observed the aerial acrobatics of the raven clan and wondered if Malia were among them. Now the cavorting birds had broken into performing pairs and, locking talons, were falling free, one erect, one upside down. The upright flier hurtled through space like a daring trapeze artist balancing on a partner whose feathered head seemed in imminent danger of cracking like a clamshell on the boulders below. They plummeted a dizzying distance, recovering themselves just a second before what appeared to the watching demon dog to be an inevitable crash landing. Then disengaging easily, they skydanced upward and tried the trick all over again, this time reversing positions.

Maybe the Nokk is right, after all, thought Puk as he contemplated the death-defying ravens. Like himself, the daredevil birds were playing hide-and-go-seek with Yamu. Each time they escaped, they were free from death for one immortal moment, until they rose high into the air, only to fall again.

The Nokk promised me freedom if I let him take me from the Netherworld, thought Puk. But now the runaway dog realized the freedom the shapeshifter had promised him was the escape itself. Puk was free only so long as he ran from Yamu. Like the ravens, he was doomed to escape over and over again.

One of the tumbling ravens had a silvery streak on one

wing, where its feathers, injured by frost, had grown in as bleached as snow. Puk sighed as he recognized Slash, bodyguard to Malia and her loyal partner. And then he saw her, larger than the others, her feathers glinting in a sudden shaft of sunlight. There was no question about it now. Malia was the other performer, playing with wild abandon—and for keeps.

Malia had run away from Yamu more than a hundred times. But each time, the Lord of the Dead found her and punished her. Eventually, there would be no desire to sky dance left in her, just a taste for cruelty and the need to be feared. Soon, she would be all harpy and no longer a raven at all. Some day, if the Nokk had his way, would Puk become a shapeshifter and no longer a dog at all?

Puk sighed again, licking the worn pads on his paws. He was tired of running and climbing and scouting for danger. The game of escape had lately become more dangerous. He knew the Lord of the Dead would be furious with him for giving in to the Nokk. Surely if Yamu found Puk, the punishment would be terrible. The hound shivered and closed his eyes, trying to block out the thought of what Yamu might do to him.

No one, he comforted himself, can look everywhere, not even the Lord of the Dead. But not to be found might join him irrevocably to the Nokk. Perhaps that would be even worse. Did the Nokk have the answer? Was it better to be everything and nothing all at once than to be found? If my Lord never finds me I may be truly lost and disappear into the Nokk forever, thought Puk uneasily. But if he *does* find me . . . A violent shudder ran through his massive body. If he does find me, what will become of Kuan?

As if in answer to his name, the boy's sleek head appeared over the ridge. He had been running to catch up. Panting, he threw himself down on a patch of yellow swale grass and wrapped his arms around Puk's neck. "There you are!" he exclaimed. "I was worried about you, boy," he puffed, patting the dog all over. "Look at that giant flock of birds squabbling and swooping down. When I couldn't see you, I feared it was you they were after. Are they vultures?"

Puk shook his huge head. "Stop calling me 'boy.' I'm the dog, you're the boy. And those somersaulting fools are ravens," he growled crossly. "But there's a harpy among them."

In spite of Malia's presence nearby and the frigid wind in his face, Puk began to feel warm all over as he let Kuan rub his coat. He put his heavy head in Kuan's lap and allowed the child to caress him between the ears. He felt comforted, as he had when he was a pup, before he had been sold to Yamu. Yet Kuan was the youngest and weakest outlaw, no protection at all from the nightmare that stalked them. Why then did he feel so much safer when the lad was near? Puk's eyelids drooped as he let his entire body relax. He had the feeling this was a question neither Yamu nor the shapeshifter nor any demon would be able to answer. And if no demon could answer it, he wondered sleepily if any demon had ever dared ask it before.

"Harpy?" inquired Kuan, cutting into Puk's half-dozing meditation. The boy gazed with more interest at the diving flock. His father had told him stories of the cruelty of harpies, but Kuan had not really believed in the existence of the legendary birds until this moment. His father had always been so sure of what was good and what was evil in the world, Kuan thought sadly, yet he had not known that evil crouched on his own doorstep, ready to strike. And what would his father have thought of Puk, who was, after all, a demon?

"Keep your eye on the harpy," answered Puk wearily. "Just be sure she doesn't see you. Stand guard, Kuan. I was built for the sea, not these blasted peaks. And I've been thinking too much. My brain is worn out. I need a nap." And so saying, he let himself relax again in the sweet cradle of the boy's embrace and immediately began to snore.

As soon as Puk was asleep, Kuan noticed the moving black shape on the face of the faraway cliff—a human struggling to reach the peak.

If his eyes had been a little sharper or T'sao T'sao a little closer, the boy would have seen the bloodstained band of leopard's fur wrapped around the climber's arm and realized that one of the men he and Puk had been tracking was almost within range.

Kuan was sorry Puk had fallen asleep, but he decided to let the dog rest. The dark figure was far away and he had no real excuse to wake his companion. They had been traveling for days, and it was Kuan's fault Puk was here in this wasteland instead of home beside a warm fire. He had convinced the dog to come with him when he had decided to run away.

Kuan knew White Streak would be angry with him for taking Puk, his most valuable tracker, and for going out on his own. The outlaw leader considered Kuan untrained, but the boy had to go. If he had lived at the Golden Phoenix under Mother Gu's vigilant watch for one more night, he thought he might have burst apart.

It's not that he wasn't grateful to Mother Gu. She was a strict taskmaster, but she had taught him well, and he was much stronger than when he had come to her a few weeks ago. She said he was smart, a quick learner, but he knew that she still had a lot to teach him. When she showed him her fighting techniques, he was filled with admiration. Also, she was a great cook and generous with her food.

But there was hardly a moment that passed that he did not think about his family and their terrible fate. Kuan missed his father and his little sister more with each passing day, and he talked to no one but Puk about this, keeping mostly to himself. He went about from dawn to dusk dutifully doing his morning exercises, waiting on tables at the inn, cleaning endless stacks of pots and bowls, sweeping the floors, shoveling horse and camel dung, and in the evenings, more deep knee bends and wrestling practice with Mother Gu.

He had seen more in a few weeks at the inn than he had seen in his entire lifetime in Banpo village. The men he had known until now were all farmers or fisherman with nothing to show for their labors but the brown water in their flooded fields and the holes in their nets. But passing through the Golden Phoenix were an endless parade of itinerant merchants from the western steppes, fire-worshipping traders and cameleers wearing tall cone hats and high brocade boots, speaking strange guttural languages Kuan had never heard before. They were carrying cargoes of gold and gems, gossamer silks, Arabian spices, and bales of wool from the fat-tailed dumba sheep that grazed in the Pamirs, weighted with the black sands of the Gobi desert.

The nomads brought their own drummers and dancing

girls with tight-sleeved blouses and long, flowing skirts of rainbow-colored gauze decorated with tiny silver bells that jingled in pleasing contrast to the deep beat of their drums. In the evenings, the men got drunk and took over the entire tavern, spending their money freely and clapping raucously in time to the music. The dancers' supple waists and belted bellies glowed like flowing oil in the candlelight, undulating softly and slowly at first and then gyrating wildly while their slippered feet kept up with the rhythm, moving faster and faster until they looked to Kuan like tiny red hummingbirds' wings.

Scattered among the customers at the Golden Phoenix were rugged Tibetan soldiers, fierce horsemen carrying bows slung across their backs and daggers displayed in their leather belts. Some brought their falcons and hunting dogs with them and most would not trust Kuan with their mounts, so fond were they of their horses. The heavy-lidded eyes of these men resembled those of the desert camels, eyes that had seen destruction of all kinds. Although he could not understand their words, Kuan could imagine the barren vistas they had come through where burnt and abandoned villages like Banpo were nothing more than useful landmarks on an otherwise blank and featureless terrain, of no more significance than petrified trees and animal bones.

Sometimes, at night, before he went to sleep, Kuan would take out the abacus he had found in the ruins of his home, and slowly slide the beads back and forth, listening dully to the hollow sound of random unrecorded sums. *Click, click, click.* The smooth little spheres had calculated without cease, but had failed to arrive at the figures decreed by fate. He wondered how this humble object could be so unchanged, functioning precisely as it always had, although it had been buried in an upheaval that had irreversibly altered his world.

Kuan had watched White Streak from a distance, waiting for a chance to come closer. The outlaw leader seemed to be listening for something in the wind, often scanning the skies or taking long walks in the woods, confiding in no one, not even Mother Gu. Puk told Kuan that White Streak's father had placed the burden of an important mission upon White Streak's shoulders.

"What mission?" Kuan had wondered.

Kuan started to eavesdrop on White Streak when Black Whirlwind visited, because the wielder of the double ax was known to speak his mind so loudly that everyone within a radius of a mile could hear him. But all that Kuan could make out from skulking around doorways and crouching on low rooftops, from putting in extra hours helping Mother Gu tend bar at the Golden Phoenix, and attempting to trail White Streak on his private forays into the woods, was that the outlaw's father had told White Streak about some kind of god on earth or Starlord, and had instructed his son to find this person without giving him much of a hint about where to look.

Kuan remembered his own father's tales of a Starlord who had ruled long ago in a golden age of justice, and his mother's belief that some day another Starlord would come to earth, righting the wrongs of the present oppressive government. But Kuan had not paid too much attention to the stories, for he had been content with his life in those days and did not know who his father meant by "the poor" or what he meant by "injustice."

The Starlord might be on this very mountain, thought Kuan as he watched Puk sleep, for Purple Mountain was part of the Kunlun range, and many mystical souls in the past had found their way here. Apparently, White Streak did not even know if this Chosen One who was to save the world from demons was a child or a grown man! But Kuan knew. He was sure the new Starlord was a child, no older than himself. And somehow he was convinced that if he went out hunting for the gang who had destroyed Banpo village, he might also just possibly find the boy who was said to wear an imperial golden necklace stamped with the sign of the phoenix.

CHAPTER TWENTY-SIX

Lord of the Dead

Death is like a clear pool—it can be entered from any side.
—The Master Hand

Far beneath the Purple Mountains, in the shadowy caverns of the Netherworld, the Lord of the Dead had retired to his throne room to think. On all four eroded walls surrounding him was a faded but lifelike mural dripping with beads of rusty moisture, depicting his ancient army of Spellbinders—demon archers and charioteers, demons mounted on elephants, pigs, foxes, dogs, snakes, and lizards, demons on foot, demons flying and tumbling like ravens, their heads facing earthward, their feet in the red smoky air.

And he was there too, of course, in the middle of all the glorious mayhem—Yamu draped in ceremonial leopard skin robes instead of armor for purposes of the portrait, calling forth violent claps of thunder and immense showers of rain, snow, and hail all at once, and posing with Old Bones, who was belching bolts of fire. Those were his glory days, before the Master Hand locked his demon army below the earth, damned to seething silence in the Tomb of the Turtle, and sealed all exits with a blessed incantation. But he would set them free, if it was his last act as King of the Netherworld.

Soon Yamu's magnificent horde of fiends and monsters would roam the earth once again, destroying everything and everyone in their path, a resurrected mob advancing under the flaming black banner of the legendary Spellbinders. The time was ripe; he held the keys to their freedom in his hands—a dissolute Emperor in one, an ambitious bandit in the other. It was amusing that they considered themselves enemies at present. And how quaint that the brigand leader fancied himself a sorcerer and already wore the sign of the leopard, one of Yamu's own preferred trademarks. As a token of his favor, the Lord of the Dead had appeared to Spotted Leopard during one of his barbaric initiation rites and had bestowed upon him Yamu's own red jade ring. But the bandit's dull-witted general had stupidly stolen the offering.

As the King of the Netherworld settled into his racklike chair of state, the comfort of the bloody reminiscence the mural had raised in his mind receded as he reviewed the frustrations, large and small, that continued to gnaw at his innards. First and foremost, Yamu was not pleased with the Nokk for absorbing his favorite demon dog. The slippery shapeshifter had gambled and lost, and as a result the Lord of the Dead had to make do without Puk for an entire year while a bunch of fishermen got to use his fine tracker's nose for their own misguided purposes. Saving a child from a wahwee, for example. What was the point of that? The boy was supposed to die that day and be united with his family and his entire village in the Netherworld. Now those bunglers had interfered and Kuan was a dangerous leftover, an arrow tightly strung and aimed in the wrong direction, inconveniently tainted with the urge for revenge.

As for his cruelest harpy, Malia, she had failed him miserably as well. Yamu was still no closer to capturing Prince Zong. Both servants had shamefully bungled their assignments and would have to be disciplined, although Yamu had not yet decided what the proper punishments might be. He smiled to himself as he mentally reviewed the tortures that awaited them, especially the Nokk. He suspected that obsequious jellyfish was a traitor at heart, preparing to betray his lord in some profoundly devious way.

How could the wily creature sustain allegiance when he hadn't even the concentration to retain his own shape for any length of time? Concentration was the key, was it not? Now Yamu focused on the hated image of the Nokk, sending his dark beam out over the darker depths of the Four Seas, searching.

Of course, no matter how well the creature had hidden itself, Yamu would certainly find the Nokk, sooner or later. And he would find that wretched harpy and her aerial tribe of red-beaked ravens as well. It was only a matter of time. And time was nothing to the Lord of the Dead, for everything in his world of ghosts was already too late.

"My dear Nokk," Yamu said to himself, relishing the imagined moment when he passed judgment on the shapeshifter, "your crime may have taken place some days or weeks ago. You have perhaps made the mistaken assumption that you have been forgiven. But I find no need to be punctual, and of course, I never forgive. It is not too late for you to regret your unfortunate meeting with the outlaws, and to suffer extreme anguish forever more."

But the proper punishment escaped him still. The mortar and pestle perhaps was best. The Nokk hated his original shape worst of all and would be humiliated beyond all salvation should he be ground to a pulp like an ordinary sea blob and pickled in his own brine.

But what then? How can one torture a shapeshifter for all eternity if one deprives him of shape? Could the Nokk, who had many selves, be mashed into a million pieces and still retain enough of its identity to feel anything at all? "It is a profound question," said Yamu to himself, "and worthy of further contemplation."

And then there was Puk. How should he punish Puk? It would be a tricky business to separate him from the shapeshifter now. Should the demon dog share the Nokk's fate, then? Ah, poor Puk. Surely the Nokk was entirely to blame, but the pup would still have to be taught a lesson, and a cruel one at that. At the end of his servitude to the outlaws, he must be broken of his love of mortals.

Tired of searching, and yielding to the soothing darkness within his mind, Yamu closed his eyes. "Dear Puk, you will suffer so," he crooned, smiling to himself. "But first, you must help me take Kuan. He should be an easy one to capture, don't you think, with his parents and grandparents newly arrived in the spirit world, so eagerly waiting to embrace him?" And Yamu's inflamed eyes fluttered and rolled back in his head as he moaned with anticipatory pleasure at the thought of that bittersweet family reunion. But he would have to wait.

Time. Yes, he had time. The master of hide-and-go-seek had all the time in the universe, and more. But his memory was short, and he had so little patience. He needed something deliciously brutal this very day, this very moment, and what would it be? Ah, where was that accursed thieving assassin Han had hired? What was his name?

Yamu clawed his own chest in frustration. The quick raking pain made him more clearheaded for a moment. T'sao T'sao, that was it. Like his demons, he could recall most of what he had said and done for the past several centuries, but he could not remember names. Well, names were of no importance. A servant was a servant, no matter the name. If he did his job, he would be rewarded. And if not, why remember his name, for he would soon be ground into dry dust and his soul would blow away leaving not a trace, like a bat in a sandstorm.

CHAPTER TWENTY-SEVEN

Malia

It is as hard to see oneself as to look backward
without turning around.—The Tattooed Monk

For the past several days T'sao T'sao had been plagued by a queasiness in the pit of his stomach, and a sense of doom. He could not stop thinking about the runt of an outlaw who had thrown him into the palace moat after beating him almost senseless. As unlikely as it seemed, he had been haunted by the feeling that, wherever he went, even into this remote and unpopulated wilderness, the small man was close behind, spying on him.

But if Day Rat were indeed tracking T'sao T'sao as he crab-walked over the chill terrain, his were not the only wary eyes trained upon the bandit. The hostile eyes of the newly home-less of Purple Mountain did not miss the telltale sign of the leopard as they watched T'sao T'sao struggling toward them.

After Monkey's cry of warning, every man, woman, and child among the huddled group below followed the brigand's progress into their valley with dread, willing him to take one hair's breadth of a step in the wrong direction and fall.

Oblivious to being watched by so many, T'sao T'sao paused again to rest, listening to the sound of his own uneven panting. The mountain's silence, broken only by the unsettling noise of that hellish flock, less distant now, weighed oppressively upon his heaving chest.

Suddenly, the largest of the ravens let out a shrill *quork*, broke out of the squadron's tight formation, and barrel-rolled downward. Closing both wings to her sides, Malia shot straight toward Yu Yu in her bright new patchwork coat.

The girl screamed and tumbled over, kicking her legs and whirling her arms like the spokes of a windmill, but Malia, certain she had finally captured the Starlord, held the child firmly in her strong beak and made straight for the cliff where she had earlier seen Puk. Her keen vision had picked out the demon dog, and she thought to enlist him. The squirming child was too heavy for her to carry any distance at all. She was certain she could bully the pup into helping her bring him to Yamu. But who was that screaming *now*?

Startled by wild, earsplitting banshee yells that seemed too loud to be coming from the small boy kneeling by Puk's head, Malia was momentarily caught off guard just at the moment she had to manage a tricky landing. She careened a little too far to the side as she deposited the burdensome girl but misjudged the distance and caused the child to topple onto Kuan, knocking him flat.

Later, when Yu Yu told the story, she always claimed that Kuan caught her in midair as she fell, and he never denied it. But at the time, it was he who felt caught beneath the weight of the struggling hostage. For several heartbeats, they just stared at each other. The girl's round face was as bright as the harvest moon and her large eyes were filled with tears, which streamed down her cheeks, tracing jagged trails. When he had regained his presence of mind, Kuan gently lifted her off his chest and stood her on her wobbly feet beside him.

Surmising that the famous patchwork jacket had been used as a decoy, Malia was now relentlessly beating Puk about the head with her wings, intending to recruit him as soon as he was fully awake into bringing up the rear of her attack on this impostor's family. Yu Yu's friends and relatives were running about aimlessly down below, yelling at one another and trying to decide what to do. It suddenly occurred to Malia that they might be hiding the true Starlord among them.

Puk reared up and roared to attention, legs stiff, paws splayed, like an angry lion protecting its young. Too late, Malia realized she had doubly miscalculated. Not only had she captured a child in a stolen jacket instead of the son of Emperor Han, but from the instant Puk's eyelids fluttered open, she could see he was bonded to the boy by his side, just like an ordinary idiotic dog, ready to lay down his life for a human.

Disgusted, Malia speedily veered away from the mastiff, for though he had somehow mysteriously been conquered by slobbering sentiment, he was, unfortunately, still endowed with demonic brute strength. Even with her brass claws, she was no match for Puk when he was in a blind, protective rage. And he was frothing at the mouth now. What Puk saw in that pathetic little bundle of skin and bone by his side Malia could not imagine. She fancied herself clever and had always considered Puk rather dumb, but she never guessed he would be so dumb as to fall for a child.

Malia had always had a certain soft spot for the rebellious Puk and had interceded on his behalf several times with Yamu. She saw in him potential for a most spectacular defiance, even more brazen than her own. But he had stepped over the line now. From just one look at him, it was clear, except perhaps to Puk himself, that he had fallen in love with a mortal.

Malia let out a ringing *krok* as she reeled through the clouds, turning a few reckless somersaults. *In love with a mortal.* And a child to boot. Well, that was news. And delivering news at the right time in the right place was one of her specialties. Once she had found the Starlord and could show her face in the Netherworld again, Malia couldn't wait to tell Yamu.

"*Shih, shih,* my lord," she murmured under her breath with just the right tone of servile tenderness and regret, "he has broken the demon code."

Yet in the very act of relishing her imagined moment of triumphant revelation and the reward her evil gossip would earn, Malia felt a sharp twinge. She tried to pinpoint what was eating at her as she rose swiftly up into the air again, slavishly followed by the raven tribe. The best fliers always knew what was happening in their hearts—it was essential when you were so out in the open, subject to every shift in weather.

Yes, Malia had to admit, there was something heavy slowing her flight, dragging at her wings. Disappointment, perhaps.

Sadness. Yearning. She wasn't the raven she used to be. But then, perhaps she was no longer a raven at all. She was a harpy now. There was no point in regretting what she had lost along the way. The only cure for what ailed her was risk—high risk, over and over again. But the real danger in her dangerous game was only just beginning to dawn on her. If escape was her true goal, she would have to come up with greater and greater feats of ingenuity and endurance until at last, inevitably, one slip of attention would deliver her into Yamu's kingdom forever. The odds were entirely in his favor. But hadn't she known that to be true all along?

What had begun as a twinge suddenly turned into a searing pain in her heart. Was it possible that she, who did such extraordinary things in the air every day would not, in the end, make any difference at all in the universe? Would she, who could soar so high, become just another ghost, erased for all eternity?

Puk, oh Puk, Malia thought as she executed yet another dizzying series of five breathtaking somersaults into the wind, one after another. Why have you turned soft just when I need you?

Slash, her mate for life, appeared above her, calling hoarsely for her attention, *rrraaap rrrraaap!*, and waiting for instructions. He was all brawn and no brains, trained to defer to her. And her tribe of ravens relied upon her for everything. In all important matters, Malia was entirely alone, flying solo, a general in the company of rank and file with no second in command.

She sighed as she wheeled away and with a loud caw led her red-beaked army in a fast plunge toward the group of victims below. There's nothing like defying death to draw a crowd, she thought bitterly, suddenly contemptuous of their innocence. In a moment or two, she would rip the gawking humans apart. *Rrrrackrrackrrack.* Yamu must be served, she told herself sternly. Wherever the Starlord was hiding, he must be captured and brought to the Netherworld.

She was picking up speed. The high-pitched notes of a winter wren called languidly from the conifers below. Then the chickadees joined in, the fluting hermit thrush answering above the whistling of the woodcock as it rose into the sky. The cheerful sounds seemed magnified, mocking Malia as one apart from all winged creation. She was not a warbler but a streamlined weapon, careening toward her destiny, moving too swiftly for song.

And although the others sang brightly, their sunny concert was only a murmur compared to what Malia could hear of the clamorous rustling of Yamu's wings as he waited in the distant darkness for the contest to begin. He was there, always there, if you knew how to listen for him.

CHAPTER TWENTY-EIGHT

The Wishing Rod

*Demons are never idle, though often their work is simply to
stand about in the dark—impatient ushers in a predictable play.*
—Yamu, Lord of the Dead

Although Yu Yu had dropped from the sky, Kuan refused to
believe that the weeping child was the Chosen One. She was
wearing the Starlord's famous patchwork jacket, yet surely this
whimpering girl could not save the universe against the invasion
of Yamu's demons any more than *he* could.

But Yu Yu was no longer paying any attention to Kuan.
When Malia dove toward Yu Yu's family with a bloodcurdling
cry, the child had fearlessly jumped up on Puk's back, riding
him like a war horse and digging her small heels into his sides.
Carrying Yu Yu on his back, the demon dog plunged recklessly
toward the humans below, trying to overtake the harpy. He had
once seen the effect of Malia's beak and claws on flesh, and the
memory spurred him furiously forward. With a flying leap, he

charged on ahead, raising billowing clouds of dust.

Kuan flung himself after them, desperately grasping Puk's tail. The strange threesome crashed down the sheer-faced cliff, Yu Yu screeching hysterically as she saw Malia swoop in on her grandmother.

To Kuan's horror, the harpy made swift work of the old woman, whose lips turned gray as she fell over into the snow. Qilin cried out, and ran to her mother-in-law, throwing herself over the corpse.

"Not her eyes!" she gasped and shielded them from the gathering ravens. Granny, who had feared very little, had always dreaded going blind in her old age and entering the Netherworld sightless.

The hollow rattle of the dark flock was deafening now. Kuan felt assaulted by the sheer volume of their ragged clanging and strident carks and whines. Behind him, the men led by Tinghong had gathered their weapons—long spears and pikes, sharpened bamboo poles and sickles, small axes, hatchets, and handsaws. Yongle, too, was ready, standing at attention with his ancient sword, the best of the shabby group's supply.

Kuan fit an arrow to his bow and sprang protectively toward Qilin. But now the harpy turned her attention to the headman just as Yu Yu crashed into him, almost falling from Puk's back. Yu Yu shook her clenched fists at the clamorous birds, yelling angry threats, but failed to distract Malia from slicing into her father's upraised arm, knocking his firebrand into the snow.

Then out of the sky dropped a huge raven with a white streak emblazoned across his wings. It hung, looming overhead.

Kuan let loose his arrow but missed. In the meantime, Malia mounted an updraft, angling for a more deadly hit.

Yu Yu's father, bleeding heavily, clasped his mangled arm. Trembling, Kuan swiftly strung another arrow, knowing instinctively it would arrive too late. It looked to the boy as if Yu Yu's father was about to join his own in the Netherworld.

And then a miracle occurred. A monkey stepped out from behind a tree and, taking a rusty metal object that looked like a sewing needle from behind his ear, waved the thing in the air a few times, chanting something incomprehensible. The needle glowed with an icy blue light and immediately began to grow in size until it was a weighty iron rod, which the ape, who was growing in stature as well, seemed to have no difficulty lifting and twirling above his head. The beast himself looked surprised at this feat and at his sudden growth spurt, and even more surprised when, as he tapped the rod on the ground, it grew yet again.

Now this strange deity moved swiftly toward Yu Yu's father and dealt the raven with the white slash a fierce blow that knocked it to the earth. And then another remarkable thing happened. From behind the tree where the monkey had appeared, a rain of stones issued, flung at the birds from a great distance. Each stone reached its mark, and for every stone cast, a raven fell from the clouds, each wounded in one wing.

Seeing her clan thus disabled, Malia cannonballed straight toward Monkey, claws bared as if intending to rip his eyes out. But Monkey calmly plucked a hair from his head, put it into his mouth and chewed, and fixing Malia with a malevolent glare, said, "Monkey, multiply!" Suddenly, there was a whole army of monkeys, leaping about, yelling like pirates, and striking the flying ravens with their iron rods identical to the Master Hand's original, except for the yellow jade handle and the two sapphires as blue as Monkey's eyes. Black feathers flew in all directions and the birds, taken by surprise, began to beat a hasty retreat, abandoning those among them who had already fallen to the bloody ground. And still the rocks kept flying from behind the tree, downing one after another of the flock's best fliers.

By this time, T'sao Tsao had landed on firm ground, and benefiting from the chaos and confusion, made straight for Qilin. With the tracking nose of a beast, he sensed she might know something of value to him. Grabbing her by the hair, he held a dagger to her throat, demanding the whereabouts of the Starlord. Weeping, she fell to her knees, pleading for mercy, and surely those would have been her last words had not one of the monkeys knocked T'sao T'sao over the head at that very moment. The bandit swooned and loosened his grip, but recovered himself enough to take a swing at his attacker before careening in another direction altogether, releasing Qilin, who crawled away toward her wounded husband.

Dripping blood, T'sao T'sao caught sight of Puk running in mad circles and, recognizing the demon dog as Yamu's pet, interpreted his presence on the scene as a breach of trust. T'sao T'sao's mind worked at a snail's pace in the best of circumstances, but stunned by the recent blow to his skull, his reasoning abilities were severely slowed. Why is Puk here? he asked himself groggily as he lumbered away, dodging a steady fuselage of rocks that seemed to come from behind the same tree from which the awful monkeys had sprung. Spotted Leopard must be checking up on him. Yes, that was it. Not believing T'sao T'sao was up to the task of finding and assassinating the Starlord, the Leopard had appealed to Yamu for help, and Yamu had sent the dog. Well, if that was the case, T'sao T'sao could use the help. Painfully, the bandit turned his steps toward the dog, trying to signal him to come closer, but Puk was ignoring him. The pup from hell seemed to have gone mad and was crazily chasing his tail, spinning faster and faster, while snapping wildly at several pursuing ravens.

Then T'sao T'sao saw that straddling Puk's back was a small figure in a patchwork jacket. Had Puk already accomplished half the job and kidnapped the Starlord? Was the demon dog dutifully bringing the assassin his victim? Signaling Puk again, T'sao T'sao stumbled toward the Starlord, but what happened next thoroughly confused the bandit.

From behind the tree sprang the Starlord's double, dressed not in his patchwork jacket but in grubby fisherman's garb, with a blue bag slung across his shoulder from which he extracted a red jade thumb ring, its heavy toad-shaped stone appearing even redder than it had on that evil night he had lost it in the palace moat.

Terror clutched T'sao T'sao's throat, for now he thought the Starlord's double was a ghost beckoning him to the Netherworld, tricking him by offering his precious good-luck charm. Yet the Prince did not beckon like a ghost. Instead, he held the bandit's stolen ring as if admiring it in the light, and cocked his head at T'sao T'sao so that the assassin could clearly see the telltale black birthmark on his cheek that identified him as the Emperor's son. And then the vision grinned.

T'sao T'sao closed his eyes for a moment to clear his brain. Were there two Starlords, then? Did the other have a birthmark too? But before he could look over in Puk's direction to check if the first Starlord was still there, the smiling marksman threw the ring, hitting T'sao T'sao squarely between the eyes with just the right force to knock him out. Like a great tree, the bandit toppled, crashing down, causing glasslike shards of ice to fly everywhere. And just as he fainted, he thought he saw the shadow of a raven, a black flat gauzy thing with wings, flutter out of the Prince's blue bag and settle on the ground like a night moth, downed in midflight.

As he fell, T'sao T'sao wondered what manner of soul the Starlord had magically trapped in his strange hunting pouch and inadvertently let escape. But even as he wondered, darkness closed in and he was suddenly sure the captured soul was his own.

The Prince did not see T'sao T'sao hit the ground, for even as he threw the ring, he ceased to notice the vanquished assassin, so sure was he of the outcome. Instead, he had locked eyes with the young boy who was standing at attention by Yu Yu's side, one protective hand resting on Puk's monstrous head. He was staring at Kuan, who, eyes wide with wonder, was staring back.

CHAPTER TWENTY-NINE

Prince of the Golden Phoenix

In our simple journey from point to point, there is more than enough for our limited understanding.
—The Immortal Beggar

"Ten thousand years," said Kuan, bowing.

The Prince bowed as well. "I wish you the same. But I am not the Emperor, if that's what you think."

"The Emperor's son, then. Prince of the golden phoenix," Kuan answered.

The Prince smiled. "Yes, the phoenix," he said sadly, fingering his heavy necklace. "A gift from my mother."

"Everyone is looking for you," said Kuan, changing the subject abruptly.

"Who is everyone?" asked Prince Zong, puzzled.

Kuan had a sudden desire to tell this boy about the fall of his village, about White Streak and the outlaws, about his narrow escape from the wahwee, and about Puk, who had saved his life and was now acting the decoy again, rudely dumping Yu Yu on the ground and running off to a safe distance from the children to fight the last of Malia's dark flock as they pecked and tore at his fur. But before Kuan could begin, T'sao T'sao began to groan and stir. Reaching for his dagger, the brigand hauled himself up on one arm and, with a savage lunge, threw the blade straight at Kuan's head.

Yu Yu opened her mouth to scream, but before the sound could leave her lips, the Starlord stepped forward and, with no effort at all, caught the weapon in midair. Then bowing politely, he threw it back at T'sao T'sao, pinning the sleeve of the murderer's throwing arm to the earth as easily as he had struck the wings of the flying ravens.

In the same instant, the light reflected from the monkeys' many wishing rods all blurred harmoniously together and the multiple fighting monkeys vanished and became one. That single monkey scooped the Prince up in his arms and strode off at top speed, disappearing into the surrounding pines, shouting "Enough!"

It all happened so quickly, Kuan was left wondering if he had actually seen the Prince and the monkey at all. But he did not have much time to wonder, for now he was facing T'sao T'sao, who had extricated himself and, ignoring the noisy girl sprawled in the snow, was advancing upon Kuan in earnest, dagger raised. Kuan swiftly reached for another arrow. But then he froze, his hand suspended in midair, his vision blurring with bitter tears of rage, for there, wrapped tightly around the killer's bulging arm, was a bloodstained scrap of leopard's fur.

Kuan's moment of hesitation would certainly have been

fatal had not the Starlord's intervention already given Tinghong and the other men a chance to reassemble. Led by Yongle with his sword, the men advanced in a tight knot, and their boiling resentment and rage for all the wrongs ever visited upon them found a perfect target in the Leopard's henchman.

Before T'sao T'sao quite knew what had happened, they had mobbed the bandit and brought him down, assaulting him with their bamboo sticks and slashing him with their spears. And all the while, they roared like a storm unleashed, as if they themselves were in agony.

Seeing T'sao T'sao in such a predicament, Malia reeled around, reversing the retreat of her severely reduced army. A few of her ravens were still pursuing Puk, and she called to them to rally around her. T'sao T'sao of course was nothing to her, but he mattered to the Leopard, who was important to Yamu, and that was enough. She could not let him bleed to death out there in the open. She would see what she could do to revive him now that the men had done their worst. To her practiced eye, his spirit had not yet departed. He was still breathing, though the beating had brought him to the brink.

Soaring and spiraling upward, she cracked a huge icicle off a nearby cliff and, holding it in her beak, hurtled down toward T'sao T'sao, who was lying there like a corpse. Hammering the ice into smaller bits on the ground she picked up several pieces and rose like a New Year's fire rocket into the sky, letting the chips drop sharply onto the man's upturned face. Again and again she did this, and her troops followed suit; until finally, pelted incessantly with sharp missiles of stinging ice, the man reluctantly began to awaken. Upon seeing the ominous black shapes of the ravens wheeling above him, T'sao T'sao immediately shut his eyes and decided to play dead for fear he was already in the Netherworld. He heard Puk yelping and wondered if the demon dog had passed to the other side as well. Yamu would certainly deal harshly with both of them for failing their missions, he thought grimly.

While T'sao T'sao struggled to orient himself, Malia retreated with her companions to a hidden ledge high above him. There she planned to rest and calculate her losses while paying a last mournful tribute to Slash. She had done her duty. The rest was up to Yamu and the Leopard. Whatever T'sao T'sao had come for, his business wasn't her affair—unless he got in her way. But he looked in no shape to do that for a long time to come.

As Malia scanned the jagged peaks, an arresting figure, clad all in white, appeared on the nearest mountain slope and strode purposefully into view. Tinghong, alerted by the others, stepped forward to meet the stranger, realizing as he took his measure that the oddly dressed man was a full head and shoulders taller and seemingly impervious to the freezing cold. Instead of a walking staff, the intruder was carrying a five-pronged harpoon, which he wielded easily and majestically, like a sea god's trident. He held out his hand in a gesture of friendship, and as he did so, the wind blew open his coat of white fox fur, revealing a bare chest beneath, branded with the black sign of the Qin.

"White Streak!" yelled Kuan, running to him joyfully. The outlaw opened his arms and received the boy, grinning broadly with relief. He glanced at Tinghong as Kuan disappeared into his fatherly embrace. "Thank you," he said. "You've kept him safe, I see."

Tinghong smiled back, although he raised an eyebrow and glanced back at Yongle and the others in warning as White Streak's fierce-looking twin came into view, a hairy brute of a man with a double ax slung across his massive shoulder and a dagger in plain sight.

"Actually, you might say it's the other way around," he answered carefully, pointing to the devastation T'sao T'sao and the ravens had wrought. "Your son fought in our defense. He protected our headman's daughter. He's a brave boy. You should be proud of him."

Kuan looked pleadingly at White Streak, knowing that Tinghong's praise would not change the fact that he had shown ingratitude by running away with Puk, but hoping White Streak would postpone his reprimand and not shame him in front of Yu Yu and the others.

The leader of the outlaws nodded solemnly at Kuan, silently acknowledging the respect he had earned from the villagers and indicating with a single stern look, brief but penetrating, that he would hold his criticism for a more private moment.

Gratefully, Kuan nodded back and then, forgetting his dignity in the excitement of seeing Black Whirlwind, hurled himself at the huge man who, oblivious to all the wordless signaling between his twin brother and Kuan, cuffed the runaway jokingly but painfully on the nose as if he were a misbehaving pup and roared, "What do you mean running away with our best tracker, you ungrateful cur?" His outburst broke the tension all around as White Streak and Tinghong burst into good-natured laughter.

Kuan laughed ruefully, rubbing his nose and glancing sideways at Yu Yu, who had sidled up to him, smiling sympathetically.

Now two more in White Streak's company hove into sight; Iron Ox, making do with his poker as a walking stick on the icy path, and Jade Mirror, who seemed almost to float as she gracefully ascended the steep trail, her beauty shining even more strikingly forth in these rough surroundings. But when her lovely eyes fastened on Yu Yu, she caught her breath. Dark brows drawn fiercely, she knelt in the snow at the girl's feet.

Frightened, Yu Yu drew back. Jade Mirror, tears forming, shook her head, struggling with emotion, but trying at the same time to reassure the girl. "I won't hurt you," she said, speaking with difficulty. "But tell me—where did you find this?" She gently touched the child's jacket.

Thinking Jade Mirror had come from Bai Ping to take the jacket and return it to the Emperor, Yu Yu began to back away, her muscles coiled to run. Who would believe her? she asked herself. These strangers were not from Purple Mountain. This woman kneeling before her must think she was a thief, for what was a poor girl who had no rice to eat doing with a beautiful red silk jacket, even if her own mother had stitched the best patch?

White Streak moved to restrain her, holding her arm lightly but firmly. Glancing questioningly at Jade Mirror, he calmly instructed Yu Yu to answer. Instead, she began to yell. Kuan, who had already heard what Yu Yu could do when she was worked up and also knew the strict limits of White Streak's patience, put his hands over her mouth, and shouted into her face, "Stop!"

Miraculously, Yu Yu did stop, too shocked to resume. "Please ask him to take his hands off my jacket," she said to Jade Mirror. "It belongs to me. The Starlord said so."

Now everyone began to speak at once, but White Streak commanded silence and asked Kuan to explain. Kuan knew nothing of how Yu Yu came to have the jacket, but he charged ahead, eager to reveal what he did know.

"He was here, I saw him, I swear it," he said. "He was behind that tree, throwing stones. And he never missed, not once. I couldn't see how he got the stones, but they seemed to just fly into his hand. He never even looked where he was shooting, but he knocked the birds out of the sky every time. And he was younger than me. But then the monkey took him away."

"What monkey? Where?" asked Jade Mirror urgently.

Kuan shrugged. "I couldn't see. One moment they were there behind the tree and the next, they were gone. They just vanished into the woods. It was so quick. . . ."

"What did the Starlord look like?" she persisted.

"Like a fisherman's son," Kuan said. "Only he was carrying a blue bag and he wore the golden phoenix necklace."

For the first time, Jade Mirror relaxed, and her smile was warm. "Ah, now I see," she said, turning happily to White Streak. "He's using Day Rat's changing bag. He knew enough to throw away the jacket and disguise himself as a peasant. Truly, he's already a fine outlaw." She laughed, as proud as any mother. "But who is this monkey?"

"He didn't throw away the jacket, lady," Yu Yu piped up

sullenly. "I told you—he *gave* it to me."

"I believe you," Jade Mirror soothed her, "It looks very well on you too." Yu Yu sat back, surprised and satisfied.

Now Jade Mirror turned to Kuan and asked him to show her the tree behind which the Starlord had been hiding. Flanked by White Streak on one side and Black Whirlwind on the other, Kuan and Puk led her there. Dropping down on their hands and knees, they searched the icy snow around the tree for a sign of the Prince's presence or a clue to where he may have gone.

A cry went up from Kuan as Puk found something black and gauzy on the ground. It was the magistrate's cap.

"He's safe," Jade Mirror whispered, clasping her hands together as if sending a prayer of thanks to the heavens. Then she continued her search for clues, working her way back to the bloodstained place in the snow where the bandit had been beaten by Tinghong and his men.

But when she reached that spot, Kuan gave a sharp gasp. Like the Starlord, T'sao T'sao too had disappeared.

CHAPTER THIRTY

Little Grandmother

A centipede dies but never falls down.—Mother Gu

Tinghong summoned the men to gather and say their last good-byes to Granny, the tribe's eldest member and matriarch, who had fallen in the attack of the ravens. Yu Yu was already at her mother's side, stroking her hand. White Streak, Black Whirlwind, and the other outlaws were paying their respects as well.

From the litter where he lay wounded, Granny's son watched weakly, his face ghostly pale. He looked as if he would follow in his mother's footsteps and cross over very soon.

Qilin spoke in clear, ringing tones: "Granny used to sprinkle salt on a tabletop and draw the stars, and the stars between the stars, so that her children knew how to see the sky. We must remember to look up and see the sparks she showed us, and show them to our children and our children's children."

Her gaze lingered on Kuan as she continued: "Granny used to say, 'From good deeds, angels are born. But from revenge are born angels without heads, and those angels are unblessed.' We must remember Granny's words."

Kuan shifted uncomfortably and lowered his eyes as she went on: "The dead are thirsty. Their country is dry. Therefore we will drink to Granny to give her comfort in the Nether-world."

Here Qilin paused, for their scarce supply of food and water had almost run out, and she was not sure how to honor the dead and satisfy her mother, who had expected a proper funeral when she finally passed beyond. Yet during wartime—and it did seem all at once to Qilin that they were at war—it was the wounded who must be served, not the dead.

White Streak, seeing her dilemma, pulled out a bulging leather pouch and from that, a fat jug of wine. With a solemn flourish, he passed it around the circle of mourners, all of whom accepted it gratefully. Qilin closed her swollen eyes as she drank deeply and when she was done, she bowed in thanks to the outlaws and invited them to sit down to a humble meal with her family and friends.

Responding to the spirit of her summons as well as to her unspoken need, White Streak dove into his provisions again, producing Mother Gu's cold sticky rice cakes filled with date paste and strips of boiled squid, their inky tendrils curled into what his mother called "lucky balls," plus a bag of her cooked shrimp and crunchy jellyfish skins, and a sack of ripe persimmons. With some ceremony, he revealed a supply of *fatsai*, the black fungus his mother said was soaked in good fortune. And last, he drew out his precious jar of dragon tea, made from the sweetest and most fragrant leaves in all the world by the now-deceased monks of the Silver Lotus monastery, who had unfailingly delivered a barrel of it each year to the Golden Phoenix.

White Streak had been saving all this for a time when, hard pressed by his enemies, he needed to renew his strength or provide a last supper before entering the Netherworld; but it seemed fitting to honor Granny by sharing the dinner and the holy brew Mother Gu had provided.

Cheered by the wine and the sight of the food, the group settled down for a feast, and soon their voices rang out across the barren valley. Tribute after tribute to Granny's wisdom rose spontaneously to the heavens, and for an hour they had no other thought but to sing her praises and pray for the recovery of her son, who seemed temporarily revived by the attention and the many cups of tea.

White Streak's generosity led to the discovery of other hidden delicacies among the tribe, which the heads of households were hoarding for a last-ditch meal. Another flask of wine appeared out of nowhere and was eagerly passed around and, amazing to all but Yongle, the ingredients for dumplings materialized from assorted saddle packs—bits of shredded pork and ginger and even a fine pot of soy sauce and vinegar! And now White Streak laughed and said he wished Mother Gu were here, for she was famous for making dumplings out of thin air, and there were no dumplings in all the world to rival hers.

"That's exactly what Granny always said," Qilin answered.

White Streak smiled and conceded that had he ever tasted

Granny's dumplings, perhaps he would be willing to grant hers equal status with Mother Gu's. But since he had never experienced the good fortune of sampling them, he had to stick to what he knew, which was that Mother Gu's ranked first.

Now a loud gasp went up from the men seated closest to the body. Still White Streak didn't realize what was happening until a strident voice trumpeted in protest: "Then you *shall* eat my dumplings or my poor ghost will never rest!"

And with those words, Granny's eyes flew open, and her corpse sat up, just like that! Before anyone could run away in terror, she began to scold: "So, Yongle, you were holding out on me, eh, saving these treats for after I was dead and gone? And you, Qilin, were left empty-handed and at the mercy of strangers to provide your mother with some small comfort as she passes. Had you fed every last scrap to this plump little daughter of yours?" And here she stuck out a wraithlike hand and tickled Yu Yu, who squealed in fright and hid behind Kuan.

"And who is *this?*" asked Granny, glaring at the newcomer.

Kuan, eyes wide in fascination rather than fear, took a step closer to the ghost and kneeled before her. "Granny, are you truly a ghost or have you visited with ghosts and decided to return?"

"I'm not *your* granny," snapped the resurrected matriarch with a loud sniff. Then crossly she said: "Yu Yu, how is it you are scared of your own granny? Come and kiss me, child. I'm no ghost. When that vicious harpy dropped down on me, I must have fainted dead away, that's all!" But the girl continued to cower, and no one made a move toward the scolding dead woman except Qilin.

"Mother, you're bleeding again," she said solicitously, wrapping her own shawl around the old woman's head wound.

But Kuan pushed himself forward now and faced Granny, bowing respectfully. "Please, did you see any ghosts in the Netherworld when you were there?" he asked again urgently. "My father and mother and little sister are new arrivals there. And my brothers too. Perhaps they asked after me?"

Granny gave Kuan a long look and wrinkled her brow as if trying to remember. "What did you sister look like?" she asked, more gently now.

"She was seven years old . . . and pretty, everyone said so, with long black hair. Her favorite slippers had little fire-red pompoms and bright green dragons. . . ." He stopped, his voice cracking. "No, well, I suppose those would have fallen off. . . ."

And now a general wailing went up from all those who had recently lost their loved ones and they pressed forward, crowding Granny, touching her hair, her clothes, her hands, her feet, and each had a question about someone lost, someone missing, someone they believed to be in the Netherworld.

Granny shook her head sadly, holding Kuan in her line of vision. "There *was* a child there," she said quietly, "a pretty young thing, about the age you describe. She had no memory of how she had died." Granny closed her eyes to picture the ghost, but Qilin shook her to make her open them again. "Don't go back there, Mother," she said. "Kuan, don't ask her anything more. All of you, give her some air. Can't you see how weary she is?"

But Granny beckoned White Streak to come closer. White Streak knelt, his head almost to the ground. Then Granny whispered fiercely in his ear. "Son of Chac, your mother's dumplings are good. But mine are better!"

White Streak rocked back on his heels, laughing. Then he turned to Tinghong and said, more seriously: "Your people and mine have a common enemy now. We invite you to join our small outlaw band. Granny is suggesting a dumpling contest. I accept the challenge in my mother's name. Return to the marsh with us. We can provide protection on your journey and put you up at the Golden Phoenix. Then we'll see if Granny can cook as well as she talks."

Tinghong's face twisted with doubt and pain. "Ah!" he muttered, shaking his head. "I don't know. . . . Outlaws. . . ." But Granny cut him short.

"Yes, you fool, *outlaws*. We're all outlaws now, like it or not. Haven't you learned that yet? How many stinging scorpions does it take to teach you to sting back?"

And then her son spoke up for the first time since he had been attacked by the harpy. Seeing his mother climb up out of the grave before his very eyes had given him new hope. If she could muster the strength and energy to survive and fight back, so could he. He looked to Qilin for confirmation as he thanked White Streak for the offer and solemnly accepted.

Granny nodded peremptorily at White Streak, showing her strong teeth in a wide grin. "Mother Gu, old friend, make way for Granny. Ha! Didn't we vow our paths would cross again some day?"

And so it was decided, and the funeral feast became a celebration of the induction of a new clan into White Streak's outlaws of Moonshadow Marsh. Yet Kuan stood apart, feeling uneasy and more in peril than ever. He removed himself from the group, drawn toward the forest and to the spot in the snow where he had last seen the fallen T'sao T'sao. Puk trailed him, but catching his mood, kept a respectful distance. Jade Mirror too noticed the boy's nervousness and, pulling away from the now raucous gathering around the fire, followed him to the clearing.

"You've not known White Streak very long," she said, studying his face. "You needn't be afraid while he's nearby."

"And what about me?" growled Puk. "Who saved him from the wahwee, the big brave twin or yours truly?"

Suddenly, a pebble sailed out from behind the tree that had hidden the Starlord during the battle with the ravens. It fell at Jade Mirror's feet, followed by a second and a third, all landing exactly in the same spot, just short of her left boot. Kuan blanched, but Jade Mirror, with a cry of excitement and surprise, darted behind the tree and pulled Day Rat out by his shooting arm. Kuan and Puk looked into the distance as the two embraced. Day Rat pulled away first.

"You travel with your own blacksmith now," he said, testing her. "Why would you need a Rat when you have an Ox?"

"Didn't you know it's the Year of the Rat, sir?" she answered, and then she kissed him, making him blush.

"Then I have you for the year at least?" asked the spy, with a smile.

"Are you asking for a more permanent pledge?" Jade Mirror countered.

"Would I be accepted?"

"Is a lady supposed to say 'yes' before the proposal is made?"

"And since when is an outlaw a lady?"

"Ah, if you do not know the answer to that, then the answer is no. Besides, you should be grateful to Iron Ox. If not for him, my head would be on display at the end of some imperial soldier's lance in front of the Gate of First Snow by now."

Puk growled, losing patience with all this banter. "Are you a spy or some drooling servant of the Emperor's court on a mission of love?" he snarled, baring his fangs. "Have you any news?"

Day Rat cocked an eyebrow at the demon dog, measuring the size of his teeth at a glance. "None that I'm aware of needing to report to you, demon," he answered rudely.

"Don't call him that," Kuan said, stung as if the insult had been directed at him. "He's at least as loyal as you are, and Yamu is no longer his master—I am."

Now Puk regarded Kuan with a look of surprised gratitude, for although he and the boy had grown close, their bond had never been openly stated. Suddenly, the new warm feeling he had experienced when Kuan rubbed his coat suffused his entire being with such intensity, he shuddered. And although he knew that White Streak had indentured him from the Nokk for a year, he suddenly realized that the boy spoke the truth. He *was* Kuan's, utterly and forevermore until death tore them apart. And neither White Streak, nor the Nokk, nor even Yamu had anything to say about it.

Suddenly, time seemed to loop like a blazing comet from past to future across the sky, and then it came to a pinpoint in the sinking sun, reflected as a blazing spark in the boy's eyes. And suspended in that moment, Puk, with the same sun reflected in his own eyes, was free.

"And who might *you* be?" asked Day Rat of Kuan, amused by the boy's air of authority. "Aren't you a bit young to be calling yourself master of anything?"

"And who might *you* be?" Kuan countered. "Aren't you a spy, and therefore also a shapeshifter?"

Day Rat bristled. "What do you mean by that?" he asked, controlling his anger. "Are you deliberately baiting me, lad?"

But Kuan was pursuing a memory and ignored Day Rat's exasperated tone. "And wasn't the noble Starlord Hung Wu a shapeshifter as well?" He turned to Jade Mirror. "My father used to tell me a story he called the Faces of Wu—about how the Starlord used to get tired of the palace, so he had a magic blue bag made, like the one the little Starlord was carrying when I spotted him behind the tree. And after that, when Emperor Hung Wu was weary of the daily round of rituals in the imperial palace, he'd just pick a disguise and slip out among the people, dressed as a common laborer, or as a beggar."

Day Rat exchanged a long look with Jade Mirror. "The boy knows much more than he should at his age," he said.

"Kuan is in training with Mother Gu," she interposed. "So, in a way, you're brothers." She put her hand on Day Rat's sleeve. "He came to the Golden Phoenix by the same road you did," she added softly.

Day Rat studied Kuan with new sympathy.

"Hello, so you're one of Mother Gu's strays, eh?" he said bluntly. He extended his hand. "Then we *are* brothers," he acknowledged warmly. Kuan didn't appreciate being called a stray but reciprocated the handshake in the spirit in which it was offered.

Turning to Jade Mirror, Day Rat took something out of his sleeve. "Do you recognize this?" he asked. It was one of the beautiful combs Jade Mirror had so often placed in her lady's hair, with a delicate butterfly about to take flight, carved out of white jade. Jade Mirror reached for it and turned it over and over in her hand. "Where did you find it?" she breathed.

"It was almost buried beneath the snow near the old fox shrine just outside Bai Ping," Day Rat answered. "Silver Lotus seems to have stopped there and she wasn't alone. My guess is that she is traveling over these mountains accompanied by someone who knows the trails and they're headed for the desert. She was hurt, but then the wound must have stopped bleeding and it grew harder to trace their path. Nothing in the shrine was disturbed and there were no signs of a struggle. In fact the place had a peaceful air, and someone had made up a rough pallet on the floor and even swept the floor around it a bit. I think she's in good hands."

"I hope you're right," said Jade Mirror fervently. "I pray some honest soul has taken her under his wing and is leading her to safety. Will you go after her?"

"No, my duty is to follow the Starlord and his odd animal companion. But there is a true beast loose in these woods, and I hope to bring his leopard heart home as a trophy before I'm through."

Jade Mirror shivered. "The assassin," she whispered.

"Let me go with you," Kuan pleaded.

Day Rat shook his head. "I work alone," he said. Kuan

thought he heard a touch of regret in his voice. "Besides, you're too young for revenge. Didn't you hear what Qilin said at Granny's funeral about those angels without heads?"

Kuan sighed. Everyone thought he was too young, but everyone was wrong. He would exact his own price from those who had killed his family. If no one but Puk would help him, then he and the dog would find the murderers alone and somehow, he would make them pay. Or he would die in the attempt.

Jade Mirror was bidding a hasty good-bye to her beloved Day Rat, and before Kuan could say farewell, the spy vanished into the trees. She raked the comb through her hair as if intending to wear it; then, thinking better of it, tucked the precious object into the lining of her boot. Jade Mirror stooped and picked up one of the pebbles Day Rat had thrown at her and fingered it, holding it up as if it were a jewel to be appraised. Frowning, she pocketed it, and signaling Kuan to follow, returned to the camp.

Kuan stood with Puk, gazing into the plum-colored light as it faded into darkness. Glinting like a crimson eye from the middle of a bloodied depression in the icy earth not far from where they stood lay a toad-shaped ring, which Jade Mirror would have recognized at once as the one she had dropped into the changing bag the night Day Rat rescued her from T'sao T'sao. A thin snake of red smoke was steaming up from its center like a miniature eruption, obscuring the amphibian's emerald green eyes and burning a black hole in the snow beneath it. Crimson smoke thickened around this blazing portal until it hovered like a cloud of fog. And into that seething mist, a dark-winged shape emerged like a hawk swiftly rocketing upward through an opening in the earth. And then another, and another escaped into the creaking forest, myriad hawklike shadows mingling with shadows of shadows in a flutter of exploding wings.

Suddenly, Puk howled, his short hairs standing on end. He shivered convulsively. Something evil had entered the woods. Through some unknown passage, demons had arrived— demons much more powerful than the harpy Malia, whom he sensed was also nearby. And where Yamu's demons blazed a trail, the Lord of the Dead was never far behind.

CHAPTER THIRTY-ONE

The Water Curtain Cave

The wall itself is both inside and outside.
—The Master Hand

"Enough! Enough! I said I've had enough!" yelled Monkey to nobody in particular as he sped away from the valley battleground. He was ascending as speedily as he could while carrying the Prince, climbing swiftly from one jagged peak to another, balancing the unhappy Starlord in his arms.

"I order you to let me down!" cried the Starlord, trying to maintain some dignity as he bounced along. "We look ridiculous. Especially you. And, as I've demonstrated, I can climb much faster on my own."

Monkey held on tightly. "You've also demonstrated your talent for running away and I can't afford to risk it. I could have lost you back there, and then where would I be? Now that you can talk, won't you be silent just a bit longer? Try the everlasting joys of meditation, why don't you? Just until I get you far away from those outlaws and that troublemaking boy."

"Kuan? I liked him," said the Prince. "And I liked his dog, too."

Monkey snorted disdainfully through his nose. "The dog's a demon, and the boy's a fool for trying to steal him. Stay away from both of them, or you'll have Yamu on your tail before you can spit."

"I don't have a tail. And I can't spit either—never tried it."

"Well, don't start now. At least wait until you're free and clear of my head."

"Then put me down!"

"Aiiiieee! I never knew you'd be so irritating when you learned how to talk. I'll let you go when I'm good and ready and not before. You've caused me no end of trouble, not to mention almost getting yourself killed. Didn't I tell you not to stop for those people? Didn't I tell you not to show your gold necklace? Didn't I tell you to mind your own business and just keep on going? What a mess you've got us into. Where would we have been if I hadn't figured out the wishing rod?"

"But you *did* figure it out, didn't you?" said the Prince. Then he grew thoughtful and frowned. "We left too soon, Monkey. I don't think they were safe. What was the hurry?"

Choosing not to answer, Monkey rolled his eyes in exasperation and sighed, toiling ever upward.

"You know you can't fight when you're carrying me," the Prince pointed out. "The wishing rod is useless stuck behind your ear if you can't put me down and get to it. We're sitting ducks out here if someone should want to pick us off with an arrow."

"Then let's hope nobody does," said Monkey grimly, trudging on. But his eyes darted about anxiously, scanning the underbrush on each side of the trail.

They came to a narrow makeshift bridge of logs hastily lashed together, spanning a gorge. Monkey looked down into the chasm of icy, churning water. Floods had cut deeply into the land and the eroded mountain path had crumbled away. The rushing current was treacherous, but clearly the only way to go forward was to cross. Still stubbornly holding the Prince in his arms, Monkey advanced cautiously, one step at a time. The Prince sighed and fell silent, afraid to break Monkey's concentration. When the ape was about halfway to the opposite shore, the platform began to sway wildly. Grimly, Monkey continued on.

"Look out!" yelled the Prince, as a heavy floating branch suddenly catapulted down the ravine, crashing into them and almost pitching Monkey over the side. The bridge shuddered and began to crack. Clutching the Prince so tightly that the boy could hardly breathe, Monkey leapt toward the opposite bank. But just as he landed, a grotesque head popped out of the thicket on the other side, barring his way.

The brigand's face was a pulpy horror, blackened with welts and bruises. The long matted hair bound up in a filthy rag and the band of bloodstained leopard's fur loosely wrapped around his arm identified the gargoyle as the resurrected T'sao T'sao.

"Dung beetle!" Monkey shouted. "No one can seem to squash you for good. Perhaps the stink would be too great! Out of my way!" T'sao T'sao took in the ape's precarious position in one hateful beady stare and, grimacing horribly, moved in closer.

"Hideous red-assed ape, who do you think you are?" he roared, brandishing his sword. "Stand away, or go piss on yourself for all I care! It's the royal brat I'm after. Hand him over and jump, and you'll save me the trouble of running you through. I'd take my chances in the water if I were you. Better to drown and go to Yamu whole than be hacked up into little pieces, eh? Take my word for it, no one will bother to glue you back together down there! Not once I've done my work on you!"

Unsheathing Dragon Rain, Monkey sprang forward to meet T'sao T'sao's challenge, but the narrow parapet was slippery and he lost his footing, almost plunging into the freezing waters. Clutching on to a vine, he barely avoided being swept away in the raging river. Tossed abruptly into the air, the Prince caught Dragon Rain and landed gracefully on one leg, balancing on a single wet log like a dancer defying gravity before steadying himself and reaching out for his guardian.

With a roar of rage, T'sao T'sao rushed forward, slashing at the Prince, but in a flash Monkey placed himself in the way and the blow fell, wounding his arm. Crying out, Monkey recoiled in pain and the sudden movement shook the catwalk mightily. This time, the sound of splitting wood reached his ears before he realized he was, once again, falling into the flood. Pieces of the shattered scaffolding crashed into the water all around him, narrowly missing his head.

When Monkey surfaced, he looked around for the Prince. The Starlord did not yet know how to swim, but the boy had managed to scamper onto several logs still lashed together with rope, and was holding out his hand to drag Monkey on board with him. Monkey's wounded arm was on fire even in the icy water and hung limp and useless by his side. Luckily the current was carrying him toward the makeshift raft. Somehow he managed to scramble clumsily onto it before it catapulted headlong down the foaming river, sweeping them toward a steep waterfall overlooking a sheer drop into rocky rapids. Monkey had a split second to decide what to do. They could ride straight ahead into the misty waterfall or dive over the towering cliff to an almost certain death in the turbulence below. Muttering a quick prayer to the River Goddess, he crawled on top of the Prince, shut his eyes, tightened his grip, and yelling "Jump!" hurtled straight through the waterfall.

When he opened his eyes on the other side, it was dark— but dry. As his eyes adjusted to the darkness, he could see they were inside a huge stone cave with stone seats and stone bowls and hollow cups all lined up on a stone table as if set there by the Master Hand. Dimly illuminating the grotto, a silent witness to all that had transpired there perhaps for centuries, stood a carved white alabaster statue of the River Goddess, Yin Dang, balanced on an open lotus flower, her right hand raised in a gesture of benediction. And gleaming in the center of her smooth stone forehead was a luminous white pearl.

"Thank you, thank you," cried Monkey, kowtowing before the statue and banging his forehead to the cold damp floor with each expression of gratitude.

"Please don't knock yourself out," groaned the Prince, rising slowly and rubbing his bruises. "I don't have enough breath left in me to bring you around if you faint."

"Show some respect," Monkey reprimanded him sternly. Monkey looked around him, stretching and testing his limbs. He was stiff and sore and his arm throbbed, but he was glad to be all in one piece. Tentatively, he jumped up and down, shedding sheets of river water as he did so. Suddenly, he was grinning broadly and jumping higher. Then, throwing his head back, he howled and improvised a wild celebratory dance, throwing beads of water from his fur like a firecracker tossing sparks at the New Year's festival.

"Is this her temple, then?" asked the Prince, kneeling to please Monkey. He studied the statue. "Will she come alive like you did and shoot blue light out of her eyes? Perhaps if you say the proper thing, she'll answer."

Monkey stopped jumping. "What shall we call this place?" he asked in an awestruck voice, still in a paroxysm of wonder and delight at being alive. "Let's name it so that it will always be a sacred shrine to wanderers and rogues of the road like us."

"A shrine sounds all right," said the Prince, "but maybe we should limit the wandering from now on. Why not stay here for a while? We can tend the altar, and do all the praying you like. T'sao T'sao will report us dead, and nobody will come looking for us behind this waterfall."

"For a Starlord, you're a bit of a stick-in-the-mud," observed Monkey.

"Or could it be that we've *already* drowned and this is our place in the Netherworld," mused the Prince.

"For a Starlord, you're very gloomy as well," said Monkey. "We can't be dead, because I'm starving to death. Maybe it's seeing all these empty cups and bowls." Ignoring the pain in his bleeding arm, he lifted one of the cups high as if it were filled to the brim with wine and began to sing lustily, a boasting song about his brave exploits with the legendary T'sao T'sao.

"An ape there was," sang Monkey, banging his empty cup down on the stone table as if calling for a refill at a crowded inn, "a match for any demon. He crossed blades with the best of bandits o'er a raging river. . . ."

"This song is all about *you!*" interrupted the Prince with some irritation. "I did nothing, of course?"

Monkey shook his head vigorously to warn the Prince not to interrupt while he was composing. "There stood the baneful brigand, in icy ambush—" he continued.

"Is a Starlord going to show up anytime soon?" asked the Prince, crossing his arms. "Or is this a ballad honoring the heroic Monkey, Guardian to what's-his-name?"

"I'll just skip the duel then," the ape conceded, undaunted. "Here am I, brave Monkey," he rushed on, "a sea rover at rest in the temple of the River Goddess. . . ."

"Oh, please," the Prince interrupted again, shaking his head.

"In the water-curtained cave beneath the falls."

"I like 'water-curtained cave,'" admitted the Prince. He said it a few times under his breath until it sounded like "water curtain cave."

"That's it!" said the Prince. "That's the right name for this place—the Water Curtain Cave." The Starlord seemed so pleased with the phrase, Monkey sang the song again, elaborating on the fighting this time and emphasizing the three words as he drew out the final lines.

But just as Monkey finished his jolly tune of triumph, a

faint roll of thunder shook the cavern floor and a greenish ball of fire appeared in the air above his head. Monkey dropped to his knees as the brilliant apparition gained substance before him, becoming a swirling galaxy of light from which emerged a great fiery hand and a familiar voice directing Monkey to step into the flames.

"Ouch, sir, so I exaggerated a little. Don't punish me," cried Monkey, instantly remorseful.

The Master Hand repeated his command. Quivering, Monkey obeyed and was instantly engulfed in a blazing illumination that penetrated straight to his heart. Advancing bravely to the center of the fire, he was surrounded by an expanse of pure blue. Suddenly, he was bathed in a warm spicy wind that buoyed him up like fragrant waves in a calm sea. His breathing slowed and he could feel an exhilarating power pumping through his blood, making him stronger than he had ever been in all his monkey lives. Out of the flames, the Master Hand spoke sternly to him, yet he did not sound angry.

"Ape, you have kidnapped a man with a great destiny and it is yours to make sure he lives to fulfill it."

"I'm doing my best, Master. But the boy won't listen. He runs away from me and—"

"Silence!" said the Master Hand. "You are his guardian. Lead him into the fire so that he may know my voice." Monkey hesitated.

"Do not be afraid," said the Master Hand.

Still Monkey hesitated, but a dark cloud was forming on the edges of Monkey's vision, growing larger and blacker by the moment. His wound began to scald and swell. In shock, he could feel his legs shaking, but by focusing all his attention away from the encroaching darkness, Monkey managed to stand straight as a temple pillar. The shadow began to recede like an ebbing tide, rustling and whispering like the ghosts of ten thousand demons. Again, the Master Hand commanded Monkey to place the Starlord in the flames. The sound of his voice banished the last of the winged horrors that had invaded Monkey's mind a moment before.

Extending his hand to the Prince, who took it without hesitation, together they stepped farther into the blaze. They were rewarded for their obedience. This time, there were no dark visions. The conflagration immediately turned a celestial blue, like the sky on a clear sunny day, and a band of enormous monarch butterflies flew up from the ashes and fluttered around the Starlord's head.

"Starlord!" came the voice of the Master Hand. "Listen to your Monkey guardian. He has only two eyes, but he has lived many lives. The River Goddess has three eyes. Take the third. Soon you will find the holy scrolls. Never forget you are the son of the phoenix and the white tiger, born of fire and ice. Monkey will teach you to use Dragon Rain, yet he will not always be with you. The phoenix rises from its ashes. But if the wind blows its ashes to the four corners of the earth, it must wait to be born again while the world withers and dies. I am sorry we do not have more time. I must take your childhood. Perhaps you will find it again in another life. Trust Monkey. Trust the Tattooed Monk. Do not turn away from us. You are our only hope. You are the Chosen One."

Now the Prince's golden necklace gave off a blinding light

so that the phoenix appeared to be pulsing with heat and almost alive. Monkey raised his arm to protect his eyes from the glare, cringing a bit in anticipation of the pain he knew that gesture would cause him.

"Wait!" cried Monkey as the fire died, hissing as it faded into the faint smell of cinders. "What do you mean, 'Monkey won't always be with you?' Where will I *be* then? Come back, I need to know. Hey, I never really had a childhood either, you know!"

But the Master Hand was gone, and the fireball had extinguished itself without a trace. And now Monkey stood, amazed, for the searing pain he had expected from moving his arm never came. The nasty wound inflicted by T'sao T'sao had disappeared, as if it had never been there at all. But the Prince was staring wildly, flailing his arms in Monkey's direction as if he could not see his guardian standing right there by his side.

It took Monkey a moment to realize that the healing was not the purifying fire's only beneficial effect. Balanced lightly and precariously on his head was the treasure he had stolen and lost in another lifetime, restored to him now—the phoenix-plumed cap of invisibility. And there wrapped around his chest was the chain-mail vest of pure gold. And on his prancing feet appeared the precious cloud-stepping shoes.

"Look, Prince!" he cried, joyfully embracing the startled child and sweeping the cap off his head. "I'm *back!*"

CHAPTER THIRTY-TWO

The Kappa

Blood is a very special juice.
—Yamu, Lord of the Dead

Staring down into the churning waterfall, T'sao T'sao felt bone weary. His skin was tight and mottled with ugly bruises all up and down his aching body, in every variety of purple, blue, brown, black, and yellow. Looking down at his battered arms and legs, he groaned. He barely recognized himself. He had never felt so empty of energy, as if all his blood had been replaced with beggar's broth, weak and watery. He yearned for nothing more than his soldier's sleeping mat back at camp, yet he was loath to return to Spotted Leopard without the Prince's head.

T'sao T'sao was fairly sure the Starlord along with his ridiculous Monkey guardian had been smashed to smithereens in the grinding rapids, but he could not be absolutely certain the

Prince had died, and without that certainty his own life was in danger. Still, he was too sick and weary to climb down the slippery mountainside and search in the treacherous current, which by now must have carried the corpses a long way downstream.

Haunted by the persistent sense that Day Rat was lurking nearby, he was also aware of a thickening of shadows in the surrounding forest and a murmuring—or perhaps it was more like a soft moaning that just barely escaped his hearing but left a residue of sorrow in the air. He blinked, thinking for a moment that he saw the leader of the raven pack perched on one of the surrounding peaks. He dug his thumbs into his swollen eyes and rubbed his throbbing forehead. No, now she was gone, if she had ever been there at all.

He had been half dead back there before those blasted birds had showered him with ice. He supposed he had nothing much to thank them for—it would have been better to die than face Spotted Leopard empty-handed. It occurred to him that the Leopard had sent the ravens to bring T'sao T'sao back to life so that he could amuse himself by murdering him over and over again. T'sao T'sao harbored no hope of being spared upon his return to camp. If he showed himself without evidence of the Prince's death, he was a dead man—or worse, an object of scorn and ridicule, reduced to a joke.

T'sao T'sao spat into the stream and rubbed his hands together, anticipating the long climb down. He had no choice but to look for the bodies. If only he had the ravens' sharp eyes and aerial view, he could find the Starlord easily in the flood below. But the beating had left him blind in one eye, and his remaining eye was almost as damaged, bloated half shut and blurred with pain. He began to stagger down the mountain, his knees shaking and his balance challenged at every step.

From her camouflaged perch, Malia observed the brigand's progress and did not interfere. She had seen Monkey and the Starlord miraculously disappear into the waterfall. She blinked as they evaporated, registering the point at which they had merged with the silvery water and vanished. She had seen magic performed before, but never so effortlessly. A performer herself, she wondered which of them was responsible for the show, the Prince or the beast, or if perhaps the Master Hand had summarily pulled them into another dimension.

Absently, she watched to see if T'sao T'sao would, in his futile pursuit of the pair, blindly drop to his death. The brigand's fate no longer concerned her. Another movement on the mountain had captured her attention.

Almost invisible against the rugged snowcapped boulders, stealthily slipping between the stunted trees, a small man shadowed the bandit, moving when he moved. Malia had spotted this man before. She had watched him prowling in the forest during Little Grandmother's funeral, and later talking with Puk's boy. He had given the boy's outlaw friend a jade comb, which the young woman had hidden in her boot. Malia had idly wondered about the couple, guessing the girl refused to wear the valuable talisman in her hair because she did not return the spy's love, or more likely because the ornament, which looked to be of imperial quality, was stolen and would draw attention.

But it was not this little lovelorn spy's stealthy passage through the alpine woods that so fascinated the harpy, although she admired his birdlike grace. It was the dark, barely discernible demon shadowing the spy that held her riveted.

The creature resembled a small skeletal horse with one huge bloodshot eye and no skin at all. Its bones glimmered like copper and its muscles and sinews were dark and raw, pulsating as it tracked its intended victim. Through its horribly wide mouth it emitted a thin stream of white vapor, which blended with the patchy mountain snow; but Malia noticed that whatever green and growing thing the monster's breath touched immediately withered, knocked down as if by a blighting winter wind. As the raven watched, a bright canary flew too close to the chemical cloud and dropped immediately to the ground, dead before the equine beast trampled it under iron hooves.

Malia cared nothing for the little spy but found herself so repelled by his hoary adversary that it was all she could do to prevent herself from swooping in to warn him of the norn. This was no ordinary shade in pursuit of everyday misfortune but a moldy, outmoded horror, a nightmare stalker that had been dug up from the clotted depths of Yamu's dungeons in the Netherworld.

If her lord was electing to send a norn to the surface, what would be next? Perhaps it would be as the dragons of old had prophesied: ponaturi, once a seemingly insignificant infestation, would rule, first toppling Chac and destroying his kingdom, then invading the land with an army of lost souls.

And where would Malia and her ravens figure into this clumsy new world, after humanity had been sucked into the depths, surrendering to the ponaturi? This norn belonged to an unilluminated world bereft of all the harpy valued. For the first time, she knew herself to be in danger of an extinction so final she could not bear to bring it to mind.

In occasional flashes of flight, Malia had intimations of outliving the sun. Sometimes, she imagined her own black wings eclipsing all light on earth. It seemed to her in those fleeting moments that life on the planet was dead. But, although absolutely lifeless, everything somehow kept moving, unable to brake the sheer descent into nothingness.

Observing Day Rat as he slowed, unwittingly narrowing the distance between himself and the norn, Malia struggled with her terror. She had almost decided to cry out and warn him when something emerged from the treeline that caused her to choke back her cry and take flight, unwilling to risk another moment of proximity to the spy.

A thing of the swamp had joined the norn, a gaunt figure, with long white hair, a beet-red face, a beaky nose and bright blue netlike webs on its fingers and feet, each fleshy thread oozing a putrid odor that had warned the harpy against approaching. Slow drips of foul slime speckled its path as it followed the outlaw, and its large liquid brown eyes lingered on everything it saw, as if sponging in every detail down to the smallest leaf pattern and twig. It whimpered and complained in a high, whiny voice as it bumbled along the trail, dragging a hump on his back as large as a tortoise shell, and with every step it took a large bite out of a fleshy melon it held in its hand, slurping and sucking the juice with as much relish as a cannibal feasting on a human head. But its oddest feature and the one that identified it to the fleeing harpy as the demon known as the kappa, was the bowl-like indentation on top of its balding scalp filled to the brim with clear amber fluid that reflected the passing clouds.

Day Rat heard the raven's cry, cut off in midstream, and at the same moment sensed the kappa, a fetid presence more repulsive than any he had ever encountered before. He could tell from its unmistakable odor that it was very close. Weapons would be useless against the demon, he knew that much from Mother Gu. He wracked his brain for what else she had told him about the foul-smelling menace even as he wondered how it had surfaced, for no kappas had been spotted since Mother Gu was a girl. She had taught him to identify and build resistance to the creature, although he had never seen one, by thinking of all the most nauseating excrescences he could possibly imagine, both human and animal, mixed together into one sickening ball and then playing a mind game with the ball, holding his focus while envisioning that with each vigorous kick, the repugnant scent unbearably increased.

And now the entire distasteful lesson came back to him, just in time. Kappas had the reputation of feeding on their victims' livers, before reaching in and drawing out the other organs one by one and eating those at their leisure, while their unwilling donors writhed in agony. Sometimes, kappas could be temporarily appeased by offering a ripe melon with a high-ranking official's name carved into the rind, but Day Rat had no melon handy, and he had never been quite sure if Mother Gu had been joking about that particular aspect of self-defense. Besides, the kappa had already just eaten a melon, and from the look on its ratlike face as it emerged from the mossy darkness, it was still hungry.

Day Rat tried not to recoil from the creature's overwhelmingly offensive musk as it came closer. It wasn't skill with bow and arrow or his well-known talent for the weighted iron ball that would save him now. It was, as he recalled, good manners alone that could rescue him.

"Honorable One, Father of all Mercies, good day to you," he called to the approaching monster, kowtowing deeply and actively refraining from holding his nose.

The kappa, true to his reputation, imitated Day Rat's obeisance with an even lower kowtow, and as he did so, his pungent aroma increased, and a trickle of the amber liquid spilled from his head and seeped into a pile of curling leaves with a nasty hiss, leaving a sizzling acid residue.

"My unworthy self most humbly greets you, Illustrious Omnipotence," Day Rat hastened to add, groveling even lower.

The kappa, though gratified by the greeting, began to be cross, but as he was known in the Netherworld for his impeccable manners, he could not fail to return Day Rat's respectful bow. Accordingly, he bent even lower than the outlaw, almost touching his head upon the ground, whereupon more of his vital fluid poured forth and quickly disappeared into the singed earth.

Now the kappa felt himself to be weakening slightly and was irritable indeed, for he had been locked in the Tomb of the Turtle for decades, and his hunger for human entrails had not yet begun to be appeased. But Day Rat, silently thanking Mother Gu for her sound instruction, banged his forehead upon the ground nine times, as if honoring an emperor, all the while complimenting the kappa on his intelligence, good looks, and sweet fragrance.

"All-seeing Benevolence and Ever-righteous Excellence," he

said, between staccato and resounding knocks of his forehead upon the hard ground, "favor me, your unworthy servant, with your unapproachable wisdom, celestial magnificence, and perfumed purity."

And unable to resist the courtesy and flattery, the kappa, beside himself with competitive zeal, kowtowed like a trained eunuch in the Emperor's court, knocking his own head on the forest floor with pent-up fury and frustration, over and over again, until not one drop of his life juices remained in his skull, whereupon he roared a complimentary epithet at Day Rat, likening him to a heavenly constellation and, beside himself with unexpressed rage, graciously passed out.

Day Rat rose to his feet and bent over the kappa for a closer look. He knew he must not touch the creature even in its unconscious state. Its cerebral fluid regenerated quickly, and the acid coating of its feverish skin would be sufficient to burn him badly. He was congratulating himself and formulating the story of his victory over the courteous demon as he might tell it to Mother Gu upon his return to the Golden Phoenix, when the norn, recognizing its opening, attacked, filling the air with a suffocating cloud of sulfurous steam.

Coughing and choking, Day Rat instantly reached for his arrows, and sent one singing into the center of the gaseous plume, straight toward the norn's wide-open mouth. Suddenly, the outlaw was entirely wrapped in a yellow mist, so thick and pungent he panicked, clutching at his throat. From the hills came another raucous bird cry, a warning perhaps that had reached him too late. Fainting, he fell with his eyes wide open, staring up into the chalky sky. As he hit the ground, just before losing consciousness, Day Rat thought he saw a piece of the sky detach and rush toward him, an abrupt black body out of nowhere, lit from behind, like a huge flat disk placed over the sun.

With whatever breath he had left in his lungs, he screamed. Then a dark weight slammed into him, the door to his brain swung shut, and it was night with no glimmer of light at all; and the only thing that told him he was not yet a ghost was the fleeting thought that he must be dying.

CHAPTER THIRTY-THREE

Flight of the Rat

Eagles and sparrows inhabit the same sky.
—Malia

When Day Rat awoke, he pretended he was still asleep as he listened to the strange conversation going on above his head. A gruff male voice was solidly located on one side of his skull and a rasping female creature stationed herself on the other, but she changed positions incessantly, hopping about in a restless fashion that made it difficult to concentrate.

"I was taking him to Yamu when you interfered," she complained. "The Lord of the Dead does not take interference lightly."

"We don't need Yamu for this; we can handle it ourselves," the man retorted. "It was your own idea to fly him to the Netherworld, harpy. I doubt Yamu concerns himself with little spies. Nor should you."

"I bear a personal grudge against this one."

"So do I," said T'sao T'sao, grimacing. "Maybe we should rip him in half, then."

Day Rat made his breath so shallow that his chest did not rise and fall, hoping they would think he had died and would therefore lose interest in torturing him. But if it came to having to choose between the two, his instinct told him to go with the harpy, for her words had an insincere ring, and he wondered what she was hiding from T'sao T'sao.

"Your 'little spy' killed a norn with one shot and tricked a kappa into unconsciousness—what makes you think you can travel with him, chained or not? He'd just as soon put an arrow in your back than blink."

"Then I'd better not turn around. But I don't see how he'd accomplish that without arms," said T'sao T'sao, drawing his sword.

This was Day Rat's cue. He had only one advantage over T'sao T'sao at the moment and that was surprise, but he had no idea how badly he had been wounded and how much power he could put into his swing. Springing up suddenly with a shocking cry, he spun his iron balls over his head so swiftly they could hardly be seen, knocking the weapon from T'sao T'sao's hand and retrieving it for his own before it touched the ground. T'sao T'sao lunged forward, trying to throw Day Rat off balance, but it was too late.

"Cut my arms off, will you?" growled Day Rat, and with a single slash of his dagger, he cut deeply into T'sao T'sao's right arm, raising a bloody wound. But even as T'sao T'sao staggered back, howling, he retaliated and punched the smaller man in the head so hard that the spy, whose brain was still slightly befogged by the norn's lingering poison, was blinded for a moment and again began to swoon, dropping the weapon. Immediately, T'sao T'sao moved in and retrieved his sword, but before he could do further damage to the spy, the harpy dug her claws into Day Rat's leather tunic, lifting him high up into the air. Desperately struggling to stay alert after the stunning blow, the outlaw twisted around, and was about to cut himself free when the harpy said quite distinctly, "Settle down. I'm trying to help you, little spy."

Fully awake now, he hesitated, dagger poised. "I was doing just fine on my own. Do you think that clumsy oaf is any match for me? Anyway, I heard you tell him you were bringing me to Yamu. Is that what you consider helpful?"

"I'm not bringing you to Yamu," said Malia, "unless you stab me and we both fall out of the sky. T'sao T'sao may be an oaf, but you've been exposed to the Netherworld fumes of a norn *and* a kappa. After inhaling that much poison, you're in no shape to fight, whether you know it or not. You can kill me if you like, but we're high enough now so that if we drop, you'll certainly die."

"I watched you revive T'sao T'sao when he might have bled to death in the snow. Why this sudden change of heart? And what do you want with me?"

Malia didn't answer except to comment, "You're light for a human, though your sleeves are weighing us down. I suppose you won't consider dropping your weapons? If you climb on my back, you'll have a more comfortable ride."

After a few more moments of dangling dizzily from her

claws, twisting precariously with every slight change of direction, Day Rat decided to make the suggested switch. Ignoring her question about his weapons, he scissored his agile body into a radical somersault that placed him directly between her wings, where the wind flattened him securely. Tucked down low so that his chin almost rested on her feathered back, the spy who had acrobatically scaled so many impossible summits and witnessed the world from spindly pinnacles as close to the heavens as most men would ever dare to rise, found himself, for the very first time in his adventurous life, truly in the air.

In spite of the danger and ambiguity of the situation, or perhaps because of it, Day Rat was suddenly swept with a wave of intense joy. For a moment, it did not matter at all what the harpy had in mind or if her intention had been to save him from T'sao T'sao or to rescue the bandit yet again. Nor did his destination worry him. Nothing mattered except that he was soaring through gray mountains of cloud, shooting like one of his own airborne arrows on soft shafts of light. He was flying!

Malia relaxed into flight, taking a deep breath as she felt the kindred exhilaration of the captured spy flood through her. Somehow, she had known the little man would take to flying, she had sensed it. But she still hadn't decided whether to bring him to Yamu, or . . .

She could not even name the notion that had begun to take shape in her mind since the moment she had caught sight of the norn. Only yesterday, she had thought Puk a fool for breaking the demon code. Now she realized, she had been the fool for ever believing Yamu would promote and protect her. She was at the height of her powers. He would continue to use her perhaps for a little while longer, in this last and greatest campaign, until the darkest of his demon army was released upon the world. If she delivered Day Rat and told him where to find the Starlord, perhaps he would be pleased with her, but only for a little while. In the end, he would turn away while the others destroyed her.

Malia had glimpsed her future in the brutal appetite of an attacking norn, in the stench and dripping formality of a gut-starved kappa. Had she been harpy through and through, there would be no turning back. But she was still a raven, mistress of the sky dance, and she could still perform a good deed if she elected to shift with the wind.

The world was a wilderness of possible predators, now more than ever. Day Rat was a spy like herself, her counterpart on the other side, her enemy. Yet she was mysteriously and unreasonably flooded by the desire to protect him. She thought of Puk. Perhaps, after all, he wasn't crazy to love the boy.

They glided above glittering lakes, casting a complex shadow on the rippling waters. Together, they sped past sheer cliff faces and monumental peaks shaped like the heads of gods. At first, Malia was cautious, keeping level and holding back, trying to maintain an even pace so as not to alarm the outlaw. But after a while, she caught the pulse of his exultation and, abandoning herself to the rare experience of companionship in flight, she dipped and soared as the spirit moved her, following her instinct and her heart.

Day Rat discovered to his utter amazement that he did not want Malia to descend. Whenever she banked and swerved downward, he closed his eyes, tightened his grip and began to steel himself for a landing but was filled with a new wave of happiness whenever she rose again, following another wayward current up far beyond the evergreen tree tops and the ghostly mountain mist. Day Rat rode the harpy as if he had been born to fly with ravens, and oddly it did not feel like the first time. He recognized the lofty purity of the aerial landscape as the backdrop for many of his best dreams, and he did not want the journey to end.

As Malia executed a convoluted spin over a flooded canyon between two pale limestone pinnacles, her keen eye detected a gathering of spiky shadows that did not follow the fingerlike contours of the rock. As she sped past, a spiral wraith of red fog clung to her wing, and suddenly she felt sleepy. Furiously, she shook the heavy feeling off, resisting Yamu's familiar touch. Day Rat instinctively nestled his head down close to hers and stroked her back, calming her. She shivered. He pressed into her sides gently, reassuringly with his knees. Gratefully Malia wondered how the spy had known something was wrong.

As they left the twin peaks in the distance, the sluggish moment passed, and Malia regained her strength and balance. Once more, the ecstasy of unrestrained flight took over, the sky was as wide as the world and they were free.

Yes, Malia decided in that rapturous moment, if a demon dog could become an outlaw, so could a harpy. The Lord of the Dead had shown his hand much too soon. If kappas and norns were the draftees of his future army, she would save the little spy, and Day Rat's safe return would be her gift of entry to the other side.

Diving into a brief, spontaneous sky dance, Malia *quorked* and chuckled to herself. And to her surprise and delight, the sound of raspy laughter echoed hers as Day Rat hung on tightly for his first frosty somersault in the blissfully clear air.

CHAPTER THIRTY-FOUR

White Moth

The world rises and falls and never stops rolling. It is so bright yet it can be broken like glass, and inside, we never stop rolling, balls within the ball, and we too can be broken.
—The Tattooed Monk

After the Master Hand's fiery visit, the Prince began to grow with astonishing speed. Every day, he looked considerably older, until by the end of a fortnight, he was as tall as a lad of twelve. One morning, while exploring the Water Curtain Cave, he found a passage that opened into a thick, mossy, lichen-encrusted forest filled with enormous sphinx moths as large as fluttering oak leaves, and great red flying squirrels flitting between the trees.

He discovered that the waterfall where he and Monkey made their home cascaded down from the mountains into a great dense bowl of woodland where the white waters ran into a rocky streambed, eventually opening into a large tranquil lake dotted with golden water lilies and pink-spotted lotus flowers. Farther along the river in a southerly direction, between two gaunt rocky cliffs worn smooth by the passing tides, a gorge plunged downward into a vast moon-shaped basin, where another great river mixed with theirs in a tangled skein of treacherous currents and whirlpools.

The Prince took long walks, wandering aimlessly through the groves of fragrant yew and largeleaf ash, pausing to admire the flash of a fire-tailed sunbird and the flowering dove trees, pure white against the green of the forest canopy. He found a place where the river ran deep and calm, and he swam with the gentle long-nosed dolphins, listening to the surrounding chirping song of the tree frogs, the bubbling sound of the lyre-shaped sand grouse, the loud cheerful calls of the bulbuls stirring restlessly in the surrounding spruce. He watched the comical tree ducks with their newborn chicks, dropping into the water from their hidden holes in the light-dappled bamboo groves. He felt a kinship with the small fluffy babies, unceremoniously catapulted into the flowing river the instant they were born and expected to swim.

At times, the Prince and Monkey explored together. They gathered fruits and berries, mountain herbs, and odd plants of every sort and, selecting the most enticing, set out delicate offerings for the fairies and friendly spirits of the mountain. The Prince had never seen one of these creatures but had heard about them from his nursemaid, Jade Mirror, who liked to tell stories about immortal djinns and magical beings.

Monkey assured the Prince that some day when he least

expected it, a fairy or a djinn would pay him a visit. When that time came, the Starlord would be ready to say good-bye to his carefree life and devote his attention to swordsmanship, becoming Monkey's pupil, as the Master Hand had directed, in the proper deployment of Dragon Rain and the basic principles of kung fu. When the Starlord was ready, Monkey further promised to teach him the art of multiplication and other uses of the wishing rod.

But as much as the Prince loved Monkey, and wanted to please him, he often preferred his own company, traveling in isolation and disappearing for days at a time. At first, this caused Monkey much anxiety. But eventually, Monkey had to admit that the Prince was impossible to find in the woods unless he chose to reveal himself to his guardian, and that both were happier if they allowed one another the freedom of solitary discovery.

One morning, as the Prince stumbled through a massive sea of sprouting tree ferns, he was startled by the ghostly appearance of a large moth. As it fluttered aloft, a nightjar came swiftly out of the shadows and the Starlord heard the sharp click of its beak as the moth vanished.

Close to the very spot from which the unlucky moth had emerged, the Prince observed a great glittering white flower, slowly unfolding in the light and emitting an intoxicating perfume. Later, when he described the experience to Monkey, the ape was envious and amazed. The Prince described the flower in such perfect detail that his guardian was able to identify it as the silver lotus, which bloomed for one day and night only, every one hundred years.

Monkey and the Prince fell into a daily rhythm. At sunrise, the Prince would rise and, leaving Monkey snoring soundly in the Water Curtain Cave, climb into the surrounding wooded hills where tiny parrots hung upside down from the branches like bats. Shaking off sleep at his approach, the birds shared a joke in an explosive series of squawks as the sun rose higher above the distant fringe of mountains, and the thick mist coiled up into the sky.

Prince Zong never tired of watching the mist. Sometimes it looked to the Starlord like drifting strands of kelp weed under the sea, or a colony of pale misshapen trees, or the vast white graves of giants who had once walked the earth. And sometimes the mist shaped itself into land dragons battling sea dragons for domination of the smoldering sky, or a phoenix dissolving into flame.

On wet afternoons when the earth turned dark and slippery, and the hiss of a surprise downpour broke over the Prince like the wash of a wave, he would find his way back to the Water Curtain Cave. There Monkey would build a warm fire and cook a giant crock of tasty vegetable soup, roasting roots he had plucked from an improvised garden at the entrance to their home.

Like Monkey, the Prince could swing from the trees and travel lightly and easily through the underbrush, following any living creature that caught his eye and scrambling to great heights. He tracked the silent lynx and the musk deer, the red fox and the wild boar, the pangolin and the giant salamander.

Gradually, the Prince's keen eye discovered all the hidden beasts of the woods, and they came to accept his presence there, no longer troubling to hide themselves. He learned that nature was endlessly various and that to be solitary was unusual. But although he had no kin, he was never really alone in the woods. Most frequently the apes kept him company and he grew to know them all and distinguish their habits and conversation—the black-leaf from the gray-leaf monkeys, the snub-nosed from the stump-tailed macaques, the howlers from the white-browed gibbons. Even the blue-faced golden monkeys showed themselves to the Prince when he happened upon their remote glade, and after he discovered them, they followed his progress through the wood from one grove to another, as if watching out for his safety.

Sometimes, the Prince took naps in the shelter of the River Goddess, like an animal cub seeking warmth and security in his mother's shadow. When he dreamt of his mother, he pictured a tall quiet woman, just like the River Goddess of the Water Curtain Cave with eyes as radiant as the glowing pearl set in the statue's untroubled brow like the promise of everlasting peace.

One morning, as the rim of the eastern horizon turned a powdery blue and the remaining stars flickered and died, the Prince discovered a mysterious glen not far from the cave. He wandered along a rushing stream to the edge of a diminutive waterfall, a small replica of the one that hid their home. Here the stream splashed onto a litter of boulders that topped the next small waterfall, and the next and the next, like descending steps.

Among the glistening black stones grew delicate ferns tapestried with moss. On the bank, dancing lightly on tiptoe, scuttling among clouds of snow-white moths, were hundreds of tiny nut brown crabs. As the Starlord approached, they raised their claws defensively and backed away, sidestepping with infinite caution and disappearing into a colony of deep thumb-sized holes in the mud, placed at random like the remnants of a giant baby's afternoon at play.

The Prince rested all day in this enchanted place, and it was here that he unexpectedly saw his first djinn. As he lay on the bank gazing up into the leaves, the creature came casually drifting through the branches with all the airy grace of a piece of flotsam.

He was clad in a little fur coat of greenish gray, and he had a long, gently curling tail. His shapely pink hands were large for his size and his fingers were slender, with rosy, spoonlike knobs at the tips. His ears were large as well and semi-transparent. They seemed to have a life of their own, alternately crumpling and folding flat to his head like a fan, and then standing erect and upright, as straight as daffodils. His face was dominated by a pair of owl-like eyes, and when he saw the Starlord, he twittered vaguely to himself. The sound must have sent out some sort of a signal, because suddenly the Prince was surrounded by djinns and their children, some of whom were no bigger than walnuts, all twittering and gazing at him with the same dark round eyes.

The Prince watched as one of the babies batted at a drowsy locust, grabbing it around the middle. The insect kicked out with its strong hind legs, trying to tip the little djinn off balance. Each time the locust kicked, the infant would topple over, still holding on, and hang upside down from the branch, suspended by the adhesive soles of his delicate feet. The opponents seemed evenly matched, and it appeared to be an innocent game until they both hung suspended over a deep black pool, ringed with rotted leaves. The water was so dark, it looked like a hole to the Netherworld, except that it was as smooth as glass and perfectly reflected the struggling pair.

Fascinated, the Prince almost stopped breathing, and as he watched, the breeze turned suddenly frigid and all the surrounding sounds of the forest quieted. But the two playmates did not seem to notice as they continued to wrestle. And then a terrible thing happened.

Shattering the mirrorlike image of their mock battle, a hairy form rose up from the depths of the watery pit. Its bumpy head was broad, with mottled eyes and a wide gaping mouth. As it lunged for the djinn, its white underbelly flushed pink. The most astonishing thing about the froglike creature, aside from its bulk and the speed of its attack, was the hair that covered its powerful thighs and hung down in thick clumps of jellylike tentacles.

The locust leaped out of the way and disappeared into the reeds, but the poor djinn was swallowed by the demon in a flash, followed by several of his companions, including the original djinn the Prince had seen just a few moments before, suspended so calmly and peacefully above his head.

Shocked, the entire djinn community stopped twittering and silently beat a hasty retreat through the trees, vanishing as suddenly as it had appeared. After gulping down a few stragglers, the monstrous amphibian retreated too, submerging slowly toward the littered bottom of its murky hole, from which arose a belch of reddish steam.

The Prince stood rooted to the spot for a long while, unable to believe that the lithe and playful djinn, so new to the world and beautiful to behold, with its shining gossamer fur and round innocent eyes, had attracted so terrible an end. The Prince thought back to the harpy who had pursued him in the marsh and the black bear and the vipers, and for the first time, he imagined the earth after his death, going on with all its earthly activities without him. Trembling like a moth in the cold light of dawn, he inched his way back to the entrance to the Water Curtain Cave, a sickness gripping at his heart. If a young djinn could be gobbled in first flight, so could a young Starlord, he reasoned, and for the very first time since he had been forced to flee the palace in Monkey's arms, the Prince felt truly afraid.

PART THREE

Leopard

*It is a miracle to walk on water and to fly through the sky,
but the real miracle is to walk on the earth.*
—The Immortal Beggar

CHAPTER THIRTY-FIVE

White Crane

Life is a game haunted by the possibility of escape.
—The Tattooed Monk

Far from the Water Curtain Cave, on the other side of the Purple Mountains, Silver Lotus sat in the Tattooed Monk's white tent, drinking tea made from rain the monk had gathered long ago and buried in a porcelain jar beneath the earth.

She had discovered that the monk had many porcelain jars buried in caves, containing rain. He taught her to distinguish between the taste of tea from tropical raindrops gathered off palm trees in a storm and those he had plucked from plum trees during a deluge. After a few weeks, she began to wonder if he had been collecting rain for centuries.

Silver Lotus thought back to her days in the Forbidden City. Idly, she wondered what the dozens of maids who had attended her in those days were doing now that she was gone.

Were they waiting on another First Consort? She spun their names in her mind, pausing on each to remember them: Musk Moon, Snow Duck, Hot Pepper, Purple Cuckoo, Pervading Fragrance, Autumn Sky. They had been her companions, her only friends, most of them her own age or younger. But her favorite, the only one she had truly trusted, was Jade Mirror. To her, Silver Lotus had confided her dreams of finding her father, and her sickness and loathing when summoned to the Emperor's bed. And to Jade Mirror she had confessed her impossible longing for a man she could love. Quietly she drank her tea and smiled at the monk sitting beside her.

Silver Lotus longed for a friend she could talk to about the Tattooed Monk, a woman she could confide in who would understand her newfound happiness as well as her fear of losing what she had just discovered. Since that day of her son's long-awaited birth, when her whole universe had turned upside down, she had become aware of just how fragile a foundation hope was built upon, more delicate than the smallest bone in her body. For a while in Bai Ping, it had crumbled and almost disappeared. Now, a new optimism had returned to her from the edge of extinction. Somehow, although the monk's past was still a mystery to her, she sensed it was the same for him.

Sometimes she slept little, thinking she heard fast footsteps in the night, the side flap of their desert home softly ripping under the clandestine attack of a bandit's dagger. In the distance, she imagined she heard the cameleers' dogs barking a warning and the song of crickets silenced by the intrusion of strangers.

The monk, too, was restless. Although accustomed to

roaming far and wide, he now seemed reluctant to be apart from her for any length of time, afraid that when he returned, their new life together would prove to have been an illusion and she would be gone.

The monk tossed and turned in his sleep, struggling with the idea that there was some action he should be taking to protect Silver Lotus from calamity. He knew with an urgency born of old scars that he must think of what to do soon. If he waited for the present to become the past, he would, by the very act of waiting, step into the future, where he could not count on anything except that something would absolutely change. Yet he waited, and, for lack of a better plan, tried to ignore all but the present which, from moment to moment, gave him so much unexpected joy.

After his family had been murdered, the monk had cast about for something useful to do and, finding himself attracted to those in pain, had become a physician of sorts, saving lives with ancient herbal remedies. He had become an excellent self-trained doctor, and his reputation had spread, particularly in the desert, where he was credited with wrestling lost souls back from Yamu, after they had already arrived in the Netherworld.

On his journeys, the monk was in the habit of collecting ingredients for his cures. Silver Lotus had watched him counting out his cold perfume pills, the most potent of his medicines, each of which he said had taken him nine years to prepare. Inside each of the capsules resided a second chance, a restorative powder that if properly administered just after the moment the spirit exited the corpse, had the power to reverse fate and bring a person back from the dead. The pills did not result in immortality; the recipient would eventually die again. But it was the best the monk could offer a mortal who had prematurely stepped over to the other side.

To make the medicine, the monk had gathered a quantity of springtime peony to which he had added summer lotus, autumn lily, and winter plum blossom. When he had finally collected all the necessary flowers, he had waited for the vernal equinox and ground them up, mixing them with powder derived from one pulverized bone of each of the twelve animals of the zodiac. To this he had added equal parts of rainwater from the first rainfall of the year, plus early morning dew gathered from the Mountain of the Five Elements. He had buried the ingredients in a white porcelain jar under a crooked, windblown tree with branches splayed and permanently tossed in such a way that its silhouette by the light of the moon resembled a dancing monkey.

The monk had planned never to reveal this medicine except to a mortal in extreme need, but propelled by an urgent desire for Silver Lotus to know his secrets, he took the pills out to show her—three perfect iridescent circles nestling like opals in the earthy palm of his hand. Sadness shadowed his face when he thought of those he had lost—his wife and child and his friend Gong Sun, all consumed in flames and beyond the reach of his restorative powers.

Silver Lotus saw the sadness, and knowing that it was, at least in part, for her father, she took his large hand in both of hers, closing his fingers one by one until the pale pills were hidden from sight. Then slowly returning them to their container, together they buried the jar deep in the earth, beneath the monkey tree.

"My father used to drink fossil-bone powder as an elixir," Silver Lotus reminisced when they had finished.

"Ah, yes," the Tattooed Monk smiled. "Gong Sun's famous dragon-bone tea."

They stood, surveying the night sky, remembering her father. When he was alone, the monk could not yet think of his friend without thinking of Gong Sun's violent death or of his own failure to save him. But when he was standing this way with Silver Lotus, he found he remembered their wide-ranging talks in the middle of the night and the comfort they gave one another.

"Perhaps we're here only to channel sparks," said the Tattooed Monk suddenly in a hushed voice, drawing her close.

"I think when we die our sparks return to the fire," she whispered huskily after a moment. "It's up to our children and to those who share our work to continue to see them still dancing there within the flame and point them out to others."

"I have no children," said the monk, almost to himself. "I am alone."

"Hush, not alone," she said. "No longer alone. My father never thought I could learn the teachings of the Silver Lotus," she went on, softly. "Yet already, in the short time we've been together, you've taught me the Fox and the White Tiger fighting forms. Will you teach me all you know of my father's secrets?"

The monk frowned. She was asking him to initiate her into a dying art, a faith that had only one survivor. As former First Consort, she was already tracked and hunted. He could smell her pursuers at a distance. As the carrier of the knowledge locked in the lost scrolls, she would be an even more magnetic target. He had taught her the White Tiger form so that she could protect herself against the likes of T'sao T'sao and Spotted Leopard. But if he taught her more, he would place his mark of ill fortune upon her, and blend his fate with hers. She had given him new life. Would he return the favor by endangering her life even further?

"Yamu is not the master of death, you know," said the monk, brooding and avoiding her question, "nor even the master of the Netherworld. But the dead *believe* he is their master, which is almost the same thing."

"Sometimes you speak as if Yamu were *your* master," said Silver Lotus, puzzled by his evasion. "Yet you have never been dead." She looked searchingly at him, as if to make sure this was true.

"I'm no ghost," he reassured her solemnly, "although there have been times when I felt like one. Many would say I've been alive too long, Yamu among them."

"What happened to your family?" she asked quietly.

He hesitated, staring at the stars. "It's difficult to speak of, even now," he said after a while. "My wife and I had lived together only a year, when one calamity after another befell our village. It was a common chain of events: first drought, then starvation and disease. We were easy victims to bandits like Spotted Leopard. It wasn't his gang that set fire to our town, but the renegade who robbed and destroyed us could have been his twin. Mercy has many faces, but the face stamped by brutality has one identifying grimace.

"I was away when it happened. My wife and baby daughter

were among the victims. Yet because they considered me an outsider, I was suspect. Having no one else to blame for their ill
fortune except the distant gods, they blamed the stranger who
disappeared for long journeys alone into the mountains.

"I was expelled from the town, barely escaping with my life,
hunted like an animal by my own neighbors. Fevered and delirious, I had no time to mourn. I was exiled, as you were, for a
crime I had not committed. But my guilt at being away when my
wife and child most needed me mingled in my mind with their
accusations and for a few weeks, or perhaps months, I believed
I was a demon who deserved their wrath. He must be stopped,
they said. He's on his way to a new place, bearing chaos. And
because the darkest chaos was in my heart, I believed what they
were saying."

"Is that when Father found you?" she asked.

"Before he found me I tracked that bandit gang and in my
madness, murdered them, one against many. Then truly, I went
insane and wandered like a lost soul in the mountains, becoming no better than a wild beast. Briefly, I joined an outlaw band,
but mostly I was alone. Sometimes, if I was starving and could
not hunt, I turned thief and stole my supper. In that state, your
father found me, took me in and heard my mad story over and
over again. Gong Sun nursed me himself. And when I had
regained my wits, he put me to work and trained me as a monk."

"A monk of the Silver Lotus. Will you teach me?" she
repeated, touching his sleeve.

"If I do, we two will be the last to speak a disappearing language, strange to everyone but ourselves," he answered sadly.
"And when we die, our knowledge, recorded only in the scrolls

of the Silver Lotus, will no longer possess any meaning at all to anyone in the entire world. Do you wish to be so lonely, living as I do, out of time?"

"I do," she said solemnly, taking his hand. "But what about the Prince? Is it not our mission to teach him, as well?"

Again, he hesitated, then answered truthfully: "It is mine."

"And mine as well," she said firmly. "He was to learn from my father when he was old enough. I had always planned it that way. Now it must be you who teach us both."

In answer he raised his calabash, twirling it rapidly until the silver lotus once again appeared, as it had the night they had first met near the Kingfisher Inn. Then he placed it in her hands, pressing her fingers around it.

"Keep it for the Starlord," said the Monk. "It contains the ashes of five holy scrolls. From the Temple of the Five Blessings comes the wisdom of the white crane, the horse, and the bear. The scrolls of the black fox and the bat were hidden in the shrine near Bai Ping. They are now within the calabash as well. Soon the Prince will need the powers of the twelve animals of the zodiac. He must collect the ashes of all twelve scrolls inside the golden phoenix he wears around his neck, before the phoenix will rise. Only then can we defeat the demon Spellbinders."

He raised his hands to the moon, and stood there, in a crane stance. Then he moved into the White Crane form, and although worried and confused by his words, Silver Lotus fell in with him, imitating his movements.

By the time Silver Lotus and the Tattooed Monk had moved through the form several times, the sun was rising and with it, just as the monk had feared, came a ragged red cloud upon the horizon, distinct from the flames of the sunrise. Framing the approaching billow of scarlet vapor was a spiky sprinkling of black banners stamped with the sign of the leopard.

The monk's face turned as white as bone. This, then, was the moment he had anticipated with such dread, when the present would become the past, and all would change, irrevocably. He had sensed its approach in the sky, in the sands, in the caves and in the mountains. It had been creeping closer with the golden close of every peaceful day and now, he thought in despair, there would be no peace. The crimson desert sun was rising on a day of blood and battle and finally, when he was least prepared, when he had let down his guard and had once again allowed himself to hope for a future, Yamu had searched him out and found him. It had come.

CHAPTER THIRTY-SIX

Old Bones

*An earthworm may swear there is no such thing
as a flying dragon, even though it has come to know the passing
shape of its winged shadow.*—Yamu, Lord of the Dead

"It has come," whispered Yamu, waking Old Bones. "Wake up,
it is almost time." The monster stirred, hearing the ringing of
caravan bells, and the distant roar of camels, signaling a fierce
and sudden storm. Above the dusty desert wind, Old Bones
heard a deep familiar voice as well, telling the ancient story, the
kidnapping of the Starlord Hung Wu by a terrible land dragon
who breathed fire and then ice, and the subsequent sinking of
the Starlord's utopian kingdom, along with its perfectly circular
palace, now covered in hoary frost and buried in the bowels of
the earth, beneath the Emperor's dungeons.

Ah, he knew that voice too well. It was the Immortal
Beggar, telling the wintry tale again, to what purpose and to
whom? What was the point of plowing the same ground

over and over again like a broken-down beast of burden? And did Old Bones have to rouse himself every single time it was told? He groaned, rattling his scales. Then he opened one double-lidded eye. A voice was answering the Beggar, a melodic beautiful voice, familiar as well.

He had heard that sweet voice singing at night in the palace above his nest, in accompaniment to the plucked notes of a silver-stringed dulcimer. It had soothed him back to sleep when he had grown restless in his dungeon and his dreams had inclined him toward battle. Why had the voice returned? And why was Yamu waking him now when he had grown fat from lying still for centuries and his bloodlust had dwindled and almost vanished?

Old Bones dozed off once again, missing much of the conversation. He had heard the Beggar's tale too many times to care. No one told the story from the dragon's point of view. His part was always brief but dramatic, making a surprise entrance toward the end of a golden era. He bore the distinction of being Yamu's largest flying demon, the monster who had lifted the blessed Emperor Hung Wu off the face of the earth in his yellow talons, belching volcanic fire and destroying a nation. He was the hulking nightmare who had transported the only right-eous Emperor to Yamu, taking a million souls with him and bringing the curtain down on enlightened government for gen-erations to come.

Some day, perhaps, he would tell it as it had really hap-pened. The human victims were incidental and only got in the way, and the Starlord was of no real importance either. It was all a fight between dragons. Old Bones had won the war over

Chac; land had prevailed over sea. But he was tired now, and he had nothing to prove by setting the crumbling record straight.

"Have you ever seen the courtyard garden in the Temple of Pleasant Sounds?" Silver Lotus was asking the monk after hearing his story. "It was the only part of Starlord Hung Wu's palace that was not destroyed by dragon fire."

"Did the Emperor tell you that? Actually, it was the only part left aboveground," corrected the monk. "The rest still exists under the earth, befouled by Yamu's land dragons. It's said that Yamu himself makes frequent visits there."

Silver Lotus shuddered. "The garden was my sanctuary, my haven in the Forbidden City," she said. "I felt the unborn Prince was at peace when we were there. Often we sat by the ancient wishing well, and in my loneliness I would talk to the beautiful marble statue of Chac that guarded the grotto."

"I'm familiar with the statue," said the monk, frowning. "It was carved by the famous wax sculptor Zheng, the Starlord's tutor, his only work in stone and his last royal commission before being dismissed from the Emperor's services in disgrace for allowing the young Hung Wu to run away. Zheng narrowly escaped being executed in the public square for not reporting the boy's intention of fleeing the court. The Emperor spared his life at the last moment and sentenced him instead to live out his remaining years in exile."

"So the statue was the work of a master. I used to sing to it sometimes," Silver Lotus admitted, blushing. "I imagined that the Dragon King of the North Sea listened and was pleased." She hesitated. "I thought perhaps it was

Chac who sent me the dream."

"The dream?" asked the monk, carefully.

"I still believe it was he who first gave me the idea that my son was to be the new Starlord." She paused, watching his face closely. "Do you think I'm mad?" she asked.

"Not mad, no," said the monk. "No one touched by Chac is quite the same after sensing his presence," he added evasively.

"I wonder now if it *was* Chac who sent the dream," said Silver Lotus thoughtfully, and suddenly the monk did not know where to look for he did not want to meet her gaze.

"A Starlord knows Chac's power and draws upon it; a Starlord's mother . . ."

"So it's true," interrupted Silver Lotus triumphantly. "The Prince *is* the son and heir of the Starlord Hung Wu!"

The Tattooed Monk hesitated, then looking toward Heaven, shrugged apologetically as if he expected to see the Master Hand materialize in the sky, shaking a cloudy finger. "Yes, it's true," he admitted, "just as you dreamt it and just as you told him when he was a baby."

"And if we die in the desert today, who will find my son and watch over him?" she asked anxiously.

Again, the monk hesitated. "Your son is no longer a child, Silver Lotus. Heaven's need for a righteous emperor was too great," he answered, unwilling to lie or to dodge her direct questions. "There was no time for the Prince to grow wiser with the slow passage of years. He is a young man now."

She clasped her hands over her heart, crying out involuntarily. "Who can be a man without a childhood?" she asked indignantly. "He is an innocent. How will he defend himself?"

"He will learn, just as you did when your own child-hood was taken from you. Was the Forbidden City a place of innocence?"

Silver Lotus shook her head, her eyes brimming with tears. The monk cast about for something to say that would bring her some relief. "A monkey with formidable magical powers and the knowledge of ninety-nine lifetimes is the Prince's guardian. Does that comfort you a little?"

She stared at him, not comprehending. "A monkey?" she said sharply, with a mother's protective rage. "Are you saying the Prince, heir to the throne and direct descendant of the Starlord Hung Wu, is being raised by a *monkey*?"

He had never seen her like this. "Not an ordinary monkey, no," he said. Now he was in the uncomfortable position of having told her too much and yet not enough. And how was he to praise Monkey's sagacity in order to console her when he despised the ape and thought him a fool and worse? There was only one way out. He would have to reveal his own part in the Starlord's destiny.

"Well, then, I will tell you what no one else on earth knows," he said, throwing another brief mental apology to the Master Hand. She looked up at him expectantly, suspending her anger, which lingered like a black storm cloud on her brow. He took a deep breath. There was no turning back. "The Immortal Beggar is also his guardian," he said.

Her face cleared. "The Immortal Beggar," she breathed in wonder. She studied him for a long moment. "Then perhaps it was *he* who sent me the dream?" The monk did not answer.

Silver Lotus sighed, still grieving. "Oh, but it was a cruel theft to take his childhood away," she whispered.

"Cruel, yes," he agreed, seeking to turn her attention back to the task at hand, "but not as cruel as those who approach us now."

They fell silent as they watched the red cloud grow darker on the horizon. Silver Lotus gave the monk a piercing look. "Why do the nightingales follow you in the evening, even out here in the desert?" she asked. It was not what she had intended to say in what was perhaps their final hour together.

"Maybe because I listen when they sing to me," he answered, smiling.

"I'll play you a song, then," she answered, "and let us see if you listen."

Old Bones yawned. It was always the same tune among humans, even when one of them was immortal, he thought. Love, the pangs of parenthood, aging, loss, and death. As if reading his thoughts, Yamu soothed the dragon, crooning softly: "Look at them, in love! Take comfort, Old Bones. At the height of their heat their flesh will slip like mist from their bones and those bones will disappear, every last one the lost key to a fallen world, a ruined kingdom never to return through time everlasting. She thinks he is what he appears to be. Yet what does she love? His flashing eyes or the hollow skull beneath? Or the desert dust that skull will soon become?

"Demons at least know they are shapeshifters. We make no bones about it. Yes, that's rich, my dear. No bones. The Immortal Beggar has fallen in love with a mortal! Watch him, my friend, as he becomes another moldy fruit caught in the plague of infected winds blowing through my blighted orchard. Shall I show you how he decays, even as he pledges undying devotion?

"And she—the loving mother. 'Who shall look after my son when we are gone?' Yamu is looking after him, my dear, even now. Sing, nightingale, and Yamu will join you, singing the little Starlord to sleep. And who can sing more sweetly than I? And who sleeps better than those I sing to sleep?"

Confident that he could defend Silver Lotus against the Leopard's worst, the Tattooed Monk occupied himself with estimating the bandit gang's numbers, counting them as they came closer. But the red cloud hid Yamu himself. And it was coming closer as well, along with the ever-complaining Old Bones who, ignoring his master's peremptory commands, was faithfully shadowing his promised war prize, the glittering Golden Wings.

"I have mused upon the dead longer than you have been alive, which is quite a long time," Yamu told the dragon as they sped along. "What do they all have in common?"

Old Bones gave a sulfurous belch in midflight, scattering puffs of ash through the air and paying no attention to his master's lecture. Yamu pretended not to notice.

"An unhappy ending, that's what," he continued. "What begins in a generous green pocket of living space can always be relied upon to end out of luck, out of time, and pinched out of existence in a grimy, gray, messy corner as dark as any beast's underground cave." As if to illustrate, the Lord of the

Dead spurred Old Bones on with a nasty pinch to the base of his spine. "Your cave, for example," he added menacingly.

Yamu warmed to his subject. "Let's examine our monk. There he is in the distance, see? Love has revived him. But I will bind his writhing hands and force him to watch as his precious Silver Lotus wilts. She will vanish, and without her, that monk will be mine. And then, Old Bones, he will slip back out of time like a common sorcerer through the Master Hand's evergreen woods into my stagnant underground system of caves. And there he will crouch, helpless at last in a foul chamber with no exit—and there I shall corner him!

"Of course, being immortal, he may choose to fall into a senseless slumber of survival. Death in life or life in death, it doesn't much matter, does it? His heart will wither and his soul will shrink and he'll be mine, the living dead. Yes, that's what matters. When Silver Lotus breathes her last, the monk will be mine."

Yamu chuckled to himself, hugging the dragon's neck with his knees so that Old Bones choked, coughing out another blast of flame. Then the Lord of the Dead laughed thunderously.

"Just this one small fire, my dear, and then you may sleep again—for a little while longer," he said. "You're out of practice, you know—a bit rusty. Consider this a dress rehearsal."

The Tattooed Monk heard the crash of distant thunder and, remembering that sound from another time, shuddered violently. Suddenly he sensed his enemy would be much more formidable than Spotted Leopard. He closed his eyes, struggling against the tide of memory as Yamu urged Old Bones to greater and greater speeds, flying straight toward their target, the monk's sparkling bone-white yurt, glowing in the newly risen sunlight like a solitary pearl.

CHAPTER THIRTY-SEVEN

Tiger Scroll

One stroke ties a thousand knots.—The Master Hand

Monkey was true to his word. After the Starlord reported his sighting of the djinns and the destruction wrought by the hairy frog demon, the guardian enlisted the Prince in lessons of self-defense, starting with the wooden sword. Now, every morning, instead of wandering free as a misty cloud in the forests, Monkey rose with the dawn and after a humble breakfast of fruit and nuts and hot jasmine tea, taught the Starlord what it meant to work: planting and weeding in the garden, sweeping and raking its paths of stray leaves and debris, dragging heavy buckets of water from the river, scrubbing his own clothes in a wooden tub, wringing and hanging out the laundry, and swabbing the floor of the Water Curtain Cave for hours on end in slow circular movements the ape claimed would strengthen and prepare him for learning the higher martial arts.

The Prince, subdued by what he had seen and feeling newly vulnerable, obeyed Monkey, submitting to a demanding daily routine of menial tasks and repetitive exercise that kept him from worrying about harpies and the fate of djinns and fairies in a world populated by demons.

Monkey asked the Prince to imitate the animals he had seen on his long walks—a deer leaping from boulder to boulder, a bathing duck, a golden monkey hanging upside down in a tree, a glaring owl, a tiger slowly turning toward its prey, a coiling snake, a bear lumbering through the forest, a flying crane.

The Prince did as he was told, and sometimes Monkey corrected him, working on his balance and suppleness so that one posture stretched and flowed smoothly and gracefully into another. Occasionally, the animal conjured would suddenly appear and join them while they practiced, particularly the golden monkeys, who would sometimes imitate the Prince. They made a strange grouping by the sparkling waterfall: Monkey, standing tall in his golden vest and shining cloud-stepping shoes; the Starlord, his face glowing in the morning light; and a tribe of studious golden monkeys, their blue, heart-shaped faces quite solemn, all flapping their long arms in slow concentration like the wings of flying cranes.

The djinns took an interest in the Starlord's training as well, and would gather in the surrounding trees, watching as Monkey schooled the Prince in the Five Elements and taught him techniques for harvesting his inner energy. The Starlord grew tall and muscular and learned with great speed, and soon the young man surpassed his teacher in strength and agility.

Now that the Starlord had seen the djinns, he saw them everywhere, and he saw fairies as well, whirring and darting quickly by like dragonflies, or hovering in the air like hummingbirds, tiny translucent beings camouflaged in all shades of woodland green. Sometimes he felt they were mocking him, and he thought he heard tinkling laughter accompanied by streaks of flashing light in the sky as he moved slowly through his evening exercises.

Once, when the Prince was restless and could not sleep, he climbed out of the cave and stood by an ancient evergreen, raising his arms, palms upward toward the Big Dipper. He heard the fairies fluttering close by and this time, finding himself a ridiculous figure, laughed with them. Suddenly, the constellation tipped toward him, filling him slowly with starlight.

Then the Dipper tilted a little more and poured more light upon the Prince, anointing him, so that his skin glowed as brightly as the moon. The laughter in the air faded and he stood, elated, surrounded by a universe of glowing planets and stars, drinking in their light until the sky turned purple and the sun rose, awakening Monkey.

"Now you are ready for Dragon Rain," he told the Starlord that day. Ceremonially burying the wooden practice sword under the evergreen tree, he began training the Prince in the use of his own inherited weapon.

No matter how hard Monkey drilled him, however, and how proficient the Starlord became at handling Dragon Rain, the work never obliterated the Prince's memory of the hairy frog demon, and his increasingly disquieting questions about the safety and whereabouts of his mother and Jade Mirror.

The Prince found himself returning again and again, armed now, to the glade of many waterfalls where he had first seen the djinns and the water demon. There he would practice the sword form for hours, becoming so swift that his instinctive moves could no longer be anticipated even by the golden monkeys who shook their furry heads as they witnessed the growing evidence of his extraordinary gift.

While meditating in this place one morning, the Prince gazed into one of the waterfalls, and was startled to see his own reflection blend into the reflection of a beast gazing back at him. As he continued to study the apparition, it solidified into a white tiger. Baring its fangs, it roared at him. In the middle of its forehead was a round pearl, blinking like an eye. The gem was as large and flawless as the pearl in the forehead of the River Goddess, but slowly it turned as red as a ruby, issuing a stream of scarlet mist.

The Prince felt a familiar chill in the air and stepped back abruptly, drawing his sword. But no hairy demon emerged, although he remained poised and vigilant for a long while.

That night, Prince Zong had a dream in which the River Goddess spoke to him in a voice he imagined to be his mother's, urgently instructing him to pluck out the pearl, which she called her "third eye." Disturbed by the command, he adamantly refused, but immediately a fever took hold of him that made him toss and turn so violently that he woke with a cry and sat bolt upright in the moonlight, repeating the strange sounds she had whispered to him: *"Yi zhi ren li xin."*

Overcome with curiosity, the Prince took hold of Dragon Rain, and pointing it at the pearl, repeated each of the sounds three times. and then another three and then, when nothing happened, another. Instantly, a bright blue light, like the sapphire beam that had emanated from Monkey's eyes on the night his guardian had kidnapped him from the palace, issued forth from the point of the ancient sword, momentarily blinding him. And the pearl dropped from its marble socket into the palm of his outstretched hand.

He touched the rim of the staring eyehole, tracing it tentatively with the tip of his finger. Hidden inside the hollow in the middle of the River Goddess's forehead was an ancient scroll, coiled tightly. Careful not to rip the fragile parchment, he held the ragged edge gingerly, slowly working it out of the depression. At first, he could make out very little. But as he studied the weathered document, he began to understand a few words and diagrams and then a few sentences, mostly precepts Monkey had taught him, written in ancient script:

Move like a tiger, gaze like a hawk.
Where there is up there is down,
 where there is forward there is back.
Where there is left there is right.
When in motion, everything moves;
 when in stillness, everything is still.

He recognized some of the fighting stances in the diagrams as well: *Grasping the Sparrow's Tail*, for example, and the *Single Whip*. The longer he scrutinized the text, the more he could decipher: *Strumming the Lute, Finding the Needle at the Bottom of the Sea, Returning to the Mountain, Repulsing the Monkey, Cloudy Hands, Crane*

Standing on One Leg, and *Stepping up to the Seven Stars.* But there was much he did not recognize as well, and as he focused on the pictures, they began to shift under his gaze and vibrate, moving across the wrinkled page in a continuous snakelike loop, as if the small, delicate ink figures pictured in various stances and poses were alive.

Scrutinizing closely, the Starlord perceived pictures of the twelve animals of the zodiac, but as he stared at them, the horse, turtle, and toad faded into a pale yellow script and then into an acidlike stain on the paper. After that, the bear and fox blurred into a purplish black blot and slowly disappeared like a healing bruise, followed by the lizard, which flashed a sunset green and then vanished from the page. Next, the phoenix, an exact replica of the one on the Prince's golden necklace, and the yellow-winged bat both turned ruby red and disappeared, leaving only a bloodlike discoloration on the spot they had occupied. And right before his wondering eyes, the crane, white tiger, and dragon, all variously posed on a beautifully drawn representation of the moon, began to rotate like spinning wheels, so that the Prince grew slightly dizzy trying to differentiate one from the other and had to close his eyes to keep his balance. When he opened them, only the white tiger remained, plus the monkey, in a martial pose, glowing sapphire blue. Beneath these impressive painted figures the parchment was covered with minute spidery diagrams of the white tiger fighting form. And, still warming the Prince's hand, was the perfect pearl.

Careful not to wake Monkey, the Prince cradled the pearl as he left the cave and made his way by the light of the moon toward the forest glen where he had seen the ghostlike head of the white tiger appear to him in the waterfall. There was no apparition now, but the Starlord stood by the swiftly flowing water and began to move according to the illustrations in the manuscript retrieved from the third eye of the River Goddess. The pearl gave forth a soft light, illuminating the page so that he could see the drawings clearly. As soon as he progressed to the stance called *Embracing the Tiger*, the air grew turbulent, and the waterfall foamed and spouted like a fountain, whipping his brow with windblown spray.

This time, when the tiger appeared and once again, roared, the Prince, as if in a trance, opened the locket of his mother's necklace, rolled the scroll tightly, and hid it behind the golden phoenix, whose ruby eyes flashed once as he snapped the latch. Then the Starlord walked without hesitation into the tiger's wide-open mouth, still holding the glowing pearl and Dragon Rain directly in front of him to guide his way through the watery darkness.

Tribes of fairy shrimp darted here and there, trailing a phosphorescent glow and emitting a strange high-pitched vibration. Clustering around the Prince, a few of them clung to him; and although tiny, they seemed to be weighing him down. Instinctively, he directed the blue light of Dragon Rain through the center of their congregation where they gathered most thickly, and instantly, they were dispelled like leaves in a windstorm; but their moans as they vanished were ghostlike, and in their wake they left a paralyzing chill. He realized he had encountered a small band of ponaturi, servants of Yamu, one of the many tribes of demons Monkey had warned him lived in these waters.

Soon the Prince found himself in a stone cave, much smaller than his home in the Water Curtain Cave but equally dry. Here, no bowls or cups were set out for his comfort. Greeting him instead was a fiercely realistic wax statue of the frightening white tiger itself. So lifelike was the replica that when the Starlord caught sight of it, he froze in his tracks.

In the same instant, the Prince remembered the story Monkey had told him on the mountain about his true father and the origins of Dragon Rain, and in a sudden flood of relief the Prince knew himself to be under the remote and watchful eye of the notorious teacher and sculptor Zheng, who resided in Heaven. Further evidence of the presence of an immortal was the round white pearl in the center of the beast's striped waxen brow, an exact replica of the one the River Goddess had bestowed upon him. And the flickering shadow the tiger cast upon the limestone floor was not that of a four-legged beast at all, but rather of a man, the wavering silhouette of a crippled beggar, holding his rice bowl in one hand and his crooked crutch in the other.

CHAPTER THIRTY-EIGHT

Guardian Ape

Miracle is faith's favorite child.—The Master Hand

Monkey grew quite frantic as hour after hour he waited in vain for the Prince to show up for his lessons. The boy had never been late before, and Monkey was visited by a disquieting sense that he might be in danger. The guardian ape drank his jasmine tea, plagued by the morning residue of restless fears that had been pursuing him each night for the past month. Often he had been shaken awake by horrendous visions of the Starlord stampeded by a throng of horrible creatures from the depths of the earth.

The night before Monkey had dreamt that he and the Prince were living again in the Emperor's castle, built on the back of a sleeping land dragon. When the monster awoke and shook its gigantic tail, violent molten eruptions swallowed thousands. As volcanoes triggered floods and earthquakes all over the earth, disasters proliferated until not one man nor one remnant of man's civilization survived, but all was reduced to an ashy wasteland, devastated by fire and flood, polluted and poisoned for generations to come.

Immersed in dark thoughts, Monkey began to view his peaceful life with the Prince in a less favorable light. We can't go on living in this cave forever, he thought, shaking his head sadly. I'm a fine fighter for a monkey, but now I'm Monkey, Guardian of the new Starlord, the only hope for saving mankind.

He contemplated his wishing rod. "This weapon is good enough when all I do is teach sword fighting to a child and feast on fruit and nuts with djinns and fairies," he said to himself, "but some day soon we're going to have to leave this shelter and return to the dangers of the world. And what then? How will I defend the Starlord against the immortal Yamu and his demons, if I'm not immortal myself? With only this one wishing rod, what chance do I have against the Lord of the Dead?"

And so, with the shadow of Monkey's anxiety for the Prince's safety clouding his mind, the entire morning passed and still, the Prince did not return. Monkey brooded and his old longing to be the first ape to achieve immortality, submerged by his love for the Starlord since their christening in the Master Hand's ball of fire, rose up with renewed vigor. With the repetitive power of a nightmare, ambition conquered him once again. Succumbing to his Monkey nature, he began to scheme, and by the time the sun was high in the sky, he had come up with a plan to visit Heaven, temporarily leaving the Prince behind. Once there, he would humbly beg for private instruction in the mysteries of the universe, gain access to the Master Hand's divine laboratory, and figure out the famous formula for the elixir of eternal life.

Faced with the prospect of a journey, Monkey realized how restless he had become in the Water Curtain Cave and how much he welcomed the possibility of a new adventure. Enlisting the djinns, he began to repair the makeshift raft he had clung to when the bridge collapsed. Energetically, he scraped it free of lichens and moss, added logs, and lashed the platform together with strong vines. Now that he had a strategy, he was less worried about the Prince's absence, convincing himself that the lad had taken some well-deserved time to wander and explore.

But once the raft was completed and the Prince had still not made an appearance, Monkey's dark mood returned, and panic once again began to clutch at his heart. He thought of all the demons he had encountered in every lifetime and imagined them attacking the boy, one after the other. In each horrible vision, the Prince grew younger and younger, until he was once again a baby, as Monkey had first discovered him.

Finally, Monkey could stand it no longer. Taking a small bundle of provisions and using his wishing rod as a steering pole, he hopped aboard the raft and let the river take him wherever it would, praying that the River Goddess, who had protected them so well in the past, would lead him straight to the Starlord.

Monkey navigated through meandering tributaries for the rest of the afternoon, searching in vain for the Prince, until at long last he drew near the place of many waterfalls and saw a powerful blue light emanating from one of the caves. Stealthily, he maneuvered the raft right up to the entrance and peered inside.

To Monkey's shock, he saw an enormous white tiger, padding slowly and regally toward him. Without thinking, he raised his wishing rod defensively, and the tiger paused, regarding him with intelligent eyes. Then Monkey, looking past the beast, gasped. The blue light that had at first attracted him was issuing from the raised palm of a commanding figure just behind the white tiger. He had not yet noticed Monkey but was absorbed in a catlike walking meditation, gracefully moving through the difficult White Tiger form. It was none other than Prince Zong, demonstrating more knowledge than his Monkey master!

Letting out a loud "Aiiieee!" Monkey advanced aggressively on the tiger, who instantly turned into the wax statue he had been when the Prince had first entered the cave. This alarming transformation left Monkey speechless. Yet Prince Zong did not seem to notice, nor did he interrupt his practice. Looking through Monkey as if he were not there, he continued progressing evenly through the demanding form to the last deliberate move, whereupon he stood in a strange trance for a long time. Finally, he raised both arms over his head, and then brought them down very gradually, so that it looked as if he were reading his own palms like a book. Then he raised his arms again and brought them down swiftly, as if he would fly away, and the blue light faded. The Prince's eyes seemed to clear, and he saw Monkey standing there, a look of betrayal upon his face.

"You've been keeping secrets from me!" the ape said accusingly.

The Starlord shook his head. "I've been keeping secrets from *myself*," he answered, dazed.

"Who brought you here?" Monkey asked angrily. "And why didn't you tell me? I was beside myself with worry all day long."

"I'm sorry you were worried," said the Prince gently. "But there was nothing to tell until today."

"That's impossible!" snapped Monkey. "It takes years to perfect the White Tiger form. Even a Starlord couldn't learn it in one day."

Gazing at Monkey, who appeared to be wracked with jealousy and rage, the Prince decided not to mention the scroll. The River Goddess Yin Dang had bestowed it upon him, not Monkey. Besides, in addition to being a gift from the River Goddess, it was, in the Prince's mind, also a gift from his mother. She had spoken to him in a dream and had led him to the white pearl. He had no desire to reveal the scroll to anyone else, at least not until he had a chance to study it himself.

Still smarting from the Prince's elusive behavior and the mystery of his sudden acquisition of superior martial skills, Monkey revealed his intention of traveling to Heaven. "You may be happier with me out of the way for a little while," he suggested huffily, hoping the Prince would beg him to stay.

The Starlord studied his companion thoughtfully. "I will miss you, Monkey," he said.

Monkey shrugged, slightly mollified. "I suppose as soon as I'm gone, *you'll* be busy with your new teacher," he said sullenly. "Let me guess. Is it the Tattooed Monk?"

The Prince sighed and shook his head. "I have no new teacher, unless you count the River Goddess, who comes to me in my dreams. And I've never met the Tattooed Monk," he answered truthfully.

"Never fear, you shall," Monkey promised, rolling his eyes up to Heaven. "He'll show up sooner or later. Just don't believe everything he tells you about me."

"Maybe you should wait until we've finished my training and then take me with you," suggested the Prince.

Monkey hesitated, then shook his head, appeased by the Prince's respectful request. "There are dangers out there you know nothing about," he said, as if speaking to a young child. "That's why I have to go alone this time. But I'll come back a better guardian, I promise."

"You're a good enough guardian now," the Prince protested, sensing the fast fading presence of the Immortal Beggar as the tiger's strangely human shadow slowly dissolved. It suddenly dawned on him that Monkey was not thinking of leaving sometime in the indeterminate future but was planning to depart that very day. "Didn't the Master Hand tell you to watch over me? How can you leave me just like that?"

"You don't need me as much anymore," said Monkey. "If what I just saw is any indication, you know more than I do, now."

"But you decided to leave *before* today, Monkey, admit it. You've been thinking about this for a long time, haven't you?" Now it was the Prince's turn to feel betrayed, but Monkey shook his head.

"Heaven beckoned me today just as the white tiger called to you," he said. "I don't know what lies in store for me up there—trouble, most likely. But I know I can't stay here any longer."

The Prince, knowing he could not convince the ape to change his mind, came forward and hugged his teacher warmly. Impulsively, he slipped the white pearl from the River Goddess into the pocket of his guardian's vest, where it glowed brightly, illuminating the scroll Monkey had found the day Chac had saved his life at Dragon Bone Lake. Ha! thought the Prince with some satisfaction, Monkey has his own scroll he's never told *me* about!

"Come back as soon as you can," the Prince whispered with tears in his eyes. Monkey returned the Starlord's embrace and warned him to stay out of trouble while he was gone. "Monkeys do not weep," he said, his voice unsteady. "Perhaps when I'm immortal, I will learn, but then there will be no need for tears in Heaven."

Suddenly, Monkey was seized by a premonition of a long, sad separation. For an instant, he wondered if the danger would be worth the reward. Even if he did manage to become immortal, what good would it do if the Prince were to die, or if somehow they never saw one another again?

"Before I go," he said, impulsively, waving the wishing rod. "I'll teach you the defensive art of replication, should you ever need to be more than one Starlord."

So with only the waxen white tiger as witness, Monkey rashly replicated his precious wishing rod and kept the less valuable one for himself, offering the Prince the Master Hand's original with its handle of yellow jade set with two sapphires as blue as his own eyes. As they bade one another farewell, he gave the Starlord a lesson in how to multiply. But try as he might, there was always only just one Starlord gazing solemnly back at him; and as the light faded from the sky, Monkey finally pressed his parting gift into the Chosen One's hand and set off on his journey toward Heaven.

CHAPTER THIRTY-NINE

Spotted Leopard

Havoc is a necessity.—Yamu, Lord of the Dead

T he Tattooed Monk, who had never truly seen Silver Lotus fight, was filled with admiration for her skill. She combined what the monk had taught her of the White Tiger with what she had learned of the martial arts at the palace into her own graceful and elusive style, and although she had less physical power than the bandit Golden Wings, she was observant and decisive, and held her own in round after round. Truly, she is Gong Sun's daughter, thought the Tattooed Monk.

Now Silver Lotus feinted, deliberately letting Golden Wings close in. Then she drew her sword and faced the armored bandit in close combat, countering move for move. Golden Wings was strong, an impassioned fighter and skilled with her flashing twin scimitars, but the two women were evenly matched and neither could gain the advantage. Parrying the other's double blades, which whirled like the blur of snowflakes in the wind, Silver Lotus sucked the darts she had been holding between her teeth into her mouth and, gathering her breath, released them with great force. Wrapping a taut wire around the golden warrior's waist, she quickly tightened another trip cord across the girl's ankles. Deflecting the darts in midair and slicing through the cords, Golden Wings recovered herself, then came at Silver Lotus with renewed abandon, like a towering goddess of war.

Keeping one watchful eye on Silver Lotus, the Tattooed Monk struck blow after blow, downing dozens of Spotted Leopard's renegades as they charged, and holding the gang successfully at bay. His lightning staff sliced to the right and then to the left, in a maneuver that repeatedly took his opponents by surprise. Swarming like bees, the brigands rushed to reorient themselves after the monk's first brutal onslaught, tripping over one another and screaming.

By the ordinary laws of nature, the monk should have been trapped by the rogues attacking him from every side, downed by their collective strength, but as the men nearest the monk stumbled backward, they pushed the men behind them into the oncoming group and for a time they all foundered about, frightened by the monk's ferocity.

The monk fought like a swimmer battling giant waves, striking once then retreating a step or two, giving more attention to defense than to attack. He refrained from cutting down men who stumbled into his range if they were no immediate threat to his life. Although easy prey, he knew their deaths would only expose him further to his enemies' swords.

None of Spotted Leopard's men seemed eager to get too close to the monk. Whenever a knot of men came at him head on, he contrived to shift to the weakest corner of their formation, attacking obliquely and picking off one or two of them at a time. Spotted Leopard strategically positioned himself on the sidelines and tried to down the monk with a well-placed arrow, but the loud twang was followed a split second later by the glint of the monk's short sword flashing through the air, and the arrow broke in two. After that, the general started fighting with both weapons at once. If his attacker moved to the right, he brought the staff into full play, sweeping it in a broad horizontal arc. But if his enemy moved the other way, the monk trapped him, pinning the man in place with the small sword and finishing him with his staff.

Now Spotted Leopard brought his own ax down from above, only to see it knocked into the air by a powerful counterblow. On Spotted Leopard's head was a stolen imperial soldier's helmet of pure steel with a long red tassel dangling behind. He wore chain mail bound at the waist by a gold-plated girdle with a leaping-leopard clasp, also lifted from a fallen warrior in a long-ago skirmish with the Emperor's militia. A leather whip hung from his left shoulder, a bow and a quiver of arrows from his right, and animal face plates, front and back, gave him added protection. But the monk, unprotected except for his staff and short sword, lunged and lunged again and, like a god of fire and fury, moved unchallenged among the warlord's tribe, making short work of anyone who came within his range. He was in a towering rage, his lust for revenge reawakened, and in the face of his wrath, Spotted Leopard was among those who reeled back.

Silver Lotus surveyed her surroundings for a place to retreat out of the open and began to edge toward the monk's white yurt behind her. She had fought well, holding her own against the daring Golden Wings, whose lack of restraint and strength of attack was beyond anything she had ever encountered. But now Silver Lotus had begun to tire, and, seeing her opportunity, Golden Wings was moving in for the kill. The girl had kept most of Spotted Leopard's men at bay throughout the fight, enjoying the fair challenge of a well-balanced match, but the bandits, thwarted by the monk's continued resistance, smelled blood, and they swooped down on the two like vultures flying in for a feast.

Suddenly, the monk was advancing furiously toward Silver Lotus, downing bandits right and left, leaping over heads, cutting his way toward her. Madly, he smashed through a bristling mob of brigadiers wielding bludgeons, chains, hooks, truncheons, halberds, spears, and rakes, and wherever he landed, he left a mass of bleeding warriors, moaning and frantically attempting to staunch their wounds while scrambling away from the wide arc of his avenging arm.

Then Spotted Leopard himself again loomed up and attacked the monk furiously, swinging his ax. The monk pressed forward to meet him. They clashed in the center of the field of battle, each exerting his utmost strength and skill.

"Beware, Monk," shouted the Leopard. "How dare you murder my men! Watch me cut you to ribbons!"

"Demon!" answered the Tattooed Monk. "I'm surprised these many will still serve you. They're better off dead."

Roaring with rage, Spotted Leopard smote his own breast shield with the blunt end of his ax, sending forth fiery red sparks. Immediately, a black mist rose and rolled toward the monk. Waving his weapon in the air, the Leopard closed his gimlet eyes and muttered a few words under his breath. Then he raised his clawlike gloved hand in a cabalistic sign.

At this signal from their leader, each of his men put a reed whistle to his lips and blew an eerie, high-pitched blast. As the sound mounted to an almost unbearable pitch, a wild wind howled, and sand began to fly as if a dust storm had suddenly descended. The heavens shook, stones rolled, and the earth quaked.

The sorcerer's spell swept like a gale across the desert toward the place where the monk stood, and darkness covered half the sky. The effect was so alarming, many of the Leopard's own followers turned and fled in cowardly disarray, their terrified horses bolting toward the obscured horizon. Emerging from the approaching cloud came hissing streaks of vapor that took the shapes of strange black serpents, converging on the monk and wrapping themselves around his neck.

The monk lifted his staff toward the heavens and loudly intoned a holy incantation. Just as suddenly as the accursed tempest had appeared, it abated. A golden ray of sun shot out like a finger from a hovering cloud and dissipated the trails of smoke, releasing the monk. Then a single bolt of lightning burst from the sky, sending a liquid ball of flame straight toward his upraised staff. The monk pointed the blazing torch straight at Spotted Leopard, who fell back with a sharp cry, holding his face as if burnt. Yelling at the top of his lungs, the monk charged forward, intent upon finding and protecting Silver Lotus. But just as the monk reached her, the moment of confidence he had allowed himself vanished like the disastrous shift in the weather.

An inky cloud of suffocating fumes closed in around them; the skies opened up and erupted in a cataclysmic blast of fire; and everything went dark. He called out her name. Then, for the second time in his life, the monk watched his home go up in flames with an explosive roar, and glimpsed the colossal wing of a great monster, a long serpentine neck, and the baneful glare of a giant reptilian eye.

It had come again, just as the monk had feared. Again, he called her name, but at the very same moment the Tattooed Monk felt the dragon's scouring breath, he heard the voice of Yamu, reaching into his mind. *What is the point of resenting fire for its heat?* laughed the Lord of the Dead. *Ask yourself this: are you well nourished by memory? In the land of the dead, ghosts relinquish all memories, the most painful first, although a few souls do escape my probing. You, for example, have escaped me through too many generations, Monk. Give me your memories now, escape your pain.*

Resisting the voice, the monk toppled precipitously into the inferno, taking several of Spotted Leopard's men down with him. Bellowing in agony just before losing consciousness, he recognized Old Bones and knew that he had failed.

Catastrophe had once again struck his resurrected heart, consuming him in a horror as dark and irredeemable as the black volcanic ash that had buried the Temple of the Five Blessings.

CHAPTER FORTY

The Hall of Penetrating Light

The hardest thing to escape from is the wish to escape.
—The Master Hand

Monkey's journey to Heaven was swift and uneventful, and when he arrived, all the immortals were rushing toward the Hall of Penetrating Light for the Master Hand's millennial peach banquet.

Without considering the consequences, Monkey put up his paw like a director of traffic, informing everyone of a fabricated change of address.

"Halt!" he cried. "Wise ones, I've been asked by the Master Hand to tell you that the rehearsal will take place at the Pool of Green Jade."

"What rehearsal?" they asked in chorus, searching their memories in vain for any instructions they might have received about a rehearsal. "We've never had to rehearse before."

"This time you do," said Monkey with authority, rushing on before the Red-Legged Ones and some of the others who had been present at his trial arrived and recognized him.

"About face, about face," he directed as he raced through the crowd, waving the wishing rod, and they all miraculously followed his instructions, turning in the opposite direction like a herd of unsuspecting sheep. When he was sure they were safely out of sight, Monkey, grinning at his successful ruse, proceeded toward their original destination.

A magnificent feast was set out in the Hall of Penetrating Light, including an enormous porcelain bowl filled to the brim with the Master Hand's pale yellow peaches of knowledge, just plucked from the heavenly orchard where they ripened once every thousand years. Beside the tower of delicious fruit was a tall carafe of his Elixir of Eternal Life, which had been bubbling on a burning hearth in the Master Hand's inner sanctum for ten thousand years.

Standing guard around the sumptuous table were Thousand-League Eye, Down-the-Wind Ear, as well as all nine Red-Legged Ones, alert with excitement and anticipation, each scuttling back and forth officiously, scanning the corridors in every possible direction for troublemakers. Monkey was certain the Celestial Detective was lurking in a hidden corner as well, just waiting for some unwary thief to appear.

The peaches gave forth such a delicious aroma that Monkey almost swooned. He plucked a few hairs from his tail, then chewed them into tiny bits and spat them out, crying "Change!" The hairs instantly transformed into a troop of whining mosquitoes that sailed forth and stung all the servants guarding the fruit, sending them into a deep slumber. Thousand League's farseeing eyes closed, Down-the-Wind's far-reaching hearing dimmed, the Red-Legged Ones collapsed in a tangled heap, and the Celestial Detective tumbled out of his hiding place in the pantry onto the kitchen floor, where he fell asleep behind the oven, emitting noisy snores.

Now Monkey was free to eat to his heart's content, gulping peach juice down his gullet. But before he could drink one drop of the sage's elixir, he heard the angry immortals approaching, looking for the stupid beast who had sent them in the wrong direction. In his panic, Monkey dropped the pitcher of the precious formula on the marble floor, spilling the elixir and sending shards of shattered glass all over the room. Taking one last succulent peach with him, Monkey beat a hasty retreat, hiding in the royal pantry just as his pursuers burst through the doors to the banquet hall.

Monkey knelt behind the thin curtain that separated him from the immortals and, knowing he would soon be trapped like a rat in its hole, prayed aloud to the Master Hand: "The peaches were delicious, sir. I know I shouldn't have stolen them, but I didn't just eat to fill my belly, you know. It wouldn't do for the Guardian of a Starlord to be just another ignorant monkey, would it? As for the elixir, well—I couldn't bear the thought that someday I would die, Your Honor, and leave the boy behind. I know I've done wrong." Here he paused and knocked his head against the hard floor several times, adding in a choked voice, "Please be merciful."

The Master Hand, listening from his throne room, shook his head sadly. "If Monkey were still stone," he said sighing, "I would scatter him to the four quarters. But he is a guardian now, and he has sinned out of love. How shall I punish him, Calabash, without doing harm to our Starlord?"

The Tattooed Monk, standing by the Master Hand's side, scowled darkly, rubbing his itching wounds. After being left for dead in the desert, he was not happy to find himself recalled to Heaven while Silver Lotus was once again adrift among evil men in the world of mortals. He glared at the Master Hand, his dark eyes blazing under beetling brows.

"Give that monkey your arm, and he'll take your leg. Give him your leg, and he'll take the other. Give him both legs, and he'll eat your head. There is no way to satisfy that monkey," he answered gruffly. "He loves no one but himself."

"Then what would you suggest?" asked the Master Hand politely.

"I would suggest you stop asking me for my suggestions when you don't listen anyway and let me go back to the desert. Monkey does not concern me. I can think of nothing but Silver Lotus. Are you holding me here just to torture me? Haven't I suffered enough? If you're not going to let me find her, you should have let me die."

"Stop feeling sorry for yourself," said the Master Hand, "and give me an answer. If Monkey can't be guardian to the Starlord, then you must take his place. Has it never occurred to you that the Prince may soon be *your* responsibility? Here you are lamenting the loss of the former First Consort when the fate of the entire universe may hang on your sword. Where's your fighting spirit, Monk?"

"My warrior days are over, sir," said General Calabash

wearily, indicating his injuries. "I've lost to Yamu too many times. He's taken my wife and child, my closest friend, Gong Sun, and now perhaps Silver Lotus. How do you expect me to protect the Starlord against him?"

"You're still a warrior, Calabash," said the Master Hand, frowning. "You'll always be a warrior. You were once a husband and a warrior; a father and a warrior; a friend to a fellow monk and a warrior. And you were once guardian of the Starlord's mother and a warrior. Now you are no longer a husband, a father, a friend to Gong Sun. But you are still guardian to the Starlord's mother and, whether you know it or not, to the Starlord himself. And you are still, above all else, a warrior."

"I love her," answered the Tattooed Monk. "That has nothing to do with your plans for me, does it?"

"I have nothing against love."

"Then let me go to her," pleaded the General.

"I need you here," said the Master Hand. "If you go anywhere, it will be to her son. She'll be grateful to you for that."

"She's in Spotted Leopard's hands. She may not be alive to be grateful, if I don't find her soon."

The Master Hand sighed. "She is safe, sir. Unhappy but safe. She is a warrior as well. Adversity will not kill her. It will only make her stronger. You will see her again, I promise you that. More, I cannot promise, for the outcome of the war to come is unknown." He placed one hand on the Tattooed Monk's shoulder, gazing into his eyes. "You must fight for me in that war, Calabash, even if you are only fighting for her."

"And if she dies," said the Tattooed Monk, "then I will die trying to save her. And next time, you shall not bring me back."

"Is that a threat?" asked the Master Hand, raising one eyebrow.

"Call it a clumsy attempt at striking a bargain," answered the monk humbly.

"Listen to me," said the Master Hand, urgently now. "Monkey has his eyes on the pot while he is eating out of the bowl. He comes in search of immortality, not realizing it is within his grasp on earth. You wish to shed your immortality in pursuit of love, not realizing that this path, too, is entirely open to you. Ironically, both of you look to me for the answer."

He shrugged, then broke into a smile, his eyes shining with amusement. "Have you considered that perhaps you and Monkey can help one another? Why don't you give up your place in Heaven to the ape?" He looked at General Calabash expectantly, grinning broadly now.

"I'm glad my predicament amuses you," said the monk bitterly. "If you must torment me with these ridiculous riddles, my lord, then let me at least torment someone else who deserves it. Leave Monkey's punishment to me."

The Master Hand hesitated a moment, fixing General Calabash with a penetrating stare. Then he nodded. "Poor Monkey," he said. "He's all yours, sir. But remember, he must be kept alive."

"What a pity," said the Tattooed Monk, turning and limping away.

But the Master Hand noticed to his supreme satisfaction that there was a new spring to the general's step as he exited.

CHAPTER FORTY-ONE

Mountain of the Five Elements

A soul must sometimes shrink before it can find its true size.
—The Tattooed Monk

"The way out is not always through the door," said the Tattooed Monk conversationally, appearing before Monkey as he cowered in his hiding place. "But perhaps you have no intention of leaving? At least in here"—and he gave the pantry a sweeping glance—"you'd never run out of delicacies. But we have a less delicious prison in mind for you."

"Have you been sent to punish me?" asked Monkey, cringing against a shelf that held jars of the rarest dried mushrooms.

"To torture you," corrected General Calabash, looming a step closer.

"Suppose I run away?" said Monkey, cautiously rising to his feet.

"Go ahead," said General Calabash with ominous self-assurance. "It will be more amusing that way. Unfortunately, I have not been authorized to end your life but only to make it miserable for its pathetic duration."

Without another word, Monkey sprang up into the air, whipped out his wishing rod, and instantly changed himself into a replica of the Tattooed Monk. "Now I am as powerful as you, Calabash!" he laughed defiantly. "In fact, I challenge you, General, to tell us apart!" And belligerently he waved his wishing rod, which had also grown in size. "Do your worst, Monk, and I shall match it," Monkey taunted.

The monk waved his hand, and immediately Monkey was surrounded by an army of thunder deities. Beset on all sides by bristling weapons and stormy, earsplitting cracks and crashes, Monkey gave himself three heads and six arms and, multiplying the wishing rod, whirled his six magic cudgels like the spokes of a windmill, so fast and furiously that no one dared come too close.

When the thunderous noise of the frustrated deities reached the Master Hand, he decided it was time to intervene.

"Monkey!" he roared, scooping the ape into the palm of his hand. "How dare you threaten my general and his hosts of heaven? Against the advice of my council, I gave you a last chance, yet you abuse my trust. No longer shall you be guardian to the Starlord, for you have abandoned him in pursuit of your own immortality."

"Forgive me, Master," replied Monkey boldly, resuming his original shape and kowtowing. "I left him only to return a better guardian. You may tell me I am no longer his guardian, but that does not make it so. I love the Prince, sir, and I will always be his guardian. I have done wrong, but so do parents do wrong, yet for that they do not lose their children."

"You have stolen my peaches, Monkey, and brought chaos to Heaven. And you have dared to raise my own wishing rod against me, a gift you promised to use well. How can I forgive you this time?"

At the mention of the peaches, Monkey grinned. "Your peaches have made me cleverer than ever, if I say so myself, sir. How about a wager? If I can jump off the palm of your hand, and somersault to the end of the world, then I am free to return to the Water Curtain Cave and use my new knowledge to protect the Prince for the rest of my natural life. And I swear I will never leave him again, unless he orders me to, and I will never again seek a shortcut to immortality."

"The Master Hand does not make wagers with the likes of you," growled the Tattooed Monk.

But the Master Hand unfurled his palm. "Jump then," he said, encouragingly.

Monkey threw one defiant look at the Tattooed Monk and leapt with all his might, somersaulting and whirling like a mad dervish. Still whirling, he landed the next night with a tremendous crash next to five pink pillars, sticking up into a starry sky. Plucking out one of his hairs, he blew on it, changing it into a writing brush and ink pad. On the base of the central pillar by the light of the moon he wrote: MONKEY WAS HERE. Then, moving to another pillar, he relieved himself before somersaulting back to Heaven and informing the Master Hand that he had indeed been to the end of the world.

"I win," he crowed. "I saw five pillars sticking up into the sky. I even wrote on one of them to prove I was there. I'll show you."

"Nasty ape, no need of that," said the Master Hand, disgustedly wiggling his fingers and dumping Monkey out. "Just look here." And to Monkey's horror, there at the base of the middle finger of the Master's Hand were the words he had just written, and in the Master's palm was a foul yellow puddle he recognized as his own.

"Impossible!" he spluttered, turning red with shame. "How did that get there? You've tricked me. I *was* at the end of the world. Let me go back and look. Your hand is only as large as a lotus leaf. How could it stretch that far?"

"The peaches have done you no good, ape," said the Master Hand wearily. "No brute is as dumb as the mortal who does not know his own size. Perhaps I was truly mistaken and you are just a little thief and will always be one. Monk, I leave this arrogant beast to you." And, sighing mightily, he withdrew.

"Your last boasting hour has come!" said the Tattooed Monk with some relish, as soon as the Master Hand was out of sight. Summoning his army of plant-headed divinities, he directed them to raise their bows and take aim.

"Have you any last words?" he asked Monkey and, without waiting for an answer, gave the signal to shoot, watching with satisfaction as his vegetable army cast a green net of thorny vines over the ape, trapping Monkey in a strangling mass of tendrils.

Monkey's heart fluttered as the prickly trap closed over him, and, thinking quickly, he hastily shrank his cudgel back into the size of a needle, hid it under his tongue, and changed himself into a holy shrine, his mouth disguised as the door, his tongue a guardian statue of the River Goddess, his two eyes, the windows. Not knowing quite what to do with his tail, he stuck it up straight behind him like a flagpole.

"Senseless ape!" roared the Tattooed Monk. "You know my archers would never attack a holy shrine or sink their thorns into an effigy of the River Goddess. But I have seen many hearth shrines in my wanderings and never has there been one with a flagpole sticking up behind! So the River Goddess must excuse me if I just bang in these windows with my fist and kick in these doors with my foot." And he approached to do just that.

Oh no, thought Monkey. If he kicks in my teeth and blinds my eyes, what kind of a guardian will I be then? So, tensing his muscles, he abandoned his ridiculous pose and, turning into a bat, leapt up toward the ceiling. He hovered there a moment, peering brightly down at his opponent before sailing out the window and up into the firmament. Turning back into Monkey, he upset the stately rhythm of the twenty-eight lunar mansions, the orderly rotation of the nine planets, the parade of the twelve hours, and the diamond-studded map of all the divine constellations, inscribed with the battle strategies of a hundred thousand heavenly soldiers. The Tattooed Monk, twirling his gourd so that it whined, summoned a host of warrior spirits in coiling dragon formation. Drawing a diamond snare from his belt, he threw it over Monkey, toppling the ape from the sky where he landed, sprawled among the Master Hand's golden sunflowers, before being dragged off in chains.

"There is defeat in victory and victory in defeat," Monkey

moaned as he tried to make his body go limp to avoid being bruised by the unceremoniously bumpy ride back to the palace. He paused to contemplate what he had just said. "Why, that sounds very much like wisdom," he told himself. "It must be those peaches. Perhaps there's hope for me, after all." But looking down at himself and taking in his sorry predicament, he moaned again. "I only pursued the beacon light of truth," he sighed. "And here I am once again, about to burn like a moth in flame."

"No burning, this time, ape," said the Tattooed Monk. "We have something more painful in mind for you."

"But you promised you wouldn't kill me," wailed Monkey.

"And I'll keep my word," said the Tattooed Monk, "unless you die of shame, of course."

And with that, General Calabash mounted a cloud and, dangling Monkey, still trussed up helplessly in the snare like a sack of oranges, parted the heavenly mist so that the ape could look down upon the demon-infested forest of the Water Curtain Cave, where the Starlord, oblivious to approaching danger, was curled fast asleep beneath the true statue of the River Goddess.

Angry clouds of red waspish creatures no bigger than flies hovered around the Prince's head, scratching small drops of fiery venom into his skin as he slept. He tossed and turned, groaning and throwing a protective arm over his eyes. The strange insects swarmed over his pale skin so that it looked as if he were sweating blood.

"Lion ants!" breathed Monkey.

Growing in the narrow crevices and gullies outside the cave

were a number of tiny trees, their trunks twisted and crumpled by the winds, each bearing a small cluster of bright golden fruit, shining dully as the sun rose. Upon each stem perched a round-eyed djinn, alert to the changing light. In the long grasses by the base of the trees grew clusters of purple orchids and the rocks were covered with a thick mat of convolvulus, from which dangled many ivory-colored, trumpet-shaped flowers. Inside each blossom, a green fairy sat, clad in a morning robe of polished leaves, calmly watching the dawn.

As Monkey beheld the sun rising, and the gathered congregation of djinns and fairies, a wave of homesickness swept over him just as a great dark cloud spread out over the familiar landscape, trailing a heavy red shadow in its wake. The tall pile of rocks, the bright flowers, and the shaggy and misshapen trees stood out starkly for a moment against a scarlet sky. A slight wind teased the grasses, bringing forth a lisping rustle like demons whispering.

Suddenly, a lone mongoose uttered an ear-piercing shriek, and a speckled owl flew up out of the scrub pine, dropping a flurry of white feathers and whirling off into the sky as if caught in a snowstorm. It seemed a signal for the djinns and fairies to flee, whereupon their abandoned fruit and trembling white trumpet flowers turned a deep crimson, instantly covered in a crawling mass of the same tiny, red-winged army that plagued the Prince as he slept.

The tattered fringe of forest surrounding the Water Curtain Cave erupted into the tumultuous flight of a million sharp-toothed animals, pursued by ruby clouds of stinging insects, hurtling toward a hiding place in the brush. Thorns tore at the furious beasts as they scrambled and clawed their way through, feverishly racing for their lives. And through this frenzied exodus, the Prince slept on.

"In what dark tree, in which forest long vanished, was this darkest of punishments devised?" asked Monkey, stiffening with fear as he sensed what was about to happen.

"It was you who ran from him when he needed you," answered the Tattooed Monk sternly. "Should you be spared the consequences of your neglect? Watch, Monkey, and tear your heart from your guilty breast as he suffers."

And now Monkey spied Spotted Leopard and his men, dark blots on the darkening landscape, moving steadily toward the Prince's hideout, following the red cloud toward the Water Curtain Cave.

As they neared, the ape saw herds of yak and blue sheep stampeding wildly toward the forest. The sound of their thundering hooves did not reach as far as Heaven, and their undulating flight looked like a silent tidal wave, menacing and beautiful all at once.

And now all the creatures in the woods sensed what was coming and fled: lynx keeping company with tree shrews; red fox with wild boar; civets with musk deer; cobra with gray voles; bubbling grouse with honey buzzards; willow warblers with cuckoos, and then suddenly it was as if the roof of the world were blowing off and there were hares and tufted deer; leopards and porcupines; hill partridges and golden pheasants; sparrowhawks and whistling ducks; falcons and shrikes; chats and thrushes; redstarts, forktails, crowtits, and goldcrests; finches and kestrels; magpies and grebes; white storks and black storks;

ibises and purple herons; whooper swans and ringed plovers; orioles and titmice and fire-breasted flowerpeckers, all fleeing toward the rising sun as an ever-widening blood-red shadow spread out over the land.

At that moment, just as the only soul he loved in the world teetered on the brink of annihilation, Monkey felt he had never in his many lives seen nature so clearly. A hummingbird stopped still in the air for a moment, buzzing like a bee, and Monkey counted a hundred small blazingly bright feathers on its fragile neck alone as it whirred amid a thousand leaves before taking flight again. And beyond those leaves were a thousand more birds in flight.

Perhaps it was the peaches, or perhaps it was part of his punishment, but no detail did Monkey miss; never had his vision been so sharp. And suddenly, he could hear just as sharply, everything from the softest lisping and faintest trill to the bubbling cries to the deep boomings and piercing shrieks, all mixing in a terrifying concert of fear.

"Can't you stop it?" pleaded Monkey, not knowing exactly what he was asking of the monk.

"No," said General Calabash icily. "I cannot interfere."

"Release me!" yelled Monkey, struggling. "At least I can try to go to him, even if I leap to my death!"

"It's too late for heroics now," answered the monk quietly, tightening Monkey's bonds. "What you are seeing has already happened. You were stuffing yourself with peaches at the time. Your greed was so great, there was no room for anything else, was there? All that stolen knowledge, yet you had no clue the Prince was in mortal danger, did you?"

"Mortal danger?" quavered Monkey.

"And you *say* that you love him," said the Tattooed Monk accusingly.

Monkey felt at that moment that a roar as mighty as a lion's was trapped in his chest, and if he did not release it, he would burst apart. Monkey opened his mouth, inflated his chest and let loose with a long, stone-shattering howl, calling upon every monkey in the forest surrounding the Water Curtain Cave to gather and wake the sleeping Starlord.

The cry seemed to rip through time and space, burning through heaven like a green flame. Miraculously, the Prince awoke, his reddened eyes glazed, staring and wild with pain. His face, except for the birthmark and a small area around it, was inflamed and covered with bloody bites, and as he rose from his pallet of reed grass, he swiped at the thick mat of poisonous insects clinging to his arms and legs. Staggering, he made his way toward the portal that opened into the waterfall, desperate to drown the deadly pests in the torrent, and in his confusion ready to drown himself to be free of them.

Again, Monkey roared with all his might, and the Prince seemed to pause, listening. Then, reversing direction and still swinging at his own head like a bear beset by raging hornets, he backed up toward the statue of the River Goddess, stumbling like a drunken man. And now from behind the statue stepped an enormous blue-faced golden monkey, who stooped to collect the Starlord's wishing rod from the floor where it had fallen, gently placed it in his blue changing bag, and pressed the bag into his swollen hands. Delirious, the Prince accepted the gift from the ape and, whispering "Jade Mirror!" collapsed, kneeling, clutching it to his heart before falling forward and passing out.

Monkey, watching, held his breath, for he felt at that moment he had somehow become that golden monkey, giving some small comfort of memory and hope to the beleaguered Prince.

Startled by the roar and by the surprising appearance of the golden monkey in a vision he thought he controlled, the Tattooed Monk stepped back, and in that instant, Monkey pressed his advantage, reaching his long arm through the confining mesh to grab the monk's calabash, twirling it in his paws until it grew warm.

"Forgive me, Monk, but I need to see my future, for I cannot stand my past or present. Ah, I see here I am a deity perhaps or at the very least, a monkey king like the legendary Monkey King, with a dreadful commanding power beyond anything the wishing rod ever bestowed upon me. But tell me, Calabash, how shall I save the Prince?"

"If you do not return the gourd, I will disregard the Master Hand's instructions and end your thieving life right now," said the Tattooed Monk in a cold fury.

"Don't be angry, General. Please let me keep it," pleaded Monkey, gazing straight into the Tattooed Monk's unforgiving eyes. "I will find a way to give the gourd to the Starlord when the time is right. I promise."

"Your promises mean nothing, ape," said the Tattooed Monk. "And your timing is never right. The gourd is not yours to give, and you are no longer the Starlord's guardian. Why do you assume you will ever see him again? Besides, if you must know, this calabash is as empty as your heart. The one that contains the scrolls is in more trustworthy hands than my own."

"Monkey!" moaned the Prince's voice, floating up from the Water Curtain Cave. "Jade Mirror!"

"He's calling me," cried Monkey.

"Look at that!" came a deep scornful voice from the Water Curtain Cave. "He's fast asleep like a baby, calling for his Monkey and his nanny."

Circling Prince Zong was an ugly band of demonlike men, oozing mud and odors of the swamp onto the floor of the Water Curtain Cave. Following in their footsteps came a squelching band of hairy frog demons, further befouling the cave.

Looming over the helpless Starlord, Spotted Leopard came forward, reaching for the imperial necklace. Fiery light flashed from the ruby eyes of the golden phoenix, blinding and then burning him as he recoiled in excruciating pain.

Placing a pointed, mud-caked boot on the Prince's fevered chest, the bandit leader studied the Starlord for a moment before landing a vicious kick to his victim's heaving ribs. Then picking the Prince up by the hair, and shoving his own scarred face too close, he whispered hoarsely: "Listen, little Starlord. We will have that necklace if we have to cut off your head to get it." He waited patiently, watching the Prince struggling toward consciousness, his eyelids fluttering wildly. Just as the boy came to, the Leopard slapped him hard.

The Starlord slumped forward, moaning softly as Spotted Leopard pulled him to his feet, still holding him tightly by the hair. Gasping for breath, the Prince put a shaking hand to his neck, protecting the golden phoenix.

And now suddenly another distant roar sounded in the woods and the golden monkey, who had been crouching in a corner of the cave, let out a cry and danced before them like a clown, waving his spidery arms and pointing to the blue changing bag.

"Kill that idiot ape," snarled Spotted Leopard. But the Prince gathered his fading energy and spoke up: "He's a messenger. Let him . . . open the bag."

Suspiciously, the Leopard pointed his sword at the monkey's head and nodded, once. Retrieving the wishing rod, the golden monkey placed it in the Prince's hand, pointing to the Prince's necklace.

The Prince touched the rod to the necklace and Spotted Leopard watched intently, narrowing his black beady eyes. Suddenly, the heavy jewelry materialized around his own neck without leaving the Starlord's, and he slapped his knee and laughed uproariously, as his companions were one by one similarly adorned. The only discernible difference between the Starlord's original and the jewelry now worn by Spotted Leopard and his men were the eyes of the phoenix, which flashed a lizardlike emerald green instead of the Prince's ruby red. And still unique to the Starlord's own necklace was the scroll of the River Goddess hidden inside.

"Give me that!" roared Spotted Leopard, reaching for the wishing rod. But the Starlord had popped it back into the changing bag and passed it to the golden monkey. Leaping beyond the greedy bandit's grasp, the ape snatched Dragon Rain as well and was already dancing away into the forest, surrounded by identical golden monkeys so that from the back, Spotted Leopard could no longer tell which was the culprit.

"I want that wishing rod!" bellowed the Leopard.

"You have the necklace," said the Prince, smiling weakly. And swooning with the effort of speech, he was senseless to the blows Spotted Leopard and the others rained down upon his head. They wrapped him tightly in thick ropy vines and shoved him into a suffocating wooden cage, dumping a stinking mass of Yamu's hairy frog demons on top of him.

"If you have any pity, let me go! I can't bear it!" cried Monkey, watching from above. Releasing the gourd, he writhed in agony. "Of all the grievous wounds I've suffered in the pursuit of a place in Heaven, watching harm come to the Prince is the most cruel. And it's all my fault!"

"You must not look away," said the monk, placing a heavy hand upon Monkey's head and holding him in an iron grip. "The Prince is the Leopard's prisoner now, thanks to you."

Monkey closed his eyes, hot tears of remorse and regret blinding him for a moment. The swift flash of sublime power he had felt while gazing into the Tattooed Monk's calabash had faded. At least he had managed to save the wishing rod and Dragon Rain from falling into Spotted Leopard's hands. But where they were now, only the golden monkeys knew.

"Open your eyes," said the monk fiercely.

"I warn you, I'll go mad and escape that way!" cried Monkey, keeping them shut.

"You won't go mad," said the monk heartlessly. "It's not that easy to go mad from grief. It will do you good to hurt yourself with the past. You will have memories of this moment that will never cease to haunt you to the end of your monkey life."

"As your memories haunt you?" asked Monkey, suddenly turning a piercing gaze upon his captor. "Do you hurt yourself with the past, over and over again, cutting deeply and letting the wound heal only to cut again? Suddenly, I know you, monk."

"Look down and try to understand, ape," said the Tattooed Monk sternly. "Your story and mine are not important. The wind of the future blows from a new and colder continent. It has the power to freeze our universe. Perhaps it is within the Starlord's phoenix power to draw out of ashes another universe. But he does not yet know his own power, and so we do not yet know it either. For now, he is a prisoner, just like you."

"I'll make it up to him someday," whispered the ape abjectly, "He'll forgive me. If we both live to see one another again, he'll forgive me for leaving him. Tell me, monk, for I think you know—shall I ever see him again?"

The Tattooed Monk shook his head, turning away and muttering to himself, and Monkey paled and staggered back, reeling from the cruelty of the sentence until he forced himself to hear the general's words, repeated over and over again: "I don't know. I don't know." And with one of those quick flashes of insight he was just coming to recognize as his own, the ape realized the monk was thinking of himself and of someone else he longed to see again.

But now the Master Hand breathed on each of the Tattooed Monk's fingers, turning them into the five elements: metal, wood, water, fire, and earth. And the monk, following the Master Hand's instructions, pressed down upon Monkey heavily, sealing him beneath the five-peaked Mountain of Five Elements.

"Under this mountain you will do penance," intoned the Tattooed Monk. "You will have just enough air to breathe but no room to move and none to make mischief. Buried alive and sealed in iron (except for your foolish head, which sticks out like a turnip), you will have all the time in the world, ape, to think about your sins and be sorry."

And so, beneath the five-peaked mountain, the Tattooed Monk left the ape all alone, weighed down with grief and uncertain as to how long he would be held there.

"All I ever wanted was to be a better guardian," Monkey cried plaintively. But the Tattooed Monk was no longer listening. So, bowing his head, Monkey, who had never shed a single tear in ninety-nine lifetimes, wept as if his burdened heart would break.

CHAPTER FORTY-TWO

White Tiger

The soul never repeats itself.—The Master Hand

"Lead the white tiger home, and you will find between the two black strokes in the middle of her forehead, painted with a bold brush by the Master Hand, a pearl as round and bright as the moon," sang Silver Lotus, mournfully strumming on her dulcimer. "And if you tame that tiger, and take that pearl, you shall live forever."

She had slept not at all since her capture, unable to trust that she would wake again should she let her guard down even for a moment. The dulcimer had become her only distraction from her urgent need to rest. Golden Wings listened, guarding her prisoner.

"I would like to learn to play," said Golden Wings solemnly, after a while.

"I would be honored to teach you then," said Silver Lotus politely, deliberately interpreting her captor's request as a purely musical one and choosing to ignore what they both knew about the instrument's hidden barbs.

Signaling Golden Wings to move closer, she sat knee to knee with the girl warrior, balancing the dulcimer between them. "Follow me," she said gently. And Golden Wings replicated her finger movements, strumming when she strummed and resting when she rested.

"Did you spare my life in the desert so that I could give you music lessons?" asked Silver Lotus after a while, smiling slightly.

"Perhaps," answered Golden Wings, not returning her prisoner's smile. They sat peacefully close in the winter sun as if they had never confronted one another in a deadly struggle designed to send one of them to Yamu, but were just two beautiful young women, passing the time on a lazy afternoon. After a while, Golden Wings stopped playing. Silver Lotus continued to concentrate on the notes, not raising her eyes, her fingers caressing the strings.

"I did more than spare your life," said Golden Wings. "I rescued you from the fire. You would have burned with the monk."

Silver Lotus stopped playing now as well.

"It wasn't easy tearing you away from that monk. He was already dead and you seemed determined to die with him. Did you love him that much?"

Silver Lotus did not answer. Her pale face froze into a mask, cold and indifferent. She would not discuss the monk. Clearly, Spotted Leopard believed the dragon had killed him. It was better that way. But Silver Lotus did not believe he was dead.

"I wish I loved someone that much," said Golden Wings wistfully.

Again, she waited. But Silver Lotus just stared at her impassively.

"I saved you because—" Golden Wings broke off, as if she were still trying to understand her own motives for taking Silver Lotus prisoner instead of letting her die. "I saved you because there is no one here who fights as you do. I can beat all the men except for the Leopard himself—and he no longer practices with me now that I'm grown." She plucked disconsolately at the instrument.

"Lightly," Silver Lotus reminded her, breaking her silence. "Like this."

The girl adjusted her touch, bent over the strings, brooding. "If you were to sing a song just for me, what would it be?" she asked. She sounded suddenly like a child, almost innocent. Silver Lotus studied her, weaving random notes into a more melodic line, waiting for the words to come. Then she sang: "The orphan, old before her time, draws a secret honey from the blasted hive. Her voice like a dry locust sings of death."

Golden Wings listened intently and on the last note, cringed. "How do you know I'm an orphan?" she asked quietly.

"I didn't know," answered Silver Lotus, still strumming.

"I'm told Spotted Leopard spared my life in a raid on my village," said Golden Wings softly, looking down at the dulcimer and not at Silver Lotus. "I'm told I watched him slay my parents, but of course I do not remember that. I was a baby and he found me with a chert dagger clutched like a toy in my hands. Since he was superstitious, he interpreted it as a sign. I was the sole survivor of the massacre."

"I'm sorry," said Silver Lotus.

"He trained me as a warrior himself," Golden Wings went on. "When I was a child, I showed talent for handling swords, and he paid special attention to me." She trailed off and frowned. "But in the past year, he's changed. Since he tried to marry me off to T'sao T'sao and I refused, he hardly speaks to me anymore."

"I wonder how you came to have a chert dagger," said Silver Lotus carefully.

Golden Wings smiled. "One of the mysteries of my childhood," she answered. "Spotted Leopard wondered the same thing. How had a dagger so rare come to me, a peasant's daughter?"

Silver Lotus shuddered. "Before he died, the old Emperor commanded that all the chert daggers found in the kingdom be displayed near his corpse in the Gallery of Horrors," she said. "Your father must have been a master craftsman. It was a rare peasant who still owned so fine a blade when failure to register the weapons with the royal armory was a capital crime. Do you still have it?"

"Dare I confess to a former First Consort?" asked Golden Wings, laughing joylessly. "Yes, the dagger is my only inheritance and I treasure it," she said, lifting her chin proudly. "Spotted Leopard wanted it, of course. But he knew he would be sliced in the public square if they found it in his possession. So he let me keep it."

She laughed again, sharply. "He intends to claim ignorance of its existence if I'm ever caught." She paused, gazing at Silver Lotus. "And if I'm caught, I intend to use it to guide me swiftly to Yamu," she added.

As if conjured by the mention of the Lord of the Dead, a dark disheveled figure came weaving toward them, mumbling to himself. Unsheathing his own dagger, he stood there, gazing dumbly at the weapon. "The brat hasn't earned his brand," he complained loudly. "I should be the one to remove it." The brigand flicked his wrist to demonstrate the rudimentary gouging procedure he had in mind. "Cost me my reputation, didn't he?" he said, slurring his words. "I'd be glad to get rid of that nasty mark for him. I'd be doing him a service."

T'sao T'sao came to a grinding halt in front of the two women, eyeing them hungrily. He rocked back on his heels. "Eh, what's this? Learning to be an imperial consort, Golden Wings?" he asked.

"Leave us, T'sao T'sao," she warned. "You're drunk."

"I'm not," he wheedled, breathing heavily and coming closer. "I should have had first crack at the boy," he whined, finding the thread of his complaint once again. "I'm the one who followed the ape to the waterfall. That birthmark was sent to the wrong man, if you ask me. What gives a Prince the right to look like an outlaw when he's just the dregs and refuse of the royal court?" He stopped, wiping drool from his lips with his sleeve. Golden Wings recoiled in disgust.

Upon hearing the word birthmark, Silver Lotus had frozen and was staring at T'sao T'sao.

"Maybe you were too busy with that infernal instrument to

hear them come into camp last night." T'sao T'sao grinned at her, happy to be the bearer of bad news. "Or maybe you just didn't recognize your own son. His face doesn't look so pretty anymore, does it?"

Silver Lotus cast an agonized look at Golden Wings, then rose and, clutching her dulcimer, strode purposefully toward Spotted Leopard's tent. Golden Wings moved as if to stop her but then followed, ignoring T'sao T'sao, who trailed behind them like a beaten dog. When he reached his leader's headquarters, he hesitated, skulking by the entrance.

Although he heard rough voices all around him, the Prince was reluctant to discover what they wanted of him. He was in the middle of a dream, and the illusion was so soothing, he was not sure he would ever want to awaken. Perhaps, he thought, it was the pain that had sent him back in this dream to the Water Curtain Cave. The louder the bandits' taunting cries, the more intense was his distress until the agony built so unbearably he knew no way to withstand it other than to escape into his mind.

"He's waking up," came a bandit's voice, too close to his ear.

An unholy din filled the air, a loud persistent buzzing and a shrill whine. Seeking comfort and relief in his reverie, the Prince found himself at the feet of the River Goddess, hiding his swollen face in her cool, carved robes. He pressed hard against her, as if he would disappear into her shadow. To his amazement, she moved, revealing the earthen doorway to a secret underground chamber which the Prince, familiar with every marble detail of the statue, had never noticed before. Passing his hands along the smooth walls in the dim light, he crawled on hands and knees into what appeared to be a subterranean tomb. The air inside was close, making it difficult to breathe. A pungent odor of rotting leaves prevailed. Suffocating, the Prince burrowed deeper, searching for an open passageway. Suddenly, the narrow space became littered with dislodged bones and random piles of crumbling skeletal fragments.

"Slap him again," came a voice, breaking into his dream.

The Prince's head rang. Someone had struck him, hard. His mouth filled with blood. He was choking. He had to get back to the cave, to the River Goddess, to the trail of white bones leading him farther and farther away from the living into the burial ground under the statue. What was he seeking? Who was buried here? A dark tunnel opened before him, echoing with the hollow sound of the booming waterfall.

"He's fainted again," came the same voice.

"Maybe he's dead," came another.

This time, when the fist struck, an explosive burst of blackness blinded him and he fell what seemed like a long distance. When he recovered his balance, he was on his feet and spread out before him was a spiral flight of white marble stairs leading down into the depths of the mountain to a pale stone path as broad and rounded as a turtle's back. Quickly, he descended, circling down and still farther down until he reached an altar built out of nine square white jade blocks, each masterfully carved with images of the dragon and the phoenix, alternating in a predictable pattern with the exception of one, which pictured the ancient Monkey King.

"Monkey?" whispered Prince Zong faintly and touched the

Monkey King, whereupon the engraved cube gave way and the shrine opened like a hinged mouth, revealing a yawning crypt below. The thunder of the falling water receded and the sounds of singing birds filled the air. How could birds sing underground? wondered the Prince.

"He thinks he sees his monkey!" roared that same insistent voice, calling the Prince back from where he wished to be.

But a new voice sounded now, one that brought the Prince back when the others had failed to reach him. It was the voice of the River Goddess.

"Give him some air!" cried Silver Lotus, breaking into the tight circle of armed ruffians that surrounded her son. "He's dying!"

Some of the men recognized the former First Consort and leered, while a few knew her as Lady Dulcimer, the singing beggar they had accosted in the alleyway in front of the Kingfisher Inn. Quickly, they made way for her, looking around fearfully for the blind warrior monk, her traveling companion. But those who had been present in the desert knew that the monk was dead, and that she was the Leopard's prisoner, and their eyes narrowed as they turned to their leader, watching to see what he would do.

Spotted Leopard did not move. His face barely registered her outcry except that his eyes found hers, glittering expectantly.

Silver Lotus saw a man who had shaped himself into something more genuinely bestial than any beast of prey. When satiated and not involved in the hunt, a leopard may stroll unnoticed among the herd he stalks, but Spotted Leopard looked to be eternally on the prowl, a relentless soul, constantly predatory.

"Make them stop their torture," she pleaded. "Keep the Prince alive!"

"I intend to—until the Festival of Lanterns," he answered coolly.

"And then?" she asked, meeting his small, appraising eyes.

"You know how demanding an emperor can be," he said, smiling slightly. He studied her in silence as she flushed a deep rose. Then he signaled Golden Wings. "See that she takes a new name," he commanded, turning to leave.

Desperately, Silver Lotus sought to detain him if only to distract the men from further tormenting her son. "There is nothing wrong with the one I have," she said defiantly. "My name honors my father, Gong Sun."

Anger pulsed through the muscles of Spotted Leopard's battered face, darkening and expanding his surly features like a massive storm cloud. Even his earrings seemed to twist with rage, like molten metal in a blacksmith's forge.

"Your father is dead," he answered roughly. "By all reports, your monk is dead as well, although we have no head to prove it. We will not make the same mistake with your son. Yamu is at work here, and his magic tricks are robbing us of our blood price. Incineration is not what the Emperor ordered. He asked for heads. We have only ashes to show for our victory in the desert. At the Festival of Lanterns, my dear, I intend to have what was ordered—the Starlord's head. And yours as well, perhaps, but that's of course up to you. There are many things a beautiful woman like yourself can do to save her life."

Silver Lotus lowered her eyes, but still she could see him, a short loathsome figure in a bloodstained cloak flung over a leopard-skin vest patched with strange rags of leather. He came closer, emitting a sour odor of smoke and rancid oil.

"I would like to address you by name, but your name honors that which no longer exists and cannot be spoken here," he said sharply, taking her chin into his black gloved hand. "Take a name that shows your new allegiance."

Silver Lotus looked around her at the litter of ceremonial horns and drums; the leather-bound volumes of spells stamped with the sign of two snakes intertwined; the leering terra-cotta demon masks on the sooty walls. "I have no new allegiance, sir," she said.

The serpent symbol on the bandit leader's books of sorcery reminded Silver Lotus of a frightening apparition she had seen once in the Emperor's palace. Chanting and mumbling magic incantations, the Rockgatherer had appeared one day in the throne room carrying a dusty sack of shrine stones. No one had remembered ushering him in, but fear prevented the Emperor from throwing him out, lest he be one of Yamu's demons. Sickened by the old man's putrid odor, Emperor Han had commanded him to bathe before reading fortunes. But the shaman had refused to remove his clothes. Stepping into the rose-petaled water, he had vanished, leaving only his hooded cowl, floating upright like an empty tent in the steaming tub. The moment before he disappeared, one of the guards had caught a glimpse of the Rockgatherer's cadaverous chest, which bore the sign of two snakes, intertwined.

Spotted Leopard's hand slipped smoothly toward her neck, his forefinger lightly tracing her windpipe. "The lotus has no thorns, Lady Dulcimer," he said. "I am beginning to believe that you are too fierce to have ever been a flower at all, even a desert cactus. You're in the cat family, I think. A jaguar . . . or a tiger perhaps?"

She shivered, hearing the monk's voice inside her head. *I thought perhaps you were a crane, but I see the white tiger is your spirit animal,* he had said, before teaching her the fighting form that had saved her from death in the desert.

"You may call me White Tiger, then," she answered.

"White Tiger," he repeated hoarsely, never taking his eyes off her. "And what's this?" he asked suddenly.

She blocked his hand which had moved to take the monk's calabash from her belt. "That is a gourd, nothing more, sir—a gift from a friend to aid in the art of meditation."

"A gift from the meditative monk perhaps?" he asked. "Later, you shall show me how it spins. I am intrigued by sorcery, as you shall learn tonight when you are initiated into the clan."

He turned to Golden Wings and was about to say something more, but T'sao T'sao broke in, barreling toward the Leopard, dragging a mud-spattered messenger by the arm. "Listen!" he panted, bloated with self-importance by virtue of having heard the scout's communication first. "He's just come from the Golden Phoenix! White Streak has enlisted a whole village in the Purple Mountains."

Abandoning the Prince and ignoring T'sao T'sao, the bandits clamorously flocked around the messenger, who also brought alarming news of an unidentified band of armed men spotted nearby and traveling in their general direction. Under cover of the loud confusion that followed, Silver Lotus crept to her son's side, kneeling and cradling his feverish head in her arms.

"Starlord," she whispered into his ear, "By some miracle, I have found you again, and you must listen. We haven't much time." He was terribly hot, his skin burning and dry, and his heart beating very faintly.

Taking the Tattooed Monk's calabash from where it hung around her waist, she unlocked the seal. Then, leaning over him so that no one would see, she opened his phoenix locket, revealing the scroll of the white tiger inside.

"No!" he cried out in his delirium, and he grabbed her wrist with surprising force.

"You have guarded the phoenix necklace well," she whispered soothingly, stroking his brow. "The power of the white tiger resides within you. Monkey has taught you his form as well, but he can help you no longer. The monkey scroll is hidden in the yellow jade handle of your wishing rod, marked with two sapphires as blue as Monkey's eyes."

"Monkey's eyes," echoed the Prince mournfully. And now the fire in his blood seemed like an insatiable hunger, a living force that could leap and travel through his limbs, heating his bones until they turned to ash.

"I give you the ashes of the white crane," the familiar voice went on urgently, pouring the black-and-white ashes from the calabash into the phoenix locket. "Now the crane's power, too, lies within you. You will know when to fly and when to stand and fight; and when you elect to fight, the power of the black fox and the black bear will come to your aid, for they are here as well, a gift from the Tattooed Monk, who was to be your guardian."

The Prince relaxed his grip on his mother's wrist. She had the voice of the River Goddess, but who was she really? Was she a demon disguised as Yin Dang, trying to steal the phoenix? His fingers closed over hers again as she touched the phoenix, but he could not speak.

In his dream, three fairies had appeared before him in the buried crypt, waving black-and-white pennants. Clad all in green like the fairies from the Water Curtain Cave, with hair piled in tight spirals on their heads, they urged him to follow them farther along the white stone road, which now seemed to emerge into the open.

"Starlord Zong," they chorused sweetly, "follow us. The monk is waiting."

"What monk?" asked the Prince aloud, but he let them lead him out of the cavern into the night. A magnificent sky stretched overhead, full of brilliant stars and a huge flat moon, floating above them like a yellow lantern.

His question startled Silver Lotus as she emptied all the ashes from the monk's calabash into the phoenix. The last layer was the bat, as fine as sand and as rust red as the desert cliffs at sunset. She closed the locket, letting her fingers linger on its warmth. Was the monk really dead, after all? she wondered. How could that be, when she had just learned to love him? Was the Prince talking to his ghost? Surely, she would know in her heart if he was no longer alive. She began to weep softly.

The Prince heard her sobs from very far away. A distant memory stirred of a beautiful weeping woman much like this one, kneeling beside him, whispering an urgent message into his ear. *Whatever happens little one, you are a prince,* the voice had said. Yes, he could hear it in his mind more clearly now. *Never forget your heritage, as I will never forget you. . . .*

The fairies were leading him through tall grasses along the banks of a tumbling brook. They walked swiftly, slipping now and then on gemstones randomly scattered in the mud that sparkled in the moonlight—sapphires, rubies, diamonds, topaz, emeralds. He admired their beauty but he could not stop to gather them. They crossed over a blue bridge with bright vermilion railings.

Silver Lotus watched her son fading. His breath was very shallow now, and he was as pale as parchment. Struggling with her grief, she desperately tried to recall everything the Tattooed Monk had told her before the battle. The Prince heard her distant voice through a haze: "You must find the horse, the lizard, the toad and the turtle, as well as the dragon, before the phoenix will rise from its ashes to defeat Yamu's army of Spellbinders," she said, urgently repeating the monk's instructions, although the Prince looked as if he would never rise to find anything ever again.

"Monkey is the keeper of the turtle scroll," she continued. "I do not know who holds the others, but legend says Old Bones himself sits on the scroll of the dragon."

The Prince did not seem to hear her. He was far away in a place she could not know. Was the monk with him there? And now her voice caught and, swallowing her tears, she became hard and fierce: "You *will* get well, Prince. You must not die. You are the Chosen One."

In his dream, the Prince had crossed to the other side of the water, where he saw a temple, sheltered by a dense grove of green willows, and fronted by a purple gate decorated with a golden star. The fairies escorted him through a magnificent courtyard of polished flagstones, across a terrace flanked on either side by crimson pillars.

Finally, the Prince found himself in a huge hall, lit by glowing dragon lamps. Mounting the steps to a raised dais obscured by a shimmering, pearl-beaded curtain, he trembled with exhaustion as a deep voice invited him to be seated.

Bowing respectfully, the fairies raised the curtain, revealing a giant of a man, dressed in yellow silk, bald and tattooed from head to foot with sacred texts and emblems that seemed to move and flicker in the reflected light. Suddenly, the sweet song of nightingales filled the air. The monk commanded the Prince to step forward and offered him a porcelain cup filled with a delicious tea that seeped into his heart like heavenly ambrosia.

Instead of tea leaves at the bottom of the cup, there was a white pill floating in the amber liquid like an incubating silkworm, and the monk urged him to swallow it. He obeyed, and in a moment, his fever lifted, leaving his mind clear. Perhaps now, thought the Prince, he would be allowed to rest. But then the monk spoke, echoing the words that the River Goddess Yin Dang had just spoken: "You *will* get well, Prince. You must not die. You are the new Starlord, the Chosen One." And then: "The battle has just begun."

With the monk's commanding words, the temple, the fairies, the dragon lamps, and the night sky all fell away. The Prince sighed and then moaned and shuddered, twisting sharply and crying out as the excruciating pain of the poisonous bites and lacerations came washing back over him. The battle had just begun; the monk had said so.

A great weeping eye materialized from the shadows above him. It was the eye of the Master Hand, mourning the death and destruction that was to come. It was the monk's eye, weeping for those consumed in fire and for those about to be burned. It was Monkey's eye, weeping in guilty isolation. It was the sacrificed eye of Yin Dang, blind now but weeping all the same. It was his mother's eye, weeping for the pain they would both endure.

The Prince opened his eyes, wet with tears. He was alive. He would get well. He was the new Starlord, direct descendant of the Emperor Hung Wu. He was the Chosen One. There would be no rest, no sleep for him, after all.

CHAPTER FORTY-THREE

Golden Wings

The world circles us with light. Yet during every moment of life, we are entirely lit from within.—The Tattooed Monk

Golden Wings had seen the former First Consort pour ashes into the Prince's golden necklace. She intended to ask Silver Lotus to explain, but the prisoner was absorbed in attending to her son, who seemed to be hovering between life and death, and all was pandemonium around them. Spotted Leopard had not acknowledged her since receiving the news of the impending raid, but he would certainly need her in the front ranks. The plan, as far as she could tell, was to meet the rival band with a strong vanguard and head them off with a surprise attack before they could close in on the camp.

Spotted Leopard approached her now, his dark brow furled in anger. She would have to wait until after the battle to deal with the mystery of what she had just witnessed between Silver

Lotus and the Prince. For a moment, Golden Wings panicked, wondering if he had expected her to prepare their horses and gear. But he had not yet given her the order to ride. She bristled defensively as he came near, but when he spoke her heart sank, for it was clear he had not yet given her part in the upcoming fight even a passing thought.

"Tell White Tiger we need a song!" he commanded. If Silver Lotus heard, she ignored him. Golden Wings tossed Spotted Leopard a dark look. Why didn't he tell her himself?

"A victory march!" he demanded again, louder this time.

Resentfully, Golden Wings obeyed, sullenly conveying the message.

"I cannot sing for him now," said Silver Lotus impatiently, not taking her anxious gaze off her son. "Doesn't he understand?"

"He understands that you are alive because he has been merciful. He understands that you owe him a battle song," said Golden Wings, "and anything else he might ask of you before he goes to war," she added pointedly.

A look of such distress passed over her prisoner's face that Golden Wings regretted her harsh tone. Soon, Golden Wings would be gone, flashing her twin swords in the glaring sunlight and raising the bloodcurdling cry of the clan as she rode like thunder, leaving Silver Lotus and her ailing son behind. She could afford to be kind, she told herself. Besides, she did not wish to see her prisoner do anything foolish that would anger Spotted Leopard and reflect badly on her own impulsive decision to keep her alive during the desert ambush.

"If I die," said Silver Lotus, pinning Golden Wings with a

piercing look, "then you must promise to guard the Starlord. I have no one else to turn to now, and I know that you have a pure heart. You are golden, like the phoenix. Swear to protect the Prince of the golden phoenix—or we will all be lost in deepest hell."

Golden Wings stepped back, as if scalded. "Are you mad?" she asked aghast. "You are still my prisoner, and I do not swear to protect you or your son, whomever you may think you are in this world or the next."

"I am sorry," said Silver Lotus. "I forgot myself. Forgive me."

Still shaken, Golden Wings felt a slow rage building in her veins. She knew the warning signs of her own murderous temper and turned away. Next time Silver Lotus dared speak to her like that, she might cut out her tongue.

But beneath the double smart of Spotted Leopard's disrespect and the former First Consort's warning, a seed of doubt had been planted in her heart. The ghost of an old suspicion the girl had attributed to the taunting of demons rose to haunt her again. An insistent voice of conscience had inquired after each bloody battle if perhaps the youngest of Spotted Leopard's warriors might be fighting on the wrong side. Could it be that the questioning voice, which had so disturbed her peace of mind, transforming pride in the spoils of each brutal victory into a scorching red shame, had come to her from the angels instead? And if that were true, could it be that Silver Lotus was an angel herself?

"A song, one song, White Tiger!" yelled Spotted Leopard from the courtyard. "How long does a warlord have to wait?

We'll have killed the outlaws and returned home by the time you strike the first note. Where is your voice? Have you lost it?"

"I will stand guard and watch the Prince while you sing," whispered Golden Wings, shoving her prisoner forward into the yard.

Silver Lotus looked back at Golden Wings, and the younger woman nodded. "A rousing call to arms," she advised curtly.

But the first song that issued forth from the newly named White Tiger's lips was mournful, more like a dirge than the victory march Spotted Leopard had requested.

"It begins with the thing that lives in the midst of bones, the thing with no face," she sang. "He licks us with a tongue of flame. Lost in Yamu's burning wood, slowly we burn."

As her voice gained in volume, the men began to droop listlessly, sapped of their energy. A few even slumped and curled up on the ground, falling into a stupefied slumber. Silver Lotus looked toward Spotted Leopard, willing him to fall under her spell. The chieftain had been quiet, waiting for the lament to shift in tone toward celebration. Instead, White Tiger's hypnotic voice grew more deeply mournful, mounting to a full-scale wailing song. And two silver tears made their way down her face, which stayed as smooth and still as a statue as the song mounted to a crescendo and then drew to a close.

"I am black ash and white; I am red ash and yellow. I am the thing that lives in the midst of bones, the thing with no face. I am dust, yet since you have asked, I sing for you."

It was absolutely silent when she finished. Spotted Leopard looked around at his spellbound men and signaled those still standing to mount and ride out. Golden Wings whistled for her yellow horse, but Spotted Leopard caught her eye and shook his head.

"You will stay this time," he said. "I cannot risk all my good fighters in the raid. Besides, if the robbers escape us, or send some men ahead to kidnap the Prince, you must be here. Guard the Prince: that is your mission, Golden Wings."

Then, with a call to his stallion and a crack of his whip, he was gone and she was left alone in an abandoned camp with a milling group of fighters, all surly and resentful of not being chosen to ride out with the others. Silver Lotus, bent over her dulcimer, continued to weep silently as the wounded Prince slipped once again into unconsciousness.

T'sao T'sao approached Golden Wings, leering, with his infuriating sideways scuttle. She braced herself, ready to vent her frustration and rage upon him with her bare fists, but instead, she had to hurl herself out of the way as Spotted Leopard veered back and charged his former general at top speed, viciously cutting him across the cheek with his whip. T'sao T'sao screamed and doubled over, falling to the ground. Then Silver Lotus cried out in alarm as the chieftain reared and plummeted toward her and reaching down with one arm, swept her up, dulcimer and all, onto his war horse, which changed direction sharply and galloped thunderously down the mountainside.

CHAPTER FORTY-FOUR

The Starlord

Change is the law of the universe, but why there should be a
universe subject to the laws of change—or why there should be
a universe at all—are questions I cannot answer.
—The Master Hand

W hen the Prince woke again, the moon had risen. His fever
had vanished, and his mind was as clear as it had been in the
dream after drinking the monk's tea and swallowing the white
pill. The River Goddess was no longer by his bedside, but he
heard the muffled steady sound of hoofbeats. He rose and
stumbled to the door, looking out into the night, wondering
who was riding so furiously, circling the camp on a solitary
watch.

Surrounding him, the snowy mountains rose pure and cold,
and above him the galaxies spun like starry wheels in the heavens. A frozen path of moonlight seemed to signal him directly
like a thin golden beam streaming across the icy plain. Dancing

along in its glow were gigantic snowflakes, falling so slowly that the Prince thought he could see the astounding form of each as it came to earth, melting into glazed droplets that stood gleaming on the stiff tussocks of tundra grass.

The Prince breathed deeply and lifted his face to the wind. Standing in the frigid air, he felt with every pulse of his beating heart how close he had come to death.

He looked up at the Big Dipper and clearly saw the black bear looming as it had once when he was very small in a marshy place near the palace when a harpy had led him into an unknown land. He saw the Milky Way and remembered the woodland fox, friend of the fairies, dancing like a spirit through the forest near the Water Curtain Cave. And then he thought of all the creatures who danced in the woods and in the air, the golden monkeys and the white cranes.

Happy to be alive, he knew himself to be a wild thing of many faces that had miraculously climbed up out of darkness, out of ancient leaf falls, out of relentless storms that had scoured the earth for millions of years, gliding through the infinite glitter of thousands of starlit snowy nights to stand at this particular point in the universe, gazing at the constellations.

He thought of the white torrents tumbling into precipitous gorges below the Water Curtain Cave, and a wave of longing for home, for the River Goddess, for Monkey, for his lost mother swept over him.

A bitter wind tore through the bandits' encampment, and now the Prince heard Yamu's voice like shattering glass on the wind, offering him solace from his pain. *Leave your memories behind*, it said, *and rest. Forget your home, your guardian, your mother.*

You have wandered too far. You are sick and weary. Forget, sleep and forget. Yamu embraces all memory, all pain. Give them up freely. We are the spirits of the fiery air, and we will bear you away so that you may rest at last, free of memory, free of pain.

He felt himself to be at the very center of a beating universal heart. With some future contraction, he would vanish, and all that would be left would be black lava frozen into shapes like fallen angels' wings, and a swirl of star fragments. He was human, but what was he truly? Would he eventually disappear altogether or shapeshift into some other kind of being? In the isolation of the wilderness, did the Master Hand and Yamu have the same voice?

He heard the insistent sound of rhythmic hoofbeats like ceremonial drums, but could see no rider. He felt a terrible red fog move insidiously into his freezing brain. The voice of Yamu was growing fainter, until he wasn't sure he had heard it at all. Then, briefly, it was there again, very close: *It's always those who carry the greatest pain who refuse to give it up. Fascinating, really,* it whispered, and then it was gone.

What could a Starlord ultimately accomplish after all? he wondered sadly. He was only stardust, as insubstantial as the luminous vision now approaching, a steaming yellow horse appearing out of nowhere, bearing a helmeted goddess all in gold. She was beautiful, more beautiful than any creature he had ever seen. But the instant his mind registered her beauty, the solitary hoofbeats were suddenly multiplied by many.

You will know when to fly and when to stand and fight, the River Goddess Yin Dang had told him. She had reassured him that the power of the white tiger, the bear, and the fox would come to his aid. He would need those powers now, for riders were overtaking the bewitching girl and surrounding her.

You must find the horse . . . Yin Dang had said in his mother's voice, and he had pictured that horse yellow as a glowing topaz, just like this galloping stallion hurtling through the rising storm, bearing the golden warrior straight toward him.

The riders were closing in, led by a tall imposing chieftain and flanked by an equally formidable second. The latter let out a wild bloodcurdling battle cry and twirled his double ax. Golden Wings answered the challenge with a sky-rending cry of her own and veered recklessly toward the strangers at full speed, flashing her twin swords. The Prince ran forward weaponless, with no plan other than the knowledge and certainty that he must somehow save the radiant one, but suddenly she raised her arm in a strange salute. She seemed to be signaling him from afar to halt and turn around.

He whirled about just in time. Looming out of the driving snow galloped the bleeding T'sao T'sao, his face slashed and twisted into a terrible demonlike grimace, leading the ragged group of bandits Spotted Leopard had left behind to guard the camp. The assassin's sword was raised, for he had been about to strike the Prince without warning from behind. When first assigned to kill the Prince, T'sao T'sao had harbored no grudge against his intended victim. But now that he had failed so miserably over and over again, he hated the boy with a passion born of humiliation.

Leaping deftly aside, the Prince sprang like a tiger onto T'sao T'sao's horse, and taking his attacker's arm in a bear's vise-like grip, wrested the weapon from his grasp and tossed him to the snowy ground. Now the Prince saw that the intruders were a scouting party vastly outnumbered by T'sao T'sao's cutthroats. He would have to slash his way through to the golden warrior, who was so far miraculously holding her own. She had saved his life when he had planned to save hers. With renewed resolve, he charged, hacking at the howling pack of brigands and scattering them like wild dogs. Not caring how many there were, he forged ahead, attacking furiously right and left.

Seizing the shaft of the first lance thrust at him, he wrenched it loose, sending its owner flying. Then taking a firm grip on the weapon, he thrashed about, hair flying, swinging with abandon and hitting anyone who came near. Using the blunt end as a bludgeon more tellingly than the blade, he downed a dozen men before the lance splintered and broke.

And now a new opponent, a hulking man built like a bear, shouldered his way forward. Resorting again to his sword, the Prince swung horizontally with all his strength, aiming at the brigand's legs. But the huge man surprised him by jumping up just in time to avoid impact, and then throwing himself at the Prince with the force of a boulder.

Grabbing the Prince by the throat, the brigand landed a blow that made the Prince think his skull had surely cracked. He gasped for air, fighting to regain his balance. His vision blurred. Taking a blind running leap, the Prince landed squarely upon the bandit's back and delivered a heavy blow to his enemy's head. Blood spurted, and a scream pierced the night. The man's hulking frame fell to the ground with a leaden thud. He rolled over, dead.

Enraged, the bandit's companions closed in, their lances

and truncheons raised. Stunned, the Prince watched them come. He had overcome many in self-defense, but he had never killed a man before. For the first time since he had begun to fight, he realized what it meant to be a warrior. Pain welled up in his heart. He knew he must defend himself, but for a moment he could not move.

A burly silhouette appeared out of the gloom. Unhooking a heavy net from his belt, he snared those closest to the Prince and dragged them, writhing, through the snow. Flashing a long knife, he took his time dispatching them as if they were nothing more than a good day's haul of fish. Then he repeated the maneuver, calmly casting his net again. But the grisly task was interrupted by what appeared to be a snow demon, holding aloft a deadly chain-ball sickle that very nearly lopped off the fisherman's head.

The netted robbers cried out to their savior, whom they recognized as T'sao T'sao, to release them. Like a demon indeed, T'sao T'sao hesitated a moment, enjoying their helpless cries of distress. These were the very men who had mocked and tortured him when he had fallen from favor with Spotted Leopard. Clutching the sickle, he released the deadly ball in orbit on its chain, holding his enemy at bay. The chain undulated like a snake in the vibrating air, momentarily distracting the fisherman. His brief confusion allowed T'sao T'sao to move in and cut a few of the frightened survivors loose. But the outlaw recovered his bearings quickly, and T'sao T'sao reared back, grimacing, shielding those who had just escaped.

Disposing of his catch, the fisherman cleared his fishing net of the dead and fatally wounded, dumping the ruffians' bodies unceremoniously into the snow. Twisting the net and twirling it above his head like a long rope, he caught T'sao T'sao's sickle, jerking the heavy weapon from his grip and tossing it beyond the bandit's reach. Then he hitched the net to his belt and closed in on T'sao T'sao like a trained boxer, fists raised.

Now the fisherman stood anchored to one spot, staring at T'sao T'sao with great intensity. His face went deadly white; his eyes glittered. Although neither moved or spoke, T'sao T'sao felt a terrifying force attack him, like lightning splitting the clouds. He flinched and stepped back, but was caught in the fisherman's piercing gaze, captured as helplessly as his companions had been in the man's far-reaching net.

T'sao T'sao went for his dagger, but the fisherman's arm shot out, gripping the bandit's shoulder so tightly that the hand clutching the blade fell limply to his side, temporarily paralyzed. Swiftly, T'sao T'sao closed his other hand around his enemy's wrist, pulling him forward. But just as he was about to land a hit to the groin with his knee, the fisherman struck a powerful blow to his unguarded belly, causing the bandit to double over and fall to the ground, gasping. Thinking him vanquished for the moment, the fisherman turned, searching for T'sao T'sao's fallen ball and chain.

Recovering quickly, T'sao T'sao made a desperate lunge for the other's neck, closing around the fisherman's throat from behind in a strangler's vise. The outlaw pressed his chin into T'sao T'sao's arm while groping for a hold. Closing around T'sao T'sao's leg, he pulled it forward with all his force, at the same time lurching forward himself.

Both men crashed to the ground, but the fisherman fell

on top, grinding T'sao T'sao's hip into the earth and nearly breaking his bones. The vise loosened. The fisherman leapt up, just in time to dodge a dagger from one of T'sao T'sao's men who had escaped the net and crept up from behind. With one foot firmly planted on T'sao T'sao's heaving chest, the fisherman made short work of this new opponent, lifting him up with one hand and throwing him in a wide arc through the air. T'sao T'sao stumbled to his feet, and the two went at it again. But the match was destined to be shortlived, for the fisherman was hardly winded, and T'sao T'sao was stumbling about, panting and striking out wildly.

The sight of T'sao T'sao spurred the Prince once more into action. Arrows flew past him as he downed one bandit after another. He struck with such precision, his overpowered enemies began to look like goblins, swimming through a lake of gore. Seeing their comrades so easily slain by a single youth seemed to paralyze the bandits. One by one, they backed into one another in retreat. Taking advantage of their panic, the Prince continued to mow his way through their ranks, moving with the strength and speed of an enraged tiger and clearing a path toward Golden Wings.

Now the fisherman dealt T'sao T'sao a fearful blow to the side of the neck that would surely have killed the bandit had he not turned so that his jaw caught half the force. Emitting a hoarse cry, T'sao T'sao grabbed the fisherman's leg in both arms and twisted it viciously, dislocating the joint. The fishermen fell, cursing, as T'sao T'sao rolled over and over out of his way and came shakily to his knees, only to see the Prince bearing down upon him, sword raised.

For a moment, T'sao T'sao took a defensive stance as if preparing to stand and fight the Starlord. Then, sizing up the glowering young warrior at a glance, he thought better of it and fled into the forest, abandoning those bandits still engaged in battle with the outlaws and leaving Golden Wings to her fate.

The Prince moved to help the fisherman but saw he had already recovered his footing. Although moving with a slight limp, the outlaw lost no time in pursuing those who had not fled with T'sao T'sao. The Prince now realized that the man was an expert marksman, for he was throwing knives from his belt with amazing speed and unerring accuracy, moving steadily back toward the center of the battle where the outlaw chief was defending the rest of his clan.

Throwing in his lot with the fisherman, the Prince fought by his side, downing those foolhardy enough to stand in their path. As he struck and struck again, the Prince forgot his will to win as well as his desire for revenge. For the moment, he saw only the snow falling between himself and the burly fisherman, and the starlight on the snow shone as piercingly bright as his own burning heart.

"Why do you murder your own?" asked the fisherman bluntly. He was studying the Prince coldly, dispelling his illusion of camaraderie. "Are you a spy or a mercenary?"

"I am a prisoner here," answered the Prince, "and no friend of Spotted Leopard's. Those who lie dead at your feet are my former captors, who were assigned to torture me without mercy and obeyed beyond the call of duty. . . . But I will defend the girl."

"She is Spotted Leopard's ward, Golden Wings," growled

the fisherman. "Why would you care about her, unless you are lying?"

As they drew closer to the outlaw leader, the Prince could see the man's bare chest in a sudden ray of moonlight, heaving as he skillfully wielded a heavy harpoon against his enemies. "If my brother slays her, she will die young as she deserves," the chieftain shouted, overhearing them.

But the Prince hardly listened to his words, for more surprising than the leader's seaworthy weapon, out of place in the snowy mountains, was the brand emblazoned over his heart—the same sign of the Qin that had sealed the Prince's own fate!

Now the Starlord understood that he was surrounded by the very outlaws he had just missed meeting on Purple Mountain, when, forced to flee in Monkey's arms, he had turned back from an elevated distance and spied the imposing White Streak and his brother, Black Whirlwind. His stocky companion at arms must be Chiko Chin, the legendary navigator. He searched in the dark for Day Rat, who had long ago saved his life, but he was not among them, nor was the Starlord's former nursemaid, Jade Mirror. With renewed vigor, the Prince joined the outlaws in making quick work of those who attacked them, chasing the stragglers toward the forest before facing White Streak.

"I salute you in friendship, White Streak," he said. "But Golden Wings does not deserve to die young, any more than I do. If you try to stand in my way, I will fight you."

"Who are you?" asked White Streak, readying his harpoon and straining to see the Prince's face in the darkness. "And how do you know my name?"

Before the Prince could answer, Golden Wings issued an earsplitting war whoop and began to retreat, flying away on her yellow horse with Black Whirlwind in hot pursuit. White Streak faced the charging hellion, springing into action to cut off her escape.

Seeing herself about to be trapped between the two outlaw brothers, Golden Wings desperately changed direction, rearing up in the driving snow and charging back toward the camp. But the moment lost in shifting purpose cost her the narrow advantage she had gained through the swiftness of her steed, and Black Whirlwind bore down upon her, closing in from one side while his twin closed in from the other.

Leaping to a standing position on her magnificent horse, Golden Wings slashed at her attackers, manipulating her swords with such skill the two blades cut a wide protective swath, a steely blur in the frigid air. As she swayed from side to side, she moved her feet as if dancing to avoid their counter blows. She was dazzling. Yet the Prince had a sense that she knew, even as she fought so valiantly, that she was doomed.

And now he saw her make a quick movement and extract something from her boot. It was a leaf-shaped knife, which glowed amber and translucent in the eerie light of the moon. She let her swords be still by her side as she pointed the weapon at her own breast, poised to leap off her plunging steed.

"No!" screamed the Prince, loudly enough to distract White Streak. Charging across the outlaw's path, he thrust himself within reach of the other's weighty weapon. As blows rained down upon him, he blocked them furiously with his sword.

Golden Wings glowered at him in a frenzy of shock and indecision. She had been about to end her own life, and now this strange young man, Silver Lotus's son, who had been lying sick and helpless in Spotted Leopard's tent on the verge of death himself, was fighting like a soul possessed and risking his life for her. Why?

Impulsively, she tossed him the knife. "I was told to protect *you*," she said, flashing him a quick smile that penetrated straight to his heart. And then in an instant she was gone, pursued by Black Whirlwind while the Prince's hand closed around the horse-shaped hilt of the girl's dagger, still warm from her touch and glowing like a golden topaz in the snow-misted moonlight.

CHAPTER FORTY-FIVE

Outlaws of Moonshadow Marsh

All other creatures look down toward the earth,
but man and monkey turn their faces toward the stars
and gaze upon the heavens.—Monkey

The Prince felt the strength of the bear, the clarity of the fox, the speed of the horse, and the deadly accuracy of the tiger surge through him as he countered White Streak's complicated series of strikes. He was light on his feet and met the more experienced fighter with a speedy succession of quick cuts. White Streak expertly parried each of the thrusts with his harpoon, but he seemed uneasy and again asked the name of his challenger. The Prince responded with a few feints preparatory to a new attack.

White Streak was a first-class fighter, but the Prince was inspired with an inexhaustible energy. He pressed forward, keeping the outlaw off balance with blow after well-aimed blow, enticing his opponent to rougher and rougher ground. White Streak had to pay increased attention to his footwork to keep from stumbling, while the Prince moved with such speed, he seemed to be floating. The chert knife, still glowing warmly in his belt, gave him courage, and a new passion throbbed through his veins, heating his blood.

This match was his first real encounter with an opponent worthy of his newly acquired skills. The exhilaration of his training days with Monkey and the wonder of his time in the white tiger's cave seemed as distant as another lifetime. The two warriors went at it for thirty rounds, each move lasting an eternity, unfolding in a suspension of time and space.

Soon, the other outlaws stood watching, their horses abandoned to the sidelines, their breath gathering around their heads in white clouds of steam, divided between the spectacle of their leader pitted against the Prince, and Black Whirlwind matching swords with the golden one, who was continuously losing ground. The few bandits left alive fled into the evergreen forest, in the hopes of finding the rest of their band.

The Prince felt he could go on fighting White Streak forever. Then, suddenly, a loud clank of arms broke in upon them and threw both warriors off their rhythm.

A troop of horsemen bearing yellow imperial banners and flaming torches emerged out of the snowy night and in seconds had surrounded the small group of outlaws. They were the Emperor's military police, heavily armed with crossbows, swords, and pikes.

"Surrender your arms!" cried their leader, whose chain-mail jacket and spiked helmet proclaimed him a captain. "We know who you are and we shall show you no mercy if you resist."

Without any exchange of words, Black Whirlwind and Golden Wings closed ranks with White Streak and the other outlaws, melting into one tightly united band, all opposition between them instantly forgotten with the appearance of this troop of the Emperor's soldiers. Only the Prince stood apart.

Coolly, he flashed his golden necklace, and then hid it again under his sheepskin tunic before the soldiers could study it too closely. White Streak's observant eyes, however, did not miss its significance as the Prince bore down upon the barking official.

"You are mistaken as to the identity of these two men," said the Prince with an air of supreme authority. He pointed to the astonished White Streak and Black Whirlwind. "They are my assistants, disguised as the famous outlaw brothers of Moonshadow Marsh, on a mission to take the treasonous band by surprise." Taking his cue, White Streak bowed, his face a solemn mask but his eyes showing some amusement.

"Unfortunately, the leaders you seek have escaped while we were engaged with these others," the Prince continued smoothly. "As you see, we were vastly outnumbered. You and your men would do well to track those that fled into the woods." He pointed toward the place the bandits had last been seen. "They could not have gone far. You have come just in time to assist us and for that we are thankful. The Emperor is all-wise, and omnipotent. I will take these miscreants back to Bai Ping, where they will answer to his infallible justice."

At this, like trained actors in a theatrical spectacle, White Streak's followers kneeled, moaning as if in mourning for their heads, which would surely soon be separated from their unfortunate bodies.

"And who are you, sir?" asked the captain, struggling to maintain his dignity but shaken by the Prince's commanding manner and the glimpse of the imperial phoenix seal he had seen on the Starlord's golden locket. No one but those of highest nobility would bear such a symbol of rank.

"My name is of no significance to you, officer. You need only know that I am a loyal servant of the Emperor," answered the Prince impatiently. He scrutinized the soldier's face as if committing it to memory. "Would you waste precious time here, exchanging pleasantries, when the treacherous White Streak is still free and fast escaping?" he continued. The man still hesitated, unsure how to react.

"Perhaps you would like to take charge of these miscreants while I go after White Streak myself?" pressed the Prince. Still the poor man hesitated, cowed by the Prince's commanding tone. "If you tarry longer your interruption impedes our duty," concluded the Prince, cutting off all further discussion. "Shall I report you to the Emperor for obstructing our mission? Or would you like to leave us to our work and attend to yours so that more honor may be heaped upon you, and your children and grandchildren shall inherit your good name in this life and the next?" The Prince turned to his two "assistants" as if there were nothing more to say.

This speech, combined with what he had seen of the man's golden seal, convinced the captain of the royal militia that he had best obey, for the mysterious speaker was clearly not an uneducated outlaw or a bandit thief who had stolen the necklace from his betters but an officer of some influence, who far out-ranked him and could destroy his hard-earned career with one whispered word in court, if he so desired.

Turning about abruptly, the captain flung a rough com-mand at his men, and they mounted and galloped away as suddenly as they had come, heading toward the woods in the direction the Prince had indicated. When they disappeared from sight, the Prince, in high spirits, raised his sword. "Let us go on!" he said amicably, aiming a long thrust at White Streak in comradly combat. White Streak easily parried the blow, then raised his weapon above his head, leaving his bare chest emblazoned with the sign of the Qin exposed to the other's attack.

"I salute you, Starlord, and entreat you to join us and be our leader," he said, smiling. "We have searched high and low for you but never expected to find the Chosen One here, with Spotted Leopard's band. Also . . ." He paused, wondering how to phrase what he had to say next. "We were told you were a child, a boy younger than our youngest outlaw."

The Prince stood, amazed by White Streak's stunning invi-tation. It was true he had saved the outlaw leader from capture and possible imprisonment by the authorities, but he had no doubt that, had they been taken, the twin brothers would have beaten the militia against all odds and escaped from their bonds before reaching Bai Ping. Even in his isolation with Monkey he had heard a thousand stories of the victorious escapades of the outlaws of Moonshadow Marsh in the hands of the Emperor's men. Surely, they did not need a Prince to lead them.

Suddenly, the Prince felt like the child White Streak had

expected to see. And now the formidable Black Whirlwind came forward to embrace him. "It was you and the magical monkey who saved Kuan in the battle with the harpies!" Black Whirlwind said. "Had it not been for you, the boy might now be with Yamu in the underworld like the rest of his family. We owe you our allegiance just for that, Prince Zong."

"I would be glad to be your friend and to have your company on the road," replied the Prince, overwhelmed. "But I am not the Chosen One, and I have no mission other than to find my guardian, who has disappeared, and my mother, who was sent into exile at my birth." He fingered the dagger at his waist and locked eyes with Golden Wings, the only bandit in their midst, who watched the others for renewed signs of hostility.

"Your birthmark makes you one of us and the golden phoenix around your neck marks you as the Chosen One," replied White Streak. "You are the direct descendant of the Starlord Hung Wu. A great war is building. Unless you join us, we will be overpowered by Yamu and his Spellbinders."

"I will join you, White Streak, but I cannot presume to lead you. As soon as I find those I seek, I do not know where my destiny will take me."

"We will command together, then," said White Streak, "and together we will find the others and return to the Golden Phoenix where you can rest after your ordeal."

Warmly clasping White Streak's hand, the Prince turned to Golden Wings. "And you?" he asked gently.

She looked around her at the outlaws she had been raised to call her enemies and then back at the Prince, who had saved her life. Spotted Leopard had told her to guard the Prince. That was her mission. Silver Lotus had begged her to protect him as well. Besides, she had new respect for him now that she had seen him fight.

"I will follow you," she said, "and be your guardian."

At this, White Streak visibly shuddered. She would guard the Starlord only to betray him, he thought. She had been known to kill for no greater glory than gold.

"The job of guardian is open at the moment, but Monkey might be jealous," said the Prince, smiling at Golden Wings.

Chiko Chin stepped closer to the Prince. "If she is to be your guardian, then you're also stuck with me," he said.

"And I'm never going to leave your side," said Black Whirlwind, grinning but meaning it.

White Streak raised his hand for silence, poised motionless in the starlight. The north wind streamed across the peaks, carrying off great clouds of powdered snow, like spires going up in flame under a silver moon. The clouds released a pattering burst of hail into the surrounding wasteland. They all stood, listening.

Then out of the white trees came a long silent line of ice-encrusted creatures, moving surely and steadily like swift shades across the canyon. Their apish silhouettes appeared as inky cutouts against the lunar glow. A spiral of galaxies floated under the round bowl of the heavens, spinning like infinite haloes over their bowed heads.

They looked at first like a procession of cowled yetis, covered in matted coats of clinging snow, their round eyes sparkling brightly. As Orion rose, a brilliant star shot across the shimmering void, illuminating their leader as he approached through the white mist, treading so lightly on the frozen crust he left no tracks at all. It was clear as he neared them that he was a golden monkey of extraordinary size. When he reached the outlaws, he stopped and stood very still. Baring his sharp dog-like teeth, he gave a wild resounding cry. As the Prince stared, he felt he recognized the golden monkey's face from a dream. Then abruptly, the messenger reached into a leather sheath oily with grime, and from it, pulled a magnificent sword that glowed like sapphires in the starlight. Solemnly, he offered this fine weapon to the Prince. It was the Starlord's missing sword, Dragon Rain!

Lovingly, the Prince brandished the sword while the solemn monkey procession passed. The last proffered him Jade Mirror's battered changing bag, identical to when he had last seen it, except now the blue cloth was damp and blackened around the edges as if it had been dragged along the forest floor. Prince Zong accepted these lost treasures from the mysterious apes as they receded silently back into the woods. Handing T'sao T'sao's crude sword to an outlaw who had lost his own in the fray, the Prince raised Dragon Rain high in a proud salute.

"To the outlaws of Moonshadow Marsh!" he cried. "My destiny is to ride under the sign of the Qin. From this night forward, I am your outlaw brother and swear to fight for all those who most need the strength of Dragon Rain to deliver them from injustice."

"We are brothers!" cried White Streak in response, raising his harpoon and crossing it with Dragon Rain, producing a mighty metallic ring that reverberated through the forest, and a flurry of blue sparks.

"Brothers!" echoed Black Whirlwind, grinding and clashing his double ax, adding white sparks to the display.

"To the Golden Phoenix!" cried Chiko Chin and all the outlaws in one voice.

And so with White Streak and the Prince in the lead, Black Whirlwind with Golden Wings galloping not far behind, and Chiko Chin bringing up the rear, the outlaws turned their horses toward Moonshadow Marsh. There, the multiplying ponaturi, the norns, the kappas, and the hairy toads; the harpies and the bunyips; the scavenging earthquake beetles and the stinging lion ants; and hordes of Yamu's ancient demons of land and sea were fast gathering for battle, the first in a long, destructive war that would determine the fate of every living, breathing creature on the face of the Master Hand's green earth.

But before that terrible confrontation, the patient Mother Gu, having received word from Day Rat and his strange new flying companion that her son was finally on his way, was preparing a celebratory feast of her famous dumplings for the entire village; while her recent guest and ancient rival, the bossy Little Grandmother, was demanding equal space in the inn's crowded kitchen, so that she too could cook a mountain of delicious dumplings in her own manner to greet White Streak and his outlaws upon their triumphant return to Moonshadow Marsh.

A solid curtain of rain, shimmering with hundreds of silvery serpents, poured down upon the imperial gardens. As soon as they landed, the snakes slid away along the flooding paths, speeding toward the shores of Moonshadow Marsh.

Peals of thunder shook the sky, awakening Old Bones in his subterranean lair. And now the battering downpour delivered a writhing mass of frogs. Illuminated by brilliant bolts of lightning, the dragonlike spikes on their backs bristled like spiny flowers as they hit the earth.

The storm set off the wind chimes in the Garden of Pleasant Sounds. But no one was present to notice except the monumental statue of Chac, King of the North Sea.

Hidden by a jumble of fallen leaves in the wishing well, a globe of soft green jelly floated through the broken shadows. The emerald sphere, misshapen from the taut struggle within, wavered like a bag containing conflicting winds. At last, it split apart, and a giant water demon lashed its way out. With a terrible high-pitched scream, the monster hurtled explosively upward and then slithered out of the well. Newly invented by the Lord of the Dead, it had only one mission: to find the Nokk.

Slowly, the dark water rose toward the eyes of the statue of Chac. Slime clung like a cloak of moss to its shoulders. In the eerie light cast by the crackling storm, the Dragon King of the North Sea appeared to be drowning.

The flood seeped into the ruins of the Starlord Hung Wu's sunken palace, far below the Emperor's overpopulated prisons. It snaked around the shattered sun dials. It soaked into the swollen marble veins of what were once lofty altars. It circled the crumbling crimson pillars. It corroded the gilded tiles of fallen rooftops, mixing with the shards of porcelain towers, all turned to rubble by dragon fire long ago.

Old Bones twitched and yawned. An inky stream, glowing like oil, dripped from the mighty stalactites above him into his gaping maw. Yamu watched as Old Bones swallowed the bitter draught, drop by glittering black drop.

The time had come to call demons from the deserts, the mountains, the forests, and the seas. The time had come to raise the Rockgatherer and to summon the Spellbinders. The time had finally come to pay Emperor Han a long-deferred visit and to open the Tomb of the Turtle. The Lord of the Dead smiled.

"Let us go, my pet," he said. "It is time."

KEY TO CHINESE CHARACTERS

PROLOGUE

 crane, *he*

PART ONE: Monkey

 monkey, *hou*

CHAPTER ONE: Sign of the Qin

 Qin (proper name, pronounced "ch'in")

CHAPTER TWO: The Phoenix

 phoenix, *feng*

CHAPTER THREE: The Immortal Beggar

 boat, *zhou*

CHAPTER FOUR: Dragon Scroll

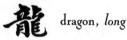 dragon, *long*

CHAPTER FIVE: Black Swans of the Red Tide

 red, *chi*

374

CHAPTER SIX: Puk

 dog, *quan*

CHAPTER SEVEN: The Guardian

 monk, *seng*

CHAPTER EIGHT: The Bunyip

 demon, *mo*

CHAPTER NINE: Dragon of the North Sea

 dragon, *long*

CHAPTER TEN: Song of the Nightingale

 jade, *yu*

CHAPTER ELEVEN: Day Rat

rat, *shu*

CHAPTER TWELVE: Lady Dulcimer

lotus, *lian*

CHAPTER TWENTY: Scourge of the Sea

犬   dog, *quan*

CHAPTER TWENTY-ONE: General Calabash

僧   monk, *seng*

CHAPTER TWENTY-TWO: First Journey

行   to travel, *xing*

CHAPTER TWENTY-THREE: Dragon Bone Lake

龍   dragon, *long*

CHAPTER TWENTY-FOUR: Yu Yu

繡   to embroider, *xiu*

CHAPTER TWENTY-FIVE: Flight

飛   to fly, *fei*

CHAPTER TWENTY-SIX: Lord of the Dead

魔   demon, *mo*

CHAPTER TWENTY-SEVEN: Malia

飛   to fly, *fei*

CHAPTER THIRTY-FIVE: White Crane

 crane, *ho*

CHAPTER THIRTY-SIX: Old Bones

 dragon, *long*

CHAPTER THIRTY-SEVEN: Tiger Scroll

 tiger, *hu*

CHAPTER THIRTY-EIGHT: Guardian Ape

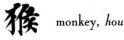 monkey, *hou*

CHAPTER THIRTY-NINE: Spotted Leopard

 leopard, *bao*

CHAPTER FORTY: The Hall of Penetrating Light

 monkey, *hou*

CHAPTER FORTY-ONE: Mountain of the Five Elements

 mountain, *shan*

CHAPTER FORTY-TWO: White Tiger

 tiger, *hu*

CHAPTER FORTY-THREE: Golden Wings

 horse, *ma*

CHAPTER FORTY-FOUR: The Starlord

 star, *xing*

CHAPTER FORTY-FIVE: Outlaws of Moonshadow Marsh

 Qin (proper name, pronounced "ch'in")

EPILOGUE

 demon, *mo*

AUTHOR'S NOTE

OUTLAWS OF MOONSHADOW MARSH is partly inspired by the true story of a small band of brave men and women who were forced by the persecution of a harsh feudal government to flee their homes and hide out as fugitives in the marshes of Shandong Province. During the Song Dynasty, a long line of corrupt rulers relentlessly pillaged and plundered the countryside. Bribery was rampant; petty tyrants ruled a deteriorating system of justice; innocent men found themselves in jail for crimes they did not commit, branded as felons while the guilty went free.

A few of the most courageous of those wrongly accused broke out of prison and banded together as outlaws. They elevated the mark of the criminal from a symbol of shame to a call to arms in defense of honor and chivalry. Starting as a handful of peasants, they became an army and fought for their rights. Like Robin Hood and his band, their names were praised by the poor and the oppressed, their deeds extolled in song and story.

Inspired in part by the classic *Shui Hu Zhuan* or *The Marsh Chronicles*, a novel published in fifteenth-century China depicting the lives of this rebel gang who lived two hundred years before, the setting of *Sign of the Qin* is not meant to be historically accurate. Some of the details of place and custom refer to the Han dynasties of the third century depicted in *The Romance of the Three Kingdoms* by Lo Kuan-Chung. The aerial acrobatics of the flying battle scenes in traditional Chinese kung fu films such as *The Dragon Gate Inn*, *The Thirty-sixth Chamber of Shaolin*, *Come Drink with Me*, and *The T'ai Chi Master* (to name a few) were also a source. Equally important as reference is the timeless classic *Hsi-yu Chi* or *Journey to the West* by Wu Ch'eng-en, describing the entertaining adventures of the Monkey King.

Although primarily inspired by Chinese legend, the gods, spirits, and demons in *Sign of the Qin* draw upon the myths and fairy tales of many nations. I have taken liberties with them, creating my own harpy, for example, who, unlike her classic Greek counterpart, is psychologically half raven, half human, but physically all bird. Similarly, I have redefined others whose characteristics do not match their original cultural sources.

I have chosen the sign of the Qin (ch'in) as the outlaws' brand as well as the title of the first book in the trilogy. There was never a band of rebels in China marked with that particular character, nor are events during the reign of the real Emperor Qin referred to in the course of the novel. But there are several reasons for my choice. The fictional outlaws in this story transcend a calamitous time of terror and manage to stand up for what is right. In that sense, they earn a measure of immortality. Emperor Qin (221–207 B.C.) was a man obsessed with immortality. He was far from a righteous leader. In fact his tyrannical rule was just the sort that called for heroes like Prince Zong,

White Streak, and Black Whirlwind, saviors of the common folk. Yet all those who have had the opportunity to view his famous army of terra-cotta warriors, frozen in time, cannot help but contemplate the mystery, grandeur, madness, and pathos of the human condition. To me, the name has transcended the man and his biography and become a symbol of our universal desire to conquer Yamu, Lord of the Dead, each in his own way. The character is also a homonym for an ancient Chinese musical instrument resembling the one Silver Lotus plays when, in exile, she finds her voice and sets out to discover her own destiny.

—L. G. Bass